Faber picked up the two pieces of paper. The page of the diary was on rice paper, obviously torn from a book. The neat swirls of the *hiragana* script were not intelligible; he read the typed translation that Tori had provided:

> Today: a seed became a bud
> a bud became a flower
> Wednesday March Eighth (sañ-ju-kyū)

Faber asked Tori Ito, "*San-ju-kyu*? What does that mean?"

"It is pencilled in on the page," she answered.

Faber looked at the original rice paper and saw where someone had made the strokes in pencil, the original writer. He asked, "What does it mean?"

She answered, "The way it is placed, it can only mean 1939."

PIKA DON

AL DEMPSEY

TOR

A TOM DOHERTY ASSOCIATES BOOK
NEW YORK

This is a work of fiction. All the characters and events portrayed in this book are fictitious, and any resemblance to real people or events is purely coincidental.

PIKA DON

Copyright © 1993 by Al Dempsey

Cover art by Alan Ayers

A Tor Book
Published by Tom Doherty Associates, Inc.
175 Fifth Avenue
New York, N.Y. 10010

Tor ® is a registered trademark of Tom Doherty Associates, Inc.

ISBN: 0-812-50939-0

First edition: March 1993

Printed in the United States of America

0 9 8 7 6 5 4 3 2 1

Dedicated to
the men who rest in BB-39

PROLOGUE

He was sweating, and he was bluffing. He looked up at the others around the table and could tell they knew he was bluffing.

He was just entering his second month as a freshman congressman from Mississippi and had been invited by the Speaker of the House for a weekend of relaxation at Breckenridge Island, the secluded government-owned island off the eastern shore of Maryland. The invitation had been a singular honor; the Speaker had found him a team player and wanted to reward him. Now he just might have blown the whole thing because he was bluffing. You simply do not bluff those craggy pros who run the House of Representatives.

The Speaker lowered his head slightly and looked, with some degree of hostility, at the young man from Mississippi. The speaker said: "You sure you want to play that kind of a game." It was not a question; the emphasis was on *that* and it carried an implied order.

The young congressman said, "Well . . . maybe I'll just fold."

All those around the table looked pleased that the neophyte had learned a lesson. As long as anyone was willing to learn to play the game their way they would support the education process. The raising continued around the table.

It was difficult to tell if the greenish pallor of the face of the Mississippian was caused by a reflection of light off the green baize of the poker table, or if it had been induced by the sudden realization that he was in a hardball, high-stakes poker game. It was only late Thursday afternoon, and he had lost thirty-seven dollars on the last hand, plus the fifty-six dollars he'd dropped on the previous hands. If he was not able to bluff he was in big trouble. He was not among his peers—he was well out of his league.

The deck slid across for him to deal; he picked up the cards with reasonable trepidation.

"Five-card stud," he announced.

As he was riffling the cards for the first time, the Speaker's administrative assistant came into the card room from the main lounge. He smiled at the others in apology for interrupting the game and said, "You have a guest arriving, Mr. Speaker."

The Speaker nodded and said, "Deal me out," as he stood and left the room.

The Speaker quickly moved out of the main lounge and paused for a moment on the wooden porch of the building. Behind him, his administrative assistant asked, "Do you want me there?" The Speaker told him no.

The Breckenridge Island congressional retreat had been built immediately after World War II as a make-work project for some surplus Corps of Engineer personnel the military did not want to dump out on the job market until there were enough civilian jobs available to avoid a high unemployment rate. The original idea had been to give federal employees a place to confer, in a quiet atmosphere away from the hectic salons of the District of Columbia. The facility quickly became an exclusive, private perk for the top members of congress. Eventually, with the growing importance of seniority in the legislative process, the use of Breckenridge Island became the private purview of the Speaker of the House; visits to the island were made only at his request or with his permission.

The Speaker looked out over his domain and felt a peace that lately had come only when he was on the island. He was tired of his political role. He was powerful—many declared him second in power only to the president—but the demands on his personal life were taking their toll; his emotions were beginning to affect his decision-making abilities, and he was giving serious thoughts to quitting.

The Speaker went down the front steps of the lodge, climbed into his golf cart, and drove to the island's landing dock. As he arrived at the pier, a Coast Guard launch smoothly eased to a mooring and discharged a passenger.

The man who emerged was clothed in black: shoes, suit, coat and hat. A white Roman collar showed at his neck. He was sixty-one-years old—one year younger than the Speaker. As he stepped onto the dock, the man extended his hand and said, "Nice to see you again, Mr. Alighieri."

The Speaker responded, "Nice to see you again, Father Venturi." The formality of the greetings was for the benefit of the Coast Guard skipper standing by the gangway. The Speaker called to him, "We will be about thirty minutes, Ensign. Not much more." The sailor nodded and moved back onto his craft.

The Speaker led the priest to the golf cart. For the rest of the visit, except for parting salutations, their conversation would be in Italian, in the Neapolitan dialect which was the native tongue of both men's grandparents. The Speaker drove down to a lagoon on the north side of the island. There the two men climbed out and began walking along in the twilight.

"Could you stay a few days?" the Speaker asked. "We could use a Mass on Sunday."

The priest smiled. "You could probably use a Mass being said tonight, my friend."

"It could never harm anything." The Speaker cut off his smile and added, "You are welcome to stay. We have seen so little of each other recently."

"We both have our duties."

"Will you stay?"

"I cannot. I leave for Rome tomorrow. There is little time for personal wants."

The two men had met forty years previous when both were students at the University of St. Louis, before Venturi had entered the Society of Jesus—the Jesuits—and Alighieri had entered civil service, then politics. Venturi had become the provincial superior of North America, the ranking member of the Jesuit order in the United States, while Alighieri had become the legislative leader of his party. Both were properly proud of their accomplishments, and each respected what the other had done.

"Sorry I had to drag you down here. The media would have been all over me if I'd come to New York to meet you," the Speaker began.

"I don't mind. I knew it was important when you called. What's the problem?"

The Speaker indicated a bench by the walkway around the lagoon; the men seated themselves. Then he said, "There's a peace rally scheduled for August just outside San Francisco. It's apparently going to be a massive thing, with three or four hundred thousand people. Some of my committee chairmen have, with good intentions but not much brilliance, managed to become involved as patrons. The committees are important—Energy, Armed Forces,

Foreign Affairs and a couple of others. The men involved are the very heart of our party structure.''

The Speaker paused, reached for a cigarette and remembered that he had quit smoking a month before. The priest picked up on this and realized that, for the first time in many years, he was seeing his friend feel insecure. Venturi reached into his coat pocket, took out a small metal box containing his tiny black cheroots and offered it to Alighieri. The two men lit up, and the Speaker continued, ''Something's going wrong with the delegation scheduled to come over from Japan.''

The priest showed his surprise. Alighieri went on: ''The Japanese delegation is the linchpin of the rally. They're sending survivors of Hiroshima to speak at the rally, there'll be a magnificent gift from the Institute For Peace and a temporary loan of displays from the Peace Memorial Museum; most of the people in this country have never seen the relics from the explosion. If anything happens to disrupt Japan's participation, the whole thing will fall apart.''

The priest, who had become the top Jesuit in America by understanding others' problems, waited and listened. The Speaker continued, ''A half dozen countries would love to have an excuse for not coming; they hate us that much. A Japanese pull out would give them an out. If the rally fails, I end up with five committee chairmen wearing political egg on their faces.''

The priest asked, ''How can I help?''

''I need some intelligence on what is going on. I need to know. I've tried through the State Department and they are useless. The FBI does not have the authority to act and I won't go to the CIA. My quiet inquiry to the Japanese embassy has given me nothing. I need some help.''

''Phalanx?''

''I'm sorry to ask.''

''Don't be.''

"But I've done it before."

"I've told you before: Don't hesitate."

"Could you have Phalanx look into it?"

"It will be done."

Phalanx is the covert intelligence-gathering arm of the Society of Jesus. Since its inception, the Jesuits have obligated each of their members to make semiannual reports on conditions within their individual areas of duty. Every six months, tens of thousands of analyses are forwarded to each priest's Provincial Superior, detailing the political, social, economic and religious climate of every community served by a Jesuit. The Provincials in turn compile a detailed report which is forwarded to the head of the Society—the Secretary General in Rome.

Historically, the Jesuits have been able to provide the Vatican with data not surpassed by any of the world's national intelligence organizations. In 1939, Pius XII realized that he was in need of other types of information and he turned to the Jesuit Secretary General, the Black Pope. By mid-1940, Phalanx was in operation in trouble spots all over Europe, using specially selected priests to gather additional intelligence on specific assignments. The group, never numbering more than sixty, continued to function for the Vatican as a special resource; their license was broad, their efforts valuable.

The priest looked at the Speaker and asked, "What is the time frame? I am going to Rome, and I will be seeing the provincial of Japan. I could have him use his people."

The Speaker asked, "Could you handle it yourself? I would rather it be someone I knew, someone who could report back to me quickly. We want to solve any problems as soon as possible."

The priest nodded and replied, "It will be done that way." After a pause, he added, "Is there anything else you need?"

The Speaker extended his hand. "No, only your blessing." The priest gave it with pleasure, because the two were true friends.

They were driving back to the dock area when the Speaker discreetly handed a manila envelope to the priest and said, "I wish you'd take this to Rome and see that it's put to a good cause." The priest took the envelope and pocketed it without looking at the contents; he knew that it was a contribution of cash. The Secretary General would see that the money went to some hospital or teaching unit. The envelope contained twenty-three thousand dollars in large bills.

The Speaker waited as the launch sped off into the night, then headed back into the poker game.

PART I

CHAPTER ONE

The Japanese immigration officer looked at the face, then down at the photograph; they matched. "You have been to Japan previously?" The English was perfect, with a tinge of a Southern accent.

"A long time ago," Bart Faber answered.

The man looked at the photograph again. Bart Faber was tall, light brown hair, with a face that could be considered attractive only by a woman who especially liked hard features. The jaw, cheekbones and forehead were defined by sharp angles. The passport stated the date of birth as December 17, 1953. The looks of the visitor tallied with the date even though the subject did look a bit younger than his age.

The officer tapped data into the computer terminal and waited. He chatted while the machine searched the records. "How long since you have been in Japan, Mr. Faber?"

Faber stated again that it had been a long time.

"And what do you do for a living?"

"I'm an educator."

The immigration officer was not pleased. He wanted to listen to English as well as speak it. But this visitor did not seem inclined to chat. The computer terminal made one of those noises which warns that the data is due in thirty seconds. The officer looked once more at the passport with a barely perceptible look of concern. Faber caught the signal and made ready for more questions. The passport was brand-new, issued only the day before. It had to have taken some effort; the man, Faber, standing there before the officer had managed to get the Japanese consul-general in San Francisco to imprint a tourist visa on the same day. That accomplishment indicated influence.

The computer terminal displayed the biographical data it contained on Bart Faber: He had been in Japan twice before; first as a U.S. Army soldier in late 1970, and second, in mid-1971, also as a soldier. The first time he had spent four months there, then shipped out for Vietnam; the second time he was only in transit, as one of the wounded on a med-evac flight bound for the States.

To the immigration officer, the four months' visit in 1970 and the brand-new passport were enough for him to alert the immigration agents on duty up on the second floor of the Arrivals area of the airport. He tapped in the code letters which would display the information on the terminal upstairs. He would let them worry about this American visitor.

When the Japanese government had constructed their controversial new airport at Nirita-Sanrizuka in the early 1970s, they anticipated a boom in jet airline travel, supersonic aircraft and terrorism in the skies; all of those matters had required creative planning. But close clandestine observation of arriving travelers was nothing new in Japan; ever since Commodore Matthew Perry had opened

Japan to the rest of the civilization, the ruling class of the nation had treated foreigners with deep suspicion.

Twenty feet above the Arrivals lounge was an office with a mirrored window for agents to look through. At a desk by the window was a computer terminal on which, at any given moment, the agents on duty could summon up data from the units on the main floor.

The agents in the security room were dividing their attentions between viewing the arrival who had triggered the alert and the terminal screen giving Bart Faber's background in Japan. They noted the speed with which Bart Faber had obtained a new passport and a tourist visa. But what really caught their attention was the four months Faber had spent in Japan in late 1970. Those were years in which antigovernment forces had been especially active, causing social and political problems. Anyone who had visited during that period was suspect.

The two men in the security room had three options: to talk directly to the suspect, to allow him to pass through, or—the most frequently used procedure—to assign surveillance to him and get a detailed report of what the visitor was up to. Manpower was no problem for the agents; apprentice detectives from the Metropolitan Tokyo Police Academy were used for the task as a routine part of their training. The detectives were required to follow any suspect visitor for a period of twenty-four hours, and then to file a report with the Ministry of the Interior. A short telephone call to the airport security office on the ground level alerted the next team of observers; they would be waiting outside the baggage claim/customs area.

"Thank you, Mr. Faber," the immigration officer at the desk said as he stamped Faber's passport and scribbled in a sixty-day permission over the ADMITTED chop.

Faber nodded his thanks, smiled and picked up his garment bag and briefcase. He followed the arrows directing him to customs.

The Japan Air Lines flight that had brought Bart Faber to Tokyo had landed at five-thirty in the morning; the arriving passengers were clearing their baggage by ten to six. Faber passed through customs after only a cursory check. Outside, taxi and limousine drivers were anxiously trying to corral their passengers for the sprint to Tokyo. Even on a Saturday morning the traffic into the city was considerable, and their hopes of beating the rush were gallant, considering the fact that they never won the race. Eternal optimists, they still persisted in trying.

Bart Faber paused, deciding which transport to use, when he felt a tug at his sleeve. A woman's voice said, "Father Faber?" He turned and was greeted with an attractive if discontented-looking face haloed in a frame of blonde hair. "I'm Bart Faber," he answered.

"I'm Sister Catherine Mary. Mother superior told me to meet you."

"Dominican?" he asked.

"Dominican," she answered. "How did you know?"

He gave a soft smile but no reply.

Faber was not pleased to be met by a nun, even if she was not broadcasting her vocation by wearing a habit. The blouse and skirt and modest blue wool overcoat did not attract attention, but the only way the mother superior of the Dominican sisters in Tokyo could have known of his arrival was if someone at Phalanx headquarters in the States had told her to meet him. Now the only way to lessen the impact of being seen with her was to leave the airport as quickly as possible.

"Shall we go?" he said. Sister Catherine Mary did not appreciate his curt manner, but then she did not appreciate having to be receptionist early on a Saturday morning. She began walking towards her car, which was parked in a loading zone.

Sister Catherine Mary was behind the wheel before Bart Faber could sling his bags into the rear seat. The engine of the aged Toyota wheezed air into its four cylinders, and was pulling away from the curb before Faber had fully closed his door.

Two hundred feet behind them, in a powerful black sedan, two neophyte detectives of the Metropolitan Tokyo Police Academy pulled out and began following their subject.

Sister Catherine Mary handled the car with a skill not anticipated in a cleric. She scooted around the buses and cars jockeying for position as they entered the main expressway leading towards Tokyo, gunned the Toyota up to sixty, and broke out of the pack well ahead of the nearest competition. Bart Faber looked over at the young woman for some sign of enjoyment; he saw only a grimly determined face.

"Where are we going, Sister?"

"We?" she came back, her voice brittle. "We are going to the convent and then you can do what you please. My orders are to meet you, come back to town and turn over this car. That's it!"

Faber was tired from the flight and he had more important goals than a quarrel with a nun. He ignored the challenge, and the young nun seemed piqued. She began driving with more intensity, and some carelessness.

Father Faber watched the scenery. Tokyo was awesome. Many people claim that Los Angeles sprawls; not so. The word *sprawl* was invented for Tokyo. Here over thirteen million people are efficiently snuggled into just under eight hundred square miles. Earthquake probabilities have inhibited any concentration of really tall buildings, and therefore low, generally wooden homes are the style. Subtracting a reasonable amount of land for factories, office buildings and streets, the average Tokyo resident has enough square footage to erect half of a single-car garage for living space. Property is valuable in Tokyo.

From the expressway, Bart Faber looked out at the

jammed-together roofs of the masses. Out of habit and
training, he occasionally glanced behind them; after the
sixth glance he was convinced they were being followed.
He said to the nun: "Let's get off this expressway, Sister.
Could we take a route through the city?"

"Look, Father. Mass is at seven o'clock at the convent. I
have to be on duty at the hospital at eight. Taking you on
a sightseeing tour is not my idea of my obligation. I'm
supposed to pick you up; I've done that. I'm supposed to
take you to the convent and give you this car. I'm doing
that! That's it! No sightseeing!"

Faber smiled at her tirade. Her cranky attitude was typical of those new young women seeking a vocation. He
replied, "Let's remember our vow of obedience, Sister."

She flashed an angry glance in his direction; there was
something she did not like about this priest. He was not
all that much older than she; he looked to be at least in
his mid-thirties, and in good physical shape. So many of
the priests she saw nowadays were not taking care of themselves, but this one looked like a jogger, and he probably
ate properly. He was out of collar; his brown sports coat
coordinated well with the rest of his outfit. She finally
realized that it was the man's confidence; it almost bor-
dered on arrogance. She was uncomfortable with his massive self-assurance. To remind her of her vow of obedience
was to show that he knew he was right; Sister Catherine
Mary did not like a man who knew he was right. "Where
do you get off?" she asked crossly.

Traveling from the international airport at Nirita, the
expressway arched in a southwesterly direction, so the
morning sun was coming up almost directly in back of
them. The house roofs undulated over the land in an end-
less wave. There was no logical place to exit without entering a labyrinth of suburban developments. Bart Faber
asked the nun, "Is the Dominican monastery still in Shibuya?"

"Yes."

He looked at his watch. It was only ten after six, and he guessed that with the lack of really heavy traffic on the expressway it would take about another thirty minutes to get to that section of Tokyo. A ten-minute detour would still get her back in time for the seven o'clock mass. He told her, "When we get to Akasaka, cut off at that exit. Just a couple of minutes, that's all. You'll get to the church on time."

She threw an angry glance at him; she did not appreciate humor, especially from a sarcastic Jesuit. She pushed her foot down on the accelerator as an indicator of her displeasure and began looking for the Akasaka exit.

In the black sedan behind them, the driver was tempted to overtake the Toyota and write out a speeding ticket. His partner told him to quit thinking like a traffic cop: "We're detectives now. Just follow them."

The Akasaka area of Tokyo is one of the new centers of business. A flush of new hotel building in the 1960s made it a focal point for visiting businessmen and tourists, blending Western influence with Oriental charm.

Sister Catherine Mary nearly overshot the exit in her effort to put Faber in his place. But she tapped the brakes effectively and coaxed the laboring car through the sweep of the exit. Faber looked back and saw that the black sedan had been taken by surprise, but had not missed getting off. Faber told the nun: "Down this street to the New Otani. There in the next block." She nodded.

There was a tour bus parked in the entrance driveway; forty-six camera-laden sightseers would soon be oozing out of the hotel. Faber said, "Drop me at the sidewalk, then take a spin around the block. If I'm not back when you get here, make another circuit; I'll be there by the time you make the second run." She opened her mouth to argue, but Faber was already opening the door. She braked to avoid him falling out.

Faber slammed the door shut and loped around the bus, then up the short flight of stairs to the hotel's entrance. He did not look back for the black sedan. Once in the lobby, he looked around for a way up to the mezzanine. A few hearty tourists were milling about the lobby, so he was not noticed by the hotel staff as he easily walked up the stairs which led to a large public area. There was a lingering odor of booze in the air, and the mezzanine looked as if it had been used for a cocktail party the night before. He worked his way around an obstacle course of tables and chairs, then reached the windows looking out on the street. The black sedan was not in sight.

None of the hotel staff were interested in this American, who was quite out of place away from the main lobby, because the tour-bus passengers were beginning to collect in a reasonably sized crowd. As he looked out the window, he saw the Toyota coming around the corner; the nun was driving a bit more quickly than was really necessary. She pulled to a stop in front of the hotel, the black sedan came into view. Only the front of the vehicle was visible from Faber's vantage point; the sedan's stop at the corner was professional, but then they blew it by easing forward a few feet so they could keep an eye on the Toyota without the inconvenience of one of the detectives getting out of their car. Then they really showed their inexperience: the man on the passenger side started to jump out. After a short hesitation, he started to close the door, then climbed back into the vehicle. The Toyota was moving again, and the sedan made itself all too obvious by increasing its speed to catch up. Faber decided they were not well trained.

Faber left the window and went back down through the lobby. He was standing on the sidewalk at the front of the bus when the Toyota came into view again.

Sister Catherine Mary pulled up, and Faber climbed

into the car. In a voice dripping with sarcasm she said, "Any other little chores, Father?"

He replied quietly, "You can get back on the main expressway, Sister." She was furious at him; she would really have enjoyed telling him off. But Faber was not paying attention; he was thinking about the black sedan behind them.

Since the two men who had been assigned to follow him were inexperienced, it was clear there was not really any high-level curiosity about what he was up to. This was just standard procedure. The immigration computer had, he guessed, showed that he had been in Japan a couple of times in the past, and, with the lack of activity on a quiet Saturday morning, some lower-level bureaucrat had suggested the monitoring. Faber was not in trouble. Not yet. But he would get rid of those who were watching.

The Nirita-Tokyo Expressway plunges into the heart of the city, then splatters out in different directions to the nine major cities that comprise the metropolitan district. Expressway Number Three is the main artery used for Shibuya, where the Dominican Monastery and Convent are located. Sister Catherine Mary was aiming the Toyota along Expressway Three with the concentration of a homing pigeon intent on returning to her hutch. Faber knew where they were going; he had studied the intricate roads and layout of Tokyo before he had left Phalanx headquarters, refreshing his memory of his visit as a member of the U.S. Army.

They exited the expressway and rushed past the Tokyo Rapid Transit Building. Faber looked back through the rear window. The nun asked, "Just what are you looking at, Father?"

"Just looking to see if we are going to get a speeding ticket." She accepted the excuse; he noted that the sedan was still following them.

The Dominican Monastery is on Nanpedidai Avenue and

about three blocks from the expressway exit. Father Faber looked at his watch; it was twelve minutes before seven. He mentioned the time to Sister Catherine Mary. She nodded, then said, "Why didn't the Society have someone meet you?"

"They did."

"I mean: Why not another Jesuit?"

"They don't like me."

She started to say that she could easily understand that point of view, but kept quiet, making a silent vow that she would have nothing more to say to this arrogant priest.

The monastery and convent occupy a full half-block of Nanpedidai Avenue. The nun pulled into a parking area beside the chapel. She took out the keys, handed them to Faber and gave a curt movement of her head that he was supposed to accept as good-bye. He told her, "Thanks for the lift." She climbed out of the car and headed into the church.

Father Faber reached across and locked the driver's door, then climbed out and locked his side. At the back of the church he found the entrance to the sacristy.

The Dominican priest inside was putting on his vestments. He stopped to accept Faber's thanks for being picked up at the airport.

The Dominican responded, "Would you like to assist at Mass, Father?"

"No, thanks, Father. I've got some things that need attention."

The other priest was an older man, in his mid-sixties. He said, "There was a time when you would have had to do your duty, Father."

"Whoops," Faber said. "I'll catch Mass tonight. What time will it be?"

"Not here," the older man said, "There is one at six o'clock over at St. Ignatius'. It's your order. You've heard of the church?"

Had Sister Catherine Mary had a chance to infect this old priest with her views on Bart Faber? The sarcasm was a little too heavy and too quick to have any reason. He left through the door leading into the church after a polite "Thank you."

The pews were about one-quarter filled, mostly with Dominicans who were probably scheduled to join Sister Catherine Mary on duty at the Catholic hospital. He avoided looking for the nun as he moved down the side aisle of the church; the congregation paid him little attention, but he was sure he could feel Sister Catherine Mary's eyes glaring in his direction.

At the back of the church, he cracked the door slightly to see where his followers had located themselves.

The black sedan was parked down the street, and two men were standing on the sidewalk, looking in his direction. As he had hoped, they were using typical lawman's logic: Their suspect was going to be tied up at Mass for a good half hour or more, so there was no sense in not getting something to eat. They walked down to the corner and went into a small *kissaten*, a Japanese version of McDonald's.

Faber headed out to the parking lot and was away, minus his surveillance, in less than a minute. Now he was free—on his own in Tokyo.

CHAPTER TWO

When Bart Faber had been assigned the task of going to Japan to compile a report on the dissension within the Institute For Peace, he had been given the usual contacts. He could touch base with U.S. embassy staff—even delicately stopping into the CIA station chief's office if need be—and he could, as a last resort, call on the two resident agents of Phalanx. The last option was to be used only in extreme circumstances; the provincial superior had made it quite clear: Faber was to be covert as long as possible. Those were the normal contacts, but Bart Faber usually used less orthodox sources.

When Faber had served in Japan at the Tokorazara U.S. Army base northeast of Tokyo, his best friend had been an American, Bernie Eby, who was especially adept at foreign languages and was working as an interpreter at base headquarters. The two young soldiers had shared a bond in skiing—they had first met during a Special Services trip to Sapporo—and in partying, which was an av-

ocation with many of the troops stationed in Japan. After
Faber had shipped out to Vietnam, the two had corre-
sponded with some vigor but the letters had tailed off when
Faber was wounded and shipped back to the States. Once
Faber had entered the seminary, the communications had
dwindled to two or three exchanges a year and, by the time
Faber was ordained, the two men were down to just annual
Christmas cards. Every now and then, there would be a
short note scribbled over the printed message "Hope to
See You Soon."

Faber knew that Eby had also been shipped to Vietnam,
and that he had married a Laotian refugee in Saigon. Eby
had taken his discharge in Japan and settled there with his
bride. He had worked at Radio Japan and the Voice of
America, then bounced around quite a bit with the sundry
English-language print publications in Tokyo. Faber knew
little else, except that Eby was a friend and friends often
help each other.

The last address Faber had for Eby was 923 Kakuco
Avenue in the Ueno section of the city; he was in the area
within ten minutes of sneaking away from the Dominican
monastery.

Finding the Eby residence was no easy chore; street
numbers in Tokyo have little correlation with logic, at least
as far as Occidental logic is concerned. On any given street
in Tokyo, the first house built was numbered 1; this system
was followed through the centuries, so that a house numbered 27 might sit between houses numbered 314 and 717.
But there is a solution—there is always a solution in Japan:
every two or three blocks there is a police substation, generally about the size of a telephone booth. The officers
manning the substations memorize house locations. Kakuco Avenue was not a long street and so Faber was directed to the proper house after having to check with
officers in only two substations.

Bernie Eby's house was not exceptional from the outside. Faber parked the wheezing Toyota by the curb and stood on the sidewalk for a moment, wondering what it would be like to see his friend after 23 years. He looked at his watch; it was just approaching seven-thirty. A smile came to Faber's lips. Years ago he would never have dreamed of visiting Bernie Eby so early on a Saturday morning: Friday nights had traditionally been their time to construct a substantial foundation for a gigantic hangover. He moved up the short path to the front door.

Tacked over the doorbell was a curled yellowed business card which identified Bernard Eby as REPORTER/WRITER— *Tokyo Times*. Faber pressed the button.

The man who answered the door was obviously Bernie Eby, but not the Bernie Eby of Bart Faber's memory. The fellow soldier who stood ramrod straight and whose face radiated joy had become a slouching dreg of a man with an obese body and an expression of fear. Large jowls rippled as the petulant mouth asked: "What the fuck do you want?"

"It's me," Faber blurted. "Bart Faber." He watched Eby try to untangle the short-circuited segments of memory.

Suddenly, there was recognition and with it a profusion of apologies and greetings. Bart Faber regretted having thought that Bernie Eby might do him some good with his mission. At age forty, Bernie Eby was obviously a lush.

They labored through the platitudes of reunion as they moved into the tiny living area of Eby's residence. Eby must have accumulated the furnishings over the years from Americans going back home; there was a motley assortment of chairs and tables and a tattered sofa. Faber was trying to cut off some of the inanities coming from Eby when the host stopped himself and offered, "How about a beer? Just for old times."

Looking at Eby's complexion, the invitation had been

predictable. "No beer for me, Bernie. You have any coffee?"

"Sure, trooper, I'll put the pot on." Eby moved to the far side of the room and started into the kitchen, but stopped, turned and asked, "Hey, where's the collar? You wrote and said you joined the Holy Joes."

"I did. I just travel out of uniform, sometimes."

"Makes it easier to pick up dames, right?"

Faber flicked a mild smile. Eby made a gesture that said he was sorry. He said, "Bad joke? Right?"

Faber shook his head. "No, Bernie. The last time we were together we were both chasing squirrels." The two men laughed; for the first time it was with some camaraderie. In the kitchen, while Eby measured coffee into the pot, Faber asked, "You still married?"

Eby responded, "Shit, yeah. Still on the old treadmill." He looked up at Faber and added, "She's down in Hong Kong looking for a brother or sister that might have come out with the boat people. She's been fuckin'-A crazy. Taning's sure some of her family made it out. I've told her she's crazy, but she's set on looking for them. What the fuck can I do?"

Faber warped back in time to a different era, when Eby and he had lived in the barracks where the *lingua franca* was made up of words of three consonants and one vowel. It had taken Faber a full six months of the seminary to get his vernacular under control. Faber asked, "You having family problems?"

Eby was getting out a cup for Faber's coffee and a beer for himself. "Naw, shit. She's great. Problem is, we live a lie; one big fucking lie, Bart."

Faber did not press: he had come for other reasons. But Eby needed no major encouragement. "The problem is that she wants to go back to Laos. Well, we can piss up a rope before they'll let a runaway and a round-eye set up housekeeping there. No way! I don't want to go back to the States; it'd be hard on Ta-ning. A slope bride has a hard time back home; I've heard what they go through.''

Faber said, ''Times have changed, Bernie.''

Eby scoffed, ''Sure, and shit don't stink. Naw, Bart, we're stuck here and, believe me, it ain't easy living in Japan. Those bastards let me hang by a thread, and they love to make sure I keep in line. No shit, Bart, it ain't easy.''

Faber tried to distract Eby by saying, ''The house is nice. You're doing okay.'' The house was not spectacular, and Eby was obviously not doing well, but it might turn the conversation.

''I did okay for a few years,'' Eby's voice had a slight whine to it, ''but not lately. No damned work worth a shit. I pick up a few bucks, crumbs they throw me.''

''Crumbs?''

Eby poured the coffee as he said, ''Sure, crumbs. It's tough living here, Bart. They don't have any use for us round-eyes except for getting things from us that they can't get from their own. The Japs have a knack for letting you know that you are just some piece of shit that they're going to use for as long as they can, then they'll toss you out with the night soil.''

Paranoia. That was the word that came to Bart Faber as he tried to shut out the complaints of his onetime friend; he was regretting coming here.

They moved from the kitchen into the living-room area. Eby, to Faber's relief, said, ''Hey, enough of my troubles, buddy. What're you doing here?''

Faber tasted the bitter coffee before he answered, ''I'm doing a magazine article for a quarterly magazine the Jesuits are starting.''

''Sounds like one of them arty intellectual rags. You like writing that shit?''

Faber smiled. ''I don't know, this is my first job with them.''

Eby asked, "You have a parish and all of that?"

"I work mostly at Fordham. Teaching."

"Hey—Professor Priest. Not bad."

"I don't think I could handle a parish, Bernie. Not to-day; too many problems."

"Ain't you supposed to have a parish?"

"Not really. The Jesuits are mainly a teaching order. We do hospital work, but the academic life gets most of our attention."

"A great way to plant that Jesuit logic in young minds."

Faber smiled. "That, too."

"So what's this article about?"

"That's why I came to you; I might need some help."

Eby gave a look that seemed to be a built-in response to an opportunity for making money; Faber caught the signal and stifled any such hope: "Just as a friend, Bernie. I don't have any budget, and I only want to pick your brain."

The look of resignation—bordering on disappointment—proved that Eby was on hard times. Faber paused, tempted to forget about talking to Eby at all. The room went quiet; Eby gulped a long draft of beer.

Eby broke the silence. "I'm not all that connected with things anymore, Bart. I've had a hard time getting work."

Faber asked, "What about Radio Japan? And the Mai-nichi newspapers? You wrote that you worked for them."

"Shit, they cut me off years ago. You've been out of touch for a long time, Bart."

Faber admitted "Sure, but we wrote. You said you were working."

Eby looked down at the floor, then gave a sad smile as he lifted the bottle of beer in a mock toast. "I had some stiff competition from my friends here."

Bart Faber had dealt with alcoholics at Jesuit hospitals; it had taken him several years to accept the problem as a sickness. He knew Bernie Eby had it. Trying to use the

knowledge of Bernie Eby would probably take more time
than it was worth, and Faber was on a schedule that allowed little time at all. He said, "I'll join you in a beer,
Bernie."

The ploy was not the kindest thing to do, but it was the
most expedient way he could think of to leave quickly.
One short beer, then out the door; Faber would use other
sources for his research.

But Eby did not move; he glared at the priest. "You
given up on your old buddy that easy, Bart? There was a
time when you'd have worried about my drinking."

Bernie Eby's mind was not as pickled as Faber had
guessed. He felt embarrassed at being caught in his ruse.
He countered, "Not really given up, Bernie. Just realistic.
You know the problem you've got, and I'm only here for
a week or ten days. There's not enough time for me to
help. I would if I could; believe me."

Eby swilled Faber's candor around in his mind the way
he would toy with the familiar sting of liquor, looking for
a defect. He gave a broad grin. " 'Pity! the scavenger of
misery.' Ain't that the fuckin' truth!"

Faber let out a loud laugh. "Was that Dryden? You
bastard."

Eby was laughing too as he stood. "Naw, Bart. It's
Shaw. You ought to know that." Eby went into the kitchen
and returned with two beers. He handed one to the priest,
who said, "Thanks, Bernie, you always have been a literate soul."

Eby sat back down across the room. "And I was always
able to read you like a book. You can bug out on me,
that's okay. But don't try to make me out as anything worse
than a good-natured drunk. If you need help on your job,
I'll pitch in. I always have; I always will."

Faber tasted his beer; it was good beer, just as most
Japanese beers were very good. He said so to Eby, who
nodded his agreement. Both men knew that Faber was

vacillating. It was not easy to turn away from an old friend; it was also not easy to ignore a possibly beneficial resource. Faber opted to leave the door open. "Maybe if I get a break then we could catch dinner or something. When's your wife due back? I'd like to meet her."

"Yeah, that'd be nice. I don't know when the shit she'll be back. I never do know because those gooks down in Hong Kong are a bunch of loonies. We'll see—maybe in the next few days."

Silence followed as each man pretended to savor the taste of an early morning beer, an uncomfortable strain between them.

The priest asked, "Whatever happened to that second lieutenant who was always on your case?"

Eby gave a sardonic laugh. "He bought it in 'nam. Probably got his ass fragged."

For the next few minutes they exchanged memories. As soon as it was seemly, the priest put down his beer and said, "I'd better get going, Bernie. I'll be in touch."

Eby made no move to get up. "Listen, Bart," he said, "I feel like hell. You come to me and I know you're looking for help, and now you're leaving and you're pissed at me."

Faber stood and spoke with a tone intended to squash Eby's mood. "That's not true, Bernie. I've come to do a job and, honestly, I am in a hurry. Sure, you might have helped me, but I think you have some problems that might just make my job harder. Your wife's away and you seem distracted by that, you seem to be down on your luck and I can't do a damned thing to help you. Our vow of poverty does not provide us much pocket money. The few bucks I have wouldn't do anything major for you, and I need cash just to get around. But I'll give it to you if you need it."

Eby snapped back, "You've really become a pain in the

ass, Bart Faber. I'm not looking for a handout from you. I said I'd help you if I can.''

Faber knew Eby was trying to put him on the defensive. Faber had dealt with too many drunks to miss the tactic. He said, ''Let it drop, Bernie. I'd better get going.''

Again Eby did not move; Faber stood there in that awkward moment of leave-taking when the guest is at the will of the host. Faber repeated that he would be going.

Eby said, ''Bart, Japan isn't what you and I thought it was back in the good old days. I've learned: The people who run things here are a brutal bunch of bastards. They can cut you up and serve you part of your own arm for sushi. They really do not like Americans, and if you're going to go poking around, maybe I can help you stay out of trouble.''

Faber had never seen any drunk do anything but cause trouble for the people around him. Abruptly, Faber said, ''We'll see.''

Eby stood. ''You arrogant sonofabitch! Who the fuck do you think you are?—taking that attitude with me. I offered to help you as a friend; I don't need any pontifical pronouncements out of you!'' The words were slightly jumbled together; Faber winced at the invective.

Faber countered. ''Look, Bernie''—the two men were three feet apart after Eby had crossed the room—''I don't want to add to your problems. I'll only be here a few days, then it's back to the States.''

''You don't give a shit about my problems.''

''I care about you.''

''You couldn't care less . . . you pompous ass.''

''I have a job to do.''

''Then let me help. Let me be a friend.''

Eby's voice had roller-coastered from belligerency to whines and ended up in calm challenge. Bart Faber was yanked along emotionally over the same route. In seminary, Faber had been taught that emotion has no place in logic. But the teaching brothers had not reckoned with friendship; or maybe they had, and Faber had missed the point. The pause between Eby's plea and Faber's reply was measured in feelings rather than in time. Quietly, Faber said, "I came to you hoping for help, Bernie."

"Then let me help. I want to."

There was another pause as the two men, two friends, studied each other. Faber broke the silence with a grin and said, "It's really no big deal, Bernie."

Eby answered with his own grin. "I probably couldn't help if it were a big deal."

The expression on Eby's face seemed to wash away all of the years that separated them from that time when they had been friends, close friends. Eby's jowls were still there, the face still sagged from dissipation, and the skin still had the same pallor, but the eyes reminded Faber of the joy that used to envelop his friend. Eby said, "Let's have a drink on that, Bart."

The proposition was predictable; Faber had never seen a drunk who did not think that drink was a panacea. He followed Eby towards the kitchen area again. He said, "I think I'll stick with coffee." And Eby responded, "Sure."

Faber fixed another cup of coffee while Eby ceremoniously opened a bottle of Suntory, the Japanese imitation of Scotch whisky. Faber remembered with some pleasure the number of bottles of Suntory he had split with the man across the kitchen; that number could compete with world records. Faber was surprised to feel an urge to join in the drink; he quickly sipped his coffee.

Eby was crouching down under the sink, mumbling to himself. "I know there's a bottle of club soda here someplace."

To Faber that was a good sign; drunks don't need mixers. Eby found the bottle and was looking for an opener when he asked, "So what's the name of your magazine? It's new, right?"

"I think they're going to call it *Vector*. Mostly they'll deal with topical subjects on a current-affairs basis."

"Brainy stuff, huh?"

"Not really," Faber said, "but probably on the egg-headed side." Faber hated lying, but Phalanx headquarters had come up with the magazine as a cover for his asking questions in Japan; he hoped he would not be challenged too much on his writing credentials.

Eby asked, "So what's the article about?"

"The editor heard there was some problem with the peace groups—especially with the Institute For Peace; he wants me to find out what's going on."

Eby was stirring the drink with his finger, and Faber was able to catch a moment, an instant of hesitation. He looked up and could see that Eby's eyes, full of joy a few minutes before, now flickered with another emotion: Fear. Eby could not hide the strain in his voice as he said, "You checking on the IFP?"

"Just looking to see if anything is going wrong. The Jesuits have an interest in peace groups."

Eby leaned back against the countertop. "When that editor hands out a bucket of shit, he really makes sure it's full to the brim. He must not like you."

"What's that mean?"

"It means that the IFP is in such a mess that it will take you a month just to put their stupid asses into the right pigeonholes."

Faber led the way back into the living room. As they walked, Eby said, "There are about twenty thousand card-carrying members of the IFP, and there are about that many opinions on how the organization should be run. It is the most fractured of all the peace groups."

"Every cause has its factions, Bernie, but they all still work for the common goal. That's what's important."

Eby sipped his drink. "That's the problem, trooper; the

factions seemed to be splitting up the goal. Sometimes they don't seem to know where they're going."

"Come on, Bernie, methods might change but not the goals. The whole movement is founded in Hiroshima; how can they move away from trying to prevent another disaster like that?"

There was another moment of hesitation and in Eby's eyes a flash of fear. Faber felt he was touching a sensitive nerve.

Eby recovered, hoping his reaction had slipped unnoticed past his friend. He argued, "On the surface, sure; but the IFP is Japanese, and they have their own problems. The two main factions of the IFP are the pacifists and the peace activists. The first bunch wants to combat violence of any kind, and the other bunch is willing to cause mayhem. I don't really know if they'd be above fatal mayhem in their efforts to stop war. There's a big fuckin' difference in their methods."

"I understand that there can be differences in tactics, but those are only nuances," said Faber.

"Nuances, hell, Bart. The peace activists here in Japan are determined. You go and watch a demonstration and you see a mass of people dressed in helmets, riot shields and bulletproof vests. You don't know if it's the fuckin' cops or the demonstrators. The word *activist* here has a special meaning. They don't go for sitting on railroad tracks in front of a train carrying nuclear weapons. Over here these shitheads bring an armored bulldozer and tear up the tracks."

"I've seen the demonstrations on TV; they're pretty violent."

"You've seen shit on TV, Bart. In one of these peace riots in Japan, if ten people get hurt you can bet that six or seven of them are the cops; the kill ratio is about fifty-fifty. The IFP are pros, real pros. At least, they used to be."

"Used to be?"

"Until about two years ago." Eby paused. "Two years ago last month. The activists lost their main leader. They have been kind of quiet lately."

Faber finished off his coffee and went to the kitchen for a refill, and to give himself time to think. Eby followed him and made another drink. Faber watched the ratio of booze to water and noticed that it was still in the area of a legitimate social drink. He calculated there would be about another half hour before Eby would be drunk. Faber said, "I was told that the IFP was being disrupted, that they were near collapse."

Eby asked, "What the fuck were you told besides that, Bart? You come traipsing in here and tell me you need help, and that you have to find out what's going on with the IFP. Why don't you level with me?"

Bart Faber had no intentions of 'leveling' with his friend. It was not Phalanx operative style to bring sources of information into a confidential situation. But it was necessary to give a little in order to gain what he wanted. He answered, "There's a peace rally scheduled for San Francisco in August; a big rally."

"I've heard about it."

"Our magazine's first issue will come out right before the rally, and we want to write about the IFP. I need to find out if their internal problems are a threat to the rally. That's it in a nutshell."

Eby said, "I'll save you a shitpot full of time and trouble. The problems are bad, so bad there's no chance that Japan is going to send a delegation to the rally. The IFP has queered the deal for all of the peace groups. There's your answer, and now you can just take the rest of the time and spend it drinking with me."

"The IFP people won't go to the rally?"

"Not a chance, Bart. You can bet on that."

Bart Faber had done enough fieldwork to know that one

opinion does not establish fact; but Eby was very emphatic. Faber had been charged only with finding out what was going on, not with trying to influence the Japanese participation. But he would need more than the word of an old Army chum, a drunken chum at that.

"Why?" Faber asked.

"Lots of reasons."

"Give me three."

"First, the notion is that the rally should be held at Hiroshima."

"Reasonable."

"Second, the people who could make that decision have been given the word: no show in the U.S."

"By whom?"

Eby ignored the question. "Third, the one guy who could have run the whole thing, the one who could have led the delegation—he's dead. He died a couple of years ago, and there's a leadership vacuum. They won't show in Frisco; I'll guarantee it."

Faber waited to hear if Eby had more to offer, then said, "Come back to point two. Who gave the word?"

"There's an old bunch in the power structure here who control the purse strings of the IFP. If Tac was alive, he would fight them. But he's dead."

"Tac?"

"Tac Okomoto. He was the one who kept the IFP moving; he was their spark plug."

Faber pulled the name up from his memory; he had heard about Tac Okomoto in his briefing at Phalanx headquarters. He made a mental note to come back to that, but there was something more important to the priest: "You mentioned the 'old bunch' who said 'no show in the U.S.' Who are they?"

There was that flicker of fear again in Bernie Eby's eyes, the same hesitation to speak. Faber put up his hand. "Hold it, Bernie. Just hold it." The priest took a swig of coffee, put the cup down and said, "Three or four times now, I have seen a look in your eyes that makes me uncomfortable, really uncomfortable, Bernie. I might be misreading you, but I think something is bothering you about talking to me. If I'm right, what's bothering you?"

This time Faber let the pause run its course. He was pleased that Eby did not gulp down his drink or even take a sip. Finally, Eby said, "There is something, Bart, but it is not you; it's Japan. The system here can tear you to pieces. I don't want to tangle with them."

"They won't know I talked with you. I won't use your name."

"They'll know. You can bet your ass they'll know."

Faber lost his patience. "Who is 'they'?"

"There's a group here in Japan that runs the whole show . . . all of it." Faber nodded. Eby continued: "They formed up around the turn of the century. They've been called different names at various times."

"The *zaibatsu*?" Faber offered.

"One of their names, an old one," Eby agreed. "Another is Economic Council. Another is International Trade Board. They control the economy, the government, the society. They *are* Japan."

"And they don't want the peace activists to go to San Francisco?"

Eby ignored the question. "Within the *zaibatsu*—or what ever name—there is a small elite clique referred to as the *Kugatsu*. The word means 'September,' and it came into use in 1945 when the Japanese officially surrendered. September, 1945. They are nationalistic, they are anti-American, and they were the driving force behind Japan's recovery."

"Then they—the *Kugatsu*—don't want the IFP to go to the rally?"

Eby smiled. "Your pronunciation isn't bad, but it isn't great. *Ku-gat-su.*"

Faber was on the verge of snapping at Eby's snide attitude. The two men looked at each other. Eby finally said, "That's right. The *Kugatsu* could control Tac Okomoto, but he's dead; they can't trust the others in the IFP."

Faber let his impatience show. "Look, Bernie, I appreciate your giving me the background. I know some of it, and the rest is interesting, but you're avoiding telling me why you show fear when I bring you near the subject. If you want to drop it, say so. I'll understand."

"It isn't fear, Bart. Well, maybe you could call it fear, but you have to understand. I'm living here, and I have to make a living." Eby struggled with the challenge his friend had placed in front of him, then admitted, "I screwed up a couple of years ago."

Faber did not press the matter. He had about given up on getting anything of value out of Eby. Faber needed information, not a sad tale of woe.

Eby ignored his drink and crossed the kitchen to pour himself a cup of coffee. He refilled Faber's cup and, with a slight nod, indicated the back door.

Property values in Tokyo are so high that large lawns and gardens are rare. Most home sites have only a bit of land, and very few backyards are larger than an American patio. Bernie Eby's was no different; it was a plot of ground about the size of a miniature-golf putting green. A wooden yard table was the only piece of lawn furniture that could fit; it looked like another piece left by an American returning to the States. An ancient tree canopied the table. The two men sat across from each other.

In a quiet voice Eby said, "It's safer out here."

"Safer?"

"There could be some bugs in the house." Eby made a sign at his ear; he meant listening devices.

Faber realized that he was seeing a case of full-blown paranoia. The realization hurt. The man across the table from him—the man who had been a jovial friend, the man

Faber had hoped would be of some help—was not mentally capable of helping, not capable of being a true friend. It hurt.

Eby sensed the change in Faber. "You think I'm exaggerating? You think such a thing is not possible? Let me ask you one question, Bart: Somebody in the Jesuits needed an article written for this new magazine—why didn't they depend on the locals? There are dozens of Japs in your order who could do the job. Why not use them?"

Faber knew why: the provincial superior in the United States did not want to compromise the two Japanese operatives in Phalanx. There was no way that Faber could share that with Eby. But Faber could understand what it must look like to his friend; he had to make some kind of reply. But Eby started speaking: "I told you I screwed up. I did, royally. Back when Tac Okomoto died there was a lot of chatter that he might have been killed on orders from the bigwigs. It seemed crazy at first, but then I began hearing some other rumors. Tac had been setting up something in the way of a big exposé. He had gotten hold of some documents and just needed one more piece of proof before he could make a big splash. From what I heard, he could have put the Institute For Peace in the driver's seat on the whole nuclear question in Japan. The day he got that last document was the day he died, or was killed."

"What do you mean: killed?"

"I mean *murdered*. Shit, Bart, don't you listen? Tac Okomoto was supposed to have died in a house fire, an accident. An accident, your ass! I started digging into the story, and that's where I screwed up. An American in Japan has to keep his ass out of trouble, but what I was digging into must have been a threat to someone, because I was waved off."

"Officially?"

"They got the message to me—loud and clear."

"What'd you find out before you quit?"

Eby said, "I found enough to convince me that Tac Okomoto did not die in some fool accident. I found out that he had collected the document before he was killed, and that that document made it necessary to get Tac out of the way."

Faber shook his head. "There's a flaw, Bernie. If the power structure was able to control your friend, then why would they have him taken out of the picture?"

"That bothered me, too, Bart, until I realized that they had lost control of Tac. He had come up with something they didn't want public and it was too much for them to let it slide. I guess they tried to make him back off, but he kept going. So they used one of their other tools: They killed him."

Faber jumped on that. "There's another illogical position. So this bunch loses control of their fair-haired boy, and someway he is taken out of the picture; now they just let the IFP collapse. I don't buy it—they have too much at stake. The Japanese are for peace. Of all the nations in the world, Japan knows the horror of nuclear war."

Eby's face showed his contempt. "Don't be so damned naive, Bart. No matter what they say publicly, the Japanese military want nuke weapons. They want them, and they'll get them."

"It's against their constitution!"

"Crap! Every American administration since Lyndon Johnson has been working to get the Japs to include nukes in their weaponry; it's going to happen. Soon."

"The proof you're wrong is in what you just said: They've failed for nearly thirty years. It won't happen."

"Bart, you're kidding yourself. This country has been dealing in military power for a thousand years. They've written the book on building a warrior society."

Faber was impressed with Eby's vehemence. Like most Americans, Faber thought that the horrific lessons of Hiroshima and Nagasaki would be enough to keep any nation from taking up the nuclear sword again. Maybe Japan was different.

But such conjecture was not part of Bart Faber's mission. His job was to see if Japan would stay away from the World Peace Rally, and he had Eby's opinion that they would. It was time to be rid of Eby; there was nothing more to be gained by listening to the rhetoric of an angry drunk. Faber finished off his coffee in a way that indicated he was going to leave; Eby pleaded, "Look, Bart, stay with me. We can do a bunch of catching up on old times. I've seen quite a few of our old drinking buddies over the past few years."

There was no temptation in the offer. Faber stood.

Eby jumped up with surprising urgency. "Look," Eby offered, "I can take you to a real source about this trouble. You could learn a lot. How about that?"

Faber looked at his watch and saw that it was only ten minutes past ten. He had a couple of hours before he should be leaving Tokyo. His plan was to drive to Osaka, where he would stay overnight before driving on to Hiroshima. He decided he could invest a bit more time.

"Who's the source?" Faber asked.

"Tori Ito." Then Eby added, "She's the gal who lived with Tac Okomoto until he died."

"A tragic, would-be widow?"

"A woman who knew every thought of Tac Okomoto. I haven't seen her for a couple of years, but she could give you the straight story on why he was murdered."

The priest hesitated. He did not want to waste time, but the background on Tac Okomoto might give him some insight into what was going on within the Institute For Peace. He said to Eby, "Let's go see her."

CHAPTER THREE

"Smooth as a baby's ass!" There was polite laughter, then Clay Morton added, "Now ain't that just the best story I've heard in a long time?" He erupted into a laugh that boomed all the way across the lounge and into the bar; heads turned, then discreetly looked away. Morton repeated, "Well, I never—'Smooth as a baby's ass.' That's really something."

Isamu Saito smiled but did not look around the room. He knew Morton's loud laughter was disturbing the other golfers taking refreshments.

The joke which had prompted Morton's outburst was a Japanese classic: A Tokyo advertising firm hired to help introduce an American brand of talcum powder to the Japanese market had translated the slogan 'Smooth as a baby's bottom!' Thus, for there is no euphemism for *derrière* in the Japanese language. The gaffe had become a favorite anecdote, although this was the first time Clay Morton had heard it.

Isamu Saito decided against another, more amusing joke. He did not want to trigger another loud laugh that would further offend the others in the Tokyo Country Club.

The rooms were crowded as usual on a Saturday morning—golf is an obsession with the men of Japan. Where else in the world could a country club charge two hundred thousand dollars for initiation and monthly dues of two thousand dollars and still have a waiting list five years long?

Morton and Saito finished off their beers and, after Saito signed the check, went out onto the terrace overlooking the eighteenth green. They had finished their play, and Morton was contemplating asking for a second round, but he knew it would place a nearly impossible burden on his friend; getting the early Saturday starting time had been a major accomplishment, considering that Morton had voiced his desire for a round of golf only the day before, when he had arrived. Morton's visit was an annual event, repaid each fall by Isamu Saito visiting Clay Morton in Houston. The two men had been associates in business ventures for nearly five decades.

Morton had first come to Japan as a member of General Douglas MacArthur's logistics staff at the end of World War II. He had been a wet-nosed, twenty-one–year–old Army captain when he arrived with the general to begin setting up the occupation government. One of Morton's first tasks had been to scramble around Japan locating competent industry managers to assume leadership positions: MacArthur would not permit the businessmen who had supplied Japan's war machine to remain in top-level categories. Eventually, MacArthur had to yield to practicality; the old industrial warlords ended up managing Japan's industrial recovery program.

But, to the benefit of the victor and the vanquished, Morton's efforts had been productive. MacArthur had sent his staff members down far enough on the Japanese cor-

porate ladder so that they found a couple dozen executives
too young to be culpable for the war crimes of industry,
yet bright enough to step into the void. There Morton had
found Isamu Saito.

The accidental encounter of the two men had been pro-
pitious; both were just beginning to move upwards. During that initial period, Morton had frequently enlisted Saito
to help structure postwar Japanese industry into a machine
for peace. That period had lasted from 1945 through 1949.
Morton had risen to the rank of lieutenant colonel when
war broke out on the Korean Peninsula. He was put in
charge of the equipment and personnel needed to build
military roads. He was just about to be promoted to full
colonel when General MacArthur crossed his military
sword with President Truman's political battle-axe. On
April 11th, 1951, Clay Morton's military fortunes dis-
solved as MacArthur was relieved of his Far East command; those with the general fell under the same blow that
finished their hero.

Morton remained in Japan during the transition of command to General Matthew Ridgeway, but he sensed his
future was dim. When Japan's sovereignty was restored by
the peace treaty of April, 1952, Clay Morton was scrambling around for some way to make a living as a civilian.
His friendship with Isamu Saito had provided the solution.

He resigned his Army commission and returned to his
native Texas, where he scouted around for potential customers of Japanese steel. In the course of his search, Morton bumped into a fledgling industry: petrochemical
products. He made Stateside contacts, went back to Japan,
and convinced Isamu Saito of the industry's potential. The
pair of them went to work. By 1955 they had obtained
government assistance in both Washington and Japan, and
by 1968 Japanese petrochemical firms were nipping at the
heels of their American competitors. Acrylics, polyesters

and polyvinyls were streaming into the world markets from Japan, in hundreds of thousands of tons.

Morton and Saito became wealthy men, and by the time Japan was ready to enter the nuclear-power age, the two men were there. Their Nippon Atomic Power Company made its mark on the scene, and by the end of the 1970s, forty-one percent of Japan's electrical power was being generated by nuclear reactors. Morton and Saito had evolved additional fortunes.

Their bond of mutual friendship passed beyond the realm of normal business associates; so if Clay Morton sometimes became a bit louder than he should have in the reserved Tokyo Country Club, Isamu Saito did not show displeasure.

Before World War II, there had been a group of influential businessmen and industrialists in Japan called the *zaibatsu*—a cartel of brutal financial wizards who had grown up within the Japanese power structures and who had provided the tools for the militarists to plunge Japan into a disastrous war. When General MacArthur steered Japan on the road back to recovery, the *zaibatsu* reorganized in a manner that was acceptable to the conquerors.

Under any moniker, old or new, the *zaibatsu* was—and is—the financial oligarchy overseeing Japan's commerce. Under a new name, the Industrial Council, fifty leaders from every facet of the economy control output, stifle unions, manage markets and see that Japan continues her conquest of the industrial world.

Japan, since entering the industrial world, has been a major manufacturer of steel and steel products. The size of the steel industry was what allowed Japan to create the guns and tanks and ships with which to wage war. After the war the steel mills were still big and the work force well trained; postwar markets were needed. Any probe for export sales to the U.S. had to be kept at a low profile, because there were still tangible hostilities against Japan;

tens of thousands of American boys had been killed by the
steel weapons of Japan. Morton became one of the low-
profile probers.

It was the Economic Council and his friendship with
Isamu Saito that had determined Clay Morton's future.

The two men on the terrace watched a foursome finish
on the eighteenth green. The morning was beautiful.

"Do you want to talk?" Saito asked.

Morton glanced at his friend with some surprise; Morton knew that Saito was referring to talk about business
and that was traditionally deferred until their first formal
business meeting, this time scheduled for Monday. Morton had always strictly recognized the Japanese manner of
not plunging right into discussions; in Japan certain con-
ventions, bordering on ritual, are to be observed before
the mundane problems of making a deal.

"Now? Here?" Morton blurted.

Isamu Saito smiled broadly, with a familial affection. "My
friend, we have been through many trials and many victories,
mostly good times. You have been patient with our customs,
and I appreciate that. But I have come to know you as a
brother, and I know when something is bursting to come out
of you. What will we speak of on Monday?"

Morton did have a major issue to discuss with Saito, but
he had already planned an elaborate and intricate presen-
tation. But Morton had not climbed to the top of an industry by being unable to improvise. He said, "We have
a chance to get the worldwide license for the Voit power-
generating plants."

Saito came back. "I thought that project was finished."

"Finished for Stateside operations, sure, but the concept is still a damned fine one. I've made contact with the
principals, and they're willing to grant us an exclusive license."

Saito began to explore the possibility. "What wattage?"

"Ten KW."

"That's small, my friend."

"You and I have been working with megawatts for the past dozen years, but there is a market for a small generator."

"I agree. But the costs are too high."

Morton gave a grin. "Three and a half cents per kilowatt hour, average, over ten years."

"Plus?"

"Plus two cents per KW hour on an order of twenty units. That will amortize the whole thing out in ten years, and we'll slip back to three or four cents. Think of it; it can be bigger than Nippon Power."

"The twenty units—who will manufacture them?"

Morton looked out at a man putting on the eighteenth green. When he felt he had stretched the suspense as long as was reasonable, he said, "We will."

Saito did not speak right away; he was weighing what he had just heard. Twenty small-capacity generators could easily be placed in areas of Japan which were in need of electrification, and that venture alone could create enough profits to keep a dozen men happy for life. What was overwhelming was the potential for Southeast Asia; that market could handle five hundred, possibly a thousand units. Isamu Saito was used to thinking of ventures calculated in the billions; he had never, however, dreamed of *profits* in the billions.

Saito glanced at Morton who was still feigning an interest in the golfers. He was feeling greedy. He had never, in all of his experience, been a greedy man, and he had prided himself in always moving forward with some goal other than personal gain. But he knew the sensation when it came, and he did not like it. He said to Morton, "I think we had better talk about this, my friend."

Morton let out a bellow that was loud enough to distract one of the golfers. "You bet your sweet ass," he boomed. "You bet we're going to talk."

CHAPTER FOUR

Bart Faber followed Bernie Eby's instructions as they drove to the Ueno District of Metropolitan Tokyo. The area is home to Tokyo University, the National Museum, many art galleries and the Ueno Zoo. It is, like all of the metropolitan complex, dense with small homes and large apartment buildings, but here large, private holdings exist as well. These places do not resemble the American suburban sprawl. They are more like those enclaves of old money outside Boston and Philadelphia and Baltimore.

Tori Ito's home was located in one of these sections, on a street right off Chuo-Dori Avenue. Faber pulled his car to a stop where Bernie Eby indicated. "I hope she's home," Eby said.

Faber studied the house and grounds and was both impressed and confused. He was impressed by the vastness of the property. Land value in Tokyo is right up there with the most expensive in the world, and he was looking at a residence sited on over one acre of land. But confusingly, the place was in a state of disrepair that conflicted with the rest of the property on the street.

Faber's face showed his question. Eby said quickly, "She's had a rough time of it, Bart. I guess she's short of money. I haven't seen her for about two years."

"Does she still live here?"

Eby replied, "I would have heard if she'd moved."

For an instant, Faber was suspicious. It did not ring true that Eby would be so well informed and yet not have seen the woman in over two years. But the question was obscured by another. Faber said to Eby, "Look around, Bernie. Every other house on this street is immaculately groomed, a showplace. And that," he pointed to the Ito property, "is a derelict."

"Shit, Bart, I told you she's had a hard time. Her folks died in a plane crash six or seven years back. They left her a trust, but property taxes have gone up and the cost of labor is out of sight. She's been fucking-well done dirt by life and that ain't no shit."

"You're sure she's still living here?"

"Let's go see. Her car's there."

Faber had already spotted the car, a 1968 yellow Mustang, but it looked as decrepit as the house: a taillight was broken, a door was dented and rust spots pocked most of the fenders. With some reluctance, Faber followed Eby out of the car and up the walk to the house.

The place was worse than it had appeared from the street. The hedges that had not died from lack of care had overgrown their borders; plants lay withered and ugly, a small pool that had probably once been home for a family of carp was dry and filled with fallen leaves. A small bridge passing over the dry creek bed looked rotten and alarmingly gave under their feet.

As they came to the wide staircase leading up to the front door, Faber heard the sound of music. Eby gave a smug smile of righteousness; Faber feinted a friendly poke of Eby's arm.

The two men went up onto a covered verandah that ran the full width of the house. To the right, under a porte cochere, stood the parked Mustang. A window was cracked, and there was another dent visible in the hood. The house paint was flaking off the wood, a rough grit had accumulated on the porch, and planter boxes that had once nourished climbing vines for the trellises sat overgrown with weeds.

Faber hung back as Eby pressed the doorbell.

The music they had heard continued, but they could hear the ringing bell over it. In less than a minute, the door opened, and a woman stood there looking at Bernie Eby. "Bernie?" was all she said, with a note of incredulity. After a long pause, she added, "It's been a long time." There was no friendliness in her voice.

She had spoken in English, and Faber noted that her pronunciation and diction were perfect. He did not dwell on that aspect of the woman, however, because her appearance demanded attention.

To Faber's way of thinking, there was a universal quality to beauty, and Tori Ito possessed that quality. Her features were flawless, and her body, clothed in a stylish skirt and blouse, was an eloquent pedestal for that beautiful face. Her eyes, mouth, cheeks, and even her hair were sculpted in a way that left no latitude for criticism. The only problem was that she radiated sadness.

It was, Faber finally realized, that her eyes, framed with soft eyelids, showed no warmth; they were cold and lacked vitality. Faber had experienced his share of sadness and he had shared it with others; but he was looking at a woman who had let sadness possess her life and who was unable to cast it away.

She was taller than Bart Faber remembered most Japanese women were, and she stood with the casual elegance of a high-fashion model. But there were those eyes, those damned sad eyes. It dawned on him that those eyes were looking at him, and that Bernie Eby was repeating something: "Hey, Bart, where's your manners? I said: This is Tori Ito."

Snapping back his attention, he responded, trying to show some grace, then added, "Sorry to barge in on you."

Her voice was throaty as she said, "There was a time, long ago, when Bernie would show up here at any hour. At least this time it is at a reasonable hour."

Faber said, "I can't place your accent; did you study in the States?"

She replied, "Berkeley.'68."

"That explains a lot."

She gave her first smile. "That does explains a lot, doesn't it?"

For an instant there was a falling away of the sadness, and Faber credited his first impression of her to loneliness. He offered, "The music that was playing: Verdi?"

She said, "Eileen Farrell," knowing that he knew.

Then he asked, "Do you see yourself as Turandot?"

Now her smile was genuine, and the sadness melted away. "Would you be Calaf?"

He laughed and said, "*Nessun dorma*. Not hardly. As a matter of fact, I have my own riddle."

Bernie Eby cut in. "What the hell are you two talking about?"

Tori Ito and Bart Faber both laughed. Eby's tastes in music ran to the Beach Boys or Led Zeppelin. They did not explain their repartee.

Tori Ito turned back to Faber and asked, "You said you had your own riddles?"

"Not really riddles, just some questions that Bernie thought you could answer."

She threw an angry glance at Bernie but came back with

her own question. "What could I give you answers to, Mr. Faber?"

"I'm here to find out what has happened to the Institute For Peace."

"And why?"

"There seems to be a chance that Japan will send no delegation to the World Peace Rally in San Francisco in August. I wanted to find out if that was true, and maybe find out why."

"You have some good reason for finding out?"

"I've been asked to do the job by my superior."

"And he has an interest."

"Don't we all have an interest in peace?"

She paused, then emphatically stated, "Japan will not send a delegation to the rally. I've heard that, but I have no direct knowledge. I'm out of the Institute; maybe Bernie forgot to tell you that."

Faber replied, "He told me that, and he told me that the Japanese delegation would not go. He thought I might gain some insight if I knew more about Tac Okomoto."

"Tac Okomoto is dead," Tori Ito said flatly. The sadness had returned to her face.

"Can you tell me about him?" Faber asked.

"Bernie knew him. He has told you about Tac."

"I'd know more if I heard from you. Do you disagree?"

She did not answer. Faber studied her as she frowned at Eby. She said, "Bernie, you have a lot of nerve. It's been two years. I've said all I can say; why do you take part in this torture?"

Eby's voice came weakly. "Look, Tori, Bart's a friend. He has a problem, and the only way I could think to help him was to come to you. Tac was your life, and he was also the guiding force of the IFP. Bart won't find out anything if he goes to IFP headquarters, because those people don't know what is happening themselves. Shit, Tori, give me some help; for old times' sake."

To Bart Faber's mind two things immediately seemed wrong with the situation. First, Bernie Eby had no right to come crashing back into Tori Ito's life after not seeing her since Tac Okomoto's death. Second, he, Bart Faber, had no right delving into the grief that enveloped this woman, especially since he had no real interest in her history. Before she could reply, Faber interjected. "Look, Tori, I've no desire to rip open the wounds you have from what is past; I don't want to see you hurt any more than you have been. I need to find out some simple facts, but if it means making you relive a difficult time, then I will find out elsewhere. I have no intention of disrupting your life." He looked at Eby and said, "I don't think that either one of us came here selfishly; I know that Bernie thinks a great deal of you and does not want to see you hurt."

There was a venom as Tori turned on Eby: "You'll never change! You come in here and—"

Eby cut in. ". . . bring a fucking buddy to—"

Tori cut back, "Well, take your fucking buddy and—"

Faber cut them off with, "Hold it!" They both looked at him, startled. "Now both of you, just hold it." He spoke to Tori Ito but kept glancing at Bernie Eby. "This was a bad idea. I'm here for only a few days and I have a job to do. I won't get my work done and you will end up as enemies if you try and help me. Now, I apologize to you, Tori, for bothering you, and I apologize to you, Bernie, for trying to do me a favor. Now, let's let it lie. We'll go now, Tori. I'm really sorry."

He faced Eby, who seemed to want to say something else, but Faber would not let him open his mouth. "Let's go, Bernie." His tone was emphatic. Eby turned and led the way from the verandah and out toward Faber's borrowed car.

Faber, following him, was about halfway to the entrance gate when Tori Ito called, "Mr. Faber."

He stopped and turned. She said, "Can I ask you something?"

Faber looked toward the car to make sure Eby was not coming back. Eby was already opening the door of the vehicle. Faber headed back to the house.

He met Tori Ito near the bottom of the stairs. She studied him, as if searching for something. Finally she said, "Who do you work for . . . Bart, isn't it?" He nodded. She continued: "I mean, Bernie never said who you were working for; he has made a living out of selling services to visiting writers, so I just figured . . ."

Faber cut in. "I'm a priest, Tori."

There was, he guessed, a moment of understandable confusion before she said, "I sure missed on that one; I had you pegged as one of the weekly magazines. A *priest*?"

He shrugged but did not speak. She had called him back, and she had something to say; he would let her do it in her own time.

The corners of her mouth turned up with a smile; it was the first time he had seen anything like happiness on her face. She said, "I could say, 'You don't look like a priest,' or 'Show me your collar,' or 'Who're you kidding?' But that would be rude. I think I believe you."

He still waited.

She continued. "I really took you for a reporter of some kind; a pretty good-looking one at that, but I'll take your word for it, because a guy wouldn't kid about being a priest . . . would he?"

"I think not, Tori."

"Well then, I'll ask again: Who sent you?"

"My boss is a man we call the provincial. He has his reasons for wanting to know what's going on here, and I was ordered to come to Japan and find out."

She said, "A 'provincial'? That's Jesuit, isn't it?"

"Right again."

"I thought so. I knew one at Berkeley. At the Newman Center."

"They do good work. I've never worked the Newman Centers. All of my work has been at universities or at hospitals."

"So he wanted to know and you came?"

"That's right."

"The vow of obedience, right?"

He nodded.

She added, "With chastity and poverty."

"You do know our order."

"Not really. Just a few bits here and there. I'm not really into religion."

She came to the point. "If you are really interested in what's going on at the Institute, I think I can give you something that might be of interest to you . . . or your boss. It's about time for me to share it with someone anyway, and, for some reason, I seem to be able to trust you."

"Part of my stock-in-trade."

"But not Bernie Eby. I won't talk with him around."

"I can come back."

"I'd rather not. Not here."

"Where?"

She thought for a moment, then said, "Do you know the Hilton?"

"I can find it."

She looked at her watch. "I've got a couple of things to do this morning, but how about meeting me there about two o'clock?"

"This afternoon?"

"Yes, at two."

He started to say that he was planning to drive to Osaka at noon, but thought better of it. He said, "I'll see you at two."

"Don't tell him you're meeting me."

"I won't lie to him."

She frowned at him. "That's your problem."

He liked her style. He said, "Maybe a little lie won't be all that bad." He extended his hand, she accepted it, and as they shook hands, he said, "I'll see you at two."

CHAPTER FIVE

From all appearances, the Institute For Peace appears to be a monolith in the cause of world peace. Actually, the organization is a hydraheaded confederation of dedicated interests, all struggling for their own goals. The IFP functions on a two-tier basis: The activist level schedules demonstrations, produces and distributes pertinent literature and invests uncountable hours in championing its position. The administrative level—a much smaller and elite group—sees to fund-raising, formulating policy and guiding the faithful. The Institute is headquartered in Hiroshima.

The IFP was born in the late 1950s, fathered by a small group of victims and relatives of victims of the atomic bomb drops on Hiroshima and Nagasaki. The common bond of horror that fostered the Institute's founders also gave them the strength to grow during the effervescent sixties, when the whole spectrum of social, economic and political reformers bubbled onto the world's center stage. The cadre of leaders of the IFP was led mainly by Minoru

Watanabe, who had been on duty as chief boilertender at the East Asia Tin Works in the Kannonmachi section of Hiroshima, about one mile from the epicenter of the bomb blast; he had survived with only radiation exposure. He also possessed a vivid memory of the historic moments, and an innate ability to relate the drama of that instant. He is credited with first using the words *Pika Don*—the bomb of lightning and thunder.

While Minoru Watanabe became one of the principle speakers for the IFP, the field people, the frontline workers, came mostly from Japanese universities.

There is a vast pool of volunteer office workers and street demonstrators available from various university *jichikai*, or student self-government associations, throughout Japan. The office workers diligently handle telephone banks, stuff envelopes, and paint placards, while the street demonstrators indulge in frequent confrontations with police over matters dealing with the environment, nuclear weapons and, quite often, anything to do with the United States.

The IFP's central operation is housed on the second floor of the Hagane Building, located on the west bank of the Ota River about a mile south of the Aioi Bridge, which was the aiming point for the dropping of the atomic bomb on Hiroshima. The headquarters are an easy ten-minute walk from the Hiroshima Peace Cultural Center and other attractions which bring pilgrims to that mecca of man's ingenious ability to kill his fellow man.

The IFP offices are huge, about seven thousand square feet, occupying half the floor. Visually, the offices are less than imposing because, as the organization expanded, they merely knocked doorways into the walls to make passageways between the various spaces. The landlord, who donated the space gratis, had complained that the IFP promised repairs would be made, but there were always more pressing causes demanding funds, and the landlord had given up complaining in July of 1971. He rationalized that it was all for a good cause.

On any given day and at any given hour, people are at work in some part of the offices. The hired staff, numbering only ten, are seldom in on the weekend, but the volunteers invariably have some project going. The volunteer personnel at the IFP turns over in relation to world events, but most students phase themselves out as they near graduation. A small number perseveres, and this group provides a continuity of purpose. Periodically, one young worker will surface from the mass as a leader, a catalyst for innovation. Susumu Kato did just that after Tac Okomoto died.

Kato had not known Okomoto well, since Kato had come into the IFP only a few months before Okomoto was lost to the cause. But over the past two years, Kato had made noticeable strides as one who could get office workers to do their jobs and street demonstrators to enter the fray. Part of Kato's success had come from knowing where the real power of the IFP rested—with that ancient activist, Minoru Watanabe, who had survived The Bomb.

Kato was in the IFP offices, nursing a considerable hangover and trying to organize transportation to Yokohama where a U.S. nuclear-powered submarine was due on a 'goodwill' visit. He still had two weeks to arrange for enough bus seats to move three hundred demonstrators to the port city but he liked to get things done early.

Susumu Kato did not look like the firebrand capable of mustering violent action from amoeboid frenzied mobs. He was short and slight: five feet six inches and one hundred forty pounds. But he had been raised on a struggling farm near Aki on the island of Shikoku, by a father who knew how to elicit productive manual labor from his children. Kato's muscles were well developed, and his voice, at the age of twenty-seven, commanded the respect of a person twice his age. It had taken well over a year before

Kato had begun to fill the void left by Tac Okomoto, but in the last six months more responsibilities had been foisted on him by the paid staff members. He was delighted. To complement his ambition he wore scars from his encounters with police on many picket lines: One gash on his forehead was the particularly proud chevron of a conflict at the Japanese Defense Force base at Nilgata, for that wound came from military, not just civilian police.

Alone at his desk, he began wondering when the other people would show up; there was to be a demonstration at the Peace Memorial Museum later in the afternoon. It did not require much advance preparation; the tourists would be impressed with the spontaneity of the display. The phone on his desk rang. He picked up and said his greeting.

The voice on the other end was gentle, soft and polite; Susumu Kato knew who was speaking and Minoru Watanabe asked, "Are you in shape to work?"

Nothing that Minoru Watanabe ever asked of his followers was questioned or denied. Kato said he was ready.

"I sent people looking for you last night. I needed to talk to you." Watanabe's voice was still gentle.

Kato explained, "I was doing research."

There was the customary pause after an admission of dalliance—Kato had spent the night introducing a coed to some of the fringe benefits of the peace movement—then the customary retort: "I've done some research in my life, boy."

The stories of Minoru Watanabe's satyric history were legion. Watanabe had lost his wife and three children in the blast of Hiroshima and had outlived two subsequent mates; he had been a widower for twenty-five years now, with a coterie of faithful women who frequently spent time, sometimes weeks on end, at the old man's home. No one ever asked what went on during that time with a seventy-seven-year-old man, but imaginations gave him much credit.

Watanabe hesitated, as if he was wondering who Kato's trysting partner had been, then continued, "I want to talk to you, my son. I would like you to come to my home."

"When would you want me there?"

"As soon as possible; I've been wanting to talk since last night."

Kato accepted the reprimand and said, "I will be there right away."

"I'd appreciate that," said Watanabe, and the click at the other end of the line cut off the conversation.

Kato sat for just a moment, savoring the new recognition bestowed on him by his leader. He had only gone to Watanabe's home once, and that had been with a group of activists who had earned the audience by a particularly bloody confrontation on an environmental issue. Kato let a wave of pride wash softly over him and began to leave the IFP offices. He gave a second or two of thought to the scheduled demonstration and then dismissed the worry; the crew that was coming in knew what had to be done.

Minoru Watanabe's home is set in the hills surrounding the bowl in which lies the city of Hiroshima. If he had owned the house back in 1945, his wife and children would not have perished, because the blast effects had vaporized only the residents living within a one-mile radius of the center of the explosion. But, back then, he had been a boiler-room worker, and could not afford the home in that area.

As he replaced the telephone in its cradle, he looked with pleasure at the woman who sat across the table from him; she was about to pour tea in that magnificent way she had of doing every chore. She was an executive secretary in the Fuji Bank in downtown Hiroshima; she had been one of his followers back when she was a student at the University Teachers College.

He said, "I will be having a visitor."

Demurely, she asked, "Do you wish me to leave?"

"You are spending the weekend."

"Yes, Watanabe-san, but I will leave if you wish."

He did not discourage the deference she still used, even after three years of intimacy; he liked the way she treated him. "Just make yourself scarce when he arrives. I don't want him to know you are here; it would not be good for your job at the bank."

"Is he one who would talk?"

"No," Watanabe replied, "I just don't want to put him in a situation where knowledge causes him jeopardy. He is a good youth."

She finished pouring the tea and the two of them sat there, sharing the companionship of silence that comes from a solid relationship.

CHAPTER SIX

The Tokyo Hilton sits with quiet dignity beside the magnificent Hie Shrine in the Akasaka district of a city well populated with Western hotels; the Hilton combines the best of Western comfort with the classical charm of the Orient. The decor pulls visitors quickly into the mood of modern Japan; the most sociable public place in the hotel is the Tea Lounge, which sits off the lobby and faces a beautiful example of the famous Japanese pond gardens. Tori Ito was waiting at an isolated table by a picture window looking out into the pond garden.

Bart Faber had spotted her easily; she was noticeable.

She was wearing a tailored linen suit, the beige color blending so well with the room that it seemed as if she had selected it purposefully to look well in that particular setting. She was wearing no jewelry, the hem of her skirt was primly set just below her knees, and the high-necked white blouse gave her an almost Victorian illusion. Faber smiled as he approached.

"You found me." Her voice carried that softness he had heard when they first met at her house.

"I looked in the coffee shop, then asked at the front desk. They know you here."

"My father was one of those instrumental in bringing the Hilton to Tokyo. It's a residual effect of having an influential father."

"It's more than that; they like you."

"They're kind."

The waitress, dressed in the traditional kimono, came for his order; Tori Ito was having tea and he ordered the same.

"Thank you for coming," she said as the waitress left them alone.

He took out a cigarette, offered her one, then said, "I wanted to talk to you. There was tension between us this morning; that does not aid conversation."

She ignored the reference to the morning. "I wanted to talk to you, too."

He looked out the window and watched the huge carp swimming in the pond, then brought his eyes back as she said, "So you're driving to Osaka."

"I was planning to," he responded. "How did that bit of information come to you?"

"I called Bernie."

"I thought you were angry with him."

"I was; I am. But I wanted to find out more about you."

"What did you find out?"

"That you were willing to lie to him and say you were driving to Osaka today." She looked at her watch. "I think you had better forget about that; it's too late."

"I'll figure out something."

She laughed and leaned over, closer. "Typical Jesuit, you are. 'It will work out.' "

"It always has."

She continued smiling. "Ignatius set a hard standard for you."

"You mean the poverty?" She nodded. He countered, "It is not all that hard. Things do have a way of working out."

"Well," she said, "you will not be able to make it to Osaka tonight. It's well over a six-hour drive, much closer to seven. It would be too late to find a room when you arrived."

"I'll manage."

He enjoyed her concern, until she said, "I've gotten you a room here for tonight."

Flustered, he was groping for a reply when she added, "And I've gotten tickets to the opera. Would you mind taking me? It's been a long time since I felt like going and had someone to take me."

"Let's back up," he said. "First, as far as taking a room here, I don't have that kind of money, and if I did I doubt I'd be willing to pay the price. I know that Tokyo hotels are expensive."

She countered, "I've taken care of the cost of the room."

"I can't let you do that, Tori."

"Don't be silly. Of course you can. Besides, the manager is a good friend of mine, and you'd be surprised how inexpensively friends can get rooms from friends."

"But I have to get to Osaka tonight. I have work to do."

"I'm helping you with your work. I have things to tell you that will make your task easier. I'm going to save you a lot of time. You can well afford to indulge in the whims of a source of information."

She added, in a low voice, "I really do have some information that will be of value to you; something that very few people know and that will make it easier for you to understand what is going on in the peace movement."

Faber knew enough not to alienate a source of information and he was beginning to believe that Tori Ito might just have something to offer. He changed his tack. "But no opera for me; not tonight."

She gave a smile that said she would win that argument, too.

He said, "Seriously, I've just zipped my body and mind through a dozen time zones. I'd probably fall asleep."

"I think not. The opera tonight is *Tannhäuser*. There's no sleeping through Venus and her bacchanal."

Faber yielded. But what accounted for her startling change in demeanor? And how could she afford to spend this money?

The waitress arrived with his tea.

He said to Tori Ito, "I've got a problem, Tori, and it is embarrassing."

"Sometimes problems are only in the mind."

He grinned. "Bernie told me that you were in financial trouble. And yet you come here, renting me a room in an expensive hotel and buying opera tickets. I saw the condition of your home, and it does seem that you are having some financial problems."

Tori Ito's face was serious, but he saw no anger. She said, "You know, it is none of Bernie Eby's business, and he surely should not have said anything of that nature to you." She accepted his nod of agreement, then continued. "My property is run-down because I want it to look that way. My parents left me well off financially but, after Tac was killed, I was determined to cut myself off from the IFP. Some of them still came around looking for money. I let it be thought that I was no longer able to give them money; they stopped coming."

"I did not mean to pry."

She said, "It is my fault. I wanted to talk to you and I have an obligation to be candid." Some of the tenseness left her face. "Seriously, you do not need to sleep in the room. It was a kindness of the manager. I told you, he is a friend. The hotel has no reservation for the room tonight. I wanted us to have a place where we could talk privately, and when we are through you can leave, if you wish. If you want to stay, feel free to use the room.''

The room was not important to Bart Faber, he would find some place to sleep, no matter what; he knew that. What was important was to hear what Tori Ito had to say. He decided not to broach the matter of her change of attitude; that explanation might surface by itself. He accepted her offer with mock humility. ''I guess you win, Ma'am. Let's look at the room.'' She handed him the key.

Tori Ito did not go up to the room immediately, but told Faber she would follow in twenty or thirty minutes, so that he would have time to settle. He picked up his bags from the car, then took the elevator up to the seventh floor. When he first entered the room he was mildly surprised to see there was no bed. There was a sofa, coffee table, chairs and a desk, but no bed. He stood in the doorway, looked at the key, then confirmed the number on the door; it was the right room. Perhaps he was to sleep on a traditional *futon* mat, that body-sized thin pad used by Japanese to sleep on the floor. But the room was Western in appearance. He finally realized the accommodation was a suite, and he found the bedroom through a doorway. A damned suite, he thought, slightly angered at her extravagance and honestly flattered by it.

He had been in the clothes he was wearing for just over thirty-one hours, and he was feeling grubby. He showered, shaved and put on a fresh shirt and slacks; he was totally refreshed when her knock came at the sitting-room door.

She was not alone.

A man in waiter's livery stood behind her with a room-service trolley. She glided in, announcing: ''You've got to eat.'' He realized he had not eaten since he had been on the airliner. She added, ''Unless you are fasting for Lent.''

He laughed. ''Lent is over.'' He liked this woman; she was a vital person.

The waiter set out the food and left before Faber could offer a tip for the service. As the door closed, Faber said, ''You're pampering me, Tori. I'm not used to this kind of attention. Only from my mother, and I see her very little.''

She motioned for him to sit. ''It's nice to worry over a man; it's what women do best.''

Faber chided her. ''That sounds like pure male chauvinism.''

''It's pure Japanese.''

She had ordered simple hamburgers, french fries and a salad. She explained her theory on jet lag: The traveler not only suffers from a time and locale disorientation but also usually indulges in strange local foods too quickly. ''A hamburger will do you well; and I haven't had one for ages,'' she admitted.

Faber was grateful for the hospitality but he was anxious to get to the purpose of their meeting. He did not press her, waiting patiently as she finished her food. He lit a cigarette and looked at her again. There was still that sadness in her eyes, but the worry lines seemed to have lessened, and her mouth looked less rigid. He did not expect to see her suddenly blossom into joy just because he had come into her life, but he hoped she could lift some of the grief from her soul. He added that project to his list of tasks in Japan.

She finished eating. ''I enjoyed that,'' she said.

He thanked her for her thoughtfulness, then waited.

Finally, she spoke. ''It is not easy for me to share a private part of my life with anyone, Bart. It is not the way I handle things. I really do not handle life very well.''

He offered, ''You seem in control of your life.''

"My life stopped two years ago when Tac Okomoto died. It was the end for me."

He did not argue. She continued; "I started going with Tac about a year before my parents were killed in the plane crash. There was hell to pay, because my parents had different plans for me, and Tac was not much help, because he saw them as everything that is wrong in our society. From my father came: 'That damned radical no-good,' and from Tac came: 'Your damned bourgeois parents.' It was a trying time for me, but I cast my lot with Tac and we lived; really lived. After my parents were killed Tac moved in with me at our house, and that caused another furor, because that lovely home in that upper-class neighborhood became sort of an annex for the IFP. The trustees even tried to break my trust, but they failed. There was no stopping us after we won."

She talked, Faber listened. He heard the story of a relationship, far from idyllic but still attractive to people who thrived on tension. She joined her lover at the proverbial barricades, listened with awe to his dissertations, and relished every small victory Tac Okomoto won. They roared through life with the frenzy of youth that let them taste even bitterness with a joyful palate. Her love for him was absolute, and her life became an adjunct to his. Then, disaster.

"It did not happen the night he died," she explained. "It started about six months before."

She had moved to the window of the suite, and Faber saw her framed against the National Diet Building in the distance. He could feel rather than see that she was developing tears in her eyes.

"He had been away for three or four nights—he had never done that before—and," she paused to take a breath, "he was different. He did not tell me where he had been, not then. His whole personality was changed. He was sullen and morose. His temper flared at me for no good reason. He stopped his involvement with the IFP but he still saw some of the more active members; friends of his, close friends.

"He did not want to talk with me, and he refused to talk on the telephone." She turned and gave a slight smile. "He finally yanked the telephone out of its cord; I didn't get it fixed until after his death." She turned back to the window. "He let the distance grow between us, and he treated me badly." There was another pause and Faber sensed she was deciding if she should share her next private memory. "And, a couple of times, he beat me . . . physically. He was not a person to do something like that; not Tac. He was gentle.

"I naturally did not understand what was happening, Bart. There was no way for me to know." She left the window and took a seat across the table from him. He lit two cigarettes and gave her one.

She continued. "The night before he died he told me, he explained."

Faber waited.

She said, "We were in the house. It was about ten at night and he was going out. He said he would be gone a couple of days. Then he told me." She reached down to the floor and picked up her purse. Faber saw that it was made from the same linen as her suit; she had expensive taste in clothing. She took out a slim tube of bamboo. "This is what caused it all," she said. "This is what took Tac away from me and ended my life." She made no move to open the tube.

She took a deep drag on the cigarette, then said, "Someone, I don't know who, found this and gave it to Tac. He was plunged into a confusion he could not handle; or maybe, he could handle it and I could not. What he went through, I cannot say, because he excluded me except for those final minutes before he left. He told me: 'Keep this, Tori; keep it safe for me. I will be back in a

couple of days. I have found the rest of the proof.' That's
how he left me. He did not even kiss me good-bye. The
next night he was killed in the fire. This is all that is left
of the great love in my life, Bart Faber. Not much, is it?''

She tossed the bamboo tube on the table. Faber made
no move to pick it up.

Tori Ito picked up the tube, eased off its delicate lid and
shook it over the table. A roll of paper fell out. She handed
it to Faber. ''There is a page from a diary, and I made a
translation. I read it right after Tac died. The diary belonged to Dr. Yoshio Nishina. He was a physicist, a famous scientist in our country. He died in the 1950s; I do
not know how Tac came to have the page. But if you read
it, or the translation, you can see what it is all about. It
caused Tac Okomoto's death.''

Faber picked up the two pieces of paper. The page of
the diary was on rice paper, obviously torn from a book.
The neat swirls of the *hiragana* script were not intelligible; he read the typed translation that Tori had provided:

> Today: a seed became a bud
>   a bud became a flower
> Wednesday, March Eighth (sañ-ju-kyū)

Faber asked Tori Ito, ''*San-ju-kyu*? What does that
mean?''

''It is penciled in on the page,'' she answered.

Faber looked at the original rice paper and saw where
someone had made the strokes in pencil, obviously not the
original writer. He asked, ''What does it mean?''

She answered, ''The way it is placed, it can only mean
1939. It makes no sense otherwise.''

''But not written by the original author?''

''I would think not.''

Faber went back to the translation:

A two-hour meeting with the War Ministry today produced the dream that I have wished for these many years. Admiral Shima has given total approval for research and development of the atomic fission project. The financing is to be provided without limits under the Rokko metallurgy contract. We are not to work on the propulsion system that I had originally proposed. The work is to be on an uncontrolled reaction. I believe I can change that direction as we proceed. Atomic propulsion can fuel our Imperial Navy; an uncontrolled reaction can only destroy. But this is the beginning. We go forward from today.

The flower becomes a garden.

Faber reread the document.

The afternoon sun was losing its battle against twilight. Faber was tired and not a little disappointed in what Tori Ito had given him. But she had been sincere, she had come to him wearing the grief that she felt from the loss of Tac Okomoto, and she thought this was an important document. He asked, "Who is this Dr. Nishina?"

"He is considered the father of Japan's nuclear industry. He died in 1951 from radiation sickness. Many claim he died from visiting Hiroshima the day after the explosion. It is well known that he was the one in charge of our atomic bomb project during the war."

Faber cut her off. "In charge of *what*?"

Tori was startled by his abruptness. She replied, "We were building an atomic bomb; Nishina was in charge of that program."

"I never heard of that, Tori. Not one word."

"It is common knowledge here. The project did not do much, because there was so little time and our resources were so limited."

"Time? According to this," Faber picked up the rice

paper diary page, "it was started in 1939. Hell, that's six damned years! The Manhattan Project in the United States did not start until after Pearl Harbor."

"Japan did not have the resources," she argued, "because the war drained the economy."

"Who said?" Faber snapped.

She was flustered for an instant. He was being an adversary and she had not expected it from him. Her voice was soft as she offered, "They said . . . it has been explained. . . . History, it is history."

Faber took hold of himself. He had plunged into an argument and had been wrong to do so. Japan, with half the population of the United States, had managed to gather enough resources to grab a healthy slice of the world by conquest; in her genius for war, she had given a considerable accounting of herself for three and a half years. Tori Ito was in no position—no one was—to present Japan as a weak sister in the family of nations. He said, "Okay, Tori, I'm sorry. Let's let that lie." He picked up the piece of rice paper again. "But you contend that Tac Okomoto died for this. A man gave up his life for what is written on this scrap of paper?"

Unshed tears glistened in her eyes. She said, "It is all too stupid, isn't it? Yes, to answer you, I do think that Tac died for that scrap of paper, and for what he was going to do after he left me. I believe that, and I think it is important for you to know that before you go off investigating the IFP."

There was a gnawing inside of his mind that she was holding something back. Faber had never considered himself a good interrogator, but he knew he was a good confessor, and if she wanted to share something he would give her the chance.

The immediate need was for him to lessen her anxiety. He asked, "What time is this opera?"

"Seven-thirty."

"That's early."

She nodded. "We're really rather provincial here in Tokyo. Maybe it's just industrious; we tend to be in bed early."

"It makes for better productivity."

"That, too."

He asked her what the appropriate dress would be, and she asked if he had a business suit. He responded, "Guaranteed polyester."

She laughed as he excused himself to go and change.

CHAPTER SEVEN

Isamu Saito had been widowed seven years before, and Clay Morton had been divorced for fifteen years; they treated their lone status as a cost of doing business, a necessary expense for men who have little time for anything other than their ventures.

Each year when Morton visited Saito in Tokyo, companions were engaged for a night of pleasure. The accommodation always took place early in Morton's visit, for neither man wanted anticipation to cloud his thoughts during corporate discussions. This year, as a novelty, Saito had arranged for imports from Manila; it was proving to be an entertaining evening.

"These little wetback gals are cute, Isamu." Morton was looking across the table at his partner; to Clay Morton, all Spanish-speaking people were "wetbacks."

Saito said, "I was concerned about what you might think."

Morton said, "Hey, good buddy, this is a great treat.

Don't worry, I expect to see one of those Tokyo gals before I head home.''

Saito gave a polite smile, but he was chiding himself for the experiment; he knew that Morton had a penchant for Japanese girls, and now he was under obligation to plan an additional evening of sport.

The two men and their companions were having a light supper on the patio of Saito's home on Tokyo Bay. Since the females had arrived, there had been some drinking, a little swimming in Saito's pool, and Morton had indulged his needs twice with the one who would be his bedmate until morning. Saito hoped his American friend would show some degree of moderation, because it would not be good for Morton to have a heart attack now; their new business opportunity was too promising.

An ancient manservant approached the table with a portable telephone and handed it to Saito, who excused himself politely before he spoke. In less than a minute Saito hung up. He said to Morton, "There is interest."

Morton's attitude switched instantly from that of roué to that of a commercial baron. He said to the young woman across the table, "Listen, honey, why don't you take that little darling friend of yours and go find something good to do for about half an hour?"

The women left.

As soon as they were alone, Morton said to Saito, "Okay, good buddy, what's up?"

Saito gave a grin that could be termed evil. "I spoke to some of the people we will need for support."

"When?"

"This afternoon, while you were napping, resting for our young friends."

Morton exploded in a laugh. "You son of a bitch, you're really interested!"

"I'm interested, and our friends are interested."

Morton was immediately serious. "I wonder if they'll go for an enrichment plant?"

"Is that necessary?"

"Why not?"

Saito gave his words a grave emphasis. "That would be very difficult."

Morton shrugged. "Ain't nothing comes easy, good buddy."

Saito's voice carried a warning, as he said, "It will be very political."

"We've handled politics before. We won each time."

"But there are treaties, international treaties forbidding Japan from generating weapons-grade plutonium."

"Fuck the treaties!" Morton spat out. "The fucking treaties are a bunch of bullshit. Listen," Morton leaned closer, "an enrichment plant is necessary: We're going to be using one hell of a lot of fuel. Remember back when that ship sank off of France with that load of enriched fuel for Japan?" Saito nodded. "Well," Morton continued, "it's just fucking lucky that the media was so hot on taking a shot at the Frogs that they let Japan off the hook. If the press had laid into Japan, who owned the load of shit, then the nuclear power industry here would be dead, dead as a fucking doornail." Saito nodded again. "We're talking about a whole new ball game. These generators can handle about five thousand customers with light industry tossed in; shit, do you know how many customers there are for that type of electric power in this part of the world?"

"I know."

"You know. I know. Now all we have to do is convince your people. You can do it."

"I don't know about the enrichment aspect. That could be impossible."

Morton glanced around, making sure no one could hear what he was going to say. "And, the plants are breeder-type reactors. We'll have more damned plutonium than we know what to do with: We could make military ordinance with the surplus.''

Isamu Saito blanched. Clay Morton had just touched a nerve. Saito blurted, ''No!''

Morton was ready for the reaction. He said, ''Take it easy. That's something just for you and me to think about. We're not going into that right away.''

Morton looked around again. His manner, the look on his face, seemed conspiratorial. The sound of his voice lowered. ''Look, Isamu, the United States is out of the game making plutonium; they've made that declaration: The Soviet Union is gone and the remaining confederation is a political eunuch. France is the only power left as a source of weapons-grade plutonium.''

''We're not going into it at all. We could never get that project off the ground, not in Japan. Not in our time.''

Morton asked, ''Do you have any idea what the friggin' French get for one of their artillery shells?''

Saito came back, ''I don't care. That is not a venture we could win.''

''We could try.''

Saito shook his head in a good-natured way and asked, ''Did I ever tell you the kamikaze joke?''

Saito did not often tell jokes, and when they were told it was with some intention. Morton knew that. He said, ''Tell me your kamikaze joke.''

''There was a new class of kamikaze pilots, and their instructor was saying to them: 'You will go out to your planes, fly out to meet the enemy and dive into the ships, killing the enemy.' One recruit in the back of the classroom stood up and said: 'Are you out of your fucking mind?' ''

Morton laughed. Then Saito said, ''That's what I want to know, Clay Morton: Are you out of your fucking mind?''

The two old friends laughed together and let the matter drop. The women were summoned back to the patio. Clay Morton knew that he could win over his friend; it would be a tough battle, but Morton would win: He was sure of it.

CHAPTER EIGHT

Minoru Watanabe sat in the dim light of his living room and suffered the aching tiredness that comes so readily with old age. He was also sick of waiting. He had sent his companion to the sleeping part of the house to wait for him. He had told her to go to sleep and he would wake her but he knew she would be waiting, patiently. She would be tired tomorrow; the old man hoped her husband would excuse her weariness. Now, as he looked at his watch, Watanabe saw that it was past ten o'clock, and he and his paramour had been waiting for six hours.

Watanabe had spent nearly four hours in the critical meeting with young Kato before dispatching him on his mission. The boy was so young that it worried Watanabe to trust such inexperience; but there was no choice, not for the moment.

Watanabe, as he had secretly been planning for some time, was going to have the Institute For Peace participate in the San Francisco World Peace Rally. The scheme had been kept from the working ranks of the organization; Watanabe had his devious reasons.

In the afternoon meeting, the old man had come slowly to the matter, letting Susumu Kato think that the idea was originating in his young, eager mind; Watanabe was a master at that sort of Machiavellian manipulation. After the subject was broached, Kato joyfully let himself be led down the course required to make all the Institute's members a part of the great event. Much of the meeting had involved the subtle moves that would be required with the media; some time had been spent on the psychology to be used on the individuals who would actually go to the United States for the rally. Kato had become light-headed when his old mentor said it was vital that Kato be the leader of the Japanese delegation; such recognition was not lightly granted in the IFP, especially not to someone who had been actively involved for only two years.

Toward the end of the meeting, Watanabe had said. "I want Yamabato."

Kato had felt a chill of excitement when Watanabe said the word. Yamabato was the statue of a stylized dove of peace that had been commissioned over a year before. When the rupture had occurred in the IFP, work on Yamabato had been halted. But the statue had become a rallying point around which the loyalists to Watanabe had gathered. Kato had said to the old man, "That will be a great moment for us."

Watanabe had waited after agreeing; then, just a bit behind the schedule Watanabe had calculated, Kato said, "Will there be time to have it ready?"

"That is a good point," Wanatabe replied, and Kato picked up no hint that he had been led to that point.

"I will begin to hunt for Raion on Monday morning," Kato offered.

Watanabe became the leader that all in the IFP followed. His voice was gentle, but left no room for question: "You will find Raion tonight." Watanabe paused in irritation. The artist who had been commissioned to create Yamabato had been arrogant enough to pick the name Raion—which meant "Lion"—as his monicker. Then the old man went on: "You will bring this artist here, to me, tonight and we will talk. Time is critical. We cannot wait until Monday."

Susumu Kato had then left to find the artist and return him to Watanabe. The old man knew the assignment would not be easy; artists the world over are not the most predictable or accessible beings.

But Kato had been gone for so long, the old man was becoming weary. He sought to distract his mind from the aches and turned to the *ikebana* flower arrangement the woman had done for him earlier. She had excited him as she placed each stem, each piece of fern, each leaf so delicately in the vase. When she glanced sideways and caught him studying her, she flicked that liquid pinkness of her tongue quickly along her upper lip; she knew how to deliver a message, she knew how to make a man need her.

His concentration on the flowers did not do the duty, and he was ready to rise and extinguish the lantern hanging beside his front door. He would go to bed, to the pleasures of his companion, and would resume his labors in the morning. He heard a car come to a stop in the driveway and then the sound of steps on the soft gravel of the walk. Someone tapped lightly on the door.

Watanabe opened it. Kato stood there, looking excited. Kato reported, "I found him, teacher. I did what you asked."

Watanabe gave a stern look as he asked, "Where is our artist friend?" He led Kato inside.

Kato's expression changed to sincere concern. "He is out in the car. There is one problem that I could not cure."

Watanabe waited. Kato explained, "Raion is stoned out of his head."

Watanabe did not try to hide his anger. "Get the fool in here. Now!"

Kato needed a little longer than was normally necessary to conduct the sculptor into the living room. Raion stood there, weaving, and slurred out, "Nice night, Grandfather."

Watanabe snapped at Kato. "He sounds drunk!"

"That, too. I'm sorry, teacher."

The old man moved close to the artist and was repulsed by the odors emanating from Raion's mouth and body; the Japanese have no tolerance for uncleanliness. In a low but firm voice, Watanabe asked: "What are you using?"

Raion admitted, "Just a little coke, Grandfather. Want some?" And the artist began to fumble in the pockets of the dirty bush jacket he was wearing.

Watanabe slapped the artist in the face.

"Watch what the fuck you're doing, old man."

Watanabe delivered the backhand of the first blow. Raion's eyes flared with hate; he raised a clenched fist. Kato made a move, but was waved off as Watanabe hissed into Raion's face: "One move, you worthless piece of dog shit, and you are a dead man."

Raion's fist froze.

Watanabe had inflicted the two most gross insults in Japanese culture: a physical attack and a verbal slur. But, immobilized by Watanabe's latent power, Raion did not retaliate. The two generations stood, glaring across the decades that separated them; Watanabe won. Raion said, "I am sorry, teacher. I lost control."

Kato quickly turned from the scene. It is not polite to watch another suffer public humiliation.

Minoru Watanabe had not kept control of a politically volatile organization for thirty years by being soft. He kept anger in his voice as he said, "You, artist, will never come to my home in this condition again. You will never speak to me except with the utmost respect. If I am within hearing distance, you will never soil any person with your filthy mouth." Then, shocking Susumu Kato, Watanabe ordered, "Get out of my house."

Fear probably acted as a neutralizer because Raion's voice now contained respect. "I have offended you, teacher. I will leave as you order."

The artist turned and went through the front door, and Watanabe motioned for Kato to follow. Then, in a surprising move, Watanabe followed them out and approached the pair at Kato's automobile. The old man said to the artist, "I want you here tomorrow morning. I want you to bring all of the paperwork on Yamabato. Tomorrow we will restart the building of our symbol."

Meekly, Raion said, "Kato told me you want Yamabato to be ready for San Francisco; that is impossible. There is not enough time."

Watanabe did not change his demeanor. "We will create the time." Then, turning to walk back into his house, he added, "Be here as you are ordered."

Once inside, Watanabe slid the door closed and enjoyed the luxury of a smile. He acknowledged to himself that he still had the ability to control subordinates. He savored the elation of power for a few moments, then turned out the lights and moved eagerly to his bedroom.

There was a dim glow from two candles in the bedroom. As he entered he saw her sitting naked on the double-sized tatami sleeping mat. She was awake; she had waited. She said, "I heard loud voices."

He was taking off his robe and he asked, "Did you think it was your husband?"

She dipped her head. "Don't tease me, please, Minoru-san."

He asked, "And what would you tell him if he came here?"

She lifted her head and smiled, realizing he was teasing; she liked that. She answered, "I would say that I love both of you . . . in different ways."

He knelt down and whispered, "Show me the way in which you love me."

CHAPTER NINE

The Fifth Division of the Army of the Republic of Korea is based five miles southeast of Taegu. Like most military posts around the world, the ROK 5th Division was on weekend status for Saturday night and all of Sunday. Perimeter security was casual; the troops were enjoying their free time.

Except in the White Area. The White Area takes its name from a time when nuclear weapons were isolated in barbed wire compounds where all the buildings were white and floodlights burned brightly. When the United States announced withdrawal of nuclear weapons from the Korean Peninsula in an effort to promote reunification of North and South Korea, storage of the weapons was turned into a covert operation. The political decision to actually keep weapons in South Korea was not all that difficult; too many memories remained of how easily the North Korean Army had invaded the south in 1950. There was no way the American forces were going to be put at that sort of risk again, even if a diplomatic fib was needed.

Contemporary White Areas are deceptive warehouses, outwardly identical to all the other drab buildings on military bases. Electronic security is now the bulwark against unauthorized entry. That works fine as long as the threat comes from those outside the class of personnel privy to the security system; danger from within is difficult to avert.

The U.S. Army's nuclear liasion officer (now called the "tactical weapons advisor") assigned to the ROK 5th Division, confident of the integrity of the security system took his wife to the base club for an evening of dancing. His backup, a career master sergeant, was in town slopping beer with the locals. Even if they had been available, it is not likely they would have detected the penetration of security, for it came from within.

Posun Pak Kee had wanted to live in Japan since he was ten years old. That was the year he had found out that his maternal grandfather was Japanese, a soldier of the Imperial Army occupying Korea before World War II. Pak Kee was not unique in his desires; to live in Japan had been the dream of millions of his countrymen, and Koreans make up the largest ethnic minority in Japan.

By the time Pak Kee was sixteen, he had tried several legal ways to immigrate, but none were successful. Then he tried an illegal attempt; like hundreds of Koreans annually, he tried to enter Japan as a tourist and then just disappear into the native population. The attempt failed, and that failure had put Pak Kee on the persona non grata list in Tokyo. His next move had been to build such an exemplary biography that he could erase the blot on his record. He entered the Korean army, specialized in computers—a skill he was sure the Japanese would eagerly desire—and applied for a labor entry visa. Tokyo rejected him. He continued to look for a chink in the Japanese immigration armor.

Four months earlier, it seemed miraculous, a proposition was made to him: His cooperation would bring his dream to fruition. All he had to do was help some Japanese steal a nuclear artillery shell from the ROK Army Munitions Depot at Fifth Division headquarters. He knew, as did most ROK troops, that nuclear weapons were stored at the depot.

He was told that the exercise was a joint Japanese-American evaluation designed to test the Korean army's security abilities. Naturally, the ROK Army would not be too pleased with his cooperation, and so the Japanese government was willing to grant him his longtime wish to immigrate, plus a sizable grant of money with which to begin his life in Japan. He was given official-looking documents granting his residency and a bank book showing a deposit in his name of twenty-five thousand dollars. It all rang true to Pak Kee; the Americans were liberal spenders and they constantly went to extremes to test their security.

A crime of such magnitude would seem impossible at first blush, but Pak Kee knew the Fifth Division's computer system, and he was a confirmed hacker who loved to sneak past the electronic safeguards in computers. In an evening of gently probing the central computer, Pak Kee was able to extract the access numbers needed before the gates and doors could be opened in the munitions depot. Then, in the necessary computerese, he instructed the memory back to neglect any entry into the White Area from eleven P.M. on any Saturday night to one A.M. the following Sunday morning. He ordered that the computer never display the new instructions. Computers are faithful slaves who have yet to be convinced that a master can perform evil; the device in the basement of the Fifth Division headquarters building obeyed the emphatic, albeit unusual, command.

At eleven-fifteen on that Saturday night, a military truck pulled up to the gate of the White Area. As soon as the vehicle rolled to a stop, the two passengers climbed out. One was Posun Pak Kee, the other was Japanese; both wore fatigue uniforms.

While Pak Kee went to the gate of the chain-link fence, the other man horsed an aluminum box, about the size of a footlocker, out onto the ground. The container was not heavy, but it was bulky and awkward to manage. With the gate opened, Pak Kee came back to help carry the box.

They moved up the walk, a light drizzle helping to hide them in the dark. At the entrance to the White Area building, they placed the box on the ground and Pak Kee tapped out the necessary code on the ten-key wall panel; there was a *click* as the door lock opened. The Japanese man urged, "Move! Quickly!"

Pak Kee moved his shoulders. "Take it easy, man. We've got this thing wired. Don't worry about it."

The other man said, "I worry. You got that, I worry. Now move!"

They carried the box into the building. Pak Kee shut the door and the other man felt a pang of fear: Suppose the damned door would not open when they wanted to come out? He did not mention his fear to Pak Kee: The reply would probably be: Don't worry.

The White Area building was forty feet wide and eighty feet long; a typical military warehouse. The first ten feet of the building were closed off, making a file room and small office area. A red light was the only illumination.

Pak Kee was looking at three doors in the far wall. He asked, "Which door?"

The Japanese said, "How the fuck do I know?"

"Didn't they tell you? The Americans who sent us in here should have told you."

"Well, they didn't."

Pak Kee hissed in anger. "I told you I should have spoken with them. I would have asked what this place looked like."

The other man said with urgency, "Go for that one. There are only three."

The door he had suggested turned out to be a bathroom, but they found the door they wanted on the second try.

The warehouse was well organized. On the right, running the whole length of the area, were boxes marked DECONTAMINATION EQUIPMENT. To the left, parked in a row, were three Jeeps laden with radiation detection equipment. At the far end were the artillery shells.

They were not an impressive sight, not considering their awesome devastating power, ready to be tickled into the millisecond that is the life span of a nuclear device. There were twenty-five shells, each wrapped in heavy plastic, each resting beside its olive drab traveling container. The lettering on each black shell was dull yellow: M-72 ASFU, Artillery Shell—Fission Unit, 1-KT. A 1-KT implement can explode with the theoretical force of one thousand tons of TNT. The temperature at the moment of detonation is four hundred times greater than that of the sun, and at the same time there is an emission of alpha and beta radiation—both deadly—in all directions at the speed of light. They sit there, they are docile, they wait only to destroy.

The Japanese man said to Pak Kee, "Look at those bastards."

Pak Kee did not respond; his mind was leaping forward to his life in Japan. He did not care about the games played in the name of security.

The Japanese man opened the aluminum case they had brought with them. Inside was a cradle of foam-rubber padding.

"Give me a hand," the Japanese man ordered.

The two men lifted the eighty-seven-pound shell into the foam rubber. Pak Kee was about to close the lid when the other man moved to the traveling case that went with the shell. He opened two clips on the end and extracted a square box that measured six inches on each side.

Pak Kee asked, "What the hell's that?"

"The fuse."

"What the hell you need that for, man? I thought you were just making a point. You gonna set that fucker off or something?"

The Japanese man did not respond. He put the fuse box in beside the shell.

They carried the aluminum container out to the truck. With a kidding smile on his face, Pak Kee asked: "Would you like me to tell the computer to let headquarters know they've been had?"

The response was a negative shake of the head, accented by a muttered response that Pak Kee could not hear; the Japanese said: "*You've* been had, idiot."

The pair was off the base within ten minutes. In that time they had transferred their treasure to Pak Kee's private car, had changed into civilian clothing, and had exited the main gate using a fake pass that Pak Kee had created on his computer.

Once clear of the base, Pak Kee drove, with due caution, to the small port town of Ulsan, thirty miles north of Pusan on Korea's eastern coast. A Japanese fishing boat was waiting at a dock near the main cannery.

The transfer was completed, and the vessel was heading out to sea by one in the morning.

Just as the boat was entering the Tsushima Strait, about ninety miles off the coast of Korea, the Japanese man shoved a knife into Pak Kee's belly. The Korean died as he was sinking into the water; the knife cut was still burning as the water flooded into his lungs.

The crossing to Hamada, on the west coast of Japan, took the ship thirteen hours.

It was a warm, sunny afternoon as the ship pulled into its home berth in Hamada. There was no inspection, because customs officials did not especially enjoy coming to the docks on Sunday afternoon. Besides, customs knew all of the fishermen were trustworthy and would make out an official report on Monday if it was necessary.

The Japanese man who had masterminded the whole operation was driving a small van out of Hamada by three in the afternoon. He stopped by a highway telephone booth and made a call.

CHAPTER TEN

Bart Faber did not fall asleep during the opera. He fell asleep while Tori Ito was driving him to the opera.

They had left the Hilton in her Mustang for an easy drive down to the theatre. The car was cozy, a cassette of a *shakuhachi* flute playing one of those classical pieces that are exciting to the Japanese ear and monotonous to an American. The soft, subtle harmony had enveloped Faber in calm peacefulness.

Tori had offered an apology that the opera was to be sung in Japanese. He had mumbled that he did not mind, and she continued: "But the inflections are different."

The last thing he remembered was when he had said, "Music is music . . . Don't worry about it."

From that point onward, the evening was a blank.

He opened his eyes and tried to figure out where he was. The room was dark; the only light came from one of those lava lamps which were so popular in the sixties. He watched the globs of heated oil ooze in distortion and yanked his eyes away; he never had liked those lamps.

In the murkiness that comes when awakening from a deep sleep, he was having difficulty organizing what he was seeing. He was lying on a couch, more like a daybed, covered with a cozy, large Afghan, his head nestled in a soft pillow that gave off a scent of jasmine. On the walls of the room, the two that he could see from his reclined position, hung the strangest collection of ornaments he had seen in a long time. There was a Japanese battle flag— the Rising Sun—and a samurai sword hung by the flag. Posters on the walls ranged from a well-faded portrait of Che Guevara to a bright, new Rio Earth Summit promotion to a Save-the-Whales appeal. Built into one wall was a stereo system that looked elaborate enough to cost thousands, and a shelf with knickknacks that looked to be in the fifty-cent category. There were also framed photographs: a man in a Japanese Army uniform, a woman holding a baby, a young girl on a horse, a college graduation photo of Tori Ito.

"How the hell did I get here?" The words came as he sat up and shook his head.

Across the room, on a chair, his suit coat and black tie lay neatly—too neatly—where they had obviously been put with some care, not the way he would have done it himself. He still wore his trousers and white shirt; his feet were bare.

"Tori," he called.

"I'll be right there," came back to him.

Tori Ito entered, carrying a tray. On the tray were a pot, two small cups and two glasses of orange juice.

Her salutation was liquid, her voice sensual. "Good morning, my sleeping prince."

He asked, "Was I drinking last night?"

She put the tray down on a table, pouring the coffee and presenting him with a glass of juice. "You had nothing to drink, sir. You managed to fall so soundly asleep that I could not wake you when we arrived for the opera. I was not about to take you back to the Hilton. I had told the manager you are a priest, and how would it look for some woman of the world to come weaving into the lobby of the hotel with a drunk-looking holy man on my arm? It would have embarrassed both of us: You, for behaving like a drunk, and me, for not having the charm to keep an attractive man, albeit a priest, interested enough to stay awake.''

''Now I'm embarrassed.'' He felt his face warm. ''I've caused you too much trouble.''

She denied that and said that it pleased her to serve him. He pointed to the coat and tie and chided her: ''You are going to spoil me.'' As if to reinforce his argument, he drank some of the juice; it was freshly squeezed.

She twisted a false pout onto her mouth and said, ''Can't I pamper you just a bit? There's no harm.''

He looked around the room and realized that there were no windows. He asked, ''Just how long did I sleep?''

''It's nearly nine. You slept just over twelve hours. Is that spoiling you?''

He was startled. ''Twelve hours! I haven't done that since . . .'' He thought, then corrected himself. ''I've never done that.''

''It's a normal reaction to jet lag, Bart. It's best not to fight it, that's what I think.''

He picked up the cup and tasted the coffee. It was good.

She said, ''I thought you'd like that better than tea.''

''You're spoiling me. You'd better quit, because I could come to expect it from you.''

He could see he had touched a nerve. She said, ''Bart, it has been two years since I let myself enjoy being a woman to a man. For eight years Tac and I had a life and a love; much of that time was spent in this room. Being here alone just dredges up the sadness of him dying. With you here I can do a bit of playacting and imagine that there are still a few good things in life."

He did not mind her pretense, and he knew he could prevent it from turning into anything more than a game. But he was uncomfortable when anyone fussed over him; his life had been too much alone. He offered, "There are many good things in life."

"And all of them are taken from you."

"And you are angry because Tac was taken from you."

"I am angry because it was not necessary. It was a waste."

He came back. "You could think he died for a cause."

She snapped, "He died for garbage. He died for nothing."

He did not speak. That look had suddenly slipped back onto her face; she was hiding something from him. The day before, in the hotel room, he had decided to let the evening play itself out, to ease her into letting her guard down and revealing what had been hidden. He had fouled up the whole thing by being a victim of jet lag. He decided to get back into that area. "Tori, just what did happen with Tac?"

She looked at him, studying his face. He felt as if he was being put on a scale and weighed on a balance of values.

It took a long time. He finished his coffee and allowed her to refill his cup. She said, "Do you see that?" She pointed to the Japanese battle flag hanging on the wall. Faber looked at the flag.

She said, "It belonged to my father's battalion during the war. After my parents died and Tac moved in with me, the first thing he did was to tear it down."

Faber said, "It is incongruous up there next to the picture of Che."

She said, "It was more than that to Tac. He hated everything to do with Japan's war venture."

Faber suppressed a retort: Japan's international conduct in the 1930s and 1940s was something more than a "venture," but he knew that Japanese historians had molded young minds into views that were less critical. Faber waited for Tori to continue. When she did, her tone of voice announced that she was beginning to open up. "Remember I told you that Tac had begun to change, about six months before he was killed?"

He nodded and said, "I remember."

"And remember I told you that the change started right after he had been gone for a couple of days?"

He nodded again.

"The first thing he did when he came back was to go out to the storage building and find the sword and flag where he had put them years before. He put them back here where they belonged. I was pleased. Before, when he had first taken them down, I felt he had desecrated a part of my family; I was proud that my father had served our country. I told Tac, and he apologized for what he had done in the first place." She stopped.

Faber encouraged her with, "And he told you what had happened to him?"

"How did you know?" She looked suspicious.

"I don't know what he told you; I only know that you've been hiding something from me. If I have no right to know, then I don't want to pry into your life. But if you want to share it with me, I'm anxious to listen."

She had stopped looking at him. Her eyes were focused down on her hands; lovely hands, Faber thought, hands that should be playing a piano rather than wringing themselves in a tangle of anguish. She said, "I have no right to keep Tac's memory from anyone. But he had changed so that I'm ashamed . . . for him."

There was another long pause. Faber waited until she continued.

"Someway, somehow, Tac had become involved with a

nationalist element here in Tokyo. We Japanese are, by nature, nationalistic; we have to be in order to survive. But nationalism died quickly after the war ended. People identified the nationalism with militarism, and neither of those forces has a place in our modern world. But, as we all knew, there was still the germ of nationalism floating around, waiting to infect a new generation. Tac became infected. Honestly''—she looked up as if to establish the truth of what she was about to say—''he never told me how he became involved, Bart.''

He gave her a smile.

She went on: "It is—was—a group of angry people who formed up in the mid-1950s, after Dr. Nishina died and after the peace treaty was signed with the United States. They called themselves *Hitori shinzo mittsu*—The Man With Three Hearts'—sort of like your cat-with-nine-lives concept. Their idea was that Japan had already died twice: once, when it lost the war and the second time when it suffered through the American occupation. They planned to struggle with all of their might to prevent Japan from dying the last time. All of their contempt for the United States pivoted around Hiroshima. They claimed there would have been no loss if the bomb had not been dropped.''

Faber argued, "Japan was going to lose the war, Tori; bomb or no bomb.''

"Their point of view was that there could have been a negotiated peace; that the war could have ended without a surrender.''

His face showed his skepticism, but he did not speak; he was not going to get into an academic debate now that Tori was talking.

She said, "Nothing is known publicly of the *Hitori shinzo mittsu* . . .''

Faber did cut her off, joking. "That is some long mouthful.''

She replied with a smile. "Bart, there are over ninety ways we write 'I' in our language. We shy away from abbreviations and acronyms; there is the danger of saying something vulgar."

He nodded.

She continued, "Anyway, the group—I'll call them 'the group'—is a secret society. You might not know this, but our Japanese men love their secret societies, and they treat them seriously. Tac had never known of them, had never been approached until six months before he was killed. It was so sad, Bart. They told him that they had been using him all of the years he was in the Institute For Peace. And he was proud—proud!—that they had used him! I could have cried when he told me, he was so honest and really so innocent. They had used him secretly for half a dozen years, and now he was thrilled when they finally deemed him worthy of joining their organization." She poured more coffee for each of them. "That page of the Nishina diary that I showed you yesterday—do you remember?"

"Was it the *Hitori shinzo mittsu* that found it?" He had mangled the pronunciation badly, and Tori laughed, nearly spilling the coffee as she passed him his cup.

"They did," she answered. "And they used that scrap of paper to pull him into their scheme."

"What scheme?"

"I don't know." She had desperation in her voice. "He told me a lot of things, but he did not tell me that. He said it would be dangerous for me to know. After all we had been to each other over the years, he decided to not trust me."

"What did he tell you?"

She gave a sigh as if she was straining to remember or hurting to recall. "It was all built around Dr. Nishina. That's why his diary page was so important. They had talked to various people, and Tac was allowed to talk to them, too. They were proving that our scientists were nearly ready with their own bomb when your country dropped the bomb on Hiroshima.''

''What would that prove? Why were they so intent on proving that?''

Tori shook her head in agreement with him. ''It would prove that our leaders should not have surrendered. The *Hitori shinzo mittsu* needs to show that Japan should not have had to surrender; that Japan could have won the war.''

Faber needed to hear what more she had to tell him. He waited.

She sensed that he wanted to argue with her, but, when he did not speak, she said, ''The Nishina diary is hidden someplace in the National Archives. They tore out one page, a damning page, they feel. When the time is right they will make a public announcement and lead journalists to the whole diary. But they need more substantial documentation.''

''Tori, you can't look on the Nishina diary as documentation. It is a personal commentary, no doubt colored by an individual's feelings. A diary is not strong proof.''

''That's what I mean.'' Tori came back with some frustration. ''That's what Tac was going after the night he died. He was going to meet a person who had stolen some documents, government papers that had been hidden for all of these years.''

''What did the papers prove?''

Her voice breaking, she said, ''I don't know! They were . . . they were . . . burned with Tac.''

Bart Faber, as a priest, knew better than to touch a woman, especially a woman weeping. He sat there, desperately wanting to comfort her, while the tears ran their course.

CHAPTER ELEVEN

Clay Morton had given Isamu Saito the boat back in that era fondly referred to as: Before Lockheed. That was when lavish gifts and substantial bribes were an acceptable part of doing business. But the whistle had been blown, the rocks had been lifted, and a government had toppled in the ensuing scandal. Isamu Saito had held onto the boat despite all the pressure, because Saito claimed—and proved—that the bauble had been an expression of friendship between two individuals. He had been honest in that respect.

The boat was a Grand Banks trawler made in Hong Kong and powered by two Japanese Ford diesels. Its forty-two feet held every possible luxury one could want on the water. The teak decking and complementary brightwork glistened; the navigation and communications gear were extraordinary.

Saito loved the craft, and Morton had enjoyed giving the gift.

But something was wrong, really wrong. They had never gone out on the boat on a Sunday when Morton was in Tokyo; they always played golf on Sunday, relaxing as a preparation for the negotiations and planning ahead. Saito had surprised Morton with the news that the two of them were going out on the boat. When Morton had awakened that morning he had found that, by some silent method, Saito had managed to extract Morton's lovely little Philippino companion from bed. She, along with the one who had been Saito's plaything, was missing from Saito's home. Morton held his peace, waiting for some explanation.

As they cleared the Magoru Yacht Club docks, Saito finally said, "We must do business today, my friend."

Through the four decades he had spent as a friend and business associate of Isamu Saito, Morton had learned that there would be some valid reason for the change in routine, so he did not ask. Saito would let him know when the time was right.

Sunday mornings on Tokyo Bay are crowded. Sailboats and pleasure craft vie for space, and a favorite pastime is to navigate in and out of the lines of ships waiting to enter Yokohama. Saito steered a course away from that, however, on a heading aimed at Chiba, a city perched on the eastern shore of Tokyo Bay, nearly twenty miles away.

They cruised for about twenty minutes, simply enjoying the morning breeze and the smooth way the boat was handling the light chop. Their talk was casual: about the boat—Saito had upgraded the loran navigation system; about their picnic lunch—Saito's housekeeper had sliced up $40.00-a-pound Kobe beef to make her version of Texas beef-barbeque sandwiches; about the puffy, white cumulus clouds, and how children, universally, can spend hours trying to see the shapes of animals in them. Morton agreed with Saito that it was too bad that adults, for some reason, stop finding enjoyment in such things. Morton agreed, but he was becoming impatient; what was Saito up to?

Saito looked at his watch, adjusted their heading slightly, and said to Morton, "Feel like having a beer?"

Morton looked at his own watch. It was only ten-fifteen, a little early. Thinking that Saito should have the right to play out his little scenario, he said, "Sure. I'll be right back."

As Morton climbed down from the flying bridge, he heard Saito talking on the ship-to-shore radio. In the galley, as Morton was extracting two beers from the refrigerator, he felt the boat turn slightly to a new heading. Back on the flying bridge, Morton said, "Okay, my friend, what's going on?"

Saito took a long draft from the frosted mug, wiped a thin line of foam from his upper lip and pointed off to starboard. Morton looked, picked up the binoculars from the ledge in front of him, and saw a long, low sailboat slicing eagerly through the water. Morton put the glasses down. "A twelve-meter?"

"It is a twelve-meter."

Mocking incredulity, Morton challenged, "You guys planning to win the America's Cup?"

"That beauty could do just that."

"You gotta be kidding, good buddy. Just about everybody in the States is pissed at you for taking the new car market; you bring the America's Cup to Tokyo and you'll see the shit fly. Believe me, you'll be in cow flops up to your elbows."

Saito's voice changed. "I'm kidding, my friend. We are meeting someone."

"Who?" Morton asked. But the Texan was to be denied for a few more minutes.

Saito said, "You'll see."

The distance between the two craft closed quickly. As the sailboat came to rest and Saito throttled back his boat, Morton saw who they were to visit.

"Hallo, Mr. Morton," called the bald, pudgy man standing in the cockpit of the twelve-meter.

Morton gave a broad grin. "Yessir," he yelled. "How you doin' this fine mornin'?"

The man in the other boat was a former prime minister. Morton had not seen him for over three years. The politician had been forced from office in a scandal, but he was known to retain the ultimate power within his party.

With a casual show of boatsmanship, the twelve-meter came alongside, then was held fast while the bald man crossed to Saito's boat. The two craft drifted apart.

Morton descended from the flying bridge quickly and faced the man he had once known so well. Morton had been privately advised to avoid contact with him after the scandal. The two greeted each other with considered politeness, first exchanging bows, then warmly shaking hands.

"I do not have too long," the bald man said.

"It's really nice to see you again," Morton responded.

Saito had switched on the autopilot and cut his power back to just above idling. He climbed down and made his greetings, then offered a beer. The visitor accepted, and the three men went into the main lounge of the Grand Banks.

Inside, Saito sat in the captain's chair in front of the main wheel and began scanning the horizon, ready to override the autopilot if necessary. Morton and the bald politician took seats across from each other at the dining table that had seen more poker than it had meals.

The politician looked dapper in his deck shoes, white ducks and expensive-looking windbreaker. Morton said so, and the other man replied, "You are looking well yourself, Morton. The Texas girls seem to be keeping you young."

Morton made a ribald comment about one of his recent conquests and there was mutual laughter.

The other man said, "I will not keep you for too long. I just wanted to see you and to have a few words."

Morton had played power politics long enough to know

that he was about to be given a message; *the* message. There are, in each society or economic bloc, certain people who are able to manifest control, and Morton knew he was sitting across from such a man.

The man asked, "Could you tell me about these small nuclear power plants?"

Morton gave a quick, concise summary of what the project would entail.

The man asked, "And they will accommodate how many customers?"

"Four thousand."

"And they are?"

"What do you mean?"

"In size?"

"Twenty-eight by fifty. About the size of a double-wide mobile home. They come on wheels and can be taken by road to any site, just as long as there is water."

"And heat pollution?"

"To the water?"

The politician nodded.

"No problem. They've come up with a helium cooling unit built into the package. No problems with heating the local water . . . none at all."

The politician stroked his bald head and digested the information. Then he said, "There will be a problem with fuel, you know that."

"I think it's time Japan did her own enrichment. These are breeder reactors, and you should control the manufacture of the fuel as we go down the road. It'd be better than having to depend on France."

The bald man said, "But that leads to a surplus eventually."

Morton knew where the conversation was going. He said, "With the enrichment process, you'll be able to end up with weapons-grade fuel. It's a natural by-product. What you do from that point onward would be up to your government."

The man finished his beer and made a silent, friendly indication that he would like another. Morton claimed one from the refrigerator, and there was silence for a full two minutes. Over the years, Morton had seen this discarded politician in action, from a distance and up close, during both crises and prosperity. Morton knew that what the man was about to say would be cast in bronze. The ex-prime minister said, "I like the basic concept, Morton. I like, even, the idea of the enrichment plant. This is a project that should go forward. I think you have brought us another benefit for our industries." As he finished speaking, the man stood.

So that was it. There was to be no further talk of Japan possibly making weapons out of the surplus fuel. There was no need to ask for clarification; the fact that it was not mentioned made it a dead issue.

The leave-taking was quick, friendly and formal. The bald man transferred back to the twelve-meter, and the boats parted. As soon as they were out of hearing, Morton turned to Saito. "You son of a bitch, you pulled one off, didn't ya? Now you're sure one good buddy!"

Saito's face showed his pride in having done so much so fast. "I felt it was a good project. I want you and me to be a part of it, Morton."

Morton thrust out his hand and they shook as the Texan said, "Good buddy, you and I are gonna set this part of the world right on their asses. You can bet on that, old friend."

Saito beamed. "Let's go someplace and finish off the beer."

"Shit, good buddy, there's more than a case in that refrigerator."

Saito said, "That should be enough."

CHAPTER TWELVE

". . . qui pro vobis et pro
multis effundètur in
remissiònem peccatorum."

As Bart Faber genuflected, then elevated the chalice, a thought tugged at his mind and he battled to push the distraction away. *"Hæc quotiescumque . . ."* he hurried, using the ritual to direct his thoughts back to the Mass.

He had used Tori Ito's telephone to call the Dominican complex. The pastor was ill, he had been told, the assistant pastor was away, serving at a church on Hokkaido, and the only priest on duty was a Japanese who had great difficulty speaking English. Tori had gotten on the line for Faber and found that, in fact, an English-speaking priest was needed for the eleven-o'clock mass.

Faber had accepted the duty with pleasure. What with his assignment here, he did not know when he might next be able to celebrate Mass.

Tori had taken him back to the Hilton for his bags and borrowed car; she had followed him to the church in Shibuya. He had thanked her in the parking lot of the church and was surprised when she asked if she could attend the service. He had told her it would be fine, and had offered to say the Mass for Tac Okomoto. She had teared at the mention of her lost love, and perhaps at Faber's thoughtfulness. He had indicated the front entrance and hurried to the back door leading to the sacristy. There he introduced himself to the young Japanese Dominican priest.

"Each Sunday we have English Mass at eleven o'clock," the priest explained. Faber was working his way into his borrowed vestment and trying to decipher what the other priest was saying; there was a great deal of banging around with the *r* and *l* sounds. It was only after several attempts that Faber discovered he was to say the Tridentine Mass, the traditional Mass, in Latin.

The Japanese stuggled to get out, "The bishop has approved this Sunday each month for the Latin Mass. . . . I do not know Latin."

Faber had nodded; his had been one of the last seminary classes educated in the Latin Mass. Faber said there would be no problem, even though it had been over a year since he had celebrated in Latin.

Now he was facing the congregation and saying, "*Ecce Agnus Dei . . .*" when he saw Sister Catherine Mary, kneeling in the front row with the other Dominican nuns from the convent. Her head was not bowed, and she was looking at him intently; her face was full of anger. He continued with his ritual, but wondered what he had done now to make the nun irritated.

As he looked out over the congregation, he was startled to see that the majority were Japanese; only about one-third were Occidental. Confusing, because the priest had told Faber that the eleven-o'clock Mass was always in English. Then it dawned on him: the Latin Mass. It was common knowledge that the Tridentine Mass, when available, was always blessed with a greater attendance. The Japanese in the church were able to take part because they were back in their universal church with the traditional liturgy.

The young Japanese priest assisting Faber was upset when Faber indicated how communion was to be distributed. Normally, the celebrant would dispense the wafers to the nuns, who were now moving to the communion rail, but Faber indicated he would take the other side. Faber was not about to mar Sister Catherine Mary's taking of the Holy Eucharist; she was obviously annoyed about something and he did not want to force her to take the Host from his hand.

As Faber moved along his half of the railing, he spotted Tori Ito standing far back in the church. Somewhere she had gotten hold of a white mantilla and looked quite in place; he was privately pleased that he could offer the Mass for her intention.

At the end of the Mass, he knelt at the foot of the altar and said a quick Hail Mary and an Our Father for the soul of his father and the health of his mother. As he rose, the Japanese priest whispered, "Will you help greet the parishioners?" Faber declined and returned to the sacristy; he felt the local priest should meet with his people without a visiting priest butting in.

Faber took his time changing from his vestments to his street clothes, savoring the quiet beauty of the whole church. The vestry was like the rest of the building, dark woods blended with elegant stonework. For an instant he felt an old longing, for a parish of his own. He had never had one: the calling assigned to him in the Society of Jesus kept him on the move too often. And the borrowed vestments he was removing were another jab; he owned one set, which had been given to him years before by his parents, when his father was still alive, but he seldom wore them, because he generally had to catch Mass on the run in some alien place. But, as he had been trained to do, he erased the regrets from his thoughts and accepted the transience those borrowed altars and the borrowed garb, as part of his calling.

He borrowed a hairbrush he found on the counter and gave a couple of quick swipes at his brown hair. Then, after a final inspection told him he looked ready to go out on the street, he took his leave of the interlude.

As he came into the parking lot, Sister Catherine Mary was waiting for him, outside the door. Her anger was still there, maybe a bit more than when he had seen her in church.

He offered a smile as he drew close.

She said, "You have one hell of a nerve, Father."

He let the thrust slip by him as he countered mildly, "Good morning, Sister."

"I try to do my job well. . . . I keep out of trouble. . . . I am just doing—"

He cut her off. "Hold it, Sister. What's your problem?"

Her face was flushed and she was actually sputtering. "Problem! I had no problems . . . not until you came here and began doing whatever you are doing." She took a breath. "What the shit are you doing here, Father?"

Faber raised his hand as he said, "First, Sister, your language leaves a great deal to be desired. I know we are to become more worldly, but a religious who spits out vulgarities might be becoming too worldly."

"Don't patronize me, Father."

"And, second, Sister,"—he jammed firmness into his voice—"what I am doing here is really none of your business."

"It is my business when the police come around interrogating me!"

Faber was off balance for an instant. "What did they want?"

Sister Catherine Mary's lips were pulled tightly across her teeth. She was making no attempt to hide her hostility. The sun had moved into the parking lot and the asphalt radiated heat, but the beads of perspiration on her upper lip were, Faber knew, from anger. The nun told him, "They wanted to know why I acted so mysteriously driving in from the airport. They wanted to know why you vanished from here yesterday morning. And they wanted to know why the car we loaned you was parked all night at the Hilton Hotel! That is what they wanted to know and they asked me; I could not tell them."

Faber said, "And nor will I tell you. You do not need to know."

Sister Catherine Mary said, "Well, you will tell Mother Superior. She had me on the carpet, and she wants to talk to you."

Faber smiled. "Mother Superior will have to wait for any explanations. You can tell her that I am doing the work of our Church and that I am acting on orders from my provincial. That is all the mother superior needs to know."

"She will not let you have the car," the nun said, her words colored with pleasure.

Faber said, "I think my use of the car depends on the authority of the pastor, Sister. The pastor has the final say in a parish, and he has been given orders to provide me with any assistance I might need. I need the car."

Faber was not pleased with the victory. He never found winning pleasant when the loser was hurt, and the nun looked hurt. He had drawn on authority, and Sister Catherine Mary was forced to yield; she had no recourse. He looked at her. She was attractive, but bore a bit too much intensity in her eyes to be really pretty. He had a feeling that she was a good nurse and would, one day, be an outstanding leader in her order. But she was going to have to learn to take defeat with a little less sting, Faber thought. He was about to voice some crumb of consolation when, from behind him, Tori Ito's voice said, "Bart; am I interrupting?"

He turned and looked at Tori, mildly grateful for her arrival. He introduced the two women. The nun rudely nodded her head and said, "I must go. I will give Mother Superior your message." She stalked across the parking lot before Faber could speak.

Tori was embarrassed. "I waited at the front of the church; I thought you would come out that way."

He explained what he had done and ended with saying, "I had to talk to the sister for a few minutes."

"I hope I didn't interrupt you."

"I was through. Did you enjoy the service?"

She responded, "I'm not much of a church goer; never have been. But it was nice. I felt close to Tac."

He was about to explain to her the beauty of that part of the Mass where he had prayed for Tac Okomoto during the Commemoration of the Dead when Tori said, "I was thinking about you going to Hiroshima."

He looked at his watch; it was ten past twelve. He said. "I'd better be getting on the road if I'm going to make Osaka in daylight."

"I delayed you a full day. I'm sorry."

"You helped me greatly, Tori. I appreciate you taking the time to give me some advance warning. I could run into a mess at the IFP."

She said, "That's what I was thinking about, Bart. There is a man in Hiroshima who was one of the founders of the Institute For Peace. I'm pretty sure he is still alive; I haven't seen him since I lost Tac. His name is Minoru Watanabe."

Faber asked, "He knew Tac?"

She nodded.

"Is he still involved in the IFP?"

"I don't really know. For his own reasons, Minoru has refused to see me or talk to me since Tac died. I even wrote to him, three times, but there was never an answer.'' She paused, and Faber watched her eyes as she grappled with still another aspect of Tac Okomoto's death. ''But he's a man who can give you a lot of background. If he's still alive.''

Faber took a pad from his coat pocket and asked Tori to spell the name. She did not remember Watanabe's address but said that the people at the IFP would know how Faber could make contact. When he had written down the information, she said, ''If he is alive and you do talk to him, would you please ask him to write to me or to call me at home? I want to find out why he cut me off without a word after Tac died. I was quite angry for a while, but time dulled that pain, too.''

Faber asked, ''You and Tac were close to the old man?''

She responded, ''He was like a father to Tac. He was the one who guided Tac; he was the one who really made all of the important decisions. I was welcomed into his home. Watanabe-san was a wise man, Bart. He was a Survivor.''

Faber took note of the inflection that capitalized the word, the same way the Japanese are able to capitalize ''The Bomb'' when it is mentioned. Faber said, ''I'll look him up.''

She said, ''Will you come back to Tokyo before you leave Japan?''

''I don't know. I could catch a flight out of Osaka.'' Then he realized that she was hopeful of seeing him before he went home and he added, ''If there is anyway for me to do it, I'll come back to Tokyo. I'd like to see you, too.''

It was a lie, not about seeing her again, but because, once done with his assignment, he would leave as quickly as possible to make his report to his provincial. He looked at his watch. ''Thanks for coming to Mass, Tori. I've got to go to the rectory and see the pastor.''

She extended her hand, it was soft and warm and the

pressure she applied indicated friendship or possibly more. He held her hand for a bit longer than he should—he knew that—but he might never see her again. They said goodbye.

Faber stood, watching her cross the parking lot and climb into her Mustang. He never enjoyed leavetakings.

He yanked his thoughts back to his assignment and walked to the rectory.

The pastor's bedroom was dimly lit, the curtains drawn closely against the warm sun. The room was filled with a musty odor of age, slightly flavored by illness. The housekeeper announced Faber and withdrew, sliding the door closed behind him.

"Come here, my son," came from the bed where the pastor lay propped up against a mound of pillows. Faber crossed the room and seated himself in the chair beside the bed. The pastor said, "How goes your trip, Father Faber?"

"I am doing just fine, Father. Sorry I could not stop by yesterday when I arrived, but I had some urgent business."

The pastor smiled. "Ah, yes, I heard about that from Mother Superior. You Phalanx chaps are always into more intrigues than is good for you."

How did this Dominican know about Phalanx? The pastor saw the reaction and said, "Father Faber, I was once nearly tempted to join the Society just so I could be a part of Phalanx. Father Venturi called me and told me to see that you obtain whatever I can give you. Is there anything you especially need?"

Absently, Faber said, "I do want to use the car for a few more days." Father Venturi, Faber's provincial secretary, was not a man to break Phalanx security lightly. Why had he done so now?

Faber heard the pastor saying, ". . . but she's a fine girl."

"Sorry, Father," Faber said, "I didn't hear you."

The pastor said, "Sister Catherine Mary is a bit of a stickler for the rules but . . ."

"Yes, sir, she is a fine nun."

The pastor asked, "And what is your schedule now?"

Faber was cautious. "I'm driving to Osaka tonight, then to Hiroshima tomorrow."

"Have you been there before?"

"Never."

"It will be an experience, Father Faber. You will walk on the same ground as Father Obrini."

Faber nodded. All modern Jesuits knew of Father Guillermo Obrini, a Jesuit who had been working in Hiroshima when the atomic bomb was dropped. Obrini survived, worked all the horrible days right after the bomb and helped to rebuild the city and the Jesuit mission. Later in life, Obrini went on to become the secretary general, the Black Pope who is the leader of the order, worldwide.

The pastor asked, "Is there anything we can do for you while you are in Hiroshima?"

"No, thank you. I will be staying at the mission."

The pastor said, "Father Venturi did not want you to stay at the Jesuit facility here; how so in Hiroshima?"

Faber paused, but the pastor already knew about Phalanx. "I did not want to become involved with the local Phalanx team. You can understand."

The pastor said, "There are only two of them here in Japan, but I guess you know that." Faber nodded. The pastor continued, "One of them is in Korea right now and the other is down on Okinawa. You won't see them for a couple of weeks."

Faber smiled. This old Dominican had his own good sources of intelligence.

The pastor paused, as if trying to gather energy, then

asked, "Is there any knowledge I can share with you, Father? I've lived here for thirty years."

Faber thought for a moment, then asked, "What about a man named Minoru Watanabe?"

The pastor said, "You pronounce that well; do you speak the language?"

"I speak kitchen Japanese; I understand more than I can speak."

"Watanabe has done great things for the peace movement, but he is a dangerous individual. Since he has tasted power he has become intoxicated with the concept of controlling people. Keep your guard up."

Faber asked, "Is there anything I can do for you, sir?"

The pastor said, "No, thank you. The young priest brought me Communion this morning. I am sure he is quite anxious to administer extreme unction."

Faber was concerned. "Are you seriously ill then?"

The pastor said, "No, not at all. Just a bad case of the flu; but my young charge is still eager to do his sacraments."

Faber rose to shake hands.

The pastor said: "I had a report on your Mass."

Faber waited.

"It seems you failed to use the *Novus Ordo* during the consecration."

Faber snapped his fingers in irritation. "I knew there was something; I felt something was different. I must have slipped back. How did you know?"

The pastor gave a grin and said, "One of the faithful who does not approve of the Tridentine ritual. He was following closely."

Faber laughed. "A spy at Mass?"

The old man said, "Not really a spy but he will report to the bishop. I will have to make a report."

"I hope I've not caused you any trouble."

"No, no, no! Old habits die slowly; I'll report that it was an honest error."

Faber apologized again, and the pastor said, "I told you: old habits die slowly; especially the good ones."

Faber did not respond. He shook hands with the pastor and turned to leave. He was at the door when the pastor said: "Keep your guard up with that Watanabe fellow. He could be a strong enemy."

Bart Faber smiled and left.

CHAPTER THIRTEEN

Bernie Eby awoke and was immediately certain that hair had begun to grow on his tongue. As he opened his eyes and saw that it was eight minutes before one, he wondered if it was midnight or midday. Then he wondered just what day he was living. He moved his arms to see if they were still controllable. His hand touched flesh, the flesh of another person.

Eby rolled quickly off the tatami mat in his bedroom and ended up on his knees while looking at a naked bundle of woman; she was curled motionless into a fetal position. Eby poked her shoulder. She did not move. He gave another poke, and was on the edge of deciding the woman was dead when she moved. She slurred out a couple of sounds that might have been words, but Eby could not understand them. In her squirming to find a position in which to continue sleeping, Eby saw that she was young, very young. Her breasts were merely buds, the rest of her body the smooth form of youth. Just how young was she?

Thirteen or fourteen was his guess. He felt a chill of disgust.

He could not remember what had happened the night before. He was pretty sure he had gone to the Ginza for something to eat. That vision came more firmly into his mind and he was able to reconstruct what probably happened because few people—save for the insipid tourists—went to the Ginza for food late at night. The Ginza, which is a section of Tokyo, not a street as is commonly thought, is a late-night spot for drugs, pachinko games or hookers. Eby was not into drugs, and he had never been fascinated by the steel ballbearings of pachinko games, but he did have an inclination towards hookers. He wondered if he had eaten anything. The thought made his stomach heave.

He went into the shower, scrubbing under scalding water while trying to figure out how to wake the girl without finding out her age. He barely heard the telephone ringing. When the noise finally reached his awareness, even though he was being deluged with nearly boiling water, he felt a painful chill: The caller might be his wife, and his companion might answer the phone.

He lunged out of the shower, not bothering to grab a towel or robe, and sprayed soap suds and water splashes through the house as he sped to the kitchen. He slid to a halt and grabbed the phone: "Hello."

There was a pause. The kitchen countertop and the table were cluttered with the remains of a Kentucky Fried Chicken dinner. So, he thought, he *had* gone to the Ginza, where Colonel Sanders had infiltrated with his red and white stripes and he had probably lured the young girl home with the promise of gourmet food.

The telephone finally made a noise, a man's voice saying, "Hello . . . Bernie Eby?"

Eby figured a male operator was connecting the call. He acknowledged.

"This is Susumu Kato."

A stranger. Probably a phone solicitation for wigs or to have his house painted. With a brittle politeness, Eby said, "Can I help you?"

"It's me . . . Susumu Kato. From the Institute For Peace."

Eby was in poor mental shape to think but he struggled and finally remembered hearing the name. He repeated, "Can I help you?"

"We've got something for you to do for us, Bernie."

Eby bristled. Kato had used the first name too familiarly, and he also sounded proprietary about the IFP. Well, the IFP had fallen apart after Tac Okomoto died, and no one had the right to represent himself as leader. *Besides*, Eby thought, *I cut that cord a long time ago; I want nothing to do with the IFP*.

Kato said, "It's a writing job, Bernie. We'd thought you'd be interested."

"I'm not."

"We could sure use your help."

"I'm pretty busy."

Kato's next words came clipped: "That's crap, Eby. You haven't worked in three months."

"That's none of your business."

"It is if I want to make it my business." His voice was a tad more gentle as he said, "There's money in this for you, Eby. Some pretty good money."

Eby smiled to himself. The IFP was stingy with money and, while Tac Okomoto had been alive, Eby had never been paid for anything he wrote for the organization. He had managed to use his relationship with Tac to write a few magazines and newspaper articles but had never gotten what could be termed good money for his talents. Kato's voice said, "Plus expenses."

Greed pushed aside a slice of the alcoholic fuzz in Eby's mind. If there was enough money he could take his wife and leave Japan. With cash in his pocket, he could find someplace to live in Southeast Asia.

"How much?" Eby asked.

"Five thousand."

Five thousand yen would not buy even a bottle of booze, so either Kato was kidding or he was talking about another currency. If it was Hong Kong dollars, then it was a fair piece of change.

Kato added, "U.S. dollars."

With that kind of money, with his current lifestyle, he could live for several months. Eby said, "I'm your man, Susumu."

Kato said, "It should take you about two weeks."

"No problem."

"This is to be mostly research. You might have to write it up for us."

"I can handle that."

Then Kato said matter-of-factly, "You will have to go to the United States."

Eby was furious, suffering a hangover and standing in his kitchen dripping wet and uncomfortably cold. He growled into the phone, "I don't go to the States, you dumb shit."

Kato argued, "You must . . . to make the money."

Eby raised his voice. "Listen, fucker: If you were half the man Tac Okomoto was, you'd fuckin' well know there ain't no money that could get me to go to the States."

There was silence on the telephone; Eby sensed that Kato was getting instructions on how to handle the call. Finally, the voice said, "Listen to me, Eby. Don't interrupt and don't hang up. We need some work done in the States and we're willing to pay you for it. If you won't do it, then you'd better start thinking about that little Laotian wife of yours down in Hong Kong. She might just get her ass shipped back to Vientiane and you might get your ass thrown out of Japan."

Eby knew the IFP had power; he had seen what Tac Okomoto had done and where help had come from when needed. Kato—or the intelligence that was guiding Kato—might well be able to reach into the Department of Immigration. An expatriate American and a refugee Laotian were insignificant mortals in Japanese society; removal would be relatively easy.

Kato's voice came through; "You are still there, friend Eby?"

Eby swallowed, hard. He needed time, not confrontation, because time could help him sort this out; confrontation could lead nowhere. But he could not retreat casually; he had lived among the Japanese long enough to understand saving face to avoid shame, the *haji* that gives an opponent a deadly weapon. Eby said, "I will talk to you," and he forced his voice to carry venom; "I have contacts in the States who could do your research. I won't go, that's definite." He took a breath. "And leave my wife out of this."

"Ah, your wife. Yes. We have talked to her in Hong Kong."

Eby blurted, "You bastard!"

Kato finished, "And she, too, does not want to be sent to her home." He added, with muffled glee, "The police there have unique ways of raping women who have married Americans. Have you heard about that?"

Eby could feel the metallic taste of bile coming up into his throat. "When can we talk?"

There was that distracting hesitation again.

The answer came: "Tomorrow night, someone will come to your home. Be there waiting."

Kato hung up. Eby felt his body quiver; never in his life had he experienced such a debilitating attack on his emotions.

In contradiction to his mood, there was a warmth on his shoulders, a gentle, soft touch. His head snapped around and the girl was there, drying his shoulders with a towel. "You will catch cold," she said as she stroked the terry cloth down his back.

She moved around in front of him and toweled his chest. He looked down at her and was as shocked as he had been when he first woke. She was tiny: maybe sixteen at the oldest, not over five feet tall. She was still naked.

In a lovely singsong lilt she said, "You look so sad. Is something wrong?"

He shook his head and heard the silent words of his mind: *Fucking slope.*

He felt her hand take hold of him. He flicked her away and said, "Go make us tea."

CHAPTER FOURTEEN

Common knowledge has it that there are two Toyota
Crown President limousines garaged in the prefecture of
Hiroshima. One is owned by the Rokko Shipbuilding
Company and is used by its managing director; the other—
it was a gift—is the property of the Institute For Peace and
is used exclusively to transport Minoru Watanabe where
he wants to go.

The vehicle is plushly appointed, even to the darkly
smoked windows that allow none to look inside. There are
periods when Watanabe does not use the limo, but sends
it out to drive around so that the local citizens can see—
or, at least, think—that he is afield and doing the work of
the Institute. On this Sunday afternoon, he was, in fact,
in the vehicle, moving slowly towards downtown Hiroshima.

There were small flags aristocratically mounted on the
two front fenders. One flag had been a personal gift from
UN Secretary-General Kurt Waldheim, given as a token

of respect during a long-past anniversary celebration; it was a replica of the white-on-blue UN flag. The other pennant was also white on blue, a copy of Picasso's *Peace Dove*. When the limo, with flags fluttering, came down the street, many pedestrians would stop and offer a respectful bow and softly mutter, *"Sensei . . . sensei."*—Teacher . . . teacher. Minoru Watanabe was well loved.

Watanabe sat in the back and gave an occasional beneficent wave of his hand even though he could not be seen through the windows; the gestures made him feel close to his fellow citizens of Hiroshima.

His thin frame was clothed in a robe that was elegant in its simplicity. On his feet were sandals that he had made himself, and the watch he wore was not fancy. Watanabe did not strive for ostentatious behavior, even if he did use the limousine with some pleasure.

His chauffeur and bodyguard was Meiji Sano, a man of tremendous proportions who was the orphan son of a Hiroshima woman who had died giving birth to him in 1953. Her radiation exposure from the 1945 explosion had not made her sterile, but had made her too weak to stand the rigors of pregnancy. Meiji had been adopted and raised by Watanabe.

Meiji drove into the downtown area through the western suburbs, crossing three of Hiroshima's seven rivers before nearing the IFP headquarters. The streets were nearly deserted in that part of town, as was normal for a bright, cheerful Sunday afternoon. The car came to rest at the curb fronting the plaza, by the Hagane Building. The driver sat behind the wheel, Watanabe sat in the back, and neither made a move to climb out into the hot air.

Watanabe began tapping his fingers on his skinny knees to display his impatience. Meiji caught the warning in the rearview mirror. They had arrived exactly on time for the meeting; he offered to go find out the cause for the delay. Watanabe said, ''No,'' but kept on tapping.

The old man looked out at the plaza and grimaced at the gigantic sculpture that was the major focus of the space. The abstract work was twenty feet tall, welded pieces of rusting scrap steel that had been salvaged from bomb-damaged buildings. The piece was supposed to convey the ugly, brute strength of the atomic bomb but merely displayed the artist's lack of talent.

"Raion!" Watanabe hissed to himself in anger at the man who had created the monstrosity. Watanabe had personally seen to the raising of several thousand yen to pay for the creation. The old man felt he had wasted his considerable talents in the effort. All of that had happened years before and Watanabe had held his peace back then, allowing himself to show adulation at the dedication and allowing Raion to be garlanded with false praise. Watanabe would have revenge; he possessed a full cup of patience.

"Here he comes," came from Meiji. Watanabe pulled his gaze away from the sculpture to see Susumu Kato walking out the front door of the Hagane Building. The old man felt a paternal comfort at the sight of Kato; here was another young activist being directed into the cause.

Kato was wearing the sterotypical garb of a nineties radical who felt a close bond with the sixties' protesters. The olive drab field jacket had the appropriate tears in the cloth and the fatigue trousers carried the required splotches and stains; all looked, at least, as though they had been caused in confrontations with the police. He wore scuffed white running shoes. The only incongruity was the Raiders baseball cap on Kato's head. Watanabe lately had allowed his disciples some latitude in their uniforms and he made a conscious note not to say anything about the cap. For the next few days, Kato would be an important link in the chain that Watanabe had been forging for the past two years.

Kato entered the back of the limo with verve. "I got him, Teacher, right by the balls."

Watanabe acknowledged his approval as he said to Meiji, "We can go."

The car moved, and Kato spoke: "I'm sorry we have to use Eby, Teacher; he is a weak person."

Watanabe responded, "What Eby has to do is nothing which requires strength, my son. It is necessary for the American to help us at this phase in the project; quite necessary, you will see very soon."

The car traveled south along the west bank of the Ota River. Two miles south of the IFP headquarters, the driver turned and crossed the first of three bridges on the route to their destination. While they rode, Kato delivered his verbatim report of the telephone encounter with Bernie Eby a few minutes before.

The old man absorbed each detail and particularly relished the discomfort caused the American by the threat of separation from his Laotian wife; Watanabe did not think that Asians should mingle with Occidentals on an intimate basis. "Doing business is one thing," he said to Kato, "but they have no right to take our women." The old man added abruptly, "Did you contact the artist?"

Kato glanced out the window as he replied, "He'll be there, waiting. He's pissed."

Watanabe's look asked *why*?

"He thinks he should come to your house, like you told him."

"I'll not have that scum in my house, ever!"

"You told him last night to come to your house, and he spent all night getting the stuff he has on Yamabato. You know, the sketches and drawings, all that shit."

Watanabe's face was grim. "I do not relish even seeing the pig. I can imagine what his home looks like after seeing what he has done to himself."

Kato said, "Well, he's there and he's waiting and he's pissed."

The old man had a way of shrugging his shoulders. All those in the IFP knew that there was a finality to the move. The matter was dropped. Watanabe went back to the subject of racial purity. Kato had heard the thoughts a dozen times before, but he was an eager student and he paid attention as the teacher spoke.

The artist Raion's workshop and residence was located at the southern tip of the city. The place was crammed in between warehouses facing out onto Hiroshima Harbor, just west of the vast complex known as the Fish Hatchery. The luxury Toyota definitely seemed out of place as it rolled to an easy halt in front of Raion's studio.

Watanabe spoke to Kato as Meiji moved around to open the door: "Is this filthy person in shape to meet us and to understand what we need?"

Kato said, "He was straight when I talked to him."

The old man said, "I hope so." He climbed out, then added, "For his good health, I hope so."

The artist Raion was coming outside, gingerly dodging around piles of metal and wood as he called his greeting; Watanabe's face twisted in annoyance at the thought of having to walk through the junkyard. At age seventy-seven he was not as agile as the younger men and he did not relish the thought of falling.

They made their way precariously through the disorder, with Raion leading and Kato following behind Watanabe, the young man ready to break the rule that no man should lay a hand on the old man, and catch him if he stumbled.

Inside the building, the huge room was cluttered, not only with the tools and materials of Raion's art, but also with piles of bagged garbage, and other food scraps just swept into heaps. Watanabe felt a swell of nausea.

"Let's talk here," Raion said. His voice and behavior lacked any hint of the animosity that Watanabe expected;

Watanabe suspected the sculptor had bolstered himself
with a mild jolt of pot.

The "here" Raion had suggested was a large worktable
with tall stools placed around it. There was a minor
amount of clutter but that was cast aside by a sweep of
Raion's arm. All that was left on the table was a two-foot-
tall clay model of Yamabato. Dove.

The figure on the table was more than just the simple
lines of a bird. A year before, Watanabe had spent ten
straight hours telling Raion what the old man envisioned
as a symbol for the peace movement. The world had accepted Pablo Picasso's simple design as the emblem of the
antiwar movement; Watanabe was determined that a Japanese design should have that honor. Japan, in Watanabe's
mind, had suffered more than any other nation because of
the horror inflicted on Hiroshima and Nagasaki. During
that exploratory session, the artist had made a sketch, rad-
ically different from any peace dove that had ever been
seen before. Watanabe had immediately commissioned
Raion to do the work. But, due to his increasing use of
drugs and the distracting need to make a living, Raion had
neglected the effort and had made only the clay model.
Watanabe, six months before, had angrily ordered Raion
to stop work. Raion had agreed. Actually, he had done
nothing of substance toward making the actual statue.

Now, for a reason known only to the old man, the venture was to be restarted. Raion was pleased. He had been
cranking out trash for the tourist market and making a bare
living. He was sure Watanabe would now provide another
large fee from the IFP treasury.

The artist asked, "When will we begin, Teacher?"

The old man, sitting erect, not allowing even his elbows
to touch the grimy worktable, said, "We began last night.
I assume you have been working today."

The artist bristled, then said, bluffing, "I've been work-

ing on the details. I had planned for the meeting at your
house for . . .''

Watanabe cut him off with a flick of the hand. "You
will not come to my house, Raion. You will be much too
busy to leave your studio from now until you finish the
work on Yamabato."

Raion waited. The old man continued, "Review your
plans for me."

Raion began: "Our magnificent symbol will measure
twenty-eight feet in height and the gentle spread of her
wings will be fourteen feet. I calculate that she will be
identifiable from a distance of two miles. She will be cast
in solid concrete with an aggregate of crushed marble that
will give her an iridescent sheen. When she is—''

Watanabe cut him off. "How long?"

The artist made a face as if he was giving serious study
to the estimate, then announced, "Six months."

The old man said, "One month."

Raion swept his hand through the air in a wave of contempt. "That would be impossible. I would have to work
day and night to get it done in three months."

"One month. How much will the final product weigh?"

Raion scoffed, "It will weigh nothing, Teacher, because
it will not be done—not in one month."

Susumu Kato moved to get up; he was sick of the artist's
arrogance and offended to hear Watanabe insulted. Before
Kato could stand, the old man was saying, "Do you see
that driver out there by my vehicle?" The artist looked
through the filthy windowpanes and gave a nod.

The old man said, "That man is an off-duty policeman
from our city. If you continue to be obstreperous, I will
call him in here, and he will take one of those welding
torches you use, and he will proceed to burn off your scro-
tum."

Raion winced; even Kato felt a slight pang of imagined
pain. Watanabe said, "You will not question my orders,

Raion. You will do as you are told. Now, how much will the statue weigh?''

The artist had paled and his eyes glowed with fear. There were stories of beatings and other abuses concerning Minoru Watanabe, there were even rumors about two people being killed when they had gotten in the old man's way. Raion did some fast figuring and said, ''Thirty-five thousand pounds.''

Watanabe said, ''It cannot weigh more than thirty thousand pounds. That is a new stipulation.''

Raion was not in an argumentative mood. ''I will have to calculate how to bring it into the requirement.'' Then, with some bravery, he asked, ''Can I ask why it is to be a certain weight?''

The old man nodded. ''It is to be flown in an airplane. There are weight regulations.''

The announcement was news even to Kato. Raion said, ''Flown? To the United States?''

Watanabe said, ''We will see about that.''

The artist said, ''It would be a great honor for my work to be displayed internationally.''

''Yes. It will be a great honor.''

Raion's mind quickly leapt forward to the day when the art world would be talking about his creation. He saw himself at the center of attention, and he envisioned massive strides forward in his career. But he had to eat. ''There will be a fee for this, Teacher?''

''We will pay your expenses until the project is completed. We will then see what you will be given as a fee by the Institute.''

Normally, Raion would have argued for an immediate advance, but he was wallowing in anticipation of world recognition and he knew he could cheat on the materials invoices. He'd get the money he wanted. One way or another.

Watanabe stood up. The old man said, "I have other things to do today, Raion. Begin work immediately. I will be by to check on your progress in a few days."

The artist stood alone as Watanabe and Kato walked out. He would have to begin work; he would show the old fool that the work could be done within a month.

CHAPTER FIFTEEN

It was dusk as the Nissan van pulled into the town of Hagi on the southwest coast of Japan. Traffic was light, because most of the Sunday drivers had already gone home.

The man in the van moved his shoulders vigorously to shake off the tiredness; he had been awake, and moving, for over twenty-four hours. But he had to keep going.

He drove through the center of Hagi, watching carefully to observe the speed limits and traffic rules; he did not want to meet some policeman who had not filled his quota earlier. On the south side of town, in a quiet residential area, he pulled up to a modest house where a young father was playing with his two small children in the front garden. The driver beeped the horn and the father, showing some visible irritation at the rudeness of such a summons, came to the driver's window.

The two men exchanged the secret greetings of the

members of the *Hitori shinzo mittsu* society. Then the driver demanded: "Where is the place?"

"As instructed," the other man responded, "I have rented the place in a busy area."

The driver nodded. "We need activity so as to avoid attention as we come and go."

"The storage space is near an apartment complex, in back of a shopping center."

"That is good."

"Let me give the children to my wife and I will go there with you."

The driver said, "You will have to walk back; this vehicle must be hidden as soon as possible."

The distance to the storage space was just over two miles, but the father said, "I will be right with you."

The men rode in silence for the two miles. The storage area was not large. It was one of those mini-storage places where it is possible to rent a garage-sized space by the month. There were twenty closed doors; they pulled the van next to the one halfway down the row away from the gate.

The driver turned off the engine. "I will stay here."

"Do you want food? I can come back."

The driver said, "I will not need food. You are to go home and forget that you have ever seen me."

The man nodded. Then he said, "I rented the place for a month only."

The driver smiled. "You did what had to be done, Brother. Now go."

They gave each other the ritualistic salutations of departure and the driver pulled down the garage door; he was in darkness.

He opened the back doors of the van and flicked on a battery lantern that bathed the back of the van in a sickly yellow glow. He unlatched the aluminum case and looked down at the plastic-wrapped metal cradled in its bed of foam rubber. He reached out and caressed the cylinder, the gesture almost sensual. He whispered, ''We will show them, my friend. We'll show the fuckers.''

He closed the case and pulled the van doors shut. He unpacked a sleeping bag, nibbled on a packet of rice cakes and drank two bottles of beer. After taking the last swig from the second bottle, he turned out the lantern, curled comfortably into the sleeping bag and went to sleep.

CHAPTER SIXTEEN

Bart Faber pulled off the highway on the southern outskirts of Osaka and parked in the gravel driveway of a
Japanese inn. The Japanese inns are the counterpart of
American motels, except that the inn in Japan has been a
hostel for travelers for thousands of years and has not
changed at the whim of the client. They only provide what
is needed: a place to sleep. Bart Faber had been introduced to them back when he had been stationed with the
army in Tokyo and the USO had encouraged the GIs to
take advantage of the clean, quiet and inexpensive facilities.

It was later in the evening than Faber had hoped to reach
Osaka: it was twenty past eight. He had been delayed leaving Tokyo because he had gone to the central police station
to clear up the problem he had obviously created for Sister
Catherine Mary the day before. Sister Catherine Mary had
been so flustered by being questioned that he felt he had
to do something to make amends.

The session at the central police station had not been easy, until a lieutenant detective appeared who had previously served with the Japanese defense forces and had had frequent liasion with American GIs. The two men were about the same age and they communicated well. The detective explained that the Metropolitan Police used by the immigration people were recruits who sometimes took their jobs a bit too seriously. When they stubbed their toes, as they had when they lost their tail on Faber, they tended to react too strongly.

Faber explained away the fact that he had lost the detectives as an accident and for the record convinced the detective that he was in Japan for a few days making an inspection of church operations. The necessary notations were made in the appropriate files, and Faber was amiably dismissed with a friendly handshake. The lieutenant detective promised to stop by the Dominican convent and put Sister Catherine Mary's mind to rest.

The uneventful drive to Osaka had been tiring, and Faber was anxious to get into his room; but once there he found he could not sleep. All Phalanx agents were trained to avoid easy, obvious analyses; no Jesuit believed that things came easy in life. But Faber felt confident that he would merely have to confirm his suspicions once he arrived in Hiroshima: The Institute For Peace had come unraveled, and its dissension was causing the problems.

The secret society that Tori Ito had mentioned—The Man With Three Hearts—did not sound as ominous as, say, The Black Dragon Society that many claim was the guiding force that led Japan into World War II. But Faber knew enough about clandestine sects to be cautious.

He would have to see for himself what power the old man named Minoru Watanabe wielded. He had an impression, mainly from Tori Ito, that the real force within the Institute For Peace had been Tac Okomoto, but maybe Okomoto had merely been the surrogate of Watanabe. That

piece of the puzzle would fit easily, once Faber had a
chance to talk to the old man in person.

Then there were the other Hiroshima groups: a full
dozen organizations vying for the paramount role in the
peace movement, a dozen fragments splintered over the
years by ideological—and political—chasms not easily
bridged. Bernie Eby had told Faber about the *Gensuikyo*
and the *Gensuikin*, the Congress and the Council—each of
Hiroshima, each against the A- and H-bombs. Those two
factions were so far divided politically that the IFP could
only bring them together from time to time, and then only
for a moment. With the IFP shunning the Frisco peace
rally, there was no hope of the other groups joining to
present a united front.

Should he try to intervene? The assignment, as set forth
by Provincial Superior Venturi in Faber's briefing for the
trip to Japan, had been only to find out what was going
on and to report back. But Faber had begun to feel that
the participation of Japan in the Frisco rally could be accomplished with a little bit of Jesuit reason and logic applied to the combatants. From all that Faber had heard so
far, the impediment was the lack of a catalyst caused by
the death of Tac Okomoto. Maybe the old man, Minoru
Watanabe, even at age seventy-seven, could be encouraged
to take up the banner of peace for one last show of soli-
darity. But intervention had not been part of Bart Faber's
charge, and he would need permission to go forward with
it.

Quite possibly, he would be able to complete his work
in a couple of days. Just before he slipped into sleep, he
made a mental note to check on available flights back to
the United States. He smiled at the thought of being home,
soon.

CHAPTER SEVENTEEN

Three hundred forty-four miles north of Osaka, Bernie Eby was as far from sleep as his rage would keep him. Frustration compounded by fear pumped adrenaline through his body at a rate that would soon induce collapse, but he would not give up trying to reach his wife on the telephone. He had made the call—an awesome expense— to Hong Kong two times previously. Each time his wife's sister had said that he should wait for a return call: "She'll call you."

He grabbed at the telephone again and dialed for the overseas operator.

To his surprise, the operator put the call right through. Frequently there was a delay in the service. Maybe, he thought, maybe things are going to start to go right. He listened to the clicks and buzzes, and finally the Hong Kong number began ringing. His sister-in-law answered.

"I need to talk to Ta-ning," he demanded.

His sister-in-law did not respond to him; he heard her

calling for her husband. The brother-in-law came on the phone with a gruff voice: "What d'you want, Eby?"

Eby did not like his wife's brother-in-law; Eby did not like many of her family. But he held his temper and said, in a quiet voice, "I must talk to Ta-ning."

"She ain't here. She won't be here for a couple of days. You know that!"

Eby's temper, short at the best of times, was lost: "What the fuck do you mean, I know that?"

"She's in Macau. . . . You know that!"

Eby exploded, "Look, shithead, I don't know what you're talking about. What the piss is going on down there?"

Hong Kong is eighteen hundred miles southwest of Tokyo but, even over that distance, Eby could sense that his wife's brother-in-law was getting ready to slam down the phone. Eby pleaded, "Hold it! I'm sorry," and he waited. The connection held. Eby went on, "Look, man, I'm tired and I'm worried. Why is Ta-ning in Macau?"

There was a hesitation at the other end, before the brother-in-law said, "Your friends, remember? I drove her to the hydrofoil myself, this afternoon. She told us that your friends had maybe found one of our cousins working in a casino on Macau and that she was to go there with them. You set the whole thing up, so why are you worried?"

The cold twist of terror grabbed hold of Eby's stomach. The *Hitori shinzo mittsu* had his wife. He was an American, not too well liked at the U.S. Embassy; his wife was a Laotian refugee. The embassy would not be much help, the Japanese would give a low priority to his problem, and he had no leverage with the Portuguese who owned Macau.

Eby said into the telephone, "Yeah, that's right. Just tell her I need her to call me when she gets back."

The voice at the other end asked, "What the hell you up to, Eby? You drunk?"

Weakly, softly, Eby responded, "No. Just have her call." And he hung up the phone.

Eby had always known the *Hitori shinzo mittsu* was powerful, but he had never dreamed that he would come up against it. He needed a drink. He might even have a couple of drinks in order to be ready for the meeting tomorrow with Susumu Kato. As he poured the liquor into the glass, he began to imagine how he would smash Kato's ugly face.

He drank.

Across Tokyo, in the plush luxury of Isamu Saito's home, Clay Morton lay in bed, alone, thinking about the next few days.

Morton had declined Saito's offer of feminine companionship for the night; he had even taken it easy with the customary after-dinner drinks. Morton wanted to savor the immediate future in privacy.

What was about to be accomplished was not a lifelong dream of Clay Morton—the business world had already provided the realization of his dreams. But getting the Japanese to initiate a new phase of nuclear power generation, a whole new era of development, was a fruit too sweet to be ignored.

Morton had taken on the cause of small-sized nuclear power generators with gusto. He was going to snatch the world market from American manufacturers, because the leadership in the United States had stupidly abdicated any right to be even a part of the venture. He was angry, furiously angry, with that segment of American management that had allowed itself to be cowed into yielding to the anti-nuclear special interests groups. Back in 1979, Morton had been flown to Harrisburg to investigate the coolant accident at the Three Mile Island power plant; he had arrived just ten hours after the incident. Morton, along with a handful of other leaders in the nuclear-power-generating business, saw the TMI event as a verification of their previous claims that nuclear power was the safest form of power. Morton and the others had argued that the plant was so well built, the equipment was so sophisticated, that the potential catastrophe was averted as a matter of routine.

Morton and the others lost. The government came in with stricter regulations, the environmentalists used millions of their subscribers' donations to launch lawsuits, and investors began redirecting their monies into less volatile enterprises. Delays—legal and emotional—caused an upward spiral in costs, and nuclear power plants became victims of a society blinded by misguided passions.

Now Russia had lived through a power plant disaster that claimed hundreds of lives, and still was adding nuclear wattage; Japan was moving near the fifty percent barrier in nuclear generation; the whole industrial world was plunging away from fossil fuel dependency, while the United States squashed an energy source so thoroughly that it was near collapse. Now he had the chance. Clay Morton was making his move.

He lay in the darkness, thinking of small nuclear plants that would bring electricity to millions, billions of people.

The fact that the venture would also introduce the by-product of nuclear enrichment meant that Japan would be capable of making nuclear weapons within five years. Morton knew that he could direct Japanese manufacturing expertise in a direction that would quickly corner the nuclear military market dominated by France and Sweden.

Aloud, in a voice that startled even himself, Morton said, "I'll show those bastards."

He willed himself to sleep. Just before he dozed off, he wished he had not rejected Saito's offer of a woman; having a female body there in bed with him would have enriched the excitement he was feeling.

In another part of Tokyo, alone in the den of her home, Tori Ito struggled against the tiredness possessing her. The night before, when she had brought Bart Faber home, she had slept little. She had gone into the den frequently to make sure that he was comfortable, secure and peaceful. Once or twice she had shivered when she realized she was happy about the priest because he was alive; too many times in the past two years she had invited the image of Tac Okomoto's dead body into her life. But the priest was gone from her life, and she was alone again.

She was dressed only in brief white underpants and a man's blue work shirt, one of the shirts left in her closet by Tac Okomoto. The shirt was part of the flotsam left by a life cut short, insignificant, but a precious memento of their love. She had never washed the shirt.

She cradled a framed photograph of Tac in her lap. "Oh, my love, why did you leave me?" A monologue with her long-lost lover was a customary ritual when Tori Ito was depressed. "I gave you all I could, Tac. I gave you one hundred percent." A soft grin came to her lips; Tac Okomoto had always criticized those activists who bragged they gave one hundred and ten percent, because, he argued, a person could only give everything and nothing more. "But the time has come for me to put you away, to turn your spirit loose. If you had lived I would be yours for all of our lives, Tac, but you are gone and I must go forward."

A tear fell on the glass of the frame and she wiped it away gently with a finger.

"If you are hearing me, then you know, don't you?" she asked. "You know what the priest has done to me. I know he cannot be mine nor can I be his; their culture is strange, Tac, that is how it is for them. But he awakened within me a desire, a longing. I do not want to be alone anymore, my love. I would take this priest if he could have me, I would give myself to him as I gave myself to you. But that is not possible. I will find another, someone I can love the way I loved you. You will always be a part of me, our love insured that. This priest is gentle like you and bright like you and considerate like you. There will be another out there for me—that I feel is certain. So, with sadness, my darling Tac, good-bye.''

The tears that flooded down onto the picture frame were too numerous to wipe clean with a finger. Tori Ito fell asleep clutching the photo tightly to her chest.

CHAPTER EIGHTEEN

Hiroshima is a port city that rests facing the Iyo Sea—the Inland Sea—nearly at the southernmost tip of the home island of Honshu. The main part of the city is actually a group of six islands in the delta of the Ota River which begins up in the Yamaguchi Mountains. Those mountains form a bowl surrounding the flatness of the city; they increased the success of the atomic bomb dropped on the city. Even though the Hiroshima bomb was considerably smaller than the one dropped on Nagasaki, the damage was greater, because the mountains concentrated the impact in the bowl.

Looking down on Hiroshima from where he had stopped in the Kumara mountain pass, Bart Faber was hard-pressed to see any reminder that Hiroshima was the birthplace of Nuclear War.

The scene was different than he remembered from his last visit to Hiroshima twenty years before. Back then, he had arrived in the city by train with a bunch of other

GIs and they had stayed in that area around the Hiroshima train station which was dense with gin mills, pachinco parlors and bordellos, although Faber and the other soldiers had been part of a planned tour designed to let the men see the first A-bomb site.

From high up in the mountains Faber was seeing tall buildings, expansive industrial sections and miles of residential areas. For the first time he saw the geography of Hiroshima, like a hand placed palm down with fingers jutting out into the harbor, the thumb carrying most of the industry and the airport stuck out on the tip of the index finger. The rivers, six of them, were laced with bridges, dozens of them. He could not identify the Aioi Bridge, that unique T-shaped bridge that was the aiming point for the bombardier in the B-29 carrying the A-bomb.

Faber started the car. His target was not buildings. His mission was to reach into the minds of people down in that city and find answers.

It was still very early in the day, just after seven. Jet lag had shoved Faber out of bed at four-thirty, a customary trick for a confused body clock. He had said his daily office and a full rosary before he heard the ancient innkeeper moving around. Faber had declined the offer of breakfast and had driven the seventy-three miles from Osaka to Hiroshima in easy time. With the early start, and beating the morning traffic in Hiroshima, he reached the Jesuit mission in the center of the city just after nine.

Faber had been briefed on the mission complex before he had left the United States. The original building had been lost in the A-bomb raid but had been reconstructed within months. The complex had grown over the years, and the older building was used mostly for storage and to house visiting priests. The mission was still staffed mostly by German Jesuits, as it had been since the mid-1930s when the American Jesuits were forced out of Japan. Even though the German Jesuits had been able to maintain an apolitical attitude during the war, resentment towards all Occidentals grew to a dangerous level after the bomb was dropped. Still, the hard-working fathers of the order managed to hold on. The city had benefited, especially from the education provided in the mission schools.

Bart Faber parked his car in a slot beside the main rectory and went inside. He introduced himself to the pastor, Father Herman Schultz.

After they exchanged handshakes, Father Schultz said, "I had a message that you would be coming here, Father Faber, but I was told it would be yesterday. We had planned to have you join us for our Sunday dinner."

Faber apologized. "I should have called you, Father. Business kept me."

"Think nothing of it, please. You merely missed an excellent German meal. Our housekeeper has become quite accomplished with Bavarian cooking."

Faber asked, "Is she Japanese?"

Father Schultz nodded. "She has been most patient in learning. Of course, we all tried to help her along with devout prayers . . . for twenty-five years."

Both men laughed.

Father Schultz obviously enjoyed volumes of rich food. The older man was carrying nearly three hundred pounds on his five feet eight inch frame; his cassock did nothing to hide the massive weight. With a wig to cover his crewcut white hair, Father Schultz could easily function as a Santa Claus.

"Well," Father Schultz continued, "there will be another excellent meal next Sunday."

Faber said, "I doubt if I will be here next Sunday."

Father Schultz looked surprised. "You just arrived."

"My assignment is simply to collect some information; I think it will not take more than a couple of days."

The older priest hesitated; a wily grin came to his face. "Could it be, Father, that you are from Phalanx?"

Faber had been trained to handle such questions. "Phalanx?"

Father Schultz gave a broad grin. "I put in my time with Phalanx, Father. In Prague, from '54 to '57. It was not easy duty."

Faber still did not commit himself.

Schultz placed his plump hands over his distended belly. "This body is not able to keep up with the Phalanx pace."

In Faber's tenure with Phalanx he had not run into any *ex*-operatives, at least none that made their background known. He decided he would not try to deceive the older priest. "My provincial has sent me out to find some information about the peace movement."

Father Schultz said, "Let's go over to the old building. We will get you settled in your room. There are no others scheduled to stay in the quarters and . . . we can talk privately."

Father Schultz led the way out of the rectory. They passed the administration building, walked through the garden at the back of the chapel and across a green lawn beside the old mission house. Halfway to the building, Father Schultz stopped and pointed with pride at the wooden structure. "This building is a great monument to our Society, Father." He made a wide, sweeping gesture as if outlining a masterpiece. He explained, "The original building, like this one, had no nails. It is made with mortises and tenons held in place with hand-carved dowels. The old building withstood the initial blast of the bomb, although we are only forty-five hundred feet—less than a mile—from where the bomb was detonated. It caught fire about two hours after the explosion. Father Kleinsorge saved the mission's money from the blaze, and that paid for the reconstruction."

Inside the building, Father Schultz pointed to a wall in the front sitting room; there was a gallery of photographs of the men who had served the order at the Hiroshima mission. The older priest observed, "We carry our scars well." Faber nodded. "I will take you to your room shortly, Father. But, first, let's sit here and talk." He indicated two chairs separated by a small table. They sat down.

Before the older priest could speak, Faber interjected: "You served in Phalanx, Father, so you know that I am under certain obligations; I cannot speak of everything."

Father Schultz said, "I know the covenants, my son. I just think that I can make your assignment less of a chore. What do you need to find out?"

"My provincial has asked me to give him a report on just why the Japanese have refused to attend the peace rally in San Francisco. He has reasons for needing to know."

The older priest smiled. "Then I know I can make your assignment easy: The Japanese *are* going!"

Faber felt his first tinge of impatience as he said, "You don't understand, Father. We know there will be Japanese going, but the official peace groups will not attend. I have to find out why."

Father Schultz held up his hand. "It was on the radio this morning. The Institute For Peace has taken a new position: They will lead the delegation to the United States."

Faber had not listened to the radio during his drive. Somewhat exasperated, he said, "What the hell is going on?"

The older priest said, "I think it was all a power play by the IFP. They do have their intrigues, you know."

Faber asked, "Maybe you had better clear this up for me."

An ancient housekeeper entered the sitting room carrying a tray laden with a coffee pot and buttered toast. Father Schultz smiled his thanks to the woman, who exited in the Japanese fashion, backing out while bowing. "She's a good woman,'' Father Schultz said. He poured the coffee, and continued: ''There are several factions that vie for preeminence in the peace movement in Hiroshima. There is good reason. Peace has become a growth industry in this city.''

The cynical remark seemed out of place to Faber. ''That sounds bad to my ear, Father.''

''It is bad; a very bad situation. What I meant by a good reason was that the groups have a real motivation for wanting to lead: there is a great deal of power involved. There is vast money connected with the A-bomb rehabilitation, many, many jobs to be allocated, and all of that pivots around the world's major platform for peace.''

''It sounds too commercial.''

''It is commercial. Monies must be generated to finance the programs needed to keep people aware of what happened here.''

''You make the various groups sound like mere business enterprises.''

''Not at all; that is not the case. The good done by these groups is important. They need funds, but the people directly involved are not mercenary. Still, you cannot eliminate the vices of human nature, and that is what causes the problems. If one group can allocate jobs, then they receive the loyalty of those getting the jobs; it is as simple as that, Father.''

''I don't mean to sound completely innocent, Father Schultz, but I would think that what happened here would unite the people in a common bond; there should be no power struggle.''

''I'm sure you are not completely innocent, Father, but you are not well informed. Right from the very beginning there was conflict. Shortly after the end of the war there rose a new word in Japan: Hiroshimaism. A new attitude in Japanese culture. For centuries, this race has been determined to hide failure or shame. The people of Hiroshima became a focus of world attention. Some of the *hibakusha*, the survivors of the bomb, began bleating about how they were the victims of a crime. Most Japanese resented those *hibakusha* who cried out publicly. There is an axiom here, *Shikata ga nai*, that means: That's life; it can't be helped. What happened here is counter to the nation's culture. Look at what goes on here each August sixth. Tens of thousands of people from around the world gather at a candlelight ceremony that culminates with the screaming chant 'No more bombs!' Conversely, in Nagasaki, where the bigger plutonium bomb was dropped and tens of thousands were killed, the August ninth anniversary of that bombing is marked by a minute of silent reflection at eleven-fifteen in the morning, that is all. Nagasaki suffered through the bomb and went on to rebuild, while Hiroshima has wrapped itself in sackcloth. Many Japanese resent that."

"Surely no one denies the rights of these victims to feel their own resentment. They do have that right."

"In Japanese culture, they have an overriding obligation to their *on*. . . . That's a concept that takes some study, Father. Just accept from me that *on*, to the Japanese, is a sacred duty to varying segments in their society. Part of that is what we Westerners have called 'saving face', it is very important to these people."

"Does this attitude have anything to do with this far-right movement, this element calling themselves . . ." To his irritation, the name would not surface. He reached for his notepad.

Father Schultz smiled. "Ah, you have heard of the *Hitori shinzo mittsu*; you have been busy. That is a very secret group."

"Yet you know of them."

The older priest gave a grin. "The confessional is a great source of information. You know that."

"Is it a threat?"

"A threat to what?"

"To the peace effort in general?"

"I think not. That group is mostly hotheads who have fixed on the idea that Japan should not have lost the war. The people of this city and especially the *hibakusha* are scared to death of war or even the threat of war. They've had enough. The group's romantic notion carries no weight with the mass of the people."

Bart Faber finished off his share of the toast and refilled his cup of coffee. This development was going to change his plans. He sat for nearly two minutes as he thought through what he would do. Obviously, he should leave Japan; there was no reason to stay when there was no work to be done. His Jesuit ethic deplored wasted effort, and there was much he could be doing for the order back in the United States. He ran over his options, then spoke his thoughts. "So there's no major threat to the peace efforts, the groups have suddenly decided to participate in the San Francisco rally, and all is well. I think I can go home. You were right, Father Schultz, you have made my tasks easier."

"Maybe," the pastor offered, "I could extend our hospitality for a day or so before you return. There is much to see here, and I would enjoy talking with you; sometimes we become so involved in our own world that it is necessary to seek outside stimulation."

Faber thought for a moment. He had gained enough information to complete a report that would satisfy the provincial superior, and even the report might not be necessary now, in light of the news about the Japanese delegations planning to go to San Francisco. But termination of a mission had to be done by the provincial, not by himself. He said, "I'll send a cable to the States and notify them of this news."

A broad smile erupted on the pastor's face. He responded, "It should take at least a day for the reply, Father Faber. Do you fish?"

It had been many years since Bart Faber had fished, so many years since he had done any personal relaxation. He replied, "I do."

"I will take you fishing. I have some chores this morning, administrative duties, but later, in the afternoon, I'll introduce you to some fine battles with our trout population. You can send your cable from the post office, do some sightseeing, and then be back here for lunch at one o'clock. I'm afraid our daily fare is native foods, we only indulge ourselves on Sundays. But you will like the meal. And then you and I will go fish and talk."

Bart Faber liked the old pastor. He was just about to accept the offer when a thought came to him: Tac Okomoto. "Did you know this activist named Tac Okomoto?"

Father Schultz answered, "Yes, of course, I knew Tac. It was a sad loss to the IFP when he died." He then hurried to add, "We can talk about Tac this afternoon, while we fish."

Faber answered, "Yes, we can talk this afternoon."

It did not take long for Faber to settle into the guest room of the old mission house, nor did it take long for him to dispatch his cable at the post office, an easy walk from the Jesuit mission. From the post office Faber wandered casually toward the Peace Memorial Park located directly under that point in space where the first A-bomb exploded.

Faber was enjoying the easy pace and the walk. He'd sent the cable at 10:40 A.M. Monday morning in Japan; that converted to 8:40 P.M. Sunday, back at headquarters. Several hours would have to pass before a reply could come back. The walking felt good, because for the past few days Faber had been sitting in airplanes or automobiles. He was also not anxious to drive because Sister Catherine Mary's car had begun to wheeze ominously during the long drive down from Tokyo. He imagined that Toro Ito's classic Mustang would have been better—Tori Ito had offered him the use of her car—but that would have probably led to another meeting with the nun, and he was hoping to avoid any further run-ins with her on this trip.

As he walked, pressing himself to a healthy pace, Faber challenged himself: Did he want to learn about Tac in order to learn more about Tori Ito? He dismissed that conjecture quickly. In the final analysis, Faber calculated that he wanted to know more about Tac Okomoto because the memory of the man caused such consternation in the people who had known him when he was alive. Maybe Father Schultz would wipe away some of the questions when they went fishing later in the day. Faber was beginning to relish the thought of such relaxation.

He arrived at the Peace Memorial Park. It was awesome, vast acres set aside in memory of the August 1945 holocaust. There were numerous monuments: the Peace Clock, the Peace Bell, the Peace Arch, the Peace Museum and even a Peace Souvenir Shop that sold grisly photographs of victims. But the one with the most dignity was the Memorial Cenotaph, which was poignantly inscribed "Rest In Peace—Man will not repeat the sin." Faber stood in front of the cenotaph, riveted by the simple beauty of the sculpture and the touching words.

Inside the Peace Museum, Faber spent a full twenty minutes studying the huge, graphic model of the city of Hiroshima on that tragic day in August 1945, that instant when tens of thousands of human beings were vaporized in the most destructive moment in the entire history of man waging war.

He left the building drained emotionally; he wanted to forget what he had seen, but he could not erase the stigma that man had placed on his own species. Mentally aching, Faber walked slowly on the path cut into the manicured grass of the park. He paused at the building which had been known as the Industrial Promotion Building in 1945, but had been renamed the Atomic Dome and left as a skeletal monument, its ironwork twisted grotesquely by the massive force of the bomb. The exfoliated granite of the building had the appearance of hideous art. Faber left the Memorial Park.

Back at the Jesuit mission, he did not comment on his morning's venture; he took his lunch with the other priests and tried to join in their banter. Father Schultz sensed Faber's mood. He had seen it many times before in those who had made their first serious visit to the Memorial Park.

CHAPTER NINETEEN

The car was a Datsun Z28, a posh sports model with every imaginable accessory. The driver negotiated the car through the parking lot of the shopping center in the town of Hagi, then around to the back, into the mini-storage compound.

The man behind the wheel was Swedish. His name was Jørg Erickson. He wore his blond hair in a pigtail that reached below the collar of his bleached Levi's jacket. In his black cord trousers and hiking boots, he looked like a young traveler having a holiday in Japan.

He pulled the car to a halt beside a Japanese man standing in front of one of the enclosed rental garages. The waiting man said, "You're late."

The Swede responded, "Hey, my friend, don't be short with me."

The other turned abruptly, pulled open the door, and made a gesture for Erickson to enter. The door slammed shut as soon as both men were inside. It was several sec-

onds before their eyes adjusted to the dark and the light
that was seeping in around the door.

The man asked, "Did you have any troubles?"

Erickson replied, "It was a piece of cake." The idiom
was lost on the other man; they were speaking in English,
which was their only common language, but neither was
totally proficient. The Swede, with some disdain, said,
"There were no problems."

The other man opened the van, turned on the lantern
and said, "It is here. It is ready."

Erickson climbed into the van and opened the aluminum case, revealing the artillery shell wrapped in plastic.
A glint came to his eyes. He said, "Well, you did it! I had
my doubts, but you damned well did it. Congratulations."

"Did you bring the necessary equipment?"

"I picked it up yesterday. They had everything I needed.
It's out in the boot of the car."

The Japanese nodded, closed the doors to the van and
went outside. Alone with the nuclear shell, Jørg Erickson
savored the culmination of years of work. He had been a
militant peace activist since his mid-teens, taking part
in demonstrations, leading riots, and battling for social
reforms all over the world. He had finally been disowned—
and financially abandoned—by his wealthy father in Stock-
holm, but by that time he had established his bona fides
as one of the truly dedicated and effective members of the
counterculture. He was trained as an explosives expert at
the Workers' Revolutionary School in El Fogaha, Libya.
By the time he graduated, he could turn a suitcase into a
death sentence for a hundred tourists at an airport baggage
claim area or turn an innocent-looking letter into a maim-
ing device for a mailroom worker. Now, after all these
years of diligent work, Jørg Erickson finally had within
his reach the ultimate political statement.

He had been able to suppress his disappointment that
the project had started with Japanese activists; he had never

felt that they were really committed to the peace movement, but it was their resources that had made the idea a reality, and it was their people who had actually obtained the weapon. He had to allow, they had been the first to do the impossible.

The door to the van opened and the Japanese handed in a black briefcase. The two men looked at each other.

Erickson said, "Listen, my friend, I could eliminate most of the mass and weight from this thing." He patted the shell with affection. "If you'll get me and this into a good machine shop for a couple of hours, I can get rid of the unnecessary parts. Two hours."

"Don't worry about the weight or size. We have allowed for that. Just hook it up."

Erickson was not used to being bossed around that way. He had not liked this particular Japanese since the two had met a year before in Amsterdam. But they were working for a common goal.

"Have it your way," the Swede said, and he opened his case.

He explained: "I'm going to rig this with three identical command devices, the ones you arranged for me to pick up. The triple triggers will insure that one of them does the job." The Japanese nodded with shallow politeness and said, "I'm sure you will do the best job."

Jørg Erickson wanted to be more a part of this grand gesture. But he knew the Japanese group was merely using him as a skilled mechanic on an undertaking of their own; he would do his work.

For the next hour, the Swede labored over the electronic intricacies of attaching a command device to the nuclear trigger. He had designed a completely fail-safe gadget that carried safeguards guaranteed to keep the bomb dormant until it was ready for detonation. The electronic gear had been expertly constructed by a member of the *Hitori shinzo mittsu* and Erickson was totally confident about it. By the

time he was finished, he was drenched in sweat, not from
nerves—because he had the sureness of an expert—but
from the heat generated within the van.

When he was done, he said, "You take this calculator
and punch the numbers one–two–three–four in order. Do
that twice in a row, and the act will take place in exactly
six hours."

He handed the calculator to the other man, who held it
delicately.

The Swede said, "Don't worry about it, my friend. It's
a standard calculator. It'll do all the normal functions. You
can carry it anywhere in the world and no one will know.
I've modified it by placing a small transmitter inside. It'll
transmit a signal without fail to the distance of one kilo-
meter. Punch in one–two–three–four, twice in that order,
and in six hours the world will know that we are serious."

The other man's eyes were still transfixed on the calculator.

The Swede said, "Turn it on; use it."

The man flicked the On switch and tapped in a simple
calculation; the result appeared in the small window.

Erickson said, "See? It works just fine. No casual inspection would reveal its purpose. Just don't use it on an
airplane. The transmitter does make some minor emission
as it sits waiting for its one–two–three–four command."

The other man nodded, then eased past Erickson to
study the wires connected to the nose of the artillery shell.
The receivers and trigger mechanism were all neatly tied
together with multicolored wires, the whole package secured tightly with heavy-duty packaging tape.

"You have done good," the man said. "We must get
you away from here now."

The Swede said, "There is a matter of some finances,
my friend."

"How much?"

"There's the airline tickets, hotel bills, the rental car . . ."

"How much?"

Erickson said, "You know, chap, I don't like your attitude one fucking bit. You've got a lot of damned nerve—"

Again he was cut off. "We will go to the money."

There was more that Erickson wanted to say, more that he wanted to tell this arrogant son-of-the-Rising-Sun, but he held his anger because of their common goal. Many times in the past fifteen years, Jørg Erickson had swallowed his own opinions because the main objective was to get on with the business of revolution. He nodded and climbed out of the van.

The Japanese asked, "Any further instructions?"

Erickson said, "None. The unit is ready. It is as secure as possible. Treat it with reasonable care, but nothing will really damage the workings." He gave a smile and offered his hand. "It's all up to you now. You haven't told me where you're going to use it. Can you tell me now?"

"No. We will go to get your money."

Erickson drove as the other man gave directions. They came to a small printing shop a couple of blocks from the center of Hagi. No sooner had they stopped than a tough-looking young man came out, wiping ink stains from his hands. Erickson listened to the foreign sounds as the two other men spoke rapidly. The printer climbed into the narrow space behind the front seats, and the other man said, "Take me back to the van. This man will take you to your money."

Back at the mini-storage garage, the other man climbed out of the car, and the printer climbed into the passenger seat.

Erickson had been doing some unpleasant thinking during the drive back. He said to the other man, "I'm not going to get my money, am I?"

The other man did not reply; he offered only a stony gaze.

"Look, man, people know I'm here. Don't fuck with me."

There was no reply.

Erickson then asked, in a calm voice, "Am I going to make it out of this alive?"

Nothing.

The Swede spat out, "Well it's too fuckin' bad when you get done in by your own. I hope the fuckin' bomb blows up in your face!"

The other man turned and went back inside the rented garage.

The body of the Swedish tourist was found just before nightfall of that evening. The investigation officer's stomach heaved as he looked at the twisted body and the wrecked car; he could not understand why visitors came to Japan and drank so much, then insisted in driving on desolate roads by the shoreline. There would be a great deal of work to do, because the diplomats would get into the act; foreigners should be more considerate.

CHAPTER TWENTY

Bernie Eby's anger turned to fear at three o'clock in the afternoon, when Susumu Kato walked into Eby's small living room and said: "You will leave tonight. Get packed. We will take you to the airport."

Eby asked meekly, "Can I ask why I have to be the one?"

Kato snapped, "You can ask nothing. Get packed!"

Eby moved to the bedroom, and he could actually feel himself slinking. He tried to walk with some pride, but there was no response from his spine. He called back, "How long will I be there?" then added, "I can ask that, can't I?" and felt a modicum of pride come to him.

"Five or six days," Kato called back.

As Eby threw some clothing into a small canvas bag, he could hear Kato out at the refrigerator in the kitchen. The sound of a bottle opening indicated that beer was being taken. "Help yourself," he called, bolstering his pride again.

Entering the living room, Eby saw Kato sitting insolently with his feet propped up on the scarred enamel of a second-hand coffee table. Anger tried to exert itself again but fear prevailed; Eby silently watched Kato swig the beer.

"Sit down," Kato ordered.

Eby obliged, then stood and, ignoring Kato's repeated command, went to the kitchen and opened a bottle of beer for himself. Back in the living room, Eby sat and drank.

Kato said, "We need information from San Francisco, Eby. You have been chosen to get it for us." Kato pulled a scrap of paper from his shirt pocket and said, "We need a description of the site for the World Peace Rally scheduled for August. We want to know everything; the terrain, the roads and the overall plan of where people will be during the rally itself."

Eby challenged, "Why the shit do you need that, Susumu? You're not going."

Kato snapped, "I'm not answering questions, Eby. You listen; you get what I want."

"But—"

"We're going. It was on the radio, it's in the newspapers. The IFP is taking part; Japan will be well represented."

Eby had not listened to the news, his thoughts had been only on his wife's disappearance in Hong Kong. The part of him that had once been a good journalist began to wonder what had caused the change within the IFP. Maybe he'd try to find out; he might be able to sell a story on the subject.

Kato went on. "You will discover for us two other things. First, what will be the customs procedures for bringing Yamabato to the United States, and second, how can Yamabato be transported to the rally site?"

Eby was caught with a swallow of beer partway down his throat: Yamabato? It couldn't possibly be ready in time. He said as much.

Kato replied, "It will be done."

Eby argued, "It can't be done. Remember, I was around

when you jerks cut Raion off. He needs five or six months to get that shitty bird of yours done. You're talking about weeks. No way!''

Kato hissed, ''You, Eby-san, let us worry about Raion and Yamabato. You just get us the information.''

Eby countered, ''Seriously, Susumu, you can't make him hurry. He'll do a piss-poor job, and you'll all be embarrassed.''

Kato's demeanor seemed to ease a bit as he said, ''Raion has been encouraged to do Yamabato in a proper manner. We are taking our symbol there and we will make a grand gesture for the cause of peace. As I said, Eby: don't you worry about that; you get us the information.''

'' 'Don't worry?' '' Eby spit out. ''You son of a bitch, you've kidnapped my wife! You're threatening me with being deported! And you say 'don't worry!' ''

Kato took a long drink of beer. ''Eby, you are a dumb shit. Now we're giving you a chance to pick up a few dollars just for this trip. You do a good job and everything will be fine. If you don't do a good job, then we might just let your little wife spend a few days in the sack with the men who have her in Macau. If you screw up completely, then her ass is shipped off back to Laos and you can go suck wind. That's it!''

Eby had no fight within himself, only the coward's excuse: What can I do?

Kato said, ''The plane leaves at seven o'clock. I have your ticket, and two thousand dollars in U.S. cash. You will be on your own.''

Kato reviewed what he wanted Eby to learn, and they left for the airport shortly after four o'clock. During the drive, Eby's dread of returning to his country kept building.

CHAPTER TWENTY-ONE

Because of his high position in Japanese industry, Isamu Saito belonged to several clubs. His favorite men's club was named simply *Kya-ku*, the 100 Club. It was the building number on the boulevard near Saito's offices; it was also the number of members allowed to join. Prospective applicants studied the newspaper obituaries, because only death created vacancies in the *Kya-ku*.

The club was the only private club to which Saito took Clay Morton during their annual visits; Morton had always liked the ambiance of the club's rooms—"Shit," he was wont to say, "can't see no sense in looking for better when this is the best."

The club was decorated in a Western manner, with dark woods, soft carpets, high ceilings and comfortable furniture. The lighting was subdued, and the hired help, most of them elderly, served members with expert quietness. To enhance privacy, the main floor was partitioned into small areas furnished with groupings of chairs and sofas.

Saito and Morton were alone in one of the small retreats relaxing after a long day of meetings. Saito was reading the Mainichi *Daily News*; he had concentrated on the financial pages and was skimming through the general news; Morton was casually thumbing through a three-day-old edition of the *International Herald Tribune*, looking for sports scores.

Their day had been productive. Morton had presented oral and written reports on the small-sized nuclear power plants to Saito and his company's executives. There had been little detailed examination during the session; the executives' staffs would be spending the night analyzing the proposal. In late morning Morton and Saito had met with three officials from the Ministry for the Environment; lunch had been a three-hour encounter with the political leaders in the Japanese Diet; and the rest of the afternoon had been devoted to a visit to the Ministry of Labor. All of the meetings had been positive. Still to be approached were the treasury and industry ministers, but Saito was confident they would be just as impressed with the potential for Clay Morton's venture.

Morton put the paper down on the small table between the two men and picked up his drink. The gin and tonic tasted just right; he was beginning to feel the glow of satisfaction that always came to him when he was in the middle of a battle—and winning. Isamu Saito caught Morton's movement out of the corner of his eye and was about to put aside his own paper when a small headline grabbed his attention. Aloud, he said, "Hello . . . what's this?"

Morton heard the words but did not react. He took another sip of his drink and eased back into the gentle luxury of the leather upholstery. He enjoyed the mood of the 100 Club—it transported him back to his own Oilman's Club in Houston; affluence seemed to have a universal common denominator. Saito hissed out an expletive; Morton grinned. The word Saito had used was one of the few in

Morton's Japanese vocabulary; it described a biological process that was impossible.

Saito said, in English, "There is a development I do not like."

Some type of damage to the nuclear power project? Morton dismissed the worry. In Japanese business, leaks from within a corporation were not as common as they were in the States. He waited.

"This article," Saito said, "has to do with a new development in the peace movement. The Institute For Peace—you remember them?" Morton nodded. "Well, they have suddenly decided they will be leading the Japanese delegation to that stupid World Peace Rally in San Francisco in August."

"I thought that IFP bunch was under control."

Saito responded, "They are . . . or were. We had even established a travel fund for quite a few individuals to go to San Francisco, but we were sure there would be no official delegation."

"Don't worry about your people causing trouble in the States, old buddy. Every fuckin' lunatic fringe group will be there beating their own drums. The thing will be on TV and in the papers for a week or so, then all of the people will go back to making a living. It's no sweat if the IFP people come."

Saito said, "That's not what bothers me, my friend." Saito leaned forward. "I do not like things to be unpredictable. I thought that the IFP had disrupted the general mood of the peace movement, but now there seems to be some unity. It is the sudden change that worries me." Saito sat back in thought. Then he reached into the inside pocket of his suit coat and pulled out a collection of small slips of paper.

Thumbing through the papers, Saito said, "I had a phone call while we were in one of the meetings today; my secretary put it on one of these message pads. I was going to answer it when I got home this evening." His fingers scurried faster then stopped. He scanned the words and looked at his watch. He said, "He will be home. I'll call him now."

Saito made a sign to one of the waiters and, as the man went off to collect a telephone instrument, said, "This call was from a friend of mine at Japan Air Lines. All it says is 'Re: IFP and JAL cargo plane.' The call did not seem important to me until I read this." Saito tapped the newspaper article. The telephone arrived and was plugged in; the waiter left them alone as he went off to pick up another drink order.

Saito punched in the number. There was a pause, then Saito spoke. Morton could tell his initial words were those used by all corporate executives who find it necessary to apologize for not returning the call sooner. A businesslike exchange of clipped phrases followed. Morton had first come to Japan forty years before and had been a more than frequent visitor to the country, but he could never bring himself to master the language; Saito had filled the gap by becoming proficient in English.

Saito hung up and told Morton, "This cannot be good. We had a fund set up, enough for two hundred militants to go to the rally in your country. Now, the IFP has called JAL and demanded thirty-one thousand pounds of cargo space and eight seats on the Cargoliner."

"They're getting pretty uppity, ain't they?"

Saito took a second to translate "uppity." "They are, but that is not unusual. What is strange is that they want the cargo space to transport a new, huge peace emblem."

Morton said, "Another fuckin' *statement*?"

Saito smiled, then his face went serious again. "We had heard that the new emblem had been given up ages ago, but now, suddenly, it will be ready to be shipped in just a few weeks. To me that means that they have been working on the project for some time. I do not like the implications."

Morton himself had little use for any of the peace groups but still, he, like Saito, had spent vast sums of his company's monies in keeping track of what was going on within them: "Know your enemy!" was an axiom Morton had learned in the military.

Saito said, "I think we had better get some help on this." He lifted the phone.

"Who you calling?"

"I have a friend at the Ministry of the Interior; they might have something for us."

"You gonna sic the spooks on them?"

Saito laughed. "I'll get somebody working; you and I have other tasks tonight."

"Oh, yes." Saito had promised an evening with an honest-to-God geisha. Not the tourist-attraction type of performer trotted out for besotted sightseers, but a real-life, all-the-way beauty of the kind reserved for the aristocracy of Japanese business. Morton thought, *Fuck the peace movement. Tonight old Saito and me, we gonna plow new ground.*

CHAPTER TWENTY-TWO

Bart Faber hung up the telephone with some impatience. He looked at his watch; it was ten minutes past seven in the evening. He had tried half a dozen times to reach Eby during the afternoon and early evening; the failure was annoying. Eby didn't have the kind of money that would allow him to go out on a binge; he'd have to drink inexpensively at home. And it was doubtful that Eby was out working on some writing assignment. Faber needed Eby's help to reach the police detective Tanaka, and to try and get a copy of Tac Okomoto's death certificate and the police report on the death. Faber did not want to have to travel all the way back to Tokyo; he was hoping to be able to leave Japan from the international airport at Osaka. With one last, frustrated look at the telephone Faber left the pastor's office and headed back to the rectory dining room.

A few minutes before, when Faber had left the dining table to try the call to Eby, the priests had been friendly, full of good-natured comments about the fish Faber and

Father Schultz had caught. The meal had been prepared
kushi ryori fashion, deep-fried. The priests had encouraged Faber to stay in Hiroshima long enough to teach Father Schultz how to fish properly; the pastor had accepted
the teasing well, and Faber tried to convince the other
priests that Schultz was an excellent fisherman.

When Faber took his seat, the mood had changed.

Father Schultz tried to veil the tension. "Did you reach
your friend, Father?"

"No. Still no answer."

Schultz added, "The fathers here are arguing about
whether the fish should be fried or served raw. I do not
yet appreciate raw fish."

Faber knew that Schultz was trying to cover up whatever
conflict had arisen in his absence. He offered no opinion
on the supposed controversy. The room fell quiet.

The elderly housekeeper brought in a fresh pot of green
tea with a tray of delicate pastries. She was the same
woman Faber had seen early in the morning and he wondered just what kind of hours the old woman put in at her
job. He had learned long before that rectory housekeepers
are a special breed of dedicated individuals, but the old
woman's obvious age made it hard to imagine that she
could have, alone, prepared the delicious meal and still
plan to clean up after the priests finished dinner. She left
the room, and the dessert was eaten in silence.

Faber looked down the table and said to the pastor, "I
fear, Father Schultz, that I have brought a tension to your
dinner. If I have done something wrong, I apologize."

Faber watched the old German priest grapple with a
silent decision; Faber knew Father Schultz would not lie.
The pastor said, "We are having a slight disagreement. It
concerns the discussions you and I had this afternoon . . .
while we were fishing."

The two men had traveled to Father Schultz's favorite
fishing spot and, once the lines were baited and in the

water, their conversation began with the peace movement in general, but Faber deftly steered Father Schultz to the life of Tac Okomoto. The old pastor had confirmed much of what Faber had already heard from Bernie Eby and Tori Ito: Tac Okomoto had been a firebrand, a militant. Father Schultz said that a neo-fascist mentality had split the Institute For Peace, and that Okomoto had been at the core of the split. Father Schultz suggested that Faber talk with Susumu Kato, who had become heir to Tac Okomoto as the head of the IFP. The two men were just about to settle down to serious fishing when Father Schultz said it was too bad that Tac Okomoto had been killed in that traffic accident; Faber was startled, for his memory told him that either Bernie Eby or Tori Ito, or both, had told him that Okomoto had died in a house fire. Faber questioned Father Schultz, who, directing his eyes towards the water, dismissed the discrepancy as unimportant; Faber decided he would follow up on that.

The fish started biting; Father Schultz promised to try and locate Susumu Kato and arrange an interview for Faber.

Faber now asked, "What part of the talk, Father?"

"About my suggestion that you talk to Susumu Kato; Father Kurt does not think it would be worth your while."

Faber turned to the priest sitting directly across the table. "Why not, Father?"

Father Kurt was also German, younger than Faber. He said, "Kato is not the real leader. You should talk, Father, to Minoru Watanabe. He is the one in power, believe me."

Faber turned back to Father Schultz. "I heard about Watanabe in Tokyo. But he must be a very old man."

Father Schultz nodded and said, "That is correct. He is old, but he is still wise about many things. But, I argue with Father Kurt because the old man spends little time at the headquarters. Things could be going on that he does not know about."

Father Kurt cut in. "That is the basis of my argument, too, Father Faber. I think pastor is wrong. I believe Watanabe is deeply involved on a daily basis."

The two priests unconsciously switched to their native tongue as they continued. Bart Faber knew enough German to stay with them, even though they were debating in the rough, guttural dialect of Bavaria.

Schultz snapped back, "Watanabe should not be bothered. He is too frail."

Father Kurt challenged, "He's strong enough to entertain several concubines."

"That has nothing to do with this matter."

The younger priest, in a quieter but triumphant tone, said, "Besides, Kato is in Tokyo."

Father Schultz nodded with some resignation. "I telephoned the IFP earlier and found that out, Father. They don't know when he will be back."

Bart Faber cut in, stumbling slightly in his German. "I would be willing to meet this Watanabe, Father Schultz, but I would not want to disturb him."

Father Kurt gave a sarcastic snort. "Watanabe lives to be interviewed. He is a professional *hibakusha*."

The pastor scolded, "Watch your charity, Father."

The younger priest made a gesture of acknowledgement but added, "Watanabe will not be taxed past his limit, Father Faber."

Father Schultz returned to English as he asked, "Would you like to talk to him tonight?"

Faber said he would.

The pastor left the dining room, and the general conversation ambled along lightly, bouncing into the other priests' encounters with Minoru Watanabe. Bart Faber decided he might enjoy talking to the old man.

Father Schultz returned in a few minutes. "Watanabe-san said he would be pleased to meet you, Father Faber.

He was just leaving his house but told me where you can find him.''

Faber said, "Can I walk, or will I drive? I don't know the city that well."

The pastor said, "We will get you there. Watanabe said he will return you to the rectory when you are through."

Father Kurt offered, "I'll drive him; I'd like to see the old geezer again."

Father Schultz said, "Watanabe will be at the studios of Raion."

"Then I *know* I want to be the one; this should be priceless."

The pastor ordered, "You will simply drop Father Faber off at the studio. Your obvious hostility might obstruct Father Faber's work."

The Society of Jesus has as a major tenet obedience, and Father Kurt knew the rule had been invoked. He did not argue. He looked at Bart Faber. "Shall we go? It's about a twenty-minute drive."

Faber responded, "I'm ready."

The drive to Raion's studio took over half an hour because Father Kurt was determined to share his own knowledge of Watanabe with Faber. By the time they had arrived, Faber was past the point of patience; he jumped out, gave his thanks and opened the studio gate while the car pulled away.

Down the block, Faber saw a long, black limousine waiting, its parking lights on. Faber let himself in through the gate.

During the ride from the Jesuit mission complex, Father Kurt had explained that their destination was the southernmost tip of the city, down in the dock area of Hiroshima Harbor; it was a bad section of the city. As Faber closed the gate, he looked at the buildings in the area and saw industrial decay. The structures seemed to be mostly abandoned warehouses. Faber knew the scene was once common in major port cities, because the container-shipping industry changed commerce drastically, with unitized containers carrying their cargo from origin to destination without the need for storage. Most ports had opted for massive rehabilitation projects, but it seemed that Hiroshima had not gotten around to demolishing the antiquated structures. Street lighting was sparse, a mist drifted in the cool evening air and it carried along the odors common to all seaports.

There was a naked, low-wattage light bulb hanging precariously high above the open area in front of the studio. Faber navigated with caution around the piles of litter which seemed to have been placed with the intention of making entry difficult. As he came to the door, he could hear loud voices coming from inside. Faber could not penetrate the rapid-fire words.

He rapped loudly on the door. The sounds inside stopped immediately.

There was a pause, then one voice gave another short burst of invective, then silence again. Faber was about to knock again when the huge front door was opened. The inside of the building was flooded in brilliant light. Faber could see ceiling rows of densely packed fluorescent shop lights, all of them burning; the area was bright as daylight.

The man who opened the door had to be, to Faber's mind, Minoru Watanabe. Standing there, offering a bow of greeting, was a man not tall or stout, but a slight figure with the posture of a teenager. Faber was surprised to see that the face lacked the normal signs of age; there were no wrinkles to speak of, and the eyes emitted an intensity that indicated an alert mind.

The man, speaking in English, said, "You must be the Father Bart Faber I was asked to meet. Is that so?"

Faber executed a bow and was careful to make it deeper

than Watanabe's, to show respect. Faber said, in Japanese, "I am pleased to meet you, Watanabe-san."

"We should talk in English, Father. It will make me more comfortable."

Faber noted that the old man had virtually no problems with pronouncing the *r* or *l* sounds which are so difficult for many Japanese when speaking English; it was obvious that Watanabe had been coached well and had studied hard.

Watanabe said, "You are thinking that I speak your language well."

Faber felt a chill on the back of his neck. He said, "You speak English very well, Watanabe-san."

"I learned many years ago that listeners in your country were distracted when we spoke in the way that is normal to us. I felt that if your people were going to benefit from my knowledge then they should not be distracted. I learned to speak your way."

Faber said, "You did. I respect your industry."

"You are very kind. But I am being rude. The evening is cool. Please come inside."

The evening chill on the street was replaced by a humid heat that made the studio uncomfortable; Faber could feel himself begin to perspire as Watanabe pushed the door closed.

The heat was startling, because the studio was easily as big as a tennis court. Then Faber saw the source of the heat: three small forges, all glowing, all of them hissing from fan-driven bellows. By one of the forges stood a man of medium stature, his hair long and untended, his clothing unkempt. Faber had been warned about the sculptor Raion.

Watanabe made a gesture to Faber and the two crossed the cluttered work area to where Raion was pretending intense interest in a piece of angle iron that was glowing orange in the bed of coals. Watanabe said, "Raion, we have a guest." Turning to Faber, the old man said, "We must speak Japanese now; our artist speaks no other language." Faber nodded; Raion did not look up from his work. Watanabe said, a bit louder, "Raion, do not be impolite to my guest."

The sculptor snapped, "In a minute." Raion took a pair of tongs and lifted the piece of metal from the forge, turned and set it on an anvil and stroked it three times with a hammer. The piece bent and twisted to the impact. He plunged it into a bucket of water. As the steam erupted, the sculptor let go of the tongs and turned to Faber. "I am Raion," he said.

Faber made a greeting bow—not as deeply as he had to Watanabe—and said, "I am Bart Faber. It is my pleasure."

The sculptor did not return the bow, nor did he say anything. Out of the corner of his eye, Faber could see a change in Watanabe. The words spilled out quickly from the old man's mouth: "You are not to act like this. Leave us now!"

Faber watched the sculptor's eyes and saw hate mingled with fear; the fear won out. Raion pulled back his lips to spit out some words when Watanabe snapped, "Now!" Raion turned, went to some electrical switches and cut the power to the fan bellows. Quiet began to settle, and the fires quickly dimmed from white-yellow to a dull red. Raion stalked angrily out through a door in the back of the studio. A slam announced his exit.

The acrid odor of carbon and ozone hung like a cloud around the forges. The vacuum was filled as Watanabe, again speaking English, said, "Artists seem to feel that vulgar behavior is a sign of their calling. I apologize for Raion's actions."

Faber responded, "I really had no right to come into his studio when he was busy."

"Nonsense! This fool would be sweeping streets if it

were not for me. Every major work he has done for the Peace Park has been commissioned by people who listened to my opinion. Raion is not a great artist, but he does have a feeling for turning the concept of Peace into monuments.''

"I guess I saw some of his works in the park.''

"Ah,'' Watanabe smiled, "you made your pilgrimage; that is good.''

"Just a short visit.''

"Were you impressed?''

"It is moving. It is a fitting memorial.''

"Then your 'short visit' was a pilgrimage. You came away with the right feeling.''

Watanabe gestured off toward the far side of the studio where a couple of folding chairs stood near a cluttered desk. He said, "Let us sit down and talk.'' The two of them walked over there, navigating around piles of steel and other mounds of rubble. On top of the desk a pot sat steaming on a small, one-burner heating element. "We can have a cup of tea,'' the old man said.

Bart Faber studied Minoru Watanabe as the ritual of pouring tea was executed. Faber had heard a lot about this old survivor, this *hibakusha*, and had formed the impression of a craggy, barely literate roué, something of an opportunist and exploiter. Now, looking at the man, Faber was beginning to wonder how such a negative impression could be held. And, Faber thought, there was some justification for Watanabe taking what he could get; he was a victim. The man had been a simple boiler-room worker when the bomb was dropped. He had lost his family, his home and his job. If he exploited his position, then could he be found at fault? What about the American scientists who made the A-bomb? Had they not exploited their knowledge and been paid handsome salaries for their demonic efforts?

This survivor had about him a grace that belied his

background. Probably, Faber thought, much of it had come from Watanabe's trips around the world lecturing in the name of peace; that sort of life tended to produce a cosmopolitan bearing. Still, Faber's training as a Phalanx agent raised a warning flag: Don't assume; find out for yourself.

The tea was poured; Watanabe spoke.

"Now then, Father Faber. My friend Father Schultz tells me that you are here doing research for a new Jesuit magazine and that you need to talk to people within the various peace organizations. What do you hope to learn?"

Faber answered, "Many of the peace groups in the United States are foundering for various reasons. We are looking at similar organizations. I hope to see if there is any similarity to what is happening here in Japan."

Watanabe smiled. "Then you come with an idea already in your mind: that our groups are in trouble?"

Faber nodded. "That's true, and what I have heard since arriving seems to support it."

Watanabe sipped his tea. "Many people think that the peace movement has grown as large as it can possibly grow. What they do not realize is that the movement is an infant. We are only experiencing growing pains as we mature. That is what people are seeing, Father. The peace movement is simply adjusting before we make our next move to rid the world of the threat of war."

"But," Faber said, "there is dissension within your groups. I heard that one section of the Institute For Peace has even become like the militarists of old; nationalism has become important again."

"Ah, do not believe all of that nonsense. You speak of the *Hitori shinzo mittsu*."

"That is one aspect. I heard that one of your followers, Tac Okomoto, died because he was doing some work that had to do with the organization." Faber had made himself ready for any reaction, since he had been told Watanabe had looked on Tac Okomoto as a son; there was none.

Watanabe replied, "Tac Okomoto died for the cause of peace. He was working hard on a new approach that would launch the peace movement into its next phase of growth."

"But he died for that."

"He died in an accident. That is all."

Faber asked, "I've heard conflicting reports about that, Watanabe-san. One person said Tac died in a house fire; another said he perished in a car crash. Which was it?"

"Neither."

Faber showed his shock.

"Tac Okomoto died in an accident involving a car and a gasoline truck. It is not important; he is gone."

Faber was even more determined to see the police report on the mysterious accident; he had now heard three versions; There was something very strange about Tac Okomoto's death.

Watanabe asked, "Where do you hear all of these different things, Father Faber? You have been talking to many people?"

Faber replied, "Some in Tokyo; some here in Hiroshima. None of them are important; what they say is, though. Was Tac Okomoto working on something that had to do with a new, militaristic movement?"

Watanabe made a delicate, polite gesture at Bart Faber's pack of cigarettes sitting on the table, "May I have one of those?"

Faber nodded, held out the pack, then offered a light. Watanabe said, "I'm not supposed to smoke—my lungs."

The old man was stalling; Faber had seen the tactic used frequently. After a couple of puffs, Watanabe said, "There is a part of the Japanese spirit unknown to the Western mind, Father Faber. We are born with certain demanding obligations that we may not ignore. The United States won the war, your people kindly supported the rebuilding of our economy, and your politicians thought they were doing us a great service by imposing a new system on our nation. Well, there are some who think you won the war by chance, that we would have rebuilt our own economy, and the system that was imposed is a farce.''

Faber offered a noncommittal response: ''I respect your opinion.''

Watanabe smiled, recognizing the parry. He said to Faber, ''For years, for decades, your government and our government have had the gall to keep secret from my people the truth that Japan could have come from the war as a victor.''

Faber kept silent. Could the old man possibly believe what he was saying?

''Victory was just a few months away, Father Faber, believe me.''

The priest waited, but Watanabe did not go on.

Faber said, ''You mean the work of Dr. Nishina?''

''You have heard about Nishina?''

''I read a page from his diary.''

Watanabe let a huge grin come to his mouth, and his eyes sparkled. ''So, so, so . . . you have been talking with the woman, Tori Ito. Is that not right?''

Faber felt control of the interview slipping away; Watanabe was a worthy adversary. ''Watanabe-san, I have talked to several people. As I said before: what they said is important. They are not.''

''Ah.'' The old man sighed. ''But there you are wrong, young person. If you talk to the wrong people, then you get the wrong information. Tori Ito is no one who should be speaking for our group. She is a woman and, in Japan, women have a proper place. She caused much trouble for me and the work of Tac Okomoto.''

Angered by Watanabe's remarks, Faber blurted, ''Tac Okomoto shared nothing with her. It was only at the last moment, when he seemed to realize he was in danger, that he told her about what he had been doing and gave her the page of the diary. If you had met her after Okomoto died you would have learned that. She tried to get in touch with you, but you refused. You cut her off completely."

Watanabe snapped back, "She was a woman who intruded in the work of men."

"That is an ancient thought."

"Your attitude is part of that system your people imposed on Japan after the war: Western thought is right! We know that it is *wrong*. There is no place in our society for your reforms."

"The world is changing."

"Father Faber, be realistic. We possess an emperor who is a direct descendant of a line that has existed for five thousand years. Think of it, young man. What civilization has lasted without interruption for that time? Greece fell, Rome fell . . . all of them collapsed because they reformed. Your nation is only two hundred years old; Anglo-Saxon civilization is, maybe, a thousand years old, and it is beginning to become unraveled just because you are changing, changing, changing—change for the sake of change. It will be your destruction. Japan will rid itself of your influence and we will return to the proper ways; we will not decay, Father. The sooner you realize that, the sooner you will leave us alone."

Faber took a deep breath, then said, "This has turned into an examination of philosophy."

Watanabe said, "I thought you members of the Society of Jesus enjoyed such intercourse."

"This is not the place, this is not the time. I will, I promise you, continue our dialogue, but I am more interested in why the peace groups are in trouble."

"Because," the old man said calmly, "the time has come for us to use violence to create peace again."

Bart Faber had heard such rhetoric many times since he

had become an operative for Phalanx; the words always made him cautious: A worn cliché.

Faber moved to pull the conversation back to his objective. "But, Watanabe-san, you ordered that the IFP not take part in the important rally in San Francisco. Then you changed, and the IFP is going. That is what I do not understand."

"I do not order the IFP to do anything, Father. The IFP is run by Susumu Kato; possibly you should be talking to him."

"I will, when he returns from Tokyo."

"But he might be very busy. He is planning a celebration for this weekend, a celebration to mark the decision to go to the World Peace Rally."

Was Watanabe delivering a threat that Kato would not talk? Faber asked, "Can you see that he talks to me tomorrow?"

The old man said, "Surely; if he returns tomorrow—he has a great deal to take care of in Tokyo."

Faber asked, "Does this man, Kato, know about the Nishina diary?"

Watanabe took another cigarette and accepted Faber's offer of a light. The old man said, "You are fascinated by the diary, is that not right?"

Faber said, "I'm not fascinated; it just seems that the troubles within the IFP begin with the diary."

Watanabe said, "That is an accurate assessment, Father. The mood was there before we came into possession of the diary, a mood of justified pride in our nation. I must admit that I was one of those who first began to support our national pride in regards to what we did during the war. It was not a popular position. All of our great military leaders had been tried for war crimes, and none were able to speak out. Some were killed by your military tribunal, some committed suicide, others were imprisoned. I had the good fortune to meet Dr. Nishina back in 1949, here in Hiroshima when he came to visit some of us survivors. He died a couple of years later, did you know that?"

"From radiation sickness—yes, I know."

"Exactly, from the sickness."

Faber asked, "And you knew about the diary in 1949?"

"No, no, no, not at all. We heard about the diary only about three years ago. It was difficult to obtain. His family had it hidden; they were ashamed."

"But they gave it to you."

"After much discussion and reasoning. Yes, they gave it to me."

"Then it was never in any national archives, as Tac Okomoto told Tori Ito?"

Watanabe laughed, "You make a joke, Father. If this document was in the national archives at any time it would have been destroyed. Our present leaders believe that heritage is less important than political expediency. I have heard, although I cannot prove it, that there was a pact between the United States and Japan committing both sides to a game of deceit, keeping Japan's atomic research secret from the world."

Faber challenged, "Such a document would be public by this time."

The old man smiled and asked, "Would it? Do you really believe that?"

The priest felt himself being drawn towards a vortex of the paranoia that seemed to surround people who clung for too long to a cause. Faber knew the danger of listening: sometimes the cause was infectious. He tried to pull Watanabe back. "The diary. How can the writing of one man be so important to you that you will let it hinder your work for peace?"

Watanabe asked, "Do you read our language, Father?"

"Only enough to struggle through the daily newspaper."

The old man said, "If you could read Japanese, then I would let you read the writings of Nishina. But it is a personal document and filled with many personal thoughts. It would be impossible for you to understand some of the meanings. But I can tell you what it says, if you will believe me."

Faber chose his words carefully to avoid an outright lie. "I have no reason not to believe you, Watanabe-san."

The old man finished off his cup of tea, stood, and said, "I do not like this place; it is hot and it smells. We should go outside, down by the water." Then, in a voice that belied his size, Watanabe bellowed: "Raion! Come here!"

The artist appeared quickly, although from his appearance, he had been sleeping. He slouched his way to Watanabe, who said, "You make the changes I ordered. We will not discuss this matter further."

Raion glared at the old patron but kept his peace. Watanabe, switching back to English said, "Can you believe that this oaf is capable of art? It is difficult to imagine. But he will be making our newest symbol of peace: Yamabato."

Faber said, "I heard about that in Tokyo."

"There is little you have not heard, Father. I am sure the article for your new magazine will be quite informative." He then swept his hand around the studio's chaos of materials. He said, "Out of this mess will come a gift from Japan to your country. A gift they will not forget." Then he added, "Please offer a friendly smile to my artist. He will think I have said something nice about him."

Faber obliged as Watanabe spoke in Japanese to Raion. "Do the changes that I told you. I will return shortly."

The old man then led Faber out of the studio into the cool, damp evening.

From the shadows at the corner of the building appeared one of the largest men Bart Faber had ever seen. The man was six feet three inches tall, he weighed three hundred eighty-six pounds, yet he moved with the ease of a dancer.

"Please meet Meiji Sano, Father Faber." Watanabe made a barely perceptible flick of his head and the man offered his hand. As Faber felt his own hand disappear in a mass of hard flesh, Watanabe added, "He is my adopted son who has the patience to drive me about."

Faber said to Sano, "You look like a Sumo wrestler, Sano-san."

Watanabe said, "He does not speak English. He was in that art form, but gave it up in the name of world peace. He also protects me."

Faber smiled. "I'm sure he could."

CHAPTER TWENTY-THREE

They were alone in the den of Isamu Saito's home.

"Do you want a woman tonight?"

Clay Morton raised his brandy snifter and said, "This is fine for me. It's the last night, remember?"

Of course Isamu Saito remembered that their custom was to abstain from females on the last night of any visit, but politeness had required him to make the offer. Saito was pleased that Morton declined, because he needed information.

Earlier in the evening, he had talked with the head of the Industrial Secret Police and told him what he wanted to know. It had been four hours with no word, and that was strange, because the men of the Industrial Secret Police moved with dispatch when instructed to do so by a member of the Economic Council. He looked at his watch again.

Morton asked, "You worried?"

Saito replied, "I always worry when I need answers."

Morton laughed. "Hey," he said, "if you're worried about what these bastards are going to do when they get to Frisco, forget it. Like I said, they'll have their big media event and in two days everybody will forget about it. Our people know how to handle these fuckers and their demonstrations."

Saito shook his head, poured another good measure of brandy in each of their glasses, and said, "I'm not concerned about that, my friend. I am confused about what is going on here, now. It is very strange, this sudden change in plans. It was positive that no official Japanese delegation was going to the rally—and now they are going en masse . . . even taking a thirty-one thousand pound statue. We've got to give them a JAL Cargoliner, for God's sake."

"So, they changed their minds. That's typical of this bunch of kids today; they don't know what the shit they want to do in life."

Saito absently studied the liquid in his glass. "It is strange . . . too strange."

There was the light tingle of the telephone bell and Saito grabbed at the instrument. He announced himself and then sat listening. It was a full two minutes before Saito said "Arigato," and hung up; he had asked no questions and made no comments during the call.

He told Morton, "Well, they got some information, but there are still questions. The decision for the delegations to change their minds came from the Institute For Peace. It was made by Watanabe."

"Is that that old bastard who used to cause you trouble?"

Saito nodded. "The same one. I thought he had taken himself out of the game; we've steered quite a few young women to him, hoping he would have a heart attack, but he seems to thrive on active sex."

Morton grinned. "Sounds like a good man."

"If he would just finish out his life it'd be good, but he keeps butting in and causing confusion."

Saito emptied his brandy snifter; Morton noted the action because he had never seen Saito turn to drink in times of difficulty. Saito poured another portion and said, "Apparently this peace statue that they want to take to the United States will not be ready in time to ship by sea. They will need air-cargo space if they are going to meet the schedule. We'll have to accommodate them."

Morton asked, "Why not tell them to go suck wind?"

"We'd love to do that, but there would be too much furor in the media. The statue is not important, it's the people who are involved."

"Bad eggs?"

"This Watanabe, we feel, is the one who had been promoting the neo-fascist position within the peace groups. If we let that genie out of the bottle, we will have more troubles than we want, especially if we're going to sell our nuclear power plant project to the people."

Now Morton's attitude became less cavalier. "Whoa, there, one minute, good buddy. What's Watanabe got to do with that?"

Saito put down his glass and pushed the decanter away from him. "This group, Watanabe's people, have been quiet, and their influence had diminished. But they're the ones who had been promoting the position that Japan should have—would have—won the war if it had lasted just a few more months."

Morton mused, "That bunch called the 'three-headed man'?"

Saito corrected him. " 'The Man With Three Hearts'."

"Right, I remember."

"Well," Saito went on, "if they get back on the political platform and start talking about how our scientists were just about finished with their A-bomb, then the other peace groups are going to begin screaming for us to shut down all of our nuclear projects. Hell, my friend, they'd like to see us cut out nuclear medicine, forget about nuclear power! And if you have any hope of getting weapons into the defense force, forget it!''

"I thought that was all under control; back when that guy fried himself.''

Saito agreed, "When Tac Okomoto died in that fire, things calmed down. We think that some of the evidence burned with him in that house.''

"What evidence?''

"We don't know." Saito's voice held some anxiety. "After the surrender there was so much chaos that many records and documents were lost, destroyed or stolen. There was a faction that had hopes of a different outcome, you know that.''

"Tell me about it, good buddy. The whole intelligence group on MacArthur's staff was sitting on eggs for the first few weeks. We didn't know when the hell it could all break loose. Like we used to say: It was all asses and elbows.''

Isamu Saito and Clay Morton had both lived through the harrowingly long months of occupation after the surrender. As vanquished and victor, they had experienced the turmoil of trying to rebuild the Japanese food chain that had been demolished in an effort to feed the war machine and, at the same time, the frantic effort to dismantle the imperial ability to wage war and initiate ventures that would provide a peace-oriented economy. The generals and admirals were punished, many of them executed as the results of the Tokyo War Crimes Trials, which were abruptly halted when world opinion began to fester against the parallel actions in Nuremburg, Germany. There had been enough killing. The demand was to let peace begin.

But old habits, like virulent infections, resist cure. Some Japanese eased themselves into the dark shadows cast by the postwar confusion; those persons—the old guard of the militarist faction—immediately began to make ready for Japan's resurrection. To lessen the scope of the War Crimes Trials, and to provide for the future, documents and records were spirited away. Some of the material was eventually turned over to the government, and some was so well hidden that it was lost forever when the concealer died, but every now and then some piece of history would surface, old wounds would be opened, and public debate would center on what had been. But, in the decades since the humiliation of defeat, little had been said about Japan's atomic research and its attempt to build a bomb; the data had been slim—and most of that hidden—and the people directly involved had not talked.

Isamu Saito, as a leader in the nuclear power industry, dreaded the day a public exposé might burst into the media. He was intent on keeping such a thing from happening.

Clay Morton was equally concerned. The two men, as they talked, agreed they did not want history injecting itself into progress towards the future. They studied the various problems they could anticipate and try to create a worst-case scenario from, but the options were too many. They decided they would handle the problems as they arose.

Morton said, "Listen, old buddy, do you want me to stay over a few more days? I can wait and see what way this mess is going to gel."

Saito replied, "My very good friend, I know I can depend on you. But what is going to happen is out of our hands at this time. As soon as I know what problems there will be, I will call you. If I need your assistance, I know you will come."

"You bet your sweet ass I'll come," Morton blustered, " 'cause you and me, good buddy, we been through a hell of a lot and we ain't gonna let some snot-nosed hippies screw things up for us now."

Saito smiled warmly. "Yes, my friend, we will handle it."

"These guys you have doing the checking, they're good?"

Saito responded, "They are very good."

"If they need any help, I can sure contact the embassy and get a couple of their Agency spooks to pitch in. If you want it."

"That will not be necessary. Our people here know what is needed. They can do the job."

The first job "they" had done had been on Susumu Kato.

The slight activist sat huddled in the corner of a stark white room that was void of furniture. He moved his tongue to the back of his lower lip and tasted the metallic sting of blood; swelling had puffed the lip against his lower teeth. One of the teeth was loose. "Dirty bastards!" spat out from his mouth as he felt a slight drool of saliva run down his chin.

He had been picked up at the airport by two plainclothes investigators from the Industrial Secret Police, but Kato did not know that. He had demanded identification from the two men, who had manhandled him into the unmarked car, but the demand was met with silence. Three miles outside the airport he was transferred to another car and another two custodians, who blindfolded him. They had driven for an hour, ignoring all his questions.

The car had driven into a basement parking garage. Kato guessed it was someplace in downtown Tokyo, but he had no way of really knowing. He was taken up in an elevator, walked down a hall and through three doors, the last of which had brought him to the stark room. Two new men took custody of him and wasted no time belting him in the mouth.

He could still feel the dampness down the front of his trousers. He had lost control of his bladder when the second blow hit him in the stomach. He had been struck a total of four times before they let him fall to the floor, where he vomited. He gave up all ideas about demanding who they were, he only wanted them to stop beating him. He talked.

Even after the lengthy series of their questions and his answers, he had no idea who they were. The questions had centered on the reasons for the IFP suddenly changing its mind about attending the World Peace Rally, and what was going on with construction of the statue of Yamabato. The answers spewed from his mouth as quickly as he could form the words, and he enhanced some of the replies with his quick imagination. Kato's sole interest was to be rid of these brutal lunatics. He convinced them that the idea to take an official Japanese delegation to San Francisco was his, and then he convinced himself that the idea had really come from Minoru Watanabe; he offered his interrogators both of those truths.

At one point during the questioning he felt he was going to get another beating, when he tried to explain that a firm schedule for activities was not available. He begged for their understanding: The decision to attend the rally was only two days old!

At last they left him alone. It had, he felt, been a long session, he guessed more than an hour. He had been sitting, slumped in the corner, for a length of time that he could not estimate.

The door opened, his two attackers came in, and Kato felt another small spurt of urine soil his trousers.

They crossed the room. One man grabbed him and pulled him to his feet. The other said, "We are through. You will forget about this meeting."

His ordeal was over! Kato summoned up some heroics. With sarcasm, he said, "Meeting?!" A sudden, swift knee to his groin erased any further words or thoughts.

The man continued. "If we need more information, we

will come to you again. If you cooperate, we will not have to bring you to our offices. Is all of that clear?''

Kato nodded, holding his head down. He did not want to look into the man's face; he wanted to forget as soon as possible.

''If someone comes to you and gives you a password, then you will answer his questions.''

Kato, still looking at the puddle of vomit at his feet, asked, ''What password? . . . I have to know what will be used.''

The man uttered a short, vulgar expression that had to do with Kato's ancestors. ''When you hear that, you talk!''

Kato nodded.

They blindfolded him again, led him out through the three doors and down to the car. They drove him for another hour, then unceremoniously dropped him near a monorail station in a far suburb of Tokyo.

Kato sat for a long time on a bench in the waiting room, thinking. He was trying to decide whether he would leave the IFP and go back to work on his father's farm. In the end he decided he would have to ask Minoru Watanabe for counsel.

CHAPTER TWENTY-FOUR

Bart Faber walked slowly along the street beside Minoru Watanabe. The chill, damp air drifting off Hiroshima Harbor was a relief after the oppressive warmth of Raion's studio. Meiji Sano followed them in the long black limo, hovering two hundred feet to the rear. The old man was doing most of the talking.

He said to Faber, "The main thrust of your magazine article should be that the dissensions we have experienced are necessary for growth, just as when a gardener disturbs the soil around the roots of a plant."

Faber's smile went unseen; Watanabe's logic fell short of any test.

The old man said, "I will give you the keystone of what you should tell your Jesuit readers. They will be instructed and educated in some truths that exist in our world."

They came to two derelict buildings that, at some time in the past, had felt the impact of the wrecker's ball: Rubble was scattered on the edge of the seawall. Watanabe stopped and said, "This used to be a lovely place to bring the family on a quiet Sunday. There is talk that, when the redevelopment is done, they will make this into a park." He gestured along the expanse of the seafront. He continued, "I used to bring my wife and children here . . ." His voice drifted off. He snapped his thoughts back and said, "But that is all past, right, Father? We should not dwell on such things."

Faber responded, "We live with those things we choose to remember; not all of them are nice memories."

Watanabe gestured toward a bench placed on top of the seawall. He said, "I wonder how this escaped the wrecking crews; they failed to destroy a place to relax."

The two men sat down and looked out over the water. To the south was the glow of the port operations on Ujina Island; the wisps of fog obscured a clear view.

Watanabe said, "I will not take long."

Faber replied, "Take as long as you wish."

"But is very cool; you may not be used to this type of weather."

"I enjoy it. The night air has a cleansing effect on me."

"I share that with you."

Faber waited. Watanabe spoke again, "You have read from the diary of Yoshio Nishina?"

"Only the translation of one page."

Watanabe turned and looked at Faber. "Do you know of Zen, Father?"

Faber answered, "Very little. We studied some of the metaphysics of other religions, but I do not claim I am an authority."

Watanabe's voice slipped down in volume as he said, "Let it be said that Zen allows one to break away the chain of words and cast aside the inhibition of logic. It is a personal, inward experience. You are not a student, but I ask you to let your imagination liberate you from what is needed for absolute proof. Give me your mind and let me take you back in time.''

Faber agreed. "I will try."

Watanabe said, "Put yourself in the place of Yoshio Nishina; let your mind go back to a day in the spring of 1939. Let me now provide the details.''

His hand feels the warmth of the large brass handle of the door then, suddenly, it is cold, chill to the touch. He pulls his hand back and pauses.

The sun is shining on the main entrance door to the Imperial Ministry of War building on Sakurada-Dori Avenue. Its warmth, reflecting back into the face of Dr. Yoshio Nishina, does nothing to lessen the chill brought on by his anxiety. He has never been in the War Ministry, and he has grave reservations about what he is doing. There is a brief moment when he feels his slight shoulders move, actually twitch, as if he is going to turn away. But he has asked for the hearing and he will be embarrassed if he does not appear. He has his On—his obligation to honor— and he will not disgrace himself or his fellow scientists.

He pulls the door open with determination. He enters.

The entrance foyer of the Ministry of War would suffice for several large laboratories. Yoshio Nishina has lately been looking at things like that, equating how others are spending their budgets when his own research budget has been shrinking. Several of his projects are dwindling down to the point where hope is futile; maybe this audience with the admirals will dam the rupture in his work.

"You are Dr. Nishina?" The man asking is dressed in the uniform of an Imperial Navy commander.

"I am."

"You will follow me, please."

Nishina is committed now, still there is a part of him that screams for him to turn, to leave and go back to his lab; he is not tuned to the military. But they have the money to spend; all of the military is spending money.

"Please be careful of the steps, they are highly polished."

"I can see that."

"Our men sometimes become too energetic and buff them so highly that one could slip."

"What is your name, please?"

"I am Lieutenant Commander Fujimoto. I am to conduct you to the meeting."

"I am pleased to meet you."

Nishina is in a vast building; he has had no idea that the Ministry of War needs so much space. The hallway is much larger than the entrance foyer. There are large glass cases displaying models of various naval ships; some of them are four feet long. Nishina looks at the replicas with some awe and some lust; he is startled to see that the navy has money to spend for playthings.

One wall of the hallway is a series of windows which looks out over a small garden and a large pond. In the distance is the sprawl of the Imperial Palace grounds. The view is restful and impressive.

"In here," the naval officer is saying. There are two armed guards at the doorway; they salute.

The office they enter has none of the affluence Nishina has seen. It is painted a dull brownish yellow; the tables and chairs are utilitarian. Three men are waiting.

Introductions are exchanged. The portly, bemedaled man behind the desk is the deputy chief of staff (Research), Admiral Tsunezo Shima; beside him is Fleet Commander Tokako Sasai; and sitting on a chair at one side of the room is Captain Shintaro Kojima, who is the most knowledgeable man in the room when it comes to naval ordinance. Nishina makes his greetings stiffly, uncomfortable because these men have a confident bearing which makes him feel like an intruder. He is told to take a seat.

"We have read your request, Dr. Nishina."

"Thank you, Admiral Shima, I would hope the Imperial Navy would benefit."

"But we have some bad news for you, Doctor."

Nishina cannot hide his reaction; they are being abrupt with him, and that is very rude. But then why did they all—all of this navy brass—come to the meeting? He waits.

Admiral Shima continues. "Just two months ago our naval attaché in Washington found out that Professor Creighton Louis and Dr. William Roberts from the Massachusetts Institute of Technology presented a similar proposal to the United States Navy Bureau of Procurement, and the concept was rejected as not practical."

Nishina says, "Admiral Shima, there are going to be problems using the heat generated by atomic fission to propel ships but, just because the Americans do not see the benefits, I do not see why we must not look into the prospect. The United States has a plentiful supply of oil; we have none. If my concept is right, then a ship could operate for months—possibly years—without refueling. I ask you to please reconsider."

Nishina, as he speaks, has become more emboldened and the admiral is not pleased; a tic under the admiral's left eye is now dancing. He says, "The matter of reconsideration is not before us, Doctor. Our decision has been made." Nishina wants to argue; he is not a man who yields easily to the authority of anyone outside the sciences. But he harnesses his hostility. He realizes that the admiral could easily have handled the rejection by letter: Something more is to come.

The admiral continues. "Our intelligence from the United States is considerable, Doctor. We do not dismiss your interest lightly. The report compiled by the U.S. Navy is damning to the scientists from MIT. The overriding consideration is the danger. That is clearly stated in the report we obtained. There would be no use in investing our en-

ergies to reinvent the wheel; the Americans did that for us.''

The admiral pauses, breathes heavily through his plump lips, wheezing. He makes an annoyed motion towards Captain Kojima, who now speaks: "Doctor, I have just returned from Germany and, as a member of the Ordinance Section of the Imperial Navy, I was invited to a lecture at the Kaiser Wilhelm Institute about a project their military scientists are presently developing. It, too, has to do with atomic fission. The German scientists are not dealing with power generation but rather with energy release.''

Nishina nods. "All that you and all that the admiral have said are one and the same thing, Captain. The Americans are concerned about danger from the rapid release of energy. It is true that if the power of a fission reaction is not controlled there can be catastrophic results. The Germans, on the other hand, are looking for ways to produce an uncontrolled reaction within a given set of circumstances. What the people working in my lab are doing is to try to generate heat from the reaction without having the uncontrolled release, which would be dangerous. If we are supported, we can build a device that will generate heat to manufacture steam; that can power ships.''

Captain Kojima raises his hand. "Go back,'' he says, "to the German approach. What would be the result of their efforts?''

Nishina's eyes are studying the wooden tabletop in front of him. He and his fellow scientists at the Imperial Academy of Science have discussed the subject in the past. He knows the answer, but he is trying to calculate the results of telling them.

Captain Kojima urges, "We are waiting, Doctor.''

Nishina now looks up. "There is no answer to that question that cannot be challenged. We are discussing a segment of physics where only theory has been advanced.

We are presently where man was before the invention of the telescope, trying to answer questions about the stars.''

Admiral Shima cuts in. *''An answer, please!''*

Nishina does not like the sound of the admiral's voice, it seems to have a death rattle. The scientist states, *''The theory is that if the natural balance of nature is disturbed, if the state of matter can be, in some way, disrupted, then a vast amount of energy will be released.''*

Captain Kojima is now impatient. *''What will happen?!''*

Nishina's voice is unsure, but his answer is full of confidence: *''There would be an uncontrolled explosion.''*

Now Fleet Commander Sasai interrupts. *''Doctor, we use a naval artillery shell that is seventeen inches in diameter and thirty-four inches long. If one of these shells was made in the way you are suggesting, what would be the result?''*

Nishina: *''I cannot say. No one can say. Much research must be done.''*

Captain Kojima inserts, *''The German scientists say that a bomb of small size could be capable of vast damage. Is this true?''*

Nishina's mind is racing. *''Then they have done more than we have done. Our effort has been on creating a source of power, a way to provide energy. If I had to guess, I would say they are correct. A release of fission energy would be enormous; an explosion could be great.''*

Fleet Commander Sasai: *''Could it be for our ships? Could you make a powerful shell for our navy?''*

''I don't know.''

Captain Kojima: *''What size would the weapon be?''*

''We need research before I can answer positively!''

Admiral Shima coughs, a gravelly sound. His face is flushed, and he swallows with difficulty. He says, *''Let this meeting come back to order. Dr. Nishina, I have made a decision, and you will abide by what I tell you.''*

The admiral looks around to each principal as he makes his point. "I want you, Doctor, to concentrate the energies of your staff at the Academy of Science on the release problem. You are to treat this matter as uppermost in priorities." Nishina starts to speak, but is halted by a sharp glance. The admiral continues, "Captain Kojima, you will see that all necessary materials are obtained by the quickest possible means. Commander Fujimoto will act as liaison among all of the parties. Fleet Commander Sasai is to be kept aware of progress at each step."

Turning back to Nishina, the admiral says, "The costs for this project are to be assumed by a special research contract that will be financed through Rokko Heavy Industries. The contract will be identified as secret work on metallurgy. Are there any questions?"

Nishina knows he faces a massive problem. He says, "I will need uranium for this; there is none in Japan, beyond the few ounces that we have been using."

Captain Kojima is saying, "I have made some preliminary arrangements with our friends in Germany. They have sources and will supply some for your work."

Admiral Shima dismisses the meeting, but Nishina is slow to leave the room, because his head is reeling. Suddenly, after years of begging and pleading for support, he has been given not only the permission but the resources to begin real work in fission. He is experiencing the joy of fruition. He has struggled for long years, and now that investment is about to deliver dividends. He is sure that he will find an immortal place in the history of science.

Bart Faber's shirt was damp. He was not sure if it was because of the moist night air or because he had perspired as Minoru Watanabe told his story. The experience had been sobering. Faber had felt transported back in time and had actually sensed the people taking part in the meeting five decades earlier. The old man looked stoically out over the harbor. Faber was reluctant to speak.

Watanabe broke the silence. "I have talked for too long. You are kind to indulge an ancient mind."

"I appreciate you taking the time to share this with me. All of that is in the Nishina diary?"

Watanabe said, "Only some of it. I was fortunate enough to talk with Dr. Nishina before he died. Also, I have read some of the documents that authenticate what did happen. I should tell you that most of what I have shared with you came from Commander Fujimoto, who survived the war, avoided prosecution before your War Crimes Tribunal and lived a quiet life. He died last year; he was a tormented man."

"How so?"

Watanabe turned. There was a slight smile on his lips. "Commander Fujimoto knew we could have won the war."

Faber, not harshly, argued, "I believe what you have told me about Nishina *starting* work on military use of atomic fission, but that does not validate the idea that Japan could have won the war. The United States invested millions, billions of dollars and uncountable hours of talent from our scientific community to develop the atomic bomb."

Watanabe countered, "Your nation started later than we did. Think back. Do you know when the United States began working on their bombs?"

Faber shook his head.

"On December 10, President Roosevelt ordered work to begin, in 1941. It did not get started until early 1942. Japan began a full two and a half years earlier."

"Japan did not have the resources."

Watanabe's smile faded as he replied, "We had the will. That is most important, Father Faber."

Faber asked, "Does Nishina's diary go on to say how much he was able to accomplish?"

Watanabe, his voice not as strong, said, "Not all of what was done. Towards the end, when the work pace picked up, he began to neglect making entries."

"Then there is no proof," Faber said. "What you have told me is conjecture."

The old man came back, "There is more. When the time is right we will make it all public."

"More documents?"

"One document, very important. When that time comes you will also know the truth."

"Can I see it now?"

"I have only a copy, a very poor one at that, and I am not free to let anyone see it. That will come later."

Faber wanted more. He had allowed himself to become greedy for what this old man could tell him. Silently, Faber scolded himself. His greed was self-serving. He wanted to know what cause, what stimulation made people like Tac Okomoto get themselves killed just to make a point, just to leave a mark in history. But he wanted to know that because of his interest in Tori Ito: What had made her stay with a man like Tac Okomoto? A danger signal tickled his conscience, and he accepted the warning. As a priest he had to avoid personal, emotional involvements; as an operative for the Jesuits' Phalanx organization, he was doubly obligated to remain detached.

Still, he wanted to know more. "Can we talk later? Maybe tomorrow?" he asked.

Watanabe replied, "I will be very busy for the next few days, Father. Tomorrow is especially difficult because we are bringing group leaders in from all over Japan to rehearse for our celebration rally on Saturday. There will be many meetings, and I will have to be involved with them. I am sorry."

Faber was disappointed, but took it as a sign that he'd gone astray from his assignment. He said, "That is probably best. I am awaiting instructions from my magazine editor; I have cabled that the conflicts between the peace groups have been settled. I think there is no need for me to stay, now that there is no more dissension."

Watanabe grinned broadly. "We have only agreed that a delegation should go to the rally; there are still strong differences among our groups. You should also talk to them."

"I will have to wait and see what my boss says; it's up to him."

Watanabe stood, "I have kept you too long, Father Faber. And I must go back and talk with my sculptor friend; he is a lout but we need him. He argues so much, and we have no time to waste on arguments."

Faber had risen and said, "Artists are a separate breed in our world."

Watanabe began walking. "That is true."

The driver, Meiji Sano, had turned the limousine around and was standing attentively at the back door. Faber offered, "I can catch a taxi, Watanabe-san."

The old man laughed. "Not in this section of town, Father. Meiji will take you back to the compound." He gave short instructions and the driver opened the door; Faber climbed in after exchanging respectful salutations.

As the car drove off, Faber looked back and watched as the old man walked up the street in the direction of the studio. He was impressed with the man's vitality. Faber hoped that he could be in that kind of shape if he ever reached Watanabe's age.

As Sano drove rapidly through downtown Hiroshima, Faber began to organize what he had to get done. He still wanted Bernie Eby to do some legwork with the police in Tokyo, but he was going to add another chore for Eby:

Faber wanted to know more about former Navy Commander Fujimoto. Eby could handle that.

Faber was impatient to get back to the Jesuit compound and its telephone. First, he'd check for any reply to his earlier cable to Phalanx headquarters. Second, he'd try to raise Eby again.

CHAPTER TWENTY-FIVE

He left the motor of the van running and walked slowly back into the rented mini-storage area. He swept the beam of the flashlight around slowly, examining each section of the space to insure that he had left no trace of his presence. Earlier, just before nightfall, he had packed all of his garbage and waste into plastic trash bags. The refuse was in the van now, sitting beside the aluminum case that held his deadly cargo. The storage space was clean.

He dropped a bundle of oiled rags and crumpled newspapers that he had prepared earlier in the day. With calculated speed, he spread the litter beside the back wall, making sure that it extended from corner to corner. He struck a match, and lit it at three places. The tinder ignited quickly and the flames were leaping up the particle-board walls in seconds. He walked out of the structure, closed the garage-type door and climbed into his van.

It was late enough in the evening so that he was sure he would not run into any traffic problems and yet it was early enough that no cruising police car would become interested in a van moving through the city.

He drove out of the mini-storage complex, around the shopping center. Some late shoppers were picking up groceries. He was tempted to stop and buy something to eat for himself, but there was too much chance that he would be seen, and someone might remember what he looked like; that would be an unnecessary risk. He decided he would stop for food a few miles south in Nogata; he could be there in under an hour.

He steered the van through downtown Hagi with care, observing all of the traffic rules and maintaining enough speed to avoid attracting attention. Three miles south of the city, on the four-lane highway running along the coast, he pulled off at a rest stop that was placed on a slight knoll. He climbed out and looked back towards that section of Hagi where the mini-storage was located; he did not see the red glow that he was hoping for.

He realized that it might take a few minutes for the buildings to really get burning—much of the structure was metal. But there was enough wood within the walls and enough junk stored in the other compartments that a fire would go once it started. He would wait.

He violated his own rule of security by opening the back of the van and lifting the lid of the aluminum case. He was charmed, nearly hypnotized by the device that rested there. He flicked on the overhead light and looked lovingly down at the nuclear shell; it was beautiful—and it was his.

There was a dim glow from the three triggering devices. The Swede had said the glow would continue for a full six months or until the device was detonated. He regretted having had to eliminate the man, but there was no way that any foreigner could have been left alive to share in the final event. That had been agreed by all concerned.

But the Swede had known his business, and the attachment of three triggers had shown that he did his best to guarantee success. Even if one of the batteries died out, there were two more ready to do the job, and if one or two of the triggers malfunctioned, there was still the final trigger to do the job. The plan had been put together with meticulous detail, and it was proceeding exactly as designed.

The man reached out and stroked the cylinder with a gentle, caressing touch; the nuclear shell had taken on an almost sensual attraction to him. His hand slid down the soft, thrilling curve of the cold metal.

"It will not be long, dear child, not long before you can come to life and show the world what you were meant to do. You and I will show the bastards."

He felt a reluctance to stop touching the metal, but he finally closed the case, turned off the light, and shut the van's door. He looked back towards the city and saw what he had been hoping for: a blaze in the right section of sky. At the same moment, he heard the first faint crying wail of sirens, the fire trucks rushing to their duty. The man let a smug grin of satisfaction creep onto his face; he had kept within the limits of the schedule he had outlined months before. He climbed back into the van and began driving south.

The man knew the road well. He had driven it three times previously in rehearsal for this night. He approached Nogata, passing through one of the major farming areas of Japan. Fields spread out from either side of the road for miles. One thing that made his project possible and nearly foolproof was that the road was excellent, made that way to handle the truck traffic carrying produce to market.

Forty minutes later, he pulled into a large, all-night truck service plaza. He did not need fuel, but he did want some food. He parked right near the front entrance of the small restaurant, pulled a loudly colored Hawaiian shirt from beneath the driver's seat, and put it on. The garish shirt would cause people to remember that and not his face. This trick was nothing he had learned at any of the five guerrilla schools he had attended over the years; this trick he had learned from watching movies.

In twenty minutes, fed, Tac Okomoto was on his way, driving along the coast road around the southern tip of the main island of Honshu. He was heading towards Hiroshima.

CHAPTER TWENTY-SIX

Minoru Watanabe was angry and slightly frightened. The sculptor Raion was raving about Watanabe's demands, and Meiji Sano had not returned from delivering Bart Faber to the Jesuit mission. Watanabe did not like people getting violent when there was no protection ready to act on his behalf.

Raion had already thrown several heavy hammers across the room in frustration. Watanabe had no illusions about what would happen if the sculptor's violence focused on him. Raion was broad in the shoulders, his arms rippled with muscles made strong by years of working with stone, iron and concrete. Watanabe knew that Raion's hamlike hands could deliver a death blow or could easily wrap their gnarled fingers around an old man's throat and squeeze out all life. Watanabe attempted to placate the sculptor, at least until Sano returned.

Watanabe shouted, "Let's stop this hostility, Raion. Let's talk quietly."

A piece of metal, the length of a small child and the thickness of a young tree, suddenly flew from Raion's hands and crashed into a table cluttered with other pieces of metal. When the din subsided, Raion said, "I feel better. Now we can talk. But, Teacher, do not ask for foolishness anymore."

Watanabe took a deep breath and knew that he would have to lessen his tension. His lungs had been damaged as an aftereffect of the bomb. Many of the *hibakusha*, the survivors, suffered respiratory problems. Watanabe's breathing had been poor for a dozen years. He sucked in air, then did it again. It seemed to give some relief.

Raion watched his mentor laboring, and a look of guilt replaced the rage on his face. He said, "I am sorry, Teacher. I am embarrassed that I lost my temper."

Watanabe said, "Do not claim shame, Raion; you have not earned it, yet. I have demanded that you compromise your art, and that is not a good thing. But in this case, in this time and place, I am forced to ask what I would not normally ask. You must try and understand."

Raion rebelled whenever anyone told him that he "must" do anything. But he might cause Watanabe another seizure. He checked his anger, but he did not respond. He would not yield to the whims of an unlearned critic.

Watanabe walked across the studio and looked down at a tangle of steel that lay on the floor. The metalwork was the structural skeleton of the IFP's new peace symbol, Yamabato. A few feet away was a pounded-steel form that would be used to mold the wet concrete into the shape of the statue. He thought, *This all is causing me such problems . . . but I cannot tell him. He cannot know.*

Raion came to stand beside him, and they both looked down at the assembly of reinforcement bars, angle irons and flat straps of steel. Raion had been working nearly constantly for the past thirty-six hours to weld and braze the metal; the urgency of the sudden deadline had sparked the effort. Watanabe knew what he wanted, what was absolutely needed, but he was having a difficult time conveying the essential modification without revealing the final purpose.

Watanabe spoke in a milder tone than the one that had caused Raion's outburst. "I am told, Raion, that there must be a cavity, a foot in diameter and six feet long. The weight demands of the plane require that."

Raion did not erupt with passion this time; he replied in a quiet voice. "And the person who told you that, Teacher, is full of dog dung. The JAL Cargoliner can carry hundreds of thousands of pounds, I know that. They just open the nose cone loading door and slide our Yamabato in and that is that."

Watanabe could not argue. He knew nothing of Japan Air Lines' cargo planes. He persisted: "Raion, you know that Susumu Kato is in Tokyo this very night, trying to get the authorities' permission. They have told him there will be a weight restriction. You must make a cavity in Yamabato."

Raion looked at his old leader. He lowered his voice to the most respectful level possible and said, "Teacher, I owe you everything I am. When others laughed at me and my ability, you made it possible for the world to see that I had a talent as an artist. I will not say that our friend Kato is lying, nor will I accuse the people at JAL of lying, but you are being misled. The plane can carry the weight. Besides, the amount of concrete that would be left out would be just a few hundred pounds. To do such a thing, to make a cavity right in the middle of our bird, I would have to cut away critical pieces of reinforcement steel. This statue is going to have to move by truck to the airport, then be loaded, then flown to the United States where the whole process will repeat in the reverse. Yamabato is going to be handled in a demanding way. If I weaken the structure, it could crack or break. I will not have that.''

"A small crack would not ruin your work, Raion. It could be patched when the statue is in place. Please, do not make me beg anymore. There is a good reason for you to do what you are being asked.''

Raion suspected that Watanabe had been avoiding telling the truth, that there was a reason other than weight. What could possibly be so important about a few hundred pounds? After a long pause, he was struck with an idea: Smuggling!

He looked at Watanabe and saw that the old man was tired. He said, "Tell me, Teacher, is there really another reason you want this modification in Yamabato? Could it be to smuggle something?''

Watanabe grasped at the new explanation. "Yes, Raion. That is it. We want to take in something secretly. Now, will you do it for me, please?''

The old man looked very tired, more tired than he should be at his age. Raion wanted to probe, to learn what contraband was going to be traveling with the peace delegation, but he decided against the move; he did not want to hurt Watanabe any more.

Instead, Raion asked for detailed instructions, and Watanabe gave them as well as he could.

There was to be allowance within the lower body to receive a cylinder nine inches in diameter and four feet long. It would be embedded within the concrete.

Raion asked, "How will it be removed once Yamabato is in America?''

Watanabe, mustering a soothing tone, replied, "It is going to stay there for the life of Yamabato, Raion. It is to be a secret gift to the people of the United States. After the deed, we will tell you about it.''

Raion was placated. He wanted to be in favor of this project. The display of such a major work, especially in the United States, would lead to his recognition as an artist of import. He asked no more questions; he made pages of notes as to what must be done to make Yamabato ready.

As soon as the burly Sano returned and came into the studio, Watanabe said to Raion, "I am very tired; I will go home."

Raion, now bursting with energy, said, "I am going to enjoy this, Teacher. I know that in your genius, you will be sending a stinging message to the Americans."

Watanabe forced an appreciative smile. "We will do that, Raion. We will all do that." Then, with a feeble hand gesture, he said, "I am leaving; we will return in a few hours."

Raion asked, "When?"

"About three or four in the morning."

Raion looked disturbed. "I cannot be ready that quickly."

Watanabe came to Raion and placed a gentle hand on the sculptor's shoulder. "I know that, my son. You do what you can, and we will give you the final measurements at that time. Do not worry yourself so much. We will see you then."

Sano was concerned; he had not seen Watanabe look this tired in many months. He tried to offer assistance, but the old man waved him off. He said, "I am not feeble. Just take me home."

CHAPTER TWENTY-SEVEN

Bart Faber sat in the dimly lit solitude of the pastor's office at the Jesuit Mission. Except for Father Schultz, the other priests had gone to bed by the time he had returned from his meeting with Minoru Watanabe. Faber had not felt like confiding in Father Schultz. He wanted to analyze the whole incident first. Father Schultz had seen that Faber was supplied with a cup of coffee and a ration of brandy, and had then retired, leaving Faber in the comfortable office.

Faber looked again at the cable that had arrived while he had been meeting with Watanabe. CLIENT PLEASED WITH YOUR FINDINGS. RETURN TO HOME OFFICE AT YOUR DISCRETION. VENTURI.

. . . at your discretion.

That was rubbing at Faber's mind—could he trust his own discretion? The cable had been sent from Rome, so Phalanx headquarters had relayed Faber's message to Venturi, involving several people and quite a few time zones.

Venturi and the people at Phalanx had arrived at the conclusion that the mission was completed. Probably it was.

. . . *at your discretion.*

Could he trust his own discretion?

Phalanx would want to have Minoru Watanabe's story in its files, and there was, according to the old man, more to be added to the history of the Japanese development of an atomic bomb. But was Faber right in staying on to flesh out the report he would be writing when he returned to the United States? There was that other document mentioned by Watanabe; he said he had a copy of the original that had been burned when Tac Okomoto died. A question: How did Watanabe get a copy? Perhaps the original source had made a copy before the accident. But the answer was only conjecture. Overriding any question was the conflicting accounts of Tac Okomoto's death; Faber could not turn loose of that.

. . . *at your discretion.*

He knew why he was troubled, why he had been so persistent in trying to reach Bernie Eby. The three calls he had made since returning from the studio had failed to locate him. He was hoping, desperately hoping that Eby would not answer so that there would be an excuse to call Tori Ito.

Faber liked the control he had over his life. He loved the priesthood and relished the assignments given to him as a Phalanx operative. He had never felt his commitment threatened, and he did not feel it threatened now. But he did feel a great sympathy for Tori Ito. She had, to his thinking, been exposed to more than a reasonable share of loss. She had lost her parents, she had lost her lover and, he felt, she had lost her purpose in life. She had been cut away from the peace movement after they had tried to milk money from her, and she had been rebuked by Minoru Watanabe, who had been like a father to Tac Okomoto. Tori Ito had been dumped on by life.

He admitted to himself that he was pleased Bernie Eby was unreachable. It gave Faber a legitimate excuse to call her.

He picked up the telephone.

Twice while he was dialing and once while the phone was ringing, he was tempted to hang up. But suddenly she was there, her voice soft and gentle, *"Kon-ni-chi-wa."*

"Tori, it's me, Bart Faber."

"I knew it was you calling, Bart. I had a feeling."

"I'm sorry to bother you. It's late."

"I was just listening to music. . . . Let me turn it off."

Through the phone he could barely hear the sound of the music. He could not make out the melody because of the poor connection. In a moment, she was back. "That was Eileen Farrell doing 'Un bel di vedremo'. So sad, so sad. I wish you were here to enjoy it."

Faber laughed. "The last time you offered music I fell asleep. I'll have to take a rain check."

"Does that mean you will be coming back to Tokyo?" Her voice carried a bit more petition than he wanted to hear.

He quickly said, "No, Tori, I'm heading back to the States, probably tomorrow night . . ."

"It was nice of you to call to say good-bye."

He said, "Well, this is not really to say good-bye; I need a favor."

With excitement she said, "Just ask, Bart. You know that I have little to do with my life."

There it was again, that reminder that she had been kicked pretty roughly for most of her adult life. Suddenly he had a pang of conscience about asking for her help; he did not want to add his name to the list of those who had used this woman. She pressed, "What can I do?"

Faber explained, "I've been trying to get Bernie Eby on the phone all day and there's been no answer. Either his phone is out of order or . . ." he cut himself off, but she finished the thought.

". . . or he may have been drinking?"

Faber smiled as he answered, "Or he may have been drinking. I do want to talk to him on the phone, and I was wondering if you could try and find him for me tomorrow."

Tori said, "I'll try tonight."

"It's late, Tori."

"Not that late, Bart. His place is only a few minutes away. I'll drive over and call you back."

Faber did not want the Jesuits' phone ringing in the middle of the night, so he suggested, "Why don't I call you first thing in the morning? Not too early."

She said, "If I find him, I'll tell him to stay by a working telephone and give you the number."

"That would be fine."

She asked, "How has your trip to Hiroshima been?"

He was glad to change the subject, because he did not want to tell Tori that he was in need of police information about the death of Tac Okomoto. Faber did not want her going down to the Tokyo police and trying to get copies of the accident report and coroner's examination; she had been through enough. So, with some interest in sharing his impressions of Hiroshima, he related most of what had happened, leaving out most of what Minoru Watanabe had said about Tac Okomoto.

He enjoyed telling her what had happened, much as he thought a traveling salesman might tell his wife about his successful business transactions. Faber had never had anyone with whom he felt inclined to share his actions; it was a nice feeling.

When he was finished, she brought him back to Watanabe: "Did Minoru have much to say about me?"

Faber lied. "No, Tori, he was only concerned with getting the IFP in the best light for any magazine article."

"How does he look?"

"He looks old, Tori. He is an old man."

She snapped, "He is an evil old man. I'm glad you are through with him. He is not a good person, Bart."

The word *evil* held a serious connotation for Bart Faber, and he was sure that Tori Ito's meaning was quite different. He merely said, "I've had more interesting interviews in my life."

His hope that she would drop Watanabe was fulfilled. She asked, "Do you mind if I ask what you need Eby to do for you? Maybe I could help."

The last thing Faber wanted was to involve Tori Ito in this aspect of his assignment; he would let the whole thing pass before he would make her party to looking into the death of her lover. He lied again. "Thanks, Tori, but I just need Eby to do some legwork for me, and it's more mundane than it sounds. If you can reach him, I'd appreciate it, though. I'll call you in the morning."

He could tell that she was wanting to carry on the conversation for talking was a way lonely people created distractions. He let her continue for a while before he said good night. The tone of her voice was warmer than he would have liked, and he resolved that when he spoke to her in the morning he would pull them back to a more businesslike level.

Still, he thought as he finished his brandy, *she does not deserve to be treated in a shabby manner; she has had enough of that in her life.*

CHAPTER TWENTY-EIGHT

Dawn was battling to shove the night away; heavy clouds to the east were not helping.

Clay Morton's company plane sat waiting for him to board. He stood talking privately with Isamu Saito on the tarmac of the General Aviation section of Haneda Airport. The plane's pilot was chatting a few feet away with Saito's ADC; they were discussing the attributes of Morton's Falcon, but their bosses were involved in more important matters.

Saito motioned for Morton to walk a few feet farther away from the others. He told Morton, "I had a call before we left the house this morning. I don't like what I was told."

Morton waited.

Saito continued. "Our investigators have been getting too many reports of sudden changes in plans. The IFP is now supporting our delegation to the World Peace Rally, there are meetings popping up all over the country, and many of the peace group leaders are being called into Hiroshima for various reasons. Everything was quiet. Now there is busy activity. Our people do not like what they are seeing.''

"Well, pardner," Morton twanged. "What do y'all want me to do? I'm sure ready to pitch in if ya tell me what ya want. Let's go git them varmints."

Saito chuckled; Morton always reverted to his Texas accent when he was getting ready to leave—Morton once told him he had to practice for when he returned to Houston. Saito said, "I'd ask you to stay a couple of days if I really thought there was something we could accomplish together, but things are in such a state of flux right now that there really is nothing to do but wait. I plan to get in touch with you in a few days, though. There might be something you need to do in the States. We might have to have your State Department reject a few visas."

"Shit, that ain't no problem, you old hoss. I'll be back in Houston on Friday or Saturday; you just give a hoot and I'll git the posse saddled up, that's fer sure."

"You won't be back until the weekend?"

Morton shook his head. "Naw, gotta steer this critter over to Riyadh 'cause the Saudis been yapping 'bout me checking up on their new cracking unit. You know, that fuckin' refinery using our power and heat generator is costing them about half what that old plant cost them. You and me gonna make us a few bucks, pardner, as soon as the word gets out. Shee-itt, we pulled one off there when we got the Saudis to come on board. You git that fuckin' bunch of bureaucrats here in Japan crackin' on that small generating unit and we'll have the whole world by their gonads; all we'll have to do is squeeze! Shit!''

Saito let out a laugh loud enough to draw the attention of Morton's pilot and Saito's ADC. While the four men were looking at each other and Saito was finishing his laugh, Morton's pilot gave a subtle nod at his watch which prompted Morton to say, "Well, I guess he's right, we got a long day of flying if I'm gonna get goat brains and lamb's eyes for dinner."

Saito made a comical grimace and they both remembered the time Morton had taken Saito to Saudi Arabia and they were treated to royal dining; Saito wanted no more of that fare.

Morton dropped his exaggerated dialect and spoke quietly, "Listen, my friend, don't let this peace thing get to you. We've weathered some bad storms together, and we'll handle anything the bastards can throw at us. You know how to get me on the phone and I'll be purely pissed if you hesitate. Just let me know what we gotta do and we'll go to work. We're a team—remember that!"

For a second time, Saito dearly wished that his friend was going to be in Japan for a few more days, but he would not broach the subject; more intelligence was needed.

The longtime friends walked to the plane. Morton's pilot had already climbed aboard and begun the preflight machinations.

In Houston, whenever Saito was arriving or leaving, the two men would exchange strong handshakes and, on occasion, familiar pats on the back. In Japan, they rigidly observed the protocol of courteous bows. With that ceremony out of the way, Morton turned, climbed into the plane and yelled to the pilot, "Let's git this bag of bolts in the air, boy." He turned to give Saito a strong, affectionate wink.

The stairs were retracted and the door closed; Saito turned and walked reluctantly to his car.

Dawn also had to struggle to work its way into Minoru Watanabe's bedroom. It was filtered by the growth of manicured shade trees in the garden outside his window, and blocked by the bamboo curtains drawn when he went to sleep. Dawn faced a battle from the old man, for he did not want to wake up and join the day.

As soon as the daylight became a conscious presence in his mind, he knew why he did not want to come out of sleep; he had been having an erotic dream. He clawed mentally, trying to hold onto the deep recesses of his mind. He was a young man again, virile and lusting. It was a time before his wife, before their children, before The Bomb; it was a time bursting with life. He was in a room which he had never seen, and he was with a woman who was young and full-bodied. She must have looked like his wife, for she was the most beautiful woman ever, and dreams only provide the best. They had coupled previously, had rested and were in the midst of arousing each other in every imaginable way. He feared he would climax before he had her ready to embrace again.

But daylight was there softly in his eyes, and he could not plunge back into that dream. There was, however, a new sensation on his body, and he kept his eyes closed tightly because this was a manifestly familiar touch. He would relish it for a few moments.

With some reluctance, he interrupted his own enjoyment when he realized it was dawn; he was supposed to have been awakened at three in the morning. He opened his eyes, looked down at the woman kneeling beside his body and demanded: ''What are you doing here?''

She told him that Sano had called her and said her talents would be needed. As she spoke, she dipped her linen rag into the bowl of warm oil again and started to caress the skin of his inner thigh. He looked down and saw that he possessed a huge erection, and that the woman was moving the rag sensually toward the base of his member. He suggested that she might stop what she was doing. ''. . . And why was I not awakened at three?''

Her hands stopped—they were especially talented

hands—and she nodded her head toward a corner of the room.

In the corner sat Tac Okomoto, asleep. His legs were pulled up and captured with his arms, and his head lay uncomfortably twisted on his knees.

Watanabe sat up quickly. He ordered the woman to leave the room and then, seeing a look of disappointment on her face, he asked, "Could you stay for a little time?" She smiled and told him she would be honored to stay. He said, "Go to the kitchen and make us some tea and something to eat. I will come out in a few minutes." She left the bedroom.

Watanabe looked down at his erection and flicked the head of his penis strongly with his thumb and forefinger. It was slightly painful but effective and instantly resulted in flaccidity. He pulled his sleeping robe about him, slid off of his *futon*, and stood up.

He looked down at the sleeping figure of Tac Okomoto and enjoyed a moment of paternal love. Watanabe reached out his foot and nudged Okomoto's shin; the young man was immediately awake.

"Good Morning, Teacher."

"Good morning, my son." Watanabe added, with mock sternness, "Why was I not awakened at the proper hour?"

Before answering, Tac Okomoto stretched his arms and legs. While he waited, Watanabe savored the youth before him. The old man was not worried, because when Okomoto was around, things went smoothly.

Tac stood and executed a bow which was returned by Watanabe. Okomoto then said, "I was delayed getting here. The damned van developed a flat tire, and I had to be very careful that some well-meaning police car did not stop to assist me. I had to drive well off the main highway. When I got here I told Meiji that we could wait a few hours."

Watanabe asked, "Was my masseuse your idea?"

Okomoto admitted, "I thought that might be a happy way to begin a promising day."

The old man giggled. "I will have to allow her to finish her performance. But first, we should get you food; you look like you can use some."

Watanabe and Okomoto settled in the dining alcove that was part of the kitchen. A glass-paneled sliding door looked out into a tiny garden that Watanabe had built over the years. He noticed that several of the delicately placed small stones had been moved, probably by some innocent bird in search of food. He also noticed that several of the plants were in need of care. Tac Okomoto impatiently glanced first to the woman in the kitchen preparing breakfast, then to Watanabe so intent on his garden. Okomoto said to the old man, "Don't you want to see it?"

Watanabe's head snapped around at Okomoto. To those who knew him, those who knew him well, Watanabe could speak with his eyes. They were bright and penetrating. The silent message was: *Be quiet. We will speak later.*

Okomoto was hurt and angry. He had been through a grueling test of nerve and ability. He had killed for this old man, and all that he was getting in return was a nasty glare. He said, "I've busted my silly ass to get that thing here, Teacher, and . . ."

Now Watanabe gave a halting hand gesture and said: "Come outside with me."

Okomoto was nonplussed; he had been through too much to be ordered around like a common worker for the IFP. He started to voice an objection, but over the years the old man had been right more times than he had been wrong. The two men rose and Watanabe led the way through the house to the front door.

The woman in the kitchen started to complain that the food was nearly ready, but she held her words back. She had not missed one innuendo of the interchange between the two men; she looked out the tiny kitchen window toward the front yard.

Watanabe's long black Toyota had been pulled out of the narrow parking spot in the front yard to make room for Tac Okomoto's Nissan van. Meiji was not in his customary post by the limo, but was standing by the van doing what all professional Japanese drivers do when they are not on the road—wiping dust from the paint and chrome.

As he and Tac approached Meiji, Watanabe ordered, "The woman has made food. Go and get something to eat." The driver made a grateful bow of respect and went into the house. The woman in the kitchen saw the action and was away from the window before Meiji entered. She could not see what was taking place outside because Meiji was anxious to talk after a long, silent night of duty.

At the van, Okomoto said, "I could have used some breakfast before we did this. You seem to have no interest."

Watanabe looked at Okomoto and saw that the young man was tense. Such a reaction was only to be expected, as Watanabe knew well, having planned the theft of the nuclear shell from Korea. For the project to succeed, the fewer people involved the better. If Watanabe had not had Tac Okomoto to use, the scheme would more than likely have failed.

Watanabe said, "You have lived through a difficult task, my son."

With bravado, Okomoto said, "It was not too hard."

"Do you want to tell me about it?"

"There's not much to tell. The Korean is shark bait, the Swede was finished in an auto accident, and I have brought you this."

Okomoto opened the door of the van and slid the aluminum case to the edge. He flicked the latches and opened the lid.

Watanabe looked down at the docile mass of metal; he was quiet for a long time as he stared at the weapon. Finally, he said, "It seems such a small thing to have such a power. To think that this innocent-looking device was what changed my life."

"This is not like the first bomb, Teacher. This one has only a yield of one kiloton. Much smaller than the Hiroshima bomb."

The old man nodded, then said, "But it will do more damage . . . more damage, the way we are to use it?"

Okomoto nodded and smiled. "It will do more." He reached to close the lid, but Watanabe moved his wrinkled hand forward and placed it delicately on the cold metal. He shared none of his thoughts with Okomoto. The silent moment passed and he let go; Okomoto closed the lid.

Watanabe's expression was grim for an instant. Then he said, "Let us go get food. There is much to do today."

Bart Faber was waiting for dawn when it arrived. He had barely shaken the residual effects of jet lag; he was fully awake an hour before the eastern sky had started to turn grey.

He had showered, shaved and dressed in the privacy of the Jesuit Mission guest house. He was still the sole resident in the three-story building, but Father Schultz had said that some visitors would be arriving later in the day. That news did not disturb Faber, because he had decided to leave Japan.

The decision had not been difficult once he had had the benefit of a solid night's sleep; a cigarette in bed before he arose had helped him to see his problem clearly. The problem was Tori Ito. As he lay there smoking, Faber scolded himself silently for allowing emotion to come into an assignment for Phalanx; he had been taught better than that. Because he had allowed his compassion for Tori Ito's sad past to enter into his analysis of his assignment, he had put things in a warped position. He had allowed Bernie Eby's paranoia to distort the importance of one small aspect of the peace movement; he had allowed Tori Ito's tragic loss to predispose him towards the leadership of the IFP; he had allowed Father Schultz's cynicism to color his thinking; and he had allowed the hyperbole of Minoru Watanabe to create in him the same paranoia that had been evident in Bernie Eby.

The fact was that there was little consequence to the confused reports of Tac Okomoto's death. *What the hell difference does that make?* he had thought. And then, *So what if the Japanese had been making an A-bomb?* He had allowed himself to become enmeshed in an intrigue that had nothing to do with his Phalanx assignment and was of no import to anyone outside a small clique, trying its best to live out a fantasy of history.

As he shaved, a ritual which always provided a mental catharsis, he had decided to leave as soon as he could get to Osaka. There would be no problem. His ticket from Tokyo was also good for boarding in Osaka; he would be able to get a seat, even if he had to upgrade to first class on the JAL 474 which would leave late that day. He had also decided that he would wear his clerical suit as a reminder to himself.

While he was putting on his Roman collar, which he acknowledged was a sort of polyester armor-plating, he worked out his schedule for his last day in Japan. He would telephone Tori Ito in Tokyo. If she had located Bernie Eby, he would thank her for her efforts; if she had not, Faber would tell her to forget it and would say good-bye. After that, Faber planned to assist at six-o'clock Mass, have breakfast with Father Schultz, then invest two or three hours talking with the leaders of the other peace groups and even with Susumu Kato at the IFP; if Kato had returned to Hiroshima from Tokyo. He would allow himself enough time to drive to Osaka so that he could check in early for a flight to the United States. That was his schedule, and the main thing to do was to hold to it. He tossed his clothing into his bag, packed his shaving gear and stripped the sheets off the bed.

He lugged the bag down the stairs and locked it in the trunk of the Toyota. That reminded him that he would have to let Sister Catherine Mary know that her car could be collected at the Osaka Airport. That should be a not-too-welcome bit of news for the good Sister.

He crossed the Jesuit Mission complex and let himself in the front door of the rectory; he could hear no sounds as he walked into the pastor's office. Faber paused, collecting his thoughts, before dialing Tori Ito's telephone number. Once he had calculated all of the she'll-say-then-I'll-say options, he picked up the phone.

He waited for a full ten rings, assuming that she might be sleeping, but there was no answer. He called again, waited for a dozen rings, and then gave up. He would try her later. If that attempt failed, he would drop her a note from Osaka. Next he tried Bernie Eby's number with no success and packed it in as far as Tokyo was concerned. He did not have to pursue the matter further; he was going back to the States.

He dialed the Japan Air Lines office in Hiroshima, found that there was space available—without having to upgrade—and booked a seat. He hung up the phone, started to move, then paused.

Faber sat looking at the telephone instrument, his thoughts on Tori Ito. His problem with her was not a sexual attraction; he had learned how to handle that early in his priesthood. But he felt an overpowering urge to help her. Yet he also knew that his good intentions could turn into something more than just friendship. His duties for Phalanx did not allow for the finesse needed to give her what she needed.

He smelled coffee brewing, strong coffee. He rose and followed the odor back to the kitchen.

As dawn was arriving in Japan, people on the West Coast of the United States were returning to their jobs from lunch and the flight from Tokyo carrying Bernie Eby was touching down at San Francisco International Airport.

The pilot had announced with pride that they were arriving a few minutes early, because they had picked up a 280-knot jet-stream tail wind. To most of the jaded travelers the news meant only that they would have to wait a few minutes longer for their baggage, because the ground crews worked on a rigid schedule.

To Bernie Eby, the message was a mixed blessing. The quicker he started his task, the sooner he would be through and his wife would be released by Susumu Kato's lunatics. But he hated being back on American soil. He had been away fourteen years and, from what he had read, things had only gotten worse. He hated the way minorities were being exploited, the way that workers were being given the short end of progress, the way the politicians kept dumping on citizens. He wanted to be in and out of this country as quickly as possible.

At the immigration desk an officious bureaucrat said, "Hey, man, welcome home! You been gone a long time." Eby smiled unwillingly through that bit of nonsense, then encountered a pompous customs agent who would not take Eby's word for the fact that he was not bringing in arms or drugs. With the insulting salutations behind him, Eby located the Japan Air Lines offices on the main floor of the terminal and, after a twenty-minute wait, introduced himself to the JAL cargo manager.

The night before, back in Tokyo, Susumu Kato had provided Eby with several bogus documents that might be used to open doors. The one Eby showed the cargo manager was a letter from Yasui Films, a nonexistent documentary film company, which was allegedly going to produce a television documentary on the transportation of the peace statue Yamabato to the World Peace Rally. According to the letter, Eby was the film's director/writer, who needed to establish camera positions and line up interviews with individuals concerned with the move. The last tidbit was all that was needed; the cargo manager harbored images of his face being in a film seen by millions on Japanese TV.

Eby's fake documents and his own intense personality did such an effective job that the JAL cargo manager personally drove him across to the Oakland airport, to the South Complex where the JAL 747 cargo plane would be landing and unloading the statue of Yamabato at the huge Federal Express cargo hangar. FedEx had loaned the facility to the JAL cargo operation because the World Peace Rally was going to be taxing the JAL facilities at San Francisco. Eby was introduced to the Federal Express cargo manager, who answered the dozen or so questions Eby had been instructed to ask.

Both the JAL and FedEx cargo men silently wondered why Eby was so insistent about the understanding that no ground personnel were to physically touch the statue. Eby did not let it show, but he was also wondering; he had no idea why Susumu Kato had demanded that that message be relayed with such emphasis. But the safety of Eby's wife was at stake and he did as he had been told.

Once that part of his assignment was completed, Eby set off after the other unfathomable details of his mission for Susumu Kato.

CHAPTER TWENTY-NINE

"I'm sorry there was no Mass this morning, Father Faber." Father Schultz reached for the silver coffee urn and filled himself a cup.

Bart Faber shrugged his shoulders and said, "I just assumed . . ." He cut himself off, not wanting to offend the old German pastor.

"On Tuesdays and Thursdays, we have no Mass because the other fathers must be at various places far from the church; they take their breakfast at the schools and hospitals on these days."

Faber nodded. "It is quite understandable, Father. I should not have presumed there would be a daily service."

The portly pastor said, "Also, attendance at the sacrament is down lately. I can remember . . ." He stopped, thinking back to when the church would be half-filled for daily Mass.

Faber sensed the pastor's thoughts. "It's the same all over, Father. The times have changed."

Faber thought the delicate matter of the *Novus Ordo* was best left undiscussed in a rectory.

Father Schultz asked, "And how was your meeting with the infamous Watanabe-san last night? You were out late; I heard you come in."

Faber said, "He's quite a character."

"Ah, he is indeed. Did you learn from him?"

Faber gave the pastor a digest of the meeting and finished with, "I don't think I've ever experienced such an engrossing recitation."

Father Schultz smiled. "He's a storyteller. I have never heard him tell a bad one."

"I'd just as soon not go through it again, Father."

Father Schultz said, "There is a mysticism out here, and it's best to stay away from such exposure. I've known susceptible people who faced quite a challenge to their souls by getting involved with some of these Oriental mystics."

Faber asked, "Do you think Watanabe is a mystic?"

"No, but he is a user; he was a common laborer who has learned how to use power. He has delved into just about everything imaginable, and I am sure that he deviously employed an illusion of Zen or one of the other exotic cults to enhance his story. He wanted to impress you. As I told you yesterday, many people here are involved in keeping the legacy of The Bomb alive, and they need publicity. He thought you would add to his legend if you came away, as I said, impressed."

Faber replied, "Well, I'm sorry to disappoint him, but his yarn will become a part of my report; it could have some bearing in the future. Maybe the local Phalanx organization should look into the matter further."

Father Schultz said, "I doubt if that will happen in the near future."

Had the remark been casual, or a jab at the Phalanx

operations in the United States? Faber gave up the conjecture quickly. He said, "I'll be leaving today, Father."

The pastor said, "That's too bad. I was hoping you could be here for Sunday dinner. As I told you, it is an excellent German meal."

"I'm sure I'll miss a fine offering, Pastor, but I can leave because my work is done. . . . Really, my work was done for me when the peace groups decided to attend the rally."

"I was surprised by that move on their part. I really thought they'd hold out to have the rally held here; it would be worth millions to the city, and the international attention would revitalize the peace movement."

"Well," Faber offered, "maybe next year."

The pastor finished his coffee. "Will you leave this morning?"

Faber was just about to give his schedule when the old housekeeper slipped into the dining room and said, "You have a visitor, Father Faber."

Father Schultz said, "It must be Susumu Kato; remember, I left a message for him?"

The housekeeper said, "It is not Kato-san."

"Well, Father Faber, you had better see who's here. I must go to the school and get them ready for classes."

Bart Faber gulped down the dregs of his coffee and blotted his mouth with the napkin as the housekeeper said, "Your visitor is in the parlor, waiting."

Waiting in the parlor was Tori Ito.

Bart Faber was jolted to see her standing there.

Tori was wearing a street kimono, an elegantly draped garment that lacked the elaborate embroidery of a formal kimono but still radiated traditional charm. It was pink with pale green trimmings, and she wore tabi socks with zori slippers; Faber had never imagined Tori Ito in the lovely costume of Japanese antiquity.

He blurted out, "I tried to call you," and he felt a fool for not being more profound.

Tori Ito was equally startled, because she had never seen Bart Faber in his black clerical garb. All she could say was, "Oh!"

The situation suddenly struck both of them as rather amusing. She gave a light laugh, which he echoed.

There was a bond between them, Faber realized. Not a bond that could tempt him from his vows, although Tori Ito was a woman, a fine woman with intelligence and a sense of humor. That she was beautiful, that her straight black hair shone, that her smile was infectious; none of those were what made the bond. It was that she had been through so many sad events and had handled them well. She was not one who collapsed the first moment things went wrong.

She said, "Cio-Cio-san has come to help with your leg-work."

Faber crossed the room to her and extended his hand. "I'll not be your Pinkerton; you know that?"

She shook his hand as she responded, "I know that; especially after seeing you so austere in your black suit."

"These will be my traveling clothes." There had been no easy way to say that and he had intentionally let it fall heavily. He wanted to establish the barriers between them.

"But you said you needed Bernie Eby to do something for you."

"That need has passed. I called you first thing this morning."

"I flew down last night after I had absolutely no luck in finding our drunken acquaintance. He was not at home nor at any of his usual drinking spots; at least none that I was aware of back when I knew him better. I thought I could help in his place."

Bart Faber was not concerned for Bernie Eby, because

his old friend knew how to take care of himself. But Tori Ito's lovely face was showing that her feelings were hurt; she was offering to help, and her offer was being cast aside. With an effort to hide his guilt, he said, "That was very kind of you, Tori."

She stood there suddenly trying to show some interest in the uninteresting room in which they faced each other. Neither wanted to be the first to speak again. Finally, in a soft voice, Tori said, "I've got a cab waiting outside; I'd better be going."

Abruptly, Faber said, "Let the cab go."

She shook her head. "No, I'd better leave. I've made you uncomfortable."

He countered, "Nonsense, Tori," then, quickly improvising, he added, "I have that terminally ill Toyota parked outside. I can drive you where you need to go."

She accepted the offer with a weak smile, but her eyes lacked their normal vitality.

Faber fumbled to cover his guilt. "I've got to make a few stops to see some of the leaders in the peace groups; could you come?"

The vitality surged back into her eyes; she really did want to help this man, because no one had needed her help for years. But then she paused. "Watanabe? Do you have to see him?"

"No. That's behind me."

She said, "It's just that I'd not like to talk to him. He was . . ."

The statement floated unfinished. Faber offered, "If being around all of this brings back bad memories, then we could just talk. I could see the others later."

She said, "No, I came here knowing there would be sad memories, and I realized after we talked last night that I have foolishly limited my life by not facing what was in the past. I need to do that before I can begin a new life. You helped me realize that there is more to life than just existing. I plan to get back to living.''

For a microsecond Bart Faber felt jealous of the man who would someday have the love of this woman, but it was quickly replaced by a surge of joy that he had contributed to her change in attitude. That, to Bart Faber, was what being a priest was all about: Helping people make the next positive step. He smiled and said, ''I'd be proud if you would come with me; I do need help sometimes with translations.''

He left the rectory with her while she dispatched the taxi. Then, after he showed her where the Toyota was parked, he went to say good-bye and thank Father Schultz for his hospitality. The pastor tried to tempt Faber to stay a few more days: ''. . . so we can get in some more fishing; I need a companion for that.'' But Faber declined. The two men parted with the fondness that can come quickly to people with a common bond.

Back at the Toyota, Faber said to Tori Ito, ''This will be a busy morning.''

''That won't bother me, Bart. I need activity.''

As Faber pulled the car out of the Mission parking lot, he said, ''We're early, but we've got a lot to do.''

''If we have time, we should go to my hotel so I can get out of this kimono.''

''I like it. More women should wear the traditional dress; it is part of the charm of Japan.''

''Well, that might be,'' she came back, ''but many women cannot afford the kimono today. As far as you liking it, that really doesn't matter, does it? Some of the women at the peace groups would not appreciate me showing up dressed this way. It is a bit ostentatious.''

''You would know that better than I.''

''I hadn't planned to be moving around town when I came to you this morning.''

Faber smiled at the brightness in her voice. He said, "Well, Madam Ito, you're moving now. Where's your hotel?"

"The Grand Hotel. . . . Four dash four Kami Hachobori."

Faber laughed. "That means less than nothing to me."

She joined in his laugh and said, "You drive, I'll tell you when to turn."

CHAPTER THIRTY

Minoru Watanabe and Tac Okomoto had driven into Hiroshima shortly after dawn, but their destination was on the other side of town, down in the harbor area: the studios of the sculptor, Raion.

Okomoto and Sano had transferred the aluminum case from the van to the limo, where it rested on the wide floor by their feet.

Okomoto sat deep in thought, savoring the power, the destruction that he had under his control. Watanabe was pleased. To Watanabe, Tac Okomoto was an heir to whom the *hibakusha*, the A-bomb survivors, had to pass the mantle of peace. If there were more in Okomoto's generation, more young men like him, who could come forth and fight the battle for peace, then Watanabe and the *hibakusha* would have done their jobs. Watanabe's only credo was carved in the Memorial Cenotaph: *Rest in Peace. Man will not repeat the sin*. The old man felt he would rest well knowing that Tac Okomoto had been taught to lead the movement.

A thought annoyed Watanabe like a gnat flitting around one's head on a summer night: Tac Okomoto would have to use the likes of Susumu Kato to keep the movement alive. For all that the old man had done, for all of the investment of time in trying to make Kato into an Okomoto, Watanabe had failed.

Watanabe was especially annoyed at Susumu Kato for not keeping in touch. Kato had been in Tokyo for two days, but the last communication had been after he had put the vulgar American, Bernie Eby, onto a plane for the United States. Kato was well past the time when he was supposed to have returned to Hiroshima, and yet he had not telephoned to say what was going on with the rest of his Tokyo tasks.

Watanabe mentioned the truant Kato to Okomoto as the limo turned down the potholed street leading to Raion's studio.

Okomoto's voice was surly as he answered, "Who needs him now? I'm back."

"Ah, yes, my son, you are back, but you cannot do the running around that we need done and there are few who have the commitment to be brought into our plan."

Okomoto's head snapped around and he hissed, "Kato is in the plan?"

Watanabe patted Tac's tense arm. "No, Kato is not in the plan; do you think I have gone senile?"

"Then why do we need him?"

"Well, for example, I need this delivered to a priest at the Jesuit Mission." The old man pointed to a wrapped packet of paper on the seat.

"What is that that's so important?"

The old man said, "It is the copy of the Fujimoto papers. I have decided to give them to this American priest who is going to write an article about our movement."

Okomoto snapped, "It is too soon. We will not be ready for two months."

"I did some checking. This priest plans to write the article for publication just before the rally in San Francisco. The timing will be perfect."

"I don't know if we can trust an American. We were going to release this through the Japanese press; we agreed."

Watanabe's voice was colored with authority as he said, "*I* have decided. The Japanese press might just be forced to quash the story. The American press will get world attention. That is what we will need if we are to succeed. Trust me."

Okomoto looked at the old man. "I have never trusted anyone the way I have trusted you, Teacher. Are you giving him the whole set of documents?"

"Everything."

"Did he ask for documents?"

"He asked for nothing. He does not even know that I am sending these papers to him. But," the old man said reflectively, "this man, this priest, was a good listener when I told him the essence of the Nishina diary. Not only is he a good listener, he absorbs what is said to him. The Fujimoto papers will be well placed with him. I just hope that Kato shows up shortly so he can make the delivery. That is a job I will not delegate lightly."

Okomoto joked, "Let me take them to him."

Watanabe did not catch the humor and snapped, "You are not to be seen in Hiroshima!" Then, as an afterthought he added, "This priest has met with Tori Ito."

The chill was sudden as Tac Okomoto dove for the emotional cocoon that he had used two years previously to shut Tori Ito out of his conscious life. Her name had never been mentioned between the two men since Tac's death was staged. Drawing inward was difficult when Tac was with

Watanabe, because their rapport tolerated no private thought.

Watanabe studied his disciple; he had placed the psychological stiletto well, with perfect timing. Both men were wrenched back to that time when the old man had decided that Tac's life with Tori Ito had to be sacrificed if the scheme was to succeed. Watanabe had explained that Tori Ito could not be expected to be brought into the plan and then asked to wait calmly for two years while Tac used a dozen different identities around the world to gain the data and skill to steal, then make ready, a nuclear weapon. Tori Ito would have broken, the old man had sensed, because she was desperately in love with Tac Okomoto. At some time she would have exposed the heart of Watanabe's intricate plot.

Watanabe jabbed the reminder into Tac Okomoto at that moment to make him aware that too much had been invested for there to be any breach of discipline. Okomoto was not to question the decision to give the Fujimoto papers to Bart Faber; Watanabe was the one to make decisions whereas Okomoto was the executor. Things were not to change.

The limo drove past the front entrance to Raion's studio and turned cautiously into an alley which lay between the sculptor's work building and a derelict warehouse to the south. Meiji Sano negotiated the turn with inches to spare and brought the vehicle gingerly to a metal roll-up door at the back of the studio.

Watanabe climbed out as he ordered the driver to stay behind the wheel; if anything was wrong, a quick departure would take Tac Okomoto and the aluminum case out of danger or discovery. Watanabe banged loudly on the metal door; there was no response. He reached down, picked up a small rock and used that as a hammer; there was still no response. He made a signal that he was going

around to the front; Sano became jittery at the thought of
his charge getting out of sight even for a few minutes.

Watanabe was bordering on rage by the time he let himself into the studio; there was no sign of Raion. The old
man called three times, the last one a crackling yell, but
there was no answer. He worked his way through the clutter of the studio, past the skeletal ironwork of Yamabato,
and then opened the metal roll-up door at the back of the
building. He labored as he pulled the heavy chain that
turned the geared wheel at the top of the door. Finally he
had it high enough to permit the limousine to drive in. Tac
Okomoto jumped out quickly and took over the job of
lowering the door.

The building in which the sculptor Raion functioned
measured seventy feet wide and two hundred feet deep.
The larger front section was where the artist did his actual
work; the back he housed his raw materials and assorted
junk. Between the two sections was a partitioned area
twelve feet deep that was supposed to act as an office, but
seldom did. Above the office space was a closed-in, private area used as living quarters.

Watanabe felt a surge of disgust as he led Tac up into
the living room of the loft; the place was filthy and reeked
of the sweet pungency of recently smoked hashish. Raion
was unconscious, his body sprawled carelessly on a frame-
less waterbed. The bed looked like a giant amoeba, Raion
a victim of an accident.

Watanabe snapped to Okomoto, "Get him up!"

Tac had been grinning at the sight. He said, "Let's let
him sleep it off. He's not in condition to work."

Watanabe growled, "I want that piece of dog dung
awake. Now!"

Tac crossed the room and bent down. For a moment he
wondered if Raion had OD'd, but a slight movement of
the chest showed he was still breathing. He gave an easy
nudge to Raion's shoulder. There was no result, and the

nudge then became a shove which produced a groan. Raion opened his bleary eyes and made a valiant effort to bring his vision into focus. His gaze finally locked on Tac Okomoto's face. There was a moment of recognition, then Raion huffed out, "Oh, shit. Bad trip!"

Okomoto said, "Our teacher is here. Get up."

Raion cried, "Fuck, man, you look just like Tac Okomoto. Anybody ever tell you that?"

Okomoto straightened up and ordered, "Get up, now, damn it."

Raion's eyes rolled back and his head slumped to the side.

Watanabe was across the room and past Tac Okomoto with a speed that would be expected from a man of younger years. The old man's foot flicked out and caught Raion in the groin. As the sculptor wrenched his body around for protection, Watanabe grabbed Raion's muscular right arm and yanked. The result was a cry of pain, and then the sculptor was on his feet, making an angry effort to focus; all he could see was the wrinkled face of the man who had guided him over the years. Raion's impulse to strike back vanished. He could never strike at Watanabe.

For the next few seconds vitriolic words poured out of the old man's mouth as he accused the artist of being an ingrate, a leech on society, a menace to mankind. Raion stood there taking the verbal abuse, accented by dollops of spittle that escaped Watanabe's lips.

Raion asked, "Who the fuck is that guy that looks like Tac?"

Watanabe released a second tirade. In a few moments though, he felt the gentle hand of Tac Okomoto on his shoulder, and Tac's voice saying, "Easy, Teacher. He's up. We'll get him right in a few minutes. Let me work on him."

Watanabe yielded not only because of the logic but because pains were beginning to make themselves known in his body; there was a pounding in his ears. He spun away from the artist and left Tac to it, but by the time Watanabe had worked his way down the narrow stairs from the loft to the cluttered office, the chest pains had increased and the thunder in his ears was beyond tolerance. He staggered and grabbed hold of the doorjamb, then he felt the powerful hands of Meiji grab his shaking shoulders. The driver led Watanabe across the room to a large workdesk covered with a jumble of papers, models, books and decaying food. In one strong motion, Meiji swept the top of the desk clean and eased the old man onto the flat surface. Watanabe was having trouble breathing.

His driver was imploring the old man for permission to call a doctor. To the man who had served Watanabe for years, the old man's health was more important than any project of the Institute For Peace. But Meiji was faithful in his service, and he knew that he had no right to do other than what he was told.

A few minutes passed before the old man was able to speak. When he did, his first words were: "No! You will call no one!" There was no argument, for fear that the tension might compound Watanabe's problems.

Upstairs, unaware of Watanabe's problems, Tac Okomoto was trying to get Raion back to reality, but with little success. Tac tried slapping, then forcing the artist to vomit, but finally had to horse the bigger man into the shower stall and turn on the cold water full blast.

As the water coursed over his body, Raion curled into a ball and began to mumble; Tac Okomoto realized the sculptor was reciting poetry. Holding his temper, Okomoto began pleading, hoping to find some connection within the brain that would override the drugs possessing Raion, but was suddenly gripped with a sense of foreboding for Minoru Watanabe. Okomoto looked around and saw that the old man was not in the room. Leaving Raion in the shower stall, Okomoto crossed the room at nearly a run. He went down the steps two and three at a time and plunged into the makeshift office. He came to a freezing halt.

Meiji Sano was leaning over the old man, speaking softly and wiping the wrinkled forehead with a damp cloth. Okomoto's feet felt as if they were encased in leaden boots; he labored to move to the desk. A flood of relief came over Okomoto as he saw the old man's eyes flicker in recognition. There was more life in those eyes than Okomoto felt in his whole body. Sano shot a hostile glance at Tac, but Watanabe spoke: "Do not be angry at Tac; it is not his fault."

Tac said, "I'm angry too. It is that fool upstairs. He will pay for this."

Watanabe lifted a hand weakly. "There will be nothing done unless I say so, my son. We need Raion now. That is all there is to this matter. I feel drained, but I will gain my strength. It is nothing for concern. Now go back up there and get that pig onto his feet. We have work to do."

Tac Okomoto was also programmed to obey Watanabe, but the sight of the old man in trouble disturbed him. He did not move.

The old man said, "Now don't cause me more anguish, Tac. I will be fine; get up there and get Raion ready to work. Please do it now."

Tac Okomoto pulled himself away and made for the stairs. As he climbed up to the loft he ran a litany of instructions to himself. He could not simply kill the sculptor for what he had done. Okomoto accepted the counsel of his mentor. He would wait until Raion had made his contribution. Then . . .

CHAPTER THIRTY-ONE

Five cups of coffee were traveling around Hiroshima in Bart Faber and they were trying to get out of his body the way water tries to get out of a squeezed sponge. He'd drunk two of the cups at the Jesuit Mission with Father Schultz, and three more cups in the coffee shop of the Grand Hotel while he waited for Tori Ito to change from her kimono to contemporary dress. He was hot and he was sweating as they walked past the city hall towards the Meniji Bridge, en route to the headquarters of the Institute For Peace.

His black suit and Roman collar were not helping his body temperature in the mid-morning sun. On the other hand, Tori seemed quite comfortable in a flimsy silk print dress that advertised her knowledge of spring weather in Hiroshima. She was wearing stockings and a pair of white shoes that matched the leather purse she carried over her shoulder. While he waited and drank too much coffee, she had also restyled her hair, lifting it off the back of her neck; she was ready for a hot, humid day.

When she had come down from her room, she had announced, "I'm sorry I took so long, but it takes time to get out of a kimono."

He had risen and pulled out a chair for her. "I've heard that the obi is just about impossible without help."

As she sat, she replied, "Ah, you have not heard of our 'instant obi.' No more struggling with thirteen feet of cloth; we use hooks and eyes now. But the whole costume does take some work. Thank you for not being angry at the wait."

He looked at his watch. "We're still early. The coffee is good."

He should have taken a cue from Tori, who had ordered only orange juice. She announced, "I've packed and had my luggage brought to the lobby. I thought I could ride to Osaka with you."

He had a moment's hesitation at the suggestion but pushed it back in his mind. "That's fine," he told her, "You can take the car back to Tokyo if you'd like. I'm sure Sister Catherine Mary would appreciate that."

Tori giggled. "I don't think the good nun would think kindly of anything I did that concerned you. I think she eyes you as her personal property."

Faber was tempted to give Tori a discourse on the vows of chastity, but that subject was especially hard to explain in Japan, where Shinto priests marry and raise families. He let the moment pass; he would be out of Japan in a few hours.

As they sat in the hotel coffee shop they worked out a schedule. They would spend the early part of the day in visits to the various peace groups, then leave Hiroshima around noon. They would find a nice place to have lunch on the road to Osaka and, even at a leisurely pace, they would be at the International Airport in plenty of time for his flight to the States.

After loading her baggage on top of his in the trunk of the Toyota, he drove to the public parking lot near the Peace Memorial Center, and they trekked around to the sundry headquarters for the peace groups. There was nominal activity at the minor groups' facilities and Faber met polite deference. At the *Gensuikyo* and *Gensuikin*, the activity was furious, but Tori Ito knew how to obtain a high-enough functionary's attention. The *Gensuikyo* is affiliated with the Japanese Communist Party and has traditionally been an adversary of the *Gensuikin* which has, since 1953, been identified as a constituency of the Japanese Socialist Party. The two organizations are equally devoted to the prohibition of nuclear war, but they are not able to reconcile their political differences in the name of peace. If the two groups are involved in any kind of nationwide congress, they are immediately at each other's throats. In the absence of substantive issues they will snipe at each other over the wording of protest banners or the seating arrangements around a conference table. Waging peace is not an easy task.

Faber found it not easy to be casual in the major peace group offices; one is expected to spend time listening.

At the *Gensuikyo* building, Faber had to endure the public relations director's efforts to promote the current version of their authentic A-bomb survivor. The *hibakusha* being offered was a woman in her mid-fifties. Back on August 11th, 1945, she had been one of the school children taking part in the Hiroshima City Council effort to create fire lanes through various neighborhoods. Hiroshima had not been attacked by American bombers during the war, but the city fathers knew that raids were inevitable. The city was a main shipbuilding facility, it was the major port of embarkation for goods and troops of the Imperial Army, and the city was the headquarters for the Second Army, charged with the defense of the homeland. After the horror stories of fire storms resulting from the incendiary raids on Tokyo and other targets in Japan, the decision was made to create firebreaks by removing all wooden structures in a pattern that would inhibit blazes from spreading through the whole city. The woman, then a child of eight, had been one of the thousands of children let out of school to aid in the removal of the buildings. She could not have known— nor could anyone in Japan have known—that the American bombers had not attacked Hiroshima during the air campaign simply because they wanted a virgin target, free of any previous damage, so that a post-A-bomb study could be conducted to see the true effects of an atomic blast.

The *Gensuikyo* survivor had received nasty radiation burns. She told of years of medical treatment needed to keep her alive, and the agonizing plastic surgery needed to cover the burn effects. She wore her scars as a badge of honor; she had endured her suffering as a loyal Japanese. Tori Ito had to interpret when the woman became emotional during her narration; Faber admitted to Tori Ito that he was duly touched by the woman's story.

The encounter had taken over an hour. Another hour was spent with the *Gensuikin* survivor.

At *Gensuikin* headquarters they were required to make a trip to the A-bomb Survivors Sanitorium at Seireien, outside of the city proper. The Seireien facility is a pleasing, lively place that looks more like a holiday motel than a hospital. Aside from the few permanent residents, many of the A-bomb survivors come to the clinic for annual physical examinations which provide historical data on just what happens when man decides to expose his fellow man to heat hotter than the sun, to an explosive compression capable of bending steel bridges, and to radiation that can deform submicroscopic genes and chromatids.

The survivor at Seireien was also a woman, but she was aged beyond a guess; Faber was told she was eighty-three, but she could have been older, by her looks. Her voice was delicately soft, and Tori Ito conducted the interview quickly and quietly; she did not translate for Faber until they had left the room. The woman had been working in the Army Garment Factory just three kilometers from the hypocenter of the explosion and had inhaled massive amounts of cotton dust along with radiated dirt; her lungs were nearly destroyed, yet still she lived.

During the ride back to the *Gensuikin* offices, Faber said, "No more survivors, Tori. It's not fair to them, and I won't really use this in my article."

Tori kept her voice low enough so that the *Gensuikin* driver could not hear what she was saying. "It is all a part of the movement, Bart. It does them good to talk about what happened."

Faber did not argue; after they had left the *Gensuikin* people, Faber spoke to the problem again, "Look, Tori, it's getting late. We can't spend much time at the IFP if we're going to leave by noon. No survivors; no side trips. All I want to hear is what made the groups agree to change their minds and attend the San Francisco rally."

That question had received a universal response at all the stops during the morning: "We always intended to go. There is no change."

Tori, in a private moment, had told Faber that the replies to his questions were polite nothings designed to save face on the part of the person giving the answer. If a group admitted they had been influenced by the leadership of the IFP, then it was admitting that it was not an autonomous organization.

As they were about to enter the IFP offices, Faber stopped, took a firm grip on Tori Ito's arm and said, "If Susumu Kato is here we can talk to him; if not: we go." He would rather spend a couple of extra hours talking with Tori Ito on this, the last day in his life he would see her, than listen to more public relations types.

She gave a broad grin that showed her lovely white teeth. "Yes, Faber-san. As you wish."

He thought, *I like this woman. I will miss her.*

Faber had expected their entrance into the IFP offices to be something of a homecoming for Tori Ito, that people would recognize and greet her. But none of the people in the big room took notice of them; the activity was frantic.

Spread on top of desks and across the floor were large sheets of paper being painted into banners for demonstrations. Some of the signs were being lettered in English script, Faber noticed; a sure sign that the Western media had been invited to the event.

Nearly a full minute passed before someone looked up and saw them standing by the door. Tori Ito asked the paint-splattered student, "Excuse me, but is Susumu Kato available for visitors?"

The student, a young man who was trying his best to look the part of a disgruntled activist, finally replied, "He's not here. His secretary is in the back."

Faber and Tori exchanged glances and she began to lead their way back through the lake of banners, the ponds of red paint pots and the flowing sea of workers. In a cluttered office in the back they finally found Kato's secretary, who told them, "No, I'm sorry. Kato-san has been in Tokyo arranging for our demonstration this weekend. He should be back in the city by now; you might find him at the home of Watanabe-san or at the studio of Raion. But, if you want to wait, you may have seats."

Faber said, "All of this activity," and he pointed out into the main offices, "is this for some special reason?"

The girl shook her head. "Oh, no. We are just getting ready for a planned demonstration."

Faber said, casually, "I understand there has been a decision to attend the rally in the United States; is that the reason for the demonstration?"

The girl replied, "Oh, no. Going to America has always

been part of our program." The girl looked at Tori for some indication of what was expected from her; she did not like talking to Occidentals, especially those dressed in funny-looking black suits. Tori gave no help. The secretary offered, "I will call the director of public information. He can help you."

Tori jumped right in. "That will not be necessary, thank you."

Faber smiled and said to Tori, "Thank *you*."

They worked their way back through the sign painters. Once outside, Tori said, "Do you want to try and find him?"

Faber said, "We could go to Watanabe's home."

Tori said, "I'd rather not." The words carried less meaning than the tone of her voice.

Faber said, "I understand. What about the sculptor's place; does that have bad memories?"

Tori replied, "All of life has bad memories, Bart. I am learning to face that. I don't want to see Watanabe-san, because he was cruel to me at a time when I needed kindness. He knew that, and I will not be able to forgive him." With that said, her face brightened. "I would not mind going to Raion's; I always thought him a lovable rogue. Did I tell you he once did a nude statue of me?"

Faber gestured to the elevator as he said, "I didn't know you were a model."

Her laugh was light and full of life. "I'm no model. It was all a bit of foolishness."

Faber liked her most when she was letting the natural joy of living come out of her inner self. Just for an instant, the image of her posing came to his mind, but she erased the thought when she said, "You might want to see the final product; most people think it is a collection of watermelons piled on a broken lobster trap. He really is a fraud as an artist; but he has moments of vitality."

Faber was laughing as he pressed the elevator button.

"Then we will allow five minutes for you to see him again. If this Kato person is not there, then we are off to Osaka."

As if she had not heard what he said, she added, "I wore a bathing suit."

Faber did not say aloud that he was pleased to hear that bit of news. He could not even explain why he was so pleased.

As the elevator door opened, she said, "I guess I'm as much a fraud as Raion. I'd like to see him."

CHAPTER THIRTY-TWO

Isamu Saito sat in the plush luxury of his executive office, trying very hard to pay attention to his aide, but the words coming to his ears could not overpower his thoughts. The aide was droning on with some data that Saito would need for a staff meeting after lunch, but the file folder sitting on Saito's desk contained a secret report from the Industrial Bureau of Investigation.

The folder had been hand-delivered, the messenger already waiting early in the morning when Saito had arrived from saying good-bye to Clay Morton at the airport. Saito had had no time to read the report, and he made an impatient gesture for his aide to hurry up the technical briefing. The aide was sensitive to the signal; he respectfully backed away as he finished his digest and announced that he would be in the outer office if needed.

''Thank you,'' Saito said, then stood and gave a proper bow of deference; Isamu Saito knew how to keep the respect of his employees.

The door closed, and the folder came open.

The first three pages were a detailed report on the interrogation of Susumu Kato, beginning with a note that Kato had been collected at the airport after seeing an American, Bernie Eby, off on a flight to San Francisco. Eby was not taken into custody, because there had been no instructions regarding people not closely identified with the IFP.

Saito was disturbed. The men from the IBI should have taken the initiative and brought in the American. It was possible to imagine that the American might be performing some devious task for Kato. Saito scribbled a reminder on his legal pad to have the IBI build a profile on this person called Bernie Eby.

The interrogation report revealed that some strange forces were coming to bear within the Institute For Peace, but found no reason why the IFP had suddenly changed its mind about going to the San Francisco World Peace Rally. The IBI closed that section with the remark that the investigation to find that reason would continue.

The next two pages gave short descriptions of related events identifiable with the other peace groups, parts of the flurry of activity that had been triggered by the IFP's mysterious decision. Saito smiled as he thought of the peace groups scrambling around so as not to be left out of the publicity and attention generated as a result of Japan's new commitment to taking part in the rally.

The next five pages reported, with little comment or suggestion, incidents which might have some obscure bearing on what might be going on at the IFP. A small plane crash at Sapporo that killed a clerk working for the *Gensuikin*; a bar fight in which a union organizer who belonged to the *Gensuikyo* was knifed in Okinawa; and two apparently separate happenings in the southwestern city of Hagi, an arson and a suspected murder. The suspected murder victim, the IBI had discovered, was a notorious peace activist suspected of terrorist activities in several countries. The report stated that, while there was no direct link between the two events, the records of the city of Hagi revealed there had not been a murder and an arson incident within a twenty-four hour period for the past forty-seven years. The IBI computer demanded that the Hagi items be recorded as unusual. IBI agents were being sent to Hagi to compile a further report.

Saito scribbled a note on his legal pad: *More needed on the terrorist!*

He sat back in his chair and pushed down an impulse to pass the findings on to the other members of the *Kugatsu* group; he would wait until the report came back from Hagi.

His fingers massaged his temples and forehead in a nervous ritual that had been a release from tension over the years. It did no good this time. Saito was fighting an ominous feeling that something terribly wrong was about to happen, and that premonition was clouding his ability to think clearly; he was concentrating with a mental ferocity that he had not experienced in all of his adult life. He did not fear for the current nuclear power project introduced by his partner, Clay Morton; Morton and he had been through trying times before and they had survived, even prospered. But Saito sensed that what was before them was going to touch each of their lives dramatically.

An idea was beginning to take root in his mind, an idea that he should retire. It would be difficult to walk away from the business, more difficult to walk away from Clay Morton. Saito felt he could not turn from his friend.

The door opened and his aide slipped into the room; the man's face was grim. Saito said, "Do not look so grim; you make me feel like Nero."

The ADC did not understand, and he frowned.

"It is said that the Emperor Nero had the habit of having any messenger of bad news put to death. I am not that stern; or am I?''

The aide smiled, but weakly. ''Mr. Ingersol is in the waiting room. He is most impatient.''

Saito felt a twitch in that part of the stomach that seems to react to bad situations. Was Ingersol's arrival part of the ill feeling? ''Show Mr. Ingersol in, and you stay here during the meeting.''

Henry Charles Ingersol was the commercial attaché at the American Embassy; that, at least was his title. Actually he was a Central Intelligence Agency specialist in international trade and a genius at finding ways to correlate seemingly insignificant bits of data about crops and rainfall and raw materials to come up with projections for future developments. Ingersol was also station chief for Japan; a visit from him seldom brought good tidings.

Ingersol entered and after a proper greeting announced, ''I've got to see you alone, Isamu.''

The CIA man was the only person from the U.S. Embassy, and one of a handful of people in all of Japan, who used Saito's first name in conversation; not even Clay Morton presumed that familiarity. But past dealings with Ingersol had been profitable for Saito. With a nearly invisible gesture, he dismissed his ADC.

As the door closed, Saito said, ''Take a seat. Would you like any refreshment?'' Then he added, ''Or should we get right to the heart of this visit?''

Ingersol said, ''Thanks for the offer, Isamu, but I got a toughie this time.''

''I think I can handle a 'toughie' today. What's the problem?''

''I need you to come to the embassy.''

Saito smarted a bit from the tone and the content of the message; Japanese businessmen had stopped being at the beck and call of the American embassy many years before. He waited, letting his silence speak volumes.

"I know," said the CIA man. "I know this is a shitty way to start off a meeting, but the ambassador needs to talk to you and he doesn't want anyone to know about it. I parked my jalopy down in your basement so nobody will see us leaving."

The U.S. Ambassador was a close, personal friend of Clay Morton, and there was no hiding the fact that many favors had been exchanged in the past. Saito resigned himself to the necessity of paying off a debt. He stood and said, "I'll tell my secretary and be right with you."

"Nope," came out of Ingersol's mouth easily, "nobody knows. You and I just ease out of here. I should have you back before you're missed."

Saito bristled and announced, "Mr. Ingersol, I do not have problems with security within my corporate family. I will tell my immediate staff what I please. You can wait here."

Saito thought for an instant that Ingersol was actually going to try to stop him, but that threat passed and Saito went to the door, called his ADC close and whispered something. Then Saito closed the door and led Ingersol to the other end of the room, where he opened the door to his private elevator. The two men entered for the ride down to the basement.

CHAPTER THIRTY-THREE

"Why me?" The question squeezed out of Susumu Kato's mouth in a whine; his face was a blend of frustration and anger. He looked from Minoru Watanabe to Tac Okomoto and then to the sculptor, Raion. Only Raion's face offered anything that could be interpreted as sympathy.

Raion had had two hours to accept the reappearance of Tac Okomoto, but Kato had been in the studio for only fifteen minutes, and his mind had yet to adjust to the shock of seeing someone who had been thought dead for over two years. Raion said, "I don't know why, man. Ask them." He nodded to Watanabe and Okomoto; neither man responded.

"Fuck!" Kato grabbed the parcel that Watanabe had placed on the table and waved it roughly as he challenged, "What's so piss-assed important about this?"

Meiji Sano stiffened, but subsided at a gesture from Watanabe. In a quiet but authoritative voice, Watanabe said, "You do not need to know, Susumu."

Kato jumped up, letting his chair crash to the floor behind him. He shouted, "There's a fucking lot I don't need to know, Teacher. That's the way it looks to me. Your hotshot Number One Boy vanishes and we all mourn because he's dead—and you've got him hidden! I've spent two years playing errand boy and wiping the noses of those shits at headquarters and listening to all the garbage from the other groups and now *he*," Kato jabbed an angry finger at Tac Okomoto, ". . . and *he* waltzes back in and takes over. It stinks!"

Tac's mouth opened, but Watanabe lifted a wrinkled hand to halt the words. The old man said, "Say what you must, Susumu."

"I take all of that shit, then I get my ass kicked around last night in Tokyo . . ."

Tac cut in, "What were you doing in Tokyo?"

Kato snapped, "None of your fucking business! I don't give—"

He was cut off again, this time by Watanabe, "Susumu was in Tokyo to send the American Eby to California."

Tac nodded, and that enraged Kato all the more. "I've had it! I'm not delivering your damned packages, I'm not taking any more shit. I'm leaving."

Watanabe reminded Kato, "You took an oath when we brought you into the *Hitori shinzo mittsu*: 'I will obey or forfeit my life.' You will obey, Susumu."

All of those present in Raion's studio had experienced the rigorous initiation into the society of The Man With Three Hearts, and all had accepted the penalties for failing to give strict obedience. Susumu Kato had no desire to walk out on the society, but he was trying to salvage some respect now that Tac Okomoto was once again in the picture. Kato had come to savor his titular role at the IFP, and he saw Tac Okomoto as the only person who could snatch the job away.

It was, in fact, Tac Okomoto who relieved the tension.

He announced to Kato, "You are still running the IFP, Su-chan, believe me. I tell you now that I have no intention of ever coming back into the Institute."

Kato was not appeased by the use of the diminutive name. He said nothing.

Finally, Watanabe broke the silence. "The vow you made when you joined the society was an oath that you are not able to reject, my young Kato. But the threat of punishment is not enough to keep you as one of us; you must want to be a part of our movement. Things are happening and about to happen that will make you proud to belong to the *Hitori shinzo mittsu*. You must have faith."

Kato said, "But so much is being asked and nothing told to me. I had to go to Tokyo and send that stupid American on a task, and I do not know why he was sent. Now, Teacher, you order me to deliver a package to a priest, and I do not know what is in the package or why he is the one to get it from my hands. Now, my brother arises from the dead and I am not allowed to know what that was about. I feel much used, Teacher."

Watanabe stood and walked to Kato, stopping when their faces were less than six inches apart. The old man said, "The book of life is written in very short sentences, Kato. Turn the next few pages with blind faith and you will have all of the answers. I promise you that, and I have never broken a promise to you, my son."

For a moment, it looked as if Kato was going to break away from Watanabe's demanding eyes, but loyalty finally overpowered Kato's emotions. "I will obey, Teacher. You have my trust."

There were smiles from all except Tac Okomoto, who felt that Susumu Kato was a weak link in the society. Before Kato could sense Okomoto's mistrust, Raion offered, "Hey, Kato, good friend, all you have to do is deliver a package; I've got to build a fuckin' statue that I don't

understand. Do you want to trade places? I will . . .
gladly.''

Kato urged a grin to his lips. He was glad for Raion's
quip, grateful for anything that helped him slip out of the
corner into which he had painted himself. He did not really want to alienate himself from the society, and he had
no idea what he would do if he did not have his work with
the Institute For Peace; it was his whole life.

Using Raion's humor as an excuse, Kato pointed at the
mass of welded steel which was to reinforce the statue,
and said, ''I want to know about that.'' He pointed to Tac
Okomoto and, still exaggerating a tone of humor, he said,
''And I want to know about him . . .'' Then, picking up
the packet that he had thrown onto the table, he finally
added, ''And after I deliver this, I want to know what it
is and why it went to the American. Do you understand
me?'' His intention was obvious. He was saving some of
his pride as he admitted defeat.

Those in the studio recognized Kato's effort at retaining
some dignity. Watanabe, mustering his best paternal voice,
said, ''All of your questions will be answered, my son.
Take the packet to the American priest at the Jesuit Mission and give it only to him. If he is not there, bring it to
me at my home. I need some rest.''

Tac Okomoto charged, ''You must stay here, Teacher.
We have work to do on Yamabato.''

The old man said, ''You do not need my help, Tac. You
know what needs to be done and Raion will be of great
assistance. I will stay a few minutes, but then I must rest.''

Susumu Kato felt a pang of envy as he heard Watanabe's
trust in Tac Okomoto. Kato resolved to reach the point
where he was given the same treatment as Tac Okomoto.
''I will be back shortly,'' he announced, as he started
toward the door with the parcel for Bart Faber.

Once he had left the studio, Watanabe and Okomoto
exchanged glances that said Susumu Kato was a danger.

Raion caught the silent exchange and quickly busied himself with work; he did not want to know about those troubles. To distance himself, he said, "I need to know how long this piece is to be."

Watanabe and Okomoto came closer to the metal and studied the prong Raion was indicating. Tac said, "I will go take a measurement."

Raion squatted down as he pulled on his welder's gloves and picked up a two-inch-wide strap of sixteen-gauge steel bar.

Watanabe said, "I will be going in a few minutes, Raion. I order you not to probe Tac about this statue. As with Kato, you will know when the time is right. Until then, you must keep your questions to yourself. I will tell you when you need to know."

Raion said, "It is difficult to work towards an end when that end is hidden in darkness."

Watanabe countered, "A blind man can make a journey if he has someone to guide him. Let Tac guide you."

"But this is terribly difficult, Teacher. We are going to hide something in my work of art and I do not know what it is; I should know. I am the only one who knows the needs for structural strength in a concrete statue; Tac might tell me something wrong, and the whole thing could collapse."

"Tac knows what is needed, and you know how to do the work. Have faith."

Tac Okomoto came back into the main studio and read off two dimensions from a scrap of paper in his hand. Raion used his welder's chalk to scribble the numbers on the piece of steel. He reached up and twisted the feed valve of the oxyacetylene torch and popped a spark that gave life to the welding flame. As he was making the flame come to the proper temperature, Watanabe said to Tac, "I will leave you two. Do you want the car back here, or do you want your van?"

Okomoto said, "Later I will need the van. Once we have the cradle built, I will take our toy away until Raion is ready to pour the concrete; I do not want it lying around this studio."

Raion said, "I know how to take care of things, you can leave it here."

There was no response except a look of contempt from Tac Okomoto.

Raion hissed, "Forget the offer. I'll do my job, then, just like Kato. But there are going to be some answers."

Watanabe made his parting bows and walked with Meiji through the back door of the studio, Meiji hovering closely behind because the old man's face was still tinted with grey.

Okomoto said, "I'll go open the freight door so they can get out."

Raion spoke loudly over the sound of the torch, "I'll need the diameter of your toy, Tac. Take those calipers and get me the exact measurement."

Tac took the calipers off the workbench and followed Watanabe. Raion lost his temper when he saw Okomoto pull the connecting door closed. He threw the piece of steel across the room and shattered the chair that Kato had knocked over earlier. He thought furiously, *They'd better start trusting me; I'm tired of this shit.*

For the next half an hour, Raion cut, bent and tacked various members of the structural skeleton, his temper growing shorter each time he had to wait while Tac Okomoto scurried to the storeroom for more measurements. Raion was just about to quit his work when there was a banging at the front door of the studio. So much dirt had collected on the panes of glass that it was impossible to see who was out there. Okomoto ran towards the back of the studio and called to Raion, "Get rid of them. Don't let them in the storeroom!"

Exasperated, Raion shut down the welding torch, flung

his gloves onto a pile of scrap and stormed to the front door. He shouted, "Who is it?" as he pulled the door open.

Tori Ito stood there with a warm, affectionate smile on her face. Bart Faber was beside her. She said, "You have not changed."

For the first instant Raion did not recognize Tori Ito, but when he did a broad, happy grin spread on his face. There was a quick exchange of polite greetings accompanied by profuse bows of respect, then an interlude of brotherly hugging which came to a halt when Raion disengaged and said, "I'm sorry, Tori-chan, I am filthy. I have gotten your clothes covered with my welding dirt."

Tori came back, "Don't worry, Raion, it has been a long time; friends cannot see dirt."

Raion took his first real look at Faber, who seemed uncomfortable at intruding in the reunion. Tori said, "This is Bart Faber . . . a friend of mine."

Raion frowned. "I've met your friend, but he was not dressed as a holy man at that time."

Faber extended his hand. Raion took it, but Faber had the feeling that the gesture was purely to please Tori. Faber offered a hello. Raion did not invite them in, instead he eased his way past the door as he said, "I have missed you, Tori-chan. You have been away for a long time."

She said quietly, "My life has been different since long ago, Raion."

Faber had been studying the sculptor during the emotional greetings. He had spotted a sinister glint in Raion's eyes.

"Why have you come?" Raion asked.

She replied, "We are looking for Susumu Kato and . . ." She moved towards the open door. ". . . I heard you were finally building Yamabato."

Raion spat out, "Don't go in!" but she was already inside. Raion might have grabbed her arm except that Faber, in an innocent-looking move, bumped into the sculptor. Faber followed quickly as Raion blustered, "You cannot go in!"

Faber stopped beside Tori Ito and saw the familiar look of remembrance on her face; from the things she had told him, she had spent many happy hours in the studio back before she had lost Tac Okomoto.

Raion came in front of them and said, "You must leave, Tori-chan. I have much work to do."

She grinned. "You had much work to do here before and I was quite welcome. Do you remember when I was your model?"

Even in his present mood, Raion could not forget the happiness that had permeated the studio back before the rupture of the organization that followed Tac Okomoto's "death." Raion had always had an affection for Tori Ito, but he had always yielded to Tac's proprietary rights. The fact that Tac Okomoto was now less than fifty feet away—and Tori Ito did not know it—gave Raion a perverse pleasure confused by affection for the woman. What Tac had done was wrong, but it was not Raion's place to set the situation right.

Faber said, "We were told that Susumu Kato might be here."

Raion snapped back, "Well, he's not; you can see that."

What Bart Faber could see was that Raion had been flicking furtive glances towards the rear door of the studio; the sculptor was hiding something.

In the back storeroom, Tac Okomoto stood, peeking between the door and the doorjamb, his main emotion rage. The rage was directed towards the man standing so close, too close, to Tori Ito.

During Tac Okomoto's exile from life, wandering through the labyrinth of revolutionary training schools and terrorist enclaves, he had envisioned Tori Ito as waiting dutifully for him to return, her body waiting for his touch, for her hands anxious to feel his skin, her entire being pleading for him to come and make her alive as only he could do. There had been other women for him during his escapades: European women with bristly hair on their legs, Latin women who ate foods which made their breath noxious, American women who did not bathe enough to rid themselves of their bodies' ugly odor. These were the women of the revolution who had to act as his receptacles during his Iliad, fantasizing about sex with Tori Ito. All during his two-year trial, he was confident that Tori Ito had been chaste; now he doubted, and rage boiled in his soul.

He wanted to rush out into the studio and kill the man with Tori Ito; no other man had the right to touch that body; no other man had the right to look on the beauty of her naked form. But Tac was commanded by his loyalty to the *Hitori shinzo mittsu*. Tac's work for the secret society was more important than anything in life; he would subjugate the urge and find another way to compensate for the insult the American had inflicted. The fist thing Tac would do, he thought, was to beat the shit out of Tori Ito. Who was she to consort with that priestly pig from America?

Tac squinted through the crack and saw Tori Ito's gentle fingers touch the left arm of the priest; the sight was another misery.

Tori Ito's touch had distracted Bart Faber from what Raion was saying, so he asked the sculptor to repeat what he had said.

"Kato has gone to the Jesuit Mission to give you a packet," Raion repeated.

"When?"

Raion looked across the studio at a clock advertising Kirin Beer, nearly obscured by dust. He replied, "Almost an hour ago."

Faber asked, "Will he come back here?"

"I don't know what he will do. That is not my business; this is my business." And he pointed to the metal frame of Yamabato.

Faber felt Tori Ito's soft touch again and looked down at her face; he saw anguish. He put an arm around her as he said, "What is it?"

She used a voice that was barely audible yet full of fear. "I don't know. . . . I feel something, Bart. . . . There is something . . . I don't . . ."

Faber gave her a fatherly hug and said, "We'd better leave; this place has bad memories for you."

Her shoulders stiffened and her head came up. There were tears on her cheeks. "No. I cannot run away for the rest of my life."

Raion had been five feet away from Faber and Tori, now he came to stand closely in front of her. He reached up and, with an easy movement, removed Faber's protective arm from Tori's shoulder. There was no rudeness in the gesture, it was apparently just meant to show that Tori must handle her problem alone. Faber yielded. Raion lifted his hand and stroked the tears away from Tori's cheeks as he said, "*Saru*, you must not cry."

More tears eased down her cheeks, she smiled; it had been more than two years since anyone had called her *saru*: monkey. That had been the nickname Tac Okomoto tagged on her because of the way she scampered around during anti-nuclear demonstrations. She said, "I can cry if I want to; I've earned that right." She reached up and patted Raion's hand. "And don't call me that name; I always hated to be called monkey."

Raion said gently, "Your friend is right, Tori; you should leave. There is nothing here, not for you at this time."

She shook her head. "No! I have a right to see your work; I was here when you first told us of your Yamabato."

Faber was relieved to see that she was fighting; she would need to fight once he left her on her own. He would be back in America, but she would have to stay and handle her own battles.

Raion argued, "There is little to see." He made a gesture at the pile of welded steel on the floor.

To help Tori Ito pull herself from the past into the present, Faber said, "It's going to be big—a very large statement."

With a mixture of impatience and pride, Raion answered, "Twenty-eight feet tall, six feet across at the base."

Faber said, "It will be heavy."

"Fifteen tons, including the steelwork. That's what I'm doing now. I must get back."

Faber observed, "You have a great deal to do, I can see that."

Tori said, "You did most of it a long time ago, Raion. I remember the forms for the body."

Raion said, "They are over there, by the front door. You can see them, and then you must leave."

Faber had been studying the steel reinforcement. "That is a great deal of interior steelwork; Yamabato will be strong."

Raion explained, "It must travel to the United States. It is to be a gift to the peace rally."

Faber resisted Raion's effort to move them towards the door. "The framework is interesting; I've never seen ferroconcrete reinforcement quite like that. I mean, that center core does not seem to contribute to the structure."

Raion had not been ready for such an observation. He started a couple of times to give an answer, but Faber could see he was groping. Finally Raion said, "That will be a pocket through the center of the statue. There is such a mass of concrete that it will take a long time to cure. I have provided that to allow it to cure faster." Briskly,

Raion added, "Come, Tori. Look at the forms and then you must leave me. I have much work to do, and we can visit another day. We will be pouring the mixture in two days, and my work is behind schedule."

The trio moved to the front of the studio where two massive sections of welded sheet steel lay like two bowls. Raion said to Faber, "I made these forms two years ago, but then the Yamabato project was stopped. It will be a beautiful memorial when it is completed. I attach the forms together with the structural steel inside, then we pour in a special mixture of concrete. It will cure in a month, in time to be presented at the rally."

After seeing the forms, Faber wanted another look at the structural frame, because there was something wrong in the story Raion had told. Faber had seen ferroconcrete sculpturing at Fordham University, and there was a basic flaw here, but Faber could not isolate it. He asked, "Could we look at the frame again?"

Raion became visibly agitated. "No! You must leave! I cannot afford the time to work."

Tori Ito offered, "We are sorry for interrupting you, Raion. I would like to spend the entire day watching you work, but we must leave the city, too. I hope to see you sometime in the future. It was nice seeing you again."

Faber said, "You can tell Kato to leave the packet at the Jesuit Mission. Father Schultz will send it to me."

Raion looked surprised. "Tori, you are leaving? You will not stay in Hiroshima?"

"No. We are going to the airport in Osaka."

Raion's face showed his confusion. "But, I thought you were back because of . . ." He cut himself off.

Faber wanted to probe, but Tori Ito said, "I only came back because I am starting a new life. I wanted to make one last visit."

Raion, maybe sensing the threat of Faber's curiosity, said, "You must go. I am sorry." He opened the door and ushered them outside. Rudely, he said, "You must go. Good-bye," and plunged back into the studio, slamming the door. Faber heard a bolt being thrown.

Tori Ito gave a laugh. "He was always a very strange person, Bart. Do not think badly of him."

"I don't. But I can tell you this: Your friend was hiding something that has him very frightened. I wish we could stay."

"I have no desire to stay, Bart." Tori took his hand. "You have given me new hope for life. All of this is in back of me now. Let me take you to Osaka. Then I must return to Tokyo. To my new life."

Faber said, "I pray that I have not caused you any undue stress."

"You have given me the will to start over; I was living a sad dream. I thank you for your prayers, and I thank you for your help." She reached up and kissed him tenderly on the cheek. She said, "This is from a sister, nothing more."

CHAPTER THIRTY-FOUR

Tucked next to the south wall of the American embassy compound in Tokyo is a two-story building which is a relic of the pre-World War II era. The structure annoys the modernists of the State Department, but no one has been able to challenge the gods of nostalgia by demolishing it. It was in that lovely building that career diplomats, under the tutelage of prewar Ambassador Joseph Grew, managed expertly to manipulate the United States into a disgusting war.

While a new breed of computer-oriented State Department functionaries ply their trade in the modern glass-and-aluminum structure of the embassy, the old building has been relegated to the Central Intelligence Agency personnel charged with the dubious honor of spying on present-day Japan.

Resident Agent Henry Charles Ingersol led Isamu Saito across the ground-floor entrance foyer. Their shoes clicked on the marble floor and echoed up to the vaulted ceilings.

A U.S. Marine security guard snapped a correct salute as Ingersol and Saito moved briskly up the curving staircase towards the sanctum sanctorum of Agency operations in Tokyo. At the top of the stairs was no spit-and-polish Marine, but rather a burly Agency guard packing a visible .357 Colt Peacemaker. The guard waved Ingersol and Saito past; they walked down the wide hall to Ingersol's office.

The door to the office was of heavy oak and framed in carved mahogany. In the middle of the door a sheet of dappled glass announced: Commercial Attaché. Incongruously, mounted carelessly on the polished face of the mahogany frame was a slotted chrome box into which Ingersol inserted a plastic card. There was a buzz, then a click, and the door opened. The two men entered.

The room was void of charm, because walls of acoustical material had been installed to insure absolute privacy; the CIA knew that their Japanese counterparts were skilled eavesdroppers.

Occupying the one comfortable arm chair was the U.S. Ambassador, who rose as soon as he saw Isamu Saito enter.

"Ah, my friend," said the ambassador, extending his hand. Saito shook it, and replied, "Admiral, it is nice to see you again."

Isamu Saito was a man skilled in the use of power, and he knew that Admiral Bob Maher dealt in power.

The admiral had served on the Joint Chiefs of Staff as Chief of Naval Operations, and had earned the respect of legislators and politicians as well as his peers in the military. When he retired from the Navy, he had been called on to serve again in this ambassadorial post. Admiral Maher's only flaw was that his background in Naval Intelligence caused him to delve a bit too much into the work of spying; he was more at home on a coding machine than he was clutching a martini at a diplomatic reception.

Saito took a seat in a wooden, hardback chair; Ingersol perched on the edge of a formica-covered office table.

Admiral Maher opened with, "Well, now. I hope you been getting enough of that sweet young stuff to keep you happy."

Saito gave a sheepish grin. "Clay was in over the weekend. A typical visit."

"I know, I got your message, but I just couldn't cut loose. We've got a wagonload of shit coming down the road and I had to stay close to home. Thanks for the offer; I could use some of that relaxation."

Saito did not reply; he was anxious to hear the reason for the meeting.

The admiral said, "I guess I'd best let Ingersol here lay it on the table. But first, I want you to know that anything you can do to help out on this bucket of worms will be greatly appreciated. I'm asking for help, my friend."

Saito replied, "That's what friends are for, Bob."

Admiral Maher nodded to Ingersol. The agent said, "I just came back from Seoul this morning. To cut through all that I could say, it's as simple as this: We've lost one of our nuke artillery shells."

The silence sat like curdled milk.

Saito's voice was hardly audible as he asked, "But the nuclear weapons have been removed from South Korea."

Admiral Maher gave a sardonic grin. "Right. Just like none of our warships bring nukes into Japanese harbors when they visit. Come on, Isamu, you know better than that."

There was a length of silence. Isamu Saito was chilled by the news; this could possibly damage his efforts with Clay Morton to begin the nuclear power project. He did not want to speak.

Finally, the ambassador said, "It's like this, Isamu. We're pretty sure the shell was stolen from one of the supply depots maintained by the ROK Army. The fuckers seem to have had a breakdown in the tightest security known to man.''

Ingersol added, ''The security system worked; the men manning it failed. It is a major fuck-up and we think the piece might have been brought here . . . to Japan.''

Saito asked, ''You have ruled out that it might have been taken to North Korea?''

''Not too likely,'' Ingersol said. ''First, the border inspections would have caught it; second, the time is wrong. They couldn't have made it up to the thirty-eighth parallel before we were alerted.''

Saito asked, ''Could it be simply misplaced?''

Admiral Maher replied, ''I wish to hell some klutz had shoved it down a latrine, but we've gone over that base until we know every piss-ant and cockroach in residence. Nope, Isamu, we might have bought the outhouse on this one. We've ruled out North Korea and the gooks on the mainland. The only ship traffic out of that shithole was to Japan. Several freighters and a whole slew of fishing boats traveled in the time frame. We need help here, and that's why I'm asking you to pitch in. We don't want a whole bunch of shit to get out in the media over this. We'll take our knocks if we have to, but I'm scared senseless that some bunch of radicals have finally pulled off the big one. How about it?''

Saito thought for a few seconds. ''We can handle this two ways. The first is for me to get right to the prime minister with the information and the proviso that we keep it quiet, or—''

Maher cut in, ''I like the second way.''

Saito, slightly startled, came back, ''I had not said the second way.''

''It has to be better than the first one you suggested. We can't get your government involved because it will mess up things in the nuke department for years. We can't go that route, Isamu.''

Ingersol asked quickly, "What about the *Kugatsu*?"

Instantly, Saito said, "I know nothing of anything called *Kugatsu*."

Ingersol's voice dripped with certainty as he charged, "We think you do, Mr. Saito, and we know pretty much what the *Kugatsu* is up to. We know that they are part of the pro-military clique that hasn't given up on losing the Big War, and we know that you are a part of it. We're just asking you to do what is obviously best for both our countries. The *Kugatsu* has the power, and that's what's needed right at this moment."

Saito looked away from Ingersol and directly into Admiral Maher's eyes. "We seem to be moving onto a new, higher level, Bob."

Admiral Maher himself did not want to escalate at that moment. He said, "I think you'd better leave us alone, Charlie. I'll call you back in a few minutes."

Ingersol blinked, but at Maher's barely discernible lifting of one eyebrow, Ingersol let himself out of the office.

As soon as the door closed, Admiral Maher said, "Look, Isamu, I don't like the way this is going, but we're really caught by the short hairs on this one. I told them to pull out the stops. I didn't know he was going to get into that September thing."

Saito's voice was low and steady but held a hint of anger as he asked, "How did he know? How do *you* know?"

Maher paused, reflecting on his professional duty and the obligation to a friend. The friendship won. He said, "Remember about three years back when Kokumaura got sick in the States and they put him in UCLA?"

Saito nodded. Zengo Kokumaura, a leader of the Japanese steel industry, had in fact died in the UCLA Medical Center. Kokumaura had also been a member of the *Kugatsu* group.

Maher continued. "Well, the Agency snuck a team into

the hospital and pumped him up with pentothal. They got the whole story.''

Saito was aghast. ''The man was eighty-three years old! How could they do such a thing?''

''Look, my friend,'' the admiral said, ''it is not important for us to delve into the past; we've got a problem. Now I have—maybe—three or four hours before I must get this information back to the State Department. I thought of going right to the president because of the leaks possible at State, but the fucking army has already advised the Pentagon, and Ingersol pulled in the CIA last night, so we've just got to hold our breath. We can only hope for no slips to the media.''

''And if I do not advise my government, and there is a leak in Washington, I look like a traitor. I will not let you put me in that position.''

They had come to a stalemate. Saito's mind was reeling. A nuclear weapon in the hands of radicals was a long-feared possibility, so he was mentally hardened to that revelation. But to hear that an old friend had been abused by the Americans, and to learn that the secret society was known to the Americans, was devastating; he tried to focus on the problem of the nuclear weapon.

Admiral Maher said, ''Okay, Isamu, let's go at it this way. You use your own good judgment on who to tell in the government, but you go to the *Kugatsu* and get them to work finding out what they can.''

Saito said, ''That is what we will do.''

Maher stood as he said, ''I hate like hell to lay this on you, old friend. We're in trouble, and I guess you turn to your friends at that time.''

Saito stood and offered a polite smile. ''That is a truth.'' He added, ''I think I can give you some data that might tie in.'' Saito told Maher of the recent, unexplained activities in the peace groups, and of the murder of an activist and the mysterious fire in Hagi. He said that he would go back and have the Industrial Bureau of Investigation probe deeper into any relationship among the events.

Maher thanked him and added, "Charlie will take you back. We've got to get on this thing."

"I agree. You will hear from me," Saito looked at his watch, "within two hours."

CHAPTER THIRTY-FIVE

Bernie Eby sat Indian-style on one of the two twin beds in the motel room, surrounded by clutter. On the chipped formica of the dresser were five empty beer cans, and empty, crumpled pretzel and potato chip bags added to the general mess. A half-full can was in his hand, and he was wiping some beer from where it had spilled on the huge topographical map spread before him.

After Eby had visited the Japan Air Lines cargo people, he had rented a car and driven to the U.S. Geological Survey office in San Francisco, where he had bought all available maps displaying Sonoma County, especially the area south of Santa Rosa and east of Cotati. He had been annoyed at the price of the maps and had said to the young woman behind the counter: "Why the fuck so much?" In her best bureaucrat-ese, she had responded, "Who the fuck knows." He had been even more irritated when he stopped in a gas station and found that road maps were no longer a giveaway item to travelers; he had exchanged vulgarities with the station attendant, too.

He had driven north from San Francisco in the rush-hour traffic and passed through the area he would be visiting the next morning, stopping in Santa Rosa for the night. Tomorrow he would have to identify himself to the farmer who was renting his land to the peace rally, and that would be about all the exposure Eby wanted during his visit to his homeland; the sooner he was away, the sooner he could be back with his wife. He had sat in the rental car as the traffic crept towards the Golden Gate Bridge and yelled out his frustration. Even with the windows closed and the air conditioning going, the driver in the next car had glared over at him.

Eby's fear for Ta-ning was the only force that kept him going. If only his own safety was involved, he would just as soon tell Susumu Kato to take a flying leap at a rolling donut. Eby was even considering returning to the United States permanently, now that he was exposed to Kato and the other kooks running the Institute For Peace; since Tac Okomoto had died things had been different—and bad. He would face that problem as soon as he had gotten Ta-ning back safely. Then he'd decide.

But, until then, he had to serve the whims of Kato.

The map showed where the fields in the area rose and fell, but he would really have to see the place and probably walk it. *Damn,* he thought, *I know what they want, but I don't know why. If I knew why the job would be easier.*

Maybe when he saw the rally site, he could figure out what he was doing. He had been told that there were to be three hundred thousand people, more or less. He had been told to get exact measurements of where the people would be, where the speaker's stand would be, where the statue of Yamabato would be placed. He had been given dozens of tasks, and they all had to do with locations and road access. He did not have to worry about things like

food locations and outdoor privies—thank God, someone
else must be handling that sordid job.

What the fuck is this all about?

He took a long swallow of the beer, made a couple of
notes on a legal pad and sat back from the map; he would
do all of that tomorrow. He decided to finish the beer,
maybe go out for another six-pack, then watch a baseball
game on the TV. It was ironic, he thought; he never, ever
went to a baseball game in Japan, and they had damned
good baseball, but the first time back and the first thing
he looked at on TV was baseball. *Maybe,* he thought,
maybe I should go out and find a hooker. "Shit," he said
out loud. "In Santa Rosa? You gotta be kidding, Eby."

There was a knock at the door and he rolled off the bed.
He thought of putting on his trousers over the undershorts
he had been wearing since he took his shower, but did
not. With the beer having some mild effect, he giggled.
Maybe it's a hooker curb service.

He opened the door. Two men stood there, and he did
not like their looks. The one wearing eyeglasses and a
bushy moustache said, "Mr. Eby."

"Yeah."

"We need to talk to you."

Eby started to shove the door closed as he said, "Not
interested."

The door flew back as both men slammed their way into
the room.

Eby had not lost his balance, so he was able to move
quickly between the beds and grab for the telephone. The
man with the eyeglasses said, "I don't think you'd better
speak into that phone, Mr. Eby. We're feds, and we need
to talk."

The other man closed the door. He was as much of a
wimp as the first man; both were dressed in suits that
looked like Attention-K-Mart-shoppers! specials.

"Who are you?" Eby demanded.

The man with the glasses said, "We're from a government agency that needs some information."

Eby snapped, "Put the questions in writing. I'll mail you the answers."

"We need to know about an American who hasn't been home for a long time, then makes a last-minute plane reservation, rents a car, and finds a motel room in Santa Rosa. We're wondering why."

"How do you know all of that?"

"Computers. It's simple."

"Fucking computers," Eby spat out. He went to the nightstand and picked up his can of beer. He finished it off and said, "So what do you need to know?"

CHAPTER THIRTY-SIX

When Tori had suggested they leave the main road leading to Osaka and take their meal at a small, seaside restaurant, Bart Faber did not argue. It was obvious to Faber that this place had some significance to her.

So, at her instructions, Faber had exited the turnpike just short of Hemeli and driven east to the old coast road that took them to an isolated oceanfront setting and the Sakura Niwa restaurant. The building had been ingeniously designed to cater to the Japanese diner's desire for privacy, built on two levels around the arc of an isolated cove that opened onto the Inland Sea. Each dining alcove was visually isolated from the other; the guests saw only a beautiful view.

Through their meal, Faber and Tori spent more time looking at the craggy shape of Awaji Island than they did in actual conversation.

Faber wanted to make sure that Tori was freed from the bond that she had maintained with the memory of Tac

Okomoto. Except for that momentary reaction in the studio, she had seemed to weather her trial with minimal difficulty.

Tori Ito was concerned that Bart Faber would be leaving Japan—and her—with a feeling that she was not grateful to him. She had evolved a fondness for this American priest, and she was willing to admit to herself that she had briefly thought of romance. But he had, in some gentle way, eased her back to a more platonic harmony. She respected him for that. She realized she had been looking for a replacement in her life, for someone who would fill the vacuum created when she had lost Tac Okomoto. But the pulse of emotion that had come to her in Raion's studio had finally made her face reality: She would not fill the vacuum but rather create another space, a new space, in her life. If that space happened to allow for a romantic attachment, then she would let it become a part of her life. But the man who sat across the table from her would never be more than a friend. A cherished friend.

They finished their meal, collected their shoes and put them on in the entrance hall, and were just outside the front door when two men, young and scruffily dressed, pushed roughly between them.

Faber had been lulled by the relaxing lunch and the anticipation of being on a homeward-bound plane in a few hours; he was caught off balance, and he and Tori were jostled into the parking lot, where two more men helped separate them. In the split seconds needed for Faber to trigger the reaction mechanism in his brain, Tori was shoved five feet away, voicing a few sounds of indignation, and then she was shoved rudely another five feet. She stumbled and fell onto the gravel. Faber made a move towards her; a strong hand grabbed his arm, and he struck back with his elbow. It came in contact with the soft flesh of a stomach and he heard a rush of air come from a mouth. There was a blow to the other side of his head, and Faber spun his body around, but there was no one there because the man had moved with the spin and Faber felt an arm closing around his own windpipe. Faber moved his eyes back towards Tori Ito and saw that two men were just about to shove her into the backseat of Sister Catherine Mary's run-down Toyota. *Good, I have the keys in my pocket. That gives me a few more seconds.*

But his time had run out. The man behind him hissed in understandable English: "Stop fighting or she dies."

The words had an unreal quality. People did not simply kill innocent young women. Then he let the tone of voice register and realized he was listening to a serious threat. To make sure, Faber made one more attempt to get free, and the voice spat: "She dies!" Faber stopped fighting.

As he let his body relax, ready to take any chance to break clear, the man let up on the pressure around Faber's throat. Tori Ito was now inside the Toyota, and one of her assailants was running towards him, gesturing for the car keys.

Only one man was with Tori Ito. If Faber could escape and get across the parking lot, then it would be one-on-one battle. But the gamble was too great; Tori's life was the wager on the table, and Faber had no right to make that decision. He plunged his hand into his pocket and held out the keys.

Faber watched the man run back to the Toyota. Who was so violently after either Tori or himself? He doubted if this was a simple mugging. He could not see Tori as the car sped out of the parking lot, and he assumed they had forced her down onto the floor. In seconds, the Toyota was out of sight.

The man holding Faber let go completely, and he turned angrily to demand, "What's going on?"

The man standing in front of Faber was Susumu Kato, but he did not introduce himself. All Kato said was, "The reason she did not fight is because she was given the same threat, Mr. Faber. We told her we'd kill you, and she did not want that, obviously. It is not good for Americans to make Japanese women feel that way."

"Listen, twerp," Faber growled, "you get her back here now or I'll rip your face off."

Kato snipped, "She is gone. You will not see her again." The sneer on his face was what finally made Faber launch a swift right fist into the man's face. Kato's feet came off the ground and his body flew a full six feet before landing in a heap on the gravel. Faber heard a soft clicking noise and turned to see the other man brandishing a long, evil-looking switchblade knife; the look on the man's face was hate.

Faber tensed for hand-against-knife combat; he had not tried that for a good many years. The man slurred, "You try, fucker. I'll slice off your balls; I'd like to do that."

Faber, his voice heavy with anger, nearly yelled, "What do you want?"

Behind him, Faber heard Kato pick himself up from the ground and utter threatening phrases in Japanese. Faber could barely make out what the threats were but they stopped suddenly as the other man snapped: *"Toh-maht-teh!"*—Stop! Kato obeyed and the other man ordered, "Open the van."

Kato turned and ran to the Nissan van parked near the entrance to the restaurant; he slid open the side door.

The other man ordered Faber, "We will get into the van."

Faber challenged, "*We* will do nothing until you tell me what's up and get Tori Ito back here."

There was a second flare of hate on the man's face. Faber studied the man standing with the knife in his hand. The face was familiar, and Faber tried to remember where he had seen it before. He began to plod through the meetings earlier in the day, the people at the various peace groups' offices. Suddenly, his brain flicked a switch back to an earlier memory bank and he saw the man's face in a photograph. Incredulously, Faber charged: "You're Tac Okomoto."

The man let his expression turn from hate to contempt. "That is very astute, Mr. Faber. But you must also realize right at this moment that your knowledge is a liability."

"I have a friend who has gone through hell because she thinks you are dead. How could you do that to a fellow human being?"

"What I do in my life and what goes on in Tori-chan's life is none of your business."

"It damned well is my business," Faber hurled back. "Hell, man, that woman has been torn apart by thinking you are dead. Why would you do that to her? She loved you!"

"She had to make a sacrifice, too."

Faber countered, "Did she make that choice?"

Silence was the embarrassed answer; for the first time Faber saw a glint of guilt. Tac broke the pause with, "It is not important."

"It is to me!"

"It is none of your concern!"

"You have no conscience."

Anger returned to Tac's face. "Get into the van."

Faber did not move; he was considering lunging at Tac.

The mean look stayed, but Tac Okomoto's voice calmed as he said, "We are taking you to the airport. Your car will be left there, and if Tori-chan wants to talk to you that will be up to her."

"I will get to the airport on my own. Right now, I demand to see Tori Ito, back here, immediately."

"That cannot be, Mr. Faber," Tac explained, "Your car is gone. You will have to come with us if you are to get to the airport."

The brutality and the mystery of the incident made no sense, and now a ghost was standing before him and talking pap. "Why?" he asked. "Why are you doing this? I have nothing to do with you."

"Get into the van; we don't have much time. I am here to see that you read something from Watanabe-san."

Faber did not move. He asked, "Watanabe knows of this?"

There was a blink of time, and Faber knew the answer was a lie: "Of course he knows. He sent me to see that you read the information." He added, "He ordered me to do this."

Faber remembered Watanabe's offer of some evidence and Raion saying a packet had been delivered to the Jesuit Mission in Hiroshima. Faber firmly doubted that Minoru Watanabe had any knowledge of what was going on at this isolated restaurant on the eastern coast of Japan; but maybe . . .

Faber said, "Let's go. I want to see Tori Ito."

Okomoto said, "If she wants to see you. Only that."

Faber did not fear for his life, because he had selected his vocation at a time when the Church was still investing priests with a strong sense of Providence. Nor was he unduly concerned for the safety of Tori Ito. This man holding the knife had once been her lover, and surely he could not let harm come to her. Faber stepped into the back of the van. But Tori was about to be given an emphatic shock. A devastating one. He vowed to be there when she was forced to come to grips with Okomoto's return from the dead.

Susumu Kato had already started the engine of the van by the time Faber climbed into the back. Tac Okomoto got in and slid the side door closed, but still kept the knife ready to cut; both sat on the floor and the van pulled out of the parking lot.

The ride was slightly uncomfortable until Faber picked up the technique of riding like a piece of cargo. He could barely see out the front, but he could tell that they were heading north towards Osaka. The trip, he guessed, would take them about an hour if Kato drove the route Faber had planned to take to the airport; it would be an hour before he could come to Tori Ito's aid—he hoped.

Tac Okomoto sat on his haunches. He did not speak for several minutes, and Faber had no desire to provide an opening. Finally, Okomoto closed the blade of the knife and reached over to lift a small package from beside the driver's seat. He carefully untied the thin white string and unwrapped a thin sheaf of papers and held them out for Faber. Okomoto said, "You are to read this."

Faber accepted the papers and slid back to brace himself against the side of the van. The first page was a poor-quality photocopy of Japanese writing. He looked up at Tac Okomoto. "Do you expect me to read this?"

Tac offered a surly grin. "You can read our language. I understand that."

Faber wondered where that information had come from: surely not Tori Ito. Faber had been speaking the language freely, and he had read documents at the various peace group offices. The remark indicated that Tac Okomoto had access to an effective intelligence network. He replied, "I can barely read a newspaper."

"Try. I will help you if you have trouble. You will find the reading very interesting."

Faber studied the face of Tac Okomoto. "What's this all about?"

Okomoto said, "I told you."

"I know what you said, but it does not ring true. You've ruined the life of a wonderful woman, and you pull a theatrical stunt like this on me and on her. Why all of the secrecy and intrigue?"

"That is no concern of yours. My leader wanted you to have this information for the magazine article you are writ-

ing. It is vital information that should be publicized in
your country. Now read what you have in your hand.''

Faber looked down at the papers in his hand and tried
to concentrate:

> *I, Kiyoshi Fujimoto, do hereby attest and swear*
> *that the following documents are exact transcriptions*
> *of the minutes recorded at a meeting on 10 March*
> *1945 at the headquarters of the Second Army in Hi-*
> *roshima. The meeting was held in the offices of Gen-*
> *eral Kumo Fukuda, Commander, Second Army.*
>
> *I further hereby attest and swear that the original*
> *minutes and the secretarial transcriptions have been*
> *in my personal custody from the date of the meeting*
> *until the present.*

The document was dated 29 November 1972 and signed
with the chop of Kiyoshi Fujimoto.

Faber had difficulty only with ''attest'' and ''swear''
which Tac Okomoto translated. Faber flicked through the
other pages and saw that they were copies of a neatly typed
transcription. The quality was poor but the words were
readable. He looked up as the truck swerved around a
bend in the road and said to Okomoto, ''This is not really
strong proof of anything, you know that?''

Okomoto snapped, ''It is strong enough proof for us.
Read what is there, then you decide.''

As Kato slammed on the brakes of the van, and Faber
felt himself being pushed forward by inertia, Tac Okomoto
was also thrown off balance, and Faber had to fight down
an urge to try and overpower the two men, or try to escape
out the back door. He decided to wait a minute and see
what was happening; Tac and Kato were exchanging
clipped phrases that Faber could not interpret.

The van came to a halt, and Kato jumped out onto the
road. Tac Okomoto flicked out the knife again. He told

Faber, "Your car has stopped by the roadside. Do not make any foolish move that might lead to sadness, Mr. Faber. I told Kato to get your baggage. You will leave Japan tonight, do not worry."

Faber asked, "Will I have a chance to talk to Tori Ito?"

Tac replied, "Right now, you read."

Faber made a feeble attempt to comply. There were two men in the van and two men with Tori; little chance that he could best all of them. In less than a minute Kato was back in the van and they were moving down the highway. Faber tried to look out the back, but Okomoto shouted, "Read!"

Faber put the papers down on the floor between his legs and demanded, "Does Tori Ito know about these?"

Okomoto spat out, "She knows nothing."

Faber argued, "But she knew you were going to get something. Back two years ago, she must have known."

Okomoto glared. "She was not allowed to know; she will never know. That is why I am here with you, and I seem to be wasting my time. I want you to take these papers and leave; you will have what you came for."

Faber was gaining confidence. "What did I come here for?"

"You came to write of our Institute. Now you have something of importance to write."

"But Tori Ito had to know. You left her to get these papers."

"Yes! But I did not tell her. Fujimoto had died, and his son was to give me the papers for our cause. Fujimoto was one of the few men in Japan who knew that we should have won the war. He just did not live to see the true victory of our Empire."

"But why didn't he make them public himself?"

Okomoto nearly yelled, "We needed the Nishina diary! We needed both documents to make our case with the public."

"Then why didn't you make these public with the diary once you had them together?"

"Because we had a new plan, something which is only our concern, not yours."

"Does this 'something else' concern Tori Ito? I must know."

Okomoto spoke in anger and impatience. "It does not deal with Tori-chan; forget her."

"She is my friend, and she has been hurt."

"She is my woman, and she is Japanese. You are now out of her life, and she is out of yours. I will worry about my woman."

"You have not worried much about her for the past two years."

"For reasons that you cannot know, I had to disappear. We were afraid the police would find out about the Fujimoto papers and then demand them. We had to make them think they had been burned."

"But you left part of the Nishina diary with Tori Ito."

"I left one page."

"But a significant page."

"We will have it back. Tori-chan will return it to us soon."

"What will happen to her?" Faber asked.

Okomoto exploded, "I am through with you, American! You will know soon what this is all about." He flicked the knife closed and looked out through the front window of the van. They were coming into the western outskirts of Kobe, where they would pick up the high-speed highway to the airport in Osaka. In a tone of finality, Okomoto said, "Read those or I will take them back to Watanabe-san."

Faber recognized the ultimatum for what it was worth; he was dealing with a man capable of irrational acts. Still, Faber had to establish one last point. "Watanabe does not know you have taken me, does he?"

Faber could see Okomoto's hesitation. Then the young man said, "No, my teacher does not know."

The van was picking up speed as it entered the multi-lane highway. Faber began reading the Fujimoto papers:

TRANSCRIPT
FOR: IMPERIAL WAR CABINET—ONLY
SUBJECT: PROJECT A
SOURCE: MEETING, 2nd ARMY HQ—10 March 1945
ATTENDING: Chairman—Neilisu Wabtsu, Deputy Prime
  Minister—War
General Kanzo Kojima, Chief, Air Force Development
Admiral Tokako Sasai, Fleet Commander—Operations
General Idko Ikeda, Chief, Military Intelligence
Dr. Fukuji Majima, Naval Technical Research Laboratory
Prince Fumimaro Konoe, Imperial Court
Commander Kiyoshi Fujimoto, Liaison, Project A

WABTSU: This meeting has been called on orders of the War
    Cabinet for the purpose of examining Project A. Two
    matters are to be examined: The unseemly delays in this
    project and the recent, unreasonable requests made by the
    Naval Technical Research Lab. We in the Cabinet are not
    at all pleased at what has transpired on this project and
    we are giving serious consideration to cancellation,
    immediate cancellation.
DR. MAJIMA: I object to the mood of this meeting if we are
    just here to cancel Project A. There are many of us who
    have worked very diligently on this assignment; it is not
    right to treat us thus.
WABTSU: You may object all you want to, Dr. Majima but the
    facts speak for themselves. This folder on Project A is
    evidence enough; you should know that, because your
    name is one of the first entered by Dr. Nishina. You have
    been a party to the failures of the project.

DR. MAJIMA: The project is not a failure; we are close to completion.

WABTSU: That is what you have been telling our government for the past six years. Results are needed, now!

DR. MAJIMA: We are in a whole new area of physics. You cannot expect instant results.

WABTSU: I hardly call the years devoted to Project A "expecting instant results." You were able to keep the former premier supporting your folly, but now there is a new government and we intend to win this war. We cannot win if we keep investing our resources in the dream of some mad scientists.

DR. MAJIMA: Nishina is not mad! He is a genius, and he will show you politicians how to win a war; the testing has been successful, and the weapon will work. We know that.

WABTSU: I have read the report of the success. The test was under controlled conditions, with no accounting for variables ...

DR. MAJIMA: You are reading a report of the first successful detonation of a fission device in the history of man. Do you not know the importance of that?

WABTSU: I will not be interrupted again! I read of the one success, but I also have in this file a list of failures. November of '42: Cyclotron failure, loss of one year's work—

DR. MAJIMA: Due to the power company's electrical failure and—

WABTSU: Do not interrupt me! September '43: there were two men killed by a thing called radiation! October '43: "trigger fuse" failure; January '44: reactor runaway with five men dying from, again, radiation exposure. Cyclotron, radiation, trigger fuses: new words for an old deed called failure! You have wasted resources. You have failed.

DR. MAJIMA: I should not have interrupted you, Deputy Minister, and I apologize, but I must convey from Dr. Nishina that the major problems have been solved and

that we will have the weapon ready soon. Dr. Nishina
promises that.

WABTSU: Dr. Nishina is a scientific dilettante who has allowed
Project A to bog down in unnecessary sophistication.

DR. MAJIMA: Nevertheless, we are very close to completion.

WABTSU: How close, Doctor?

DR. MAJIMA: We should have the weapon ready to use by the
end of the calendar year.

WABTSU: That attitude is exactly what I have been speaking
about, Dr. Majima. Nishina and you and the others have
no concept of what is going on. The Imperial military
forces are suffering great losses. The time for action is
now. I want you to hear the last report compiled by our
military intelligence. You will give your report, General
Ikeda.

GENERAL IKEDA: This report has been compiled by Military
Intelligence. There are detailed copies available for each
individual if needed. Briefly, the report reveals that the
Americans are in the advanced stages of preparation for
two main military offensives. Operation Olympic is what
they call the first. It has to do with the invasion of
Kyushu in the month of November of this year. The
second is called Operation Coronet and is scheduled for
March of 1946. The Americans are willing to expend the
lives of eight hundred thousand men for these plans. We
can calculate that our civilian and military losses will be
at least double that figure. Our agents in the United
States report to us through Mexico, and the last word we
have is three weeks old, but even then troops were being
embarked for staging areas in Australia and the
Philippines. This is serious news. It is most reliable.

PRINCE KONOE: General, while the conduct of this war is not
the jurisdiction of the Imperial Presence, it is with great
concern that I ask if our military leaders are prepared to
accept such huge losses. We are already suffering greatly

on the home front from the air raids being conducted by
the Americans.

GENERAL IKEDA: Your Excellency, it is the duty of my staff
to compile intelligence.

WABTSU: I can speak for the War Cabinet, Prince Konoe. I can
only tell you that, on the whole, we see no other recourse
than to plan for combating the enemy.

PRINCE KONOE: At the risk of millions of lives?

WABTSU: Most of the cabinet feel there would be the total
destruction of our Empire if we did not fight.

PRINCE KONOE: Is there strong dissension within the cabinet?

WABTSU: Not strong, Prince.

PRINCE KONOE: Is an opinion needed from the Imperial
Presence?

WABTSU: An opinion will be asked when the time comes,
Prince.

PRINCE KONOE: Thank you.

WABTSU: Continue, General Ikeda.

GENERAL IKEDA: I have little to add other than to remind us
all what the American war machine has done to Germany.
We can project that forward and see that November of this
year could be the beginning of the end for our Empire.

WABTSU: Thank you, General. You can see, Dr. Majima, the
people under Dr. Nishina at the Technical Research
Laboratory have put our Empire in a dangerous position.
We need Project A completed and ready for use before
November. There will be no delays.

DR. MAJIMA: I cannot offer such a guarantee, Deputy
Minister; I do not have that authority.

WABTSU: I do not ask for your guarantee, Doctor, I merely ask
you to carry the order to Nishina. The project will be
complete.

DR. MAJIMA: Is the project to be used against the invading
forces or against the bases in the Philippines? That could
be important if we could raise the weight restrictions. The
six-thousand-pound limit is one of the problems we are

having. Our test device was eight thousand pounds; if the distance was reduced, then we could easily meet the deadline.

WABTSU: Doctor, you will meet the deadline, but your question must be answered by General Kojima of the Air Force Development Group. Do not reveal the target, General.

GENERAL KOJIMA: It would be possible for the unit weight to be raised another five hundred pounds, but that is all.

WABTSU: Does that answer your question, Dr. Majima?

DR. MAJIMA: I will report to Dr. Nishina the orders you have given. That is all I can do.

WABTSU: That is all that we expect, Doctor. You can leave now; there is a plane waiting to take you back to Kanda.

(STENOGRAPHIC NOTE: Dr. Majima leaves the meeting.)

WABTSU: I am furious at those scientific fools. I would not be talking to them if we had not invested so much of our time and resources in their foolishness.

PRINCE KONOE: Do you think the project is impossible?

GENERAL IKEDA: My intelligence organization knows from our embassy people in Moscow that the Americans are working on a similar project, but, from what we can learn, we are far ahead of them. I have our people in the United States trying to find out how far the Americans have proceeded. They do not really need such a weapon, because they have the manpower and equipment to win by strength alone.

WABTSU: It is obvious that the Americans do not have such a weapon, or they would not be moving such huge forces of men and massive quantities of equipment for an invasion of our homeland. We can survive the current bombings, but we must be prepared to fight off an invasion. If these foolish scientists are able to make their weapon, then we will strike a blow against the Americans and they will not invade—if the weapon works!

PRINCE KONOE: Would it be wrong to ask what the target will
be if the bomb is finished?

WABTSU: This is to be shared only with His Imperial Presence,
you know that. The target will be either the Boeing
aircraft plant in Seattle or the naval shipyards in San
Francisco.

PRINCE KONOE: I do not know of such things, but the size of
the weapon is obviously great and the distance to the
United States is vast. Our attack on Pearl Harbor took us
to the limit of our fleet's range, and the Imperial Fleet is
considerably less than it was at the beginning of the war.

WABTSU: General Kojima is in charge of our aircraft
development. He will explain the mission so that you can
relay our hopes to His Imperial Presence.

GENERAL KOJIMA: Last October we first flew the Nakajima
G-8-N, which is named Renzan. It is a four-engined bomber
with a combat payload of six thousand pounds and a range
of seven thousand miles. By the end of this month we will
have completed construction of four of these planes. Two
of them will be used for testing, and two will be used for
the mission.

PRINCE KONOE: But that range is not enough to reach the
United States.

WABTSU: Let him finish, Prince.

GENERAL KOJIMA: Next month, the four aircraft will be
moved from the Nakajima factory in Tokyo to the Otaru
Air Base west of Sapporo. Dr. Nishina's bomb will be
moved to Sapporo as soon as it is completed and installed
in the attack aircraft. Two aircraft will be programmed for
the mission, the other two will be used for the aircrews
for simulated training. In October, the two mission aircraft
and technicians will be moved to the Shikotan Island
Naval Air Station. After the final installation and testing,
the mission will be launched.

PRINCE KONOE: But can they fly that distance?

GENERAL KOJIMA: The attack plane will strike the target,

then begin the trip homeward. The crew will abandon the
plane and be recovered by our submarines, sitting safely a
thousand miles off the West Coast of the United States,
five hundred miles south of Alaska. There will be no
problems with the mission.

PRINCE KONOE: Seattle or San Francisco?

WABTSU: One or the other. Probably San Francisco, because the
Boeing factory in Seattle is set in a densely populated
area of the city. In San Francisco the targets will be the
Naval Supply Depot, the Alameda Air Station and the
Oakland Army Base. The destruction will impress the
Americans.

PRINCE KONOE: Just how powerful is this new weapon?

WABTSU: Commander Fujimoto is Project A liaison officer; he
can tell you what the scientists hope for.

COMMANDER FUJIMOTO: From what I have been told, the
weapon carries the equivalent explosive force of twelve
kilotons; that converts to twenty-four million pounds of
dynamite. Dr. Nishina is certain that the blast effects
alone will be massive. Then there will be fires caused by
the heat, and also some radiation exposure. We have lost
men to radiation, but the scientists have not been able to
calculate what the effect will be during the actual
detonation.

PRINCE KONOE: It sounds like an effective tool of war.

WABTSU: If our physicists are right, it will be a good tool, but
we will have only one. It will take another six months to
construct another. That is why we must be prepared to
last out the horrors of an invasion.

PRINCE KONOE: Will it influence the Americans? I mean, if we
have only one weapon, they might accept the loss and still
continue the war.

WABTSU: Prince Konoe, they will not know that we have only
one bomb. We will take the position that we have several
and deliver an ultimatum: End the fighting!

PRINCE KONOE: I will relay this information to His Imperial
  Majesty.

WABTSU: Admiral Sasai, do you have anything to add?

ADMIRAL SASAI: My submarines will be there to recover the
  crew. The Imperial Navy still asks permission to carry the
  weapon to the target; we have earned the right.

GENERAL IKEDA: My intelligence sources in America tell me
  that there is no way that one of your submarines could
  get near the target. You will be lucky to reach the
  rendezvous point for the rescue.

GENERAL KOJIMA: Our bomber will have a difficult time, but
  we are estimating that the Americans will not be able to
  intercept an aircraft flying at thirty-eight thousand feet.
  They do not know we have a bomber with such a
  capability. We will succeed. I'm afraid the submarines
  would fail.

ADMIRAL SASAI: We did not fail at Pearl Harbor.

WABTSU: There will not be any more of this service conflict.
  The effort is being made on behalf of the Empire, and all
  subjects will share equally when the victory is won.

PRINCE KONOE: If the bomb is completed in time.

WABTSU: The bomb will be made. There is much work to be
  done; this meeting is closed.

Bart Faber felt trickles of sweat running down his side.
He wished it was coming from the humidity inside of the
Nissan van as it navigated through the western outskirts
of Osaka. His stomach churned. He willed it to be from
the lunch he had eaten with Tori Ito. But the sweat and
the churning came from the words he had just read.

He could not look at Tac Okomoto squatting on the
other side of the van; he did not want to look at that face
of contempt and wickedness. Faber looked out the rear
window of the van again, hoping to see the Toyota that
was supposed to be carrying Tori Ito; it had been out of

sight for the past half hour. He said to Tac Okomoto, "It's a hell of a document . . . if it is true."

"It is true. And you know it is true."

Faber had just lifted an edge of the curtain of history and peeked into a dark corner of time; he was not sure he appreciated the gift. History, to Faber, was fact; it sat there cast in bronze and was immutable. He was not prone to "what might have been," and so he was willing to discount Tac Okomoto's document as a bit of obscure trivia. But there was another aspect of history that was as important as what had been: History also left legacies. The American legacy of the dropping of the A-bombs on Japan was a national guilt complex over being the first to unleash nuclear war. Some had been able to salve their conscience by balancing the loss of Japanese lives at Hiroshima and Nagasaki against the possibly tenfold greater loss of lives if an invasion had taken place. Now Faber realized that the horror story could have been different.

He looked at Tac Okomoto and saw that the smugness was gone, replaced with hope. Okomoto said, "I want you to believe what you have read, Mr. Faber; I want you to tell your people."

Faber did not answer. What *should* be done with the Fujimoto documents?

"The meeting did not end with those last words of Deputy Minister Wabtsu. There was more."

Faber looked at the damp papers in his hand, as if to read what had not been written. "Why was it not recorded?"

"Wabtsu did not want any written record. They went on to establish San Francisco as the definite target. Before he died, Commander Fujimoto told me the decision was made because the military targets in San Francisco Bay were removed from civilian populations."

"That's crap, and you know it. If there was a miss of

the target there could easily have been hundreds of thousands killed. They could have missed.''

''We did not miss at Pearl Harbor. Our pilots knew how to hit a target; they could not have missed. Besides, Fujimoto told me that General Ikeda insisted that the raid be shortly after dawn. His intelligence people had decided the American government might just try to cover up the raid by saying an accident had happened at one of the military installations. The bomb was to be dropped in daylight, so that there could be witnesses. The crew would have made its mission with accuracy.''

Faber argued, ''It would have been impossible for our government to cover up if you had missed and taken out Nob Hill along with a million people.''

Okomoto smiled. ''Fujimoto told me there was an additional plan, to have the backup aircraft fly into Tokyo eighteen hours after the attack. They would claim they were the crew that had dropped the bomb on San Francisco and they would produce pictures that were made the year before at the test explosion. Quite a good touch, I felt.''

Faber had come to Japan on a simple mission for Phalanx, and he had lifted up a few rocks that had exposed a tangle of worms few people would ever care about. History was there, it was written as it happened. All he wanted now, once he was sure Tori was all right, was to be away from the machinations of a bunch of disgruntled activists who were losing their grip on their cause. He gave one more futile look back, hoping to see the Toyota bringing Tori Ito to the airport.

The van came to a halt and the side door was yanked open by one of the men who had been riding in the Toyota. Okomoto jumped out and slid the door halfway closed; Faber could not hear the conversation. In less than a minute, the door opened and Okomoto climbed back into the van. He said, "Tori-chan does not wish to meet with you, Mr. Faber. She will be well with her own people."

"I'd like to hear that from her."

"That is not possible," Okomoto snapped. "We have made arrangements for you to catch a flight in twenty minutes. It is a charter plane to Los Angeles but all you have to do is present your ticket; your baggage has been checked in by our people."

Faber asked, "Suppose I don't want to go?"

"If you want to see Tori-chan hurt, then you will keep up this attitude. You will go with the gift we have given you and you will publish what you have discovered."

Faber insisted, "I have a right to talk to Tori Ito. We are friends. You have no right to keep me from saying good-bye to her."

"You have no rights, Mr. Faber. We have given you a gift that you will use for the good of all the world. You must tell the people that Japan was destined to win the war, that we did not go down in defeat."

Faber gave a slight, irritable shrug that triggered a burst of anger in Okomoto, who said, "You will learn, American, that we have been denied our rightful place in history. I have given you a gift, and we will give all of your people another gift, very soon. That gift will be one that you will remember, Mr. Faber. You lodge these words in your memory: *We will not be denied.*"

Faber studied the young Japanese man opposite him. There was a venom and hostility that seemed to make the words mean more than they said. Faber did not shrug again. He merely said, "I'd like to leave. I have nothing more to say."

Okomoto nodded. "You can go. But do not let your memory fail you."

Faber opened the door and stepped out into the warm afternoon sun. He looked around for the battered Toyota; there was no sign of the car or Tori. He hated to leave without speaking personally with her. But surely she was safe; Tac Okomoto was her former lover and would do no harm.

He admitted to himself, reluctantly, that he would do more good by leaving.

On board the charter flight, an hour out of Osaka, Faber was still thinking of Tori Ito, but Tac Okomoto's words and the tone in which they were delivered would not leave his mind.

PART II

CHAPTER THIRTY-SEVEN

The Speaker of the House came down the wide staircase into the main lobby of the Bohemian Club and crossed to the dining room. Several members nodded to the Speaker, and some smiled, but none spoke. Even though he was not a member, those who did belong treated guests with courtesy. Some of those seeing the Speaker wondered who had invited him, and some also wondered why he was not a member, but curiosity was left at the entrance gate to the monastery-like club; privacy was the prime commodity in the compound.

In the dining room, the majordomo led the Speaker to a secluded table where he would meet with the two other outsiders who would be arriving shortly. The Speaker opted for coffee and juice until the other guests arrived. He put his brown folder on the table and said, "They should be here in fifteen or twenty minutes."

The majordomo said, "That should be about right. The car went to the strip a few minutes ago."

The Speaker nodded, and the majordomo left the alcove.

Five miles away, at a deserted, former Navy airstrip, an executive jet with no company markings landed and quickly taxied to the waiting station wagon. The pilot had listed on his manifest the names of John Smith and Bill Jones. Each name was followed by an asterisk that indicated the true names of the passengers were on file at corporate headquarters if the Internal Revenue Service really wanted to know who had made the flight from New York to northern California. If a dedicated auditor did pursue the matter, he would find a notation to contact the director of the IRS who was the only person, besides the corporate president and the Speaker of the House, who knew the identities of the passengers.

"John Smith" was the provincial superior of the Jesuit Order in the United States, Father Joseph Venturi, and "Bill Jones" was his aide, Father Bart Faber.

The car they approached was nothing special, a standard Ford station wagon, brown in color, with modest trim. The driver was an employee of the Bohemian Club who had held his job long enough to know that he was to ask no questions. He noticed that the older man was tall and thin and wore black garb typical of a priest, even to the long black overcoat which seemed out of place on a hot August day in California. The priest was carrying his black hat, and had thinning silver hair.

The other man, Bart Faber, was dressed in mufti. His stint in Japan just eight weeks before had left him uninterested in opening up any more relationships like the one he had allowed to evolve with Tori Ito. But today the provincial superior had ordered Faber to wear the street clothes of a modestly successful man in his mid-thirties; Faber had complied without argument. He had spent several sessions with his confessor about the involvement with

Tori Ito, and he was not inclined to open the issue with the provincial. To Faber's thinking, the matter was closed.

The driver noted that the younger man looked tired; his eyes were listless, his mouth set in a grim frown. The two men did not speak as they climbed into the backseat of the car. They watched the jet speeding down the runway. As soon as it was airborne, it would turn south for the run to Oakland, where it would land, close its flight plan, and never note the stop at the deserted landing field near the Bohemian Club.

The station wagon covered the distance to the club in less than ten minutes, and the new arrivals reached the Speaker's breakfast table in another two minutes. The Jesuit provincial introduced Bart Faber. The Speaker said, "I've heard a lot about you, Father Faber. You've done some fine work for us."

Faber responded, "Thank you, Congressman Alighieri. Anything I've done has been done for the good of us all."

The provincial superior had been taking off his coat. He said, "Is anyone else joining us?"

The Speaker, as he sat back down, answered, "No, Father, put it right there; no one is joining us."

He dropped the coat on the fourth chair.

Faber pulled out a chair, sat and took a sip of water before he lit a cigarette. The majordomo appeared and took the breakfast orders. Two silver thermos jugs of coffee were placed on the table. "Your food will be here in ten minutes, gentlemen." Faber liked the style of the Bohemian Club.

Once they were alone, the Speaker addressed Father Venturi: "I'm destined to make your life difficult. I need help finishing what you started two months ago. I thought it was all over when Father Faber brought back his findings about the peace groups, but there was a later development that might be a part of the whole picture."

Two weeks earlier, in a meeting in New York, the

Speaker had told Father Venturi about the possibility of terrorists stealing a nuclear weapon from Korea; Venturi had briefed Faber on the plane ride.

Faber asked, "But how can that tie in with the peace groups? The last thing the Japanese peace groups want is nuclear terrorist activities."

The Speaker agreed. "But there could be other forces coming to bear on the activities in Japan."

Faber asked, "You mean the *Hitori shinzo mittsu*, The Man With Three Hearts?"

The Speaker nodded. "I worked your findings back through the House Intelligence Committee, and they were able to get a firm confirmation through other channels."

Faber bristled at the notion that his data needed confirmation. The Speaker sensed the irritation and added, "I had to get our people reacting to your intelligence, Father Faber. They had let this development go completely unnoticed. You were able to get a focus on the problem: All of the people you identified in your report are, as you stated, working to make Japan proud of its role in the war."

Father Venturi said, "They seem to be having some success. From the digests of reports in the media, you'd think the United States really lost the war."

The Speaker gave a grim smile. "Our media has established the postulate that we lost by winning. I'm not suggesting that we, as a nation, have anything to be proud of by having dropped the bombs on Japan, but we were provoked. I know what I'm talking about." He unbuttoned the sleeve on his left arm and displayed an ugly, glistening red scar. "I picked that up while a Marine on Guadalcanal." He added, "Our newsmen of today did not live through that time. Their exposure to war has been a TV media event called Vietnam, and a surgical encounter in the desert of Kuwait."

The provincial superior asked, "Will you tell Father Faber how we can be of help?"

The Speaker said, "Terrorists have found ways to infiltrate the peace groups in just about every country. They are beginning to make headway with their notion that Mahatma Gandhi's civil disobedience can be interpreted as a call to indiscriminate bombings and assassinations. One school of revolutionary thought suggests that Martin Luther King's genius for peaceful demonstration was merely an initial step towards change by anarchy. It seems that in a normal progression the peace groups will promote violence to create peace."

Faber cut in. "Not to be contentious, Congressman Alighieri, but that point of view does not give much credit to the people who are out there sincerely trying their damnedest to make a better world for their children."

"That's just my point, Father Faber: We must protect the peace movements. If there is a radical group planning something horrible, then it is our duty to see that the peace movement isn't scarred."

The provincial superior said, "We will do anything that is necessary, my friend."

"Here's where we stand," the Speaker said. "The peace rally is one day away. We calculate over three hundred thousand people are arriving, close to one hundred thousand from other countries. Our intelligence community has been unable to establish who stole the nuclear weapon, but after analysis of marine traffic and computer-enhanced satellite weather photos from the day of the theft, it seems that the weapon either is still in Korea or was transported to Japan. Now, we've been able to have the Korean government put a clamp on their delegation, and the only people being given travel documents are ones who can be depended upon to support us. But Japan is another, totally different problem. There are people coming from Japan who are quite capable of anything that will hurt the image of the United States."

Faber asked, "Mostly the people in the Institute For Peace?"

"Exactly; even though there are others in other organizations who would not be unhappy to see the United States end up in trouble over this rally. The Japanese peace movement does not appreciate this rally taking place outside of Japan, believe that."

Faber said, "The people I met, the ones who told me about the Japanese A-bomb work, had a strong case. I sent you that one document and told you what I read in the Nishina diary."

The Speaker nodded. "Their case is stronger than you guessed when you sent me your report. After I read what you sent, I did some digging of my own. The State Department gave me this." He untied the strings that secured the brown folder and extracted a manila folder stamped TOP SECRET. He took out a sheet of paper and handed it to Faber. The Speaker said, "I have not been able to get them to declassify that thing, yet."

The document was a Xerox copy of a State Department protocol dated 2 September 1945, headed: State Department, Territory of the Philippines, Manila.

1) This understanding between the Republic of the United States of America and the Imperial Government of Japan is to be considered a codicil appended to the Instrument of Surrender entered into on this date and is to be classified as TOP SECRET.

2) The parties hereto signing are agreed that all research, development, work and product connected with the effort broadly identified as "Project A" is to remain privately and completely the property of the Republic of the United States. In exchange, no person or group of persons are to be prosecuted for scientific or research projects under any present or

future Order of Crimes as set forth by the Allied Governments.''

The document was signed by Leon Amoury for the State Department and by Dr. Yoshio Nishina for the Imperial Academy of Science. Affixed below Nishina's signature was an identification chop of someone from the Japanese Foreign Office.

Faber looked up. The Speaker was saying to Father Venturi, ''. . . so there was a valid premise. The Yalta Agreement set by Roosevelt and Stalin had provided for a sharing of any captured discoveries in manufacturing research of military weapons. The Russians grabbed a whopping share of the Germans' metallurgy and rocketry advances, and they wouldn't share. Truman was really angry, and he decided the Japanese A-bomb could not be shared because the knowledge would give the Soviets the keys to atomic weaponry. He did not know that the Russians had already penetrated the Manhattan Project at Los Alamos. But, Truman figured, what had been lost at Peenemünde, Dresden and Leipzig could be offset by keeping the atomic secrets out of Communist hands.''

Faber opened his mouth to ask a question but stopped as the waiter delivered the food. For the next two minutes, while the plates were set in place, the Speaker and the provincial superior chatted about old times. To anyone listening, the meeting was as innocent as any between old friends. As soon as the waiter left the table, Faber asked, ''Could I ask one question?''

The Speaker was pouring heavy syrup onto his pancakes and Faber wondered how the man kept himself so slim. The Speaker said, ''I hope you have many questions, Father Faber. Your report on Japan raised many questions in my mind.''

Faber said, ''I also referred to what might have become

of the Japanese bomb. Were you able to get anything on that?''

The Speaker cut and took a bite from a sausage patty. ''Good point you raised, Father. It took my staff a full six weeks to come up with an answer; I received the report just before I came out here to meet you. I have a copy for you, but I'd just as soon hold onto it until this mess is over.''

Father Venturi asked, ''What did happen, Dante?''

The Speaker said, ''By the time we dropped the bombs, the Japs had moved their weapon to the air base at Otaru, west of Sapporo. It was there that two of the bombers were being fitted for the mission. The Nishina people had come up with a triggering technique called 'the shotgun,' where two charges at each end of the bomb are exploded to cause the implosion of the uranium. The bomb looked like a dumbbell and required a unique rack in the bomb bay. But they were solving that problem when, on August 6, we hit Hiroshima. They were probably a month away from being ready to seat the bomb in the plane. One other problem was the Twentieth Air Force raids on the Nakajima factories outside of Tokyo; they had lost one of the training planes in a raid in June. The day after Hiroshima was hit, Nishina flew from Sapporo in a military transport to Hiroshima, and as soon as he saw the damage he knew the race was over. He was furious with the Americans for beating him to the punch. Work on Project A was stopped after the Nagasaki bomb; they did not know how many bombs the Americans had, and so they threw in the towel.''

Faber asked, ''And the bomb?''

The Speaker sipped some coffee. ''We were able to dig all I've just told you out of the old Atomic Energy Archives at Alamogordo; the facts were really well hidden in tons of other data that they'd just as soon nobody saw again. The hard part was digging out what happened to the bomb. We finally found the records buried deeply in the Air Force Historical Research Center at Maxwell Air Force Base in Alabama. It seems a B-36 from the Eleventh Bomb Wing at Carswell A.F.B., Texas, was taking part in Operation Ivy out at Eniwetok Island as part of the secret project to explode the first hydrogen bomb in 1952. Well, they flew that old monster plane up to Sapporo, picked up the bomb and dropped it at Eniwetok. It exploded with about a fourteen-kiloton capacity, but that was after our Atomic Energy Commission people worked on it to make it ready. Their Project A was a primitive device by that time, but the damned thing worked."

Father Venturi asked, "Why was all this not made public?"

"Initially, we needed to keep the mysteries of the atom from the Russians. Then, when the peace treaty was signed and Japan adopted a constitutional form of government, we insisted they make a nonmilitary commitment. Then we were trying to get Japan to join the nuclear club in military weapons; it would have done nothing to help that effort if it was known that the Japs had the intentions of A-bombing the United States during the war."

Faber asked, "Were there any influential politicians who were just interested in keeping the stigma of guilt fastened on the United States?"

The Speaker responded, "There was probably some of that, too. There's a certain charm in having our nation be a moral punching bag. Some of our biggest politicians thrive on that guilt."

As provincial superior of the United States for the Society of Jesus, Father Venturi had learned how to keep discussions on track. He said, "We are delving into Machiavellian intrigues which are, in fact, a part of history. We have a more immediate problem that should be the focus of our attention."

"Quite the contrary, old friend," the Speaker argued.

"What happened back then bears directly on the problem of today. It's quite possible that our Japanese delegates, some of them anyway, are planning a huge publicity stunt, planning to release these documents Father Faber uncovered."

Father Venturi asked, "And what about their stolen nuclear weapon, if they have it?"

The Speaker said, "If this group, The Man With Three Hearts, *does* have the weapon, then we figure they'll call a press conference, release their documents, then put the weapon on display. It'll gain them what they want: Publicity."

Faber said, "I've met some of these people, Congressman Alighieri. Publicity won't satisfy them. They are determined to force a public acknowledgment that Japan should have won the war."

The Speaker smiled. "You could be right, Father, but, from what our analysts have told me, these fanatics want most to stand on center stage before the world and make a statement. Being forewarned by what you found out in Japan, we'll be ready to let them have their say. Then we can counter quickly, and the whole thing will die."

Faber was skeptical. "You think their showing the world they have stolen a nuclear weapon from our stockpiles in Korea will die an easy death? I think not, sir; I think you'll have one pissed off population angry as hell."

The Speaker continued to smile. "That's where we hope you will come in, Father Faber."

Father Venturi said, "What do you want?"

"We're prepared to handle the revelations about the Japanese atomic bomb and the subsequent cover-up. We have a sizable congressional delegation out here for the rally and we will make the proper noises and call for the appropriate investigations by House committees. We don't think we'll be able to fully conceal the fact that one of our nuclear artillery weapons was stolen. We'd like Father Faber to go among the Japanese delegations and see if he can locate the weapon; we will do the rest. You find it; we'll get it back."

Faber replied with a hint of impatience: "First, Mr. Congressman, you are not at all sure the people within the Institute For Peace are the ones who have stolen the weapon or if it is even being brought to the rally. Second, and this is probably overriding, I duped those people one time, and I doubt if I can do it one more time. I have no credibility with them. I told them I was going to write a magazine article; there has been no article written."

The Speaker digested what had been said, then, after finishing off the dregs of his coffee, he said, "If I was a betting man, I'd say they're going to use the weapon to condemn our country. But putting that aside, I realize what you are saying. Is there no chance that they'd accept you again?"

Faber answered, "I won't predict what the chances are. Just using logic, though, I can't see them welcoming back someone who did not deliver for them. These are not stupid people, Mr. Congressman. They are bright and they are dedicated."

The Speaker asked, "Is there none in the IFP that you could trust?"

Faber snapped, "There are none that *I* could trust; there are none that should trust *me*."

Father Venturi said, "Had we known that Father Faber would need to go back into the IFP, we'd have handled things differently. But that's behind us. I must agree that there are no friends within the IFP now."

The congressman was not pleased; things were not going as he had hoped. He took a cigarette from the pack sitting in front of Bart Faber and lit it, then said, "Could you then give us some help within our operation? Advise our people."

Faber nodded. "With whom will I be working?"

The Speaker said, "We've set up a command post in Santa Rosa in the post office building. The man running our part of the show is Charlie Ingersol."

Faber asked, "From your staff?"

"No. Central Intelligence."

There was an instant exchange of glances between the two priests; Father Venturi said, "We never have our Phalanx people working directly with any other intelligence operation, Dante. You know that. We cannot expose our group. That would be impossible."

There was another pause. Then the Speaker offered, "Suppose I tell them that Father Faber is simply a priest who has served in Japan and might be able to identify some of the activists in the peace movement?"

Another set of glances flitted between the two priests. Father Venturi said, "If you can guarantee that Father Faber's Phalanx connection is not exposed. We have a strict rule of secrecy; we do not want the Agency to know that Phalanx even exists."

The Speaker said, "I apologize for letting the suggestion even come up, Joseph. I know you have given me a great trust by letting me know about Phalanx. I would never compromise your group." Then he turned to Faber. "Are you willing to go into our command post on that basis?"

Faber replied, "I will do what I am ordered to do."

It was just before nine in the morning when Faber left the Bohemian club. The World Peace Rally was exactly twenty-four hours away.

CHAPTER THIRTY-EIGHT

As Bart Faber was being driven in the bright morning sun from the Bohemian Club to Santa Rosa, it was drizzling rain and two o'clock in the morning at Osaka Airport. Cargo workers were laboring over the job of lifting the fifteen-ton statue Yamabato into a Japan Air Lines 747 Cargoliner.

Portable quartz lighting stands flooded the loading area in an eerie amber glow. Not too far away from the loading crew stood a cluster of JAL officials, media representatives and a pair of U.S. government employees, representing immigration and customs. The American bureaucrats were on hand to perform the courtesy service of pre-clearing the cargo and the IFP passengers who would accompany it on the flight to San Francisco.

Those passengers were to be Susumu Kato, Tori Ito, Bernie Eby, and Tac Okomoto—Okomoto posing as the sculptor Raion. Kato was listed as the head of the traveling delegation, Tori Ito was there as the women's representative, and Eby was accredited as the press reporter for several minor Japanese publications. Kato was slightly pleased to be noted as the IFP's leader. Tori Ito was going in a mood of strained desperation because Tac Okomoto had been unusually cruel to her since his return and she was hoping to win a place back in his life by being with him during his moment of victory. They were all standing a few feet away from the hubbub, trying to keep out of the glare of the work lights. Standing with them, protected by an umbrella, was Minoru Watanabe.

Over the lifting device there was a flurry of activity, and the loadmaster ran to the JAL officials, who dispatched an underling to the IFP delegates. "We would ask the sculptor to assist us, please," the man asked.

Watanabe said, "Go help them, Raion."

Watanabe addressed Tac Okomoto, who was clothed in a car coat with the hood drawn over his head as if against the rain. Raion had, in fact, been exterminated seven weeks before, shortly after he bragged in the golden fog of a marijuana high, that a nuclear military weapon had been hidden in the middle of his creation. He thought it was a magnificent trick to send the damned Americans back one of their own devilish weapons.

But Raion's biggest mistake had been to press Tac Okomoto as to just when the Americans were going to be told about the ruse. That was when it had dawned on him that the weapon might be exploded and destroy his work of art. As the horror appeared on his face, Okomoto killed him, then disposed of the body in Hiroshima Bay, weighting it down with some of the scrap metal littering Raion's studio. Watanabe had approved the action after the fact, and decided that Tac would assume Raion's identity for the trip. Raion had been quite a recluse for the last few years, and few people knew what he looked like. Still only Watanabe and Okomoto knew just what was planned. Susumu Kato and Tori Ito had been brought partway into the plot, but they thought the weapon was going to be made public at a news conference.

Tori Ito felt a flutter of anxiety as Tac walked towards the aircraft; she was not sure that the impersonation was going to succeed. She wanted to run to him, to be with him; she did not want to lose him from her life again.

Minoru Watanabe reached out a hand and held her back. "Do not fear, Tori. He will be safe."

She snapped a glance towards the old man. "I have reasons to fear, Watanabe-san."

He replied, "You do have reasons, my dear, but your fears are premature. Wait until you are at the rally and the world of the foreigners begins to crumble. Then you and Tac both will have a justifiable fear for the future."

Across the tarmac, Tac Okomoto approached the loading operation; he hoped there was nothing too technical to be solved.

Yamabato lay cradled in foam-rubber padding attached to a massive frame of cedar timbers. The statue in its protective nest had been forklifted onto a transport platform that now sat in front of the yawning raised nose cone of the 747 cargo plane. A scissored-jack lifter was waiting to take the load and hoist it into place so that the pallet could be rolled into the cargo bay.

A worried-looking loadmaster came timidly to Okomoto. "There is a problem that we did not cause, sir. We are sure we did not cause the problem. We are not—"

Okomoto cut off the obsequious pleading and demanded, "What is the problem?"

Yamabato was reclining in the glare, drips of water collecting in the crevasses which were the eyes, nose and mouth of the statue. Okomoto's own eyes darted quickly to a point halfway down the cylindrical body of the statue. All the time that Raion had been supervising the pouring of the concrete onto the steel form, he had been complaining that the suspending of the artillery shell in the middle of the structural steel had been a danger. Surely, Raion had argued, the shell should be encased in a steel tube. Okomoto had refused, because the radio signal that was to initiate the timing device on the trigger mechanism could not penetrate such a tube, or so Tac Okomoto had been taught at the Libyan explosives school. The signal would be just strong enough to penetrate twenty inches of concrete and some of the randomly set bars of reinforcing steel.

The argument had been one of those hints that Raion had put together into the real plan for his statue; his logic had been fatally successful.

Okomoto was relieved to see the smooth white finish of the concrete solid and unmarred over the nuclear shell. The loadmaster was gesturing at an area near the base. There was a hairline crack at the bottom of the twenty-eight-foot statue, where the statue was married to a plug of concrete four feet in diameter that was to anchor Yamabato into the pedestal waiting in California. The flaw ran around the seam between plug and statue. Okomoto shrugged. "It is nothing. Do not worry."

With great relief the loadmaster hurried his men to raise the statue up for loading.

Okomoto returned to the IFP people and told them of the problem. Knowing smiles passed between Watanabe and Okomoto. Tori and Susumu Kato accepted them as a sign of good things to come.

Moving Yamabato into the plane took only a short time. Japan Air Lines had donated this flight for transporting the gift to the United States. Actually, most of the Japanese government and a large segment of Japanese industry was relieved to have the Japanese delegation attending the World Peace Rally; everyone was walking gingerly to insure that nothing untoward happened to disrupt the participation.

Over the previous two days, nearly five thousand peace

activists had flown, at nominal cost, to San Francisco. JAL had donated the aircraft and crews—the passengers paid for the fuel—while the Japanese Travel Bureau had arranged a similar deal with a tour-bus operator in California.

Everything was going well. The JAL officials were eager to see their jumbo jet off the ground and on its way to America. The American immigration and customs men approached the IFP people and, in a perfunctory manner, completed the formality of clearance into the U.S.

Minoru Watanabe walked to the front of the aircraft where the loading platform now stood empty, waiting to take up the passengers. In the manner of their society, the four who were departing made respectful bows to the old man, who bowed in return. He approached Bernie Eby who had been included because he had actually seen the site of the rally. Eby's wife had been returned to Japan from Hong Kong as his price for participation, but there was still a silent threat; he had not yet seen her.

Eby snapped, "I'm holding you responsible for my wife, old man."

Watanabe smiled. "You will return in three days; your wife will be waiting. She will be safe if you do your tasks."

To Tori Ito, the old man said, "I will say this one more time: I do not want you to go."

She said, "You kept me from him once in my lifetime; never again. This could be my last chance with him."

To Susumu Kato, Watanabe said, "Now you have the answers you demanded, young friend. Now you have the leadership of our Institute For Peace. Do your job well; do our work well."

Kato beamed. "You never called me 'friend' before, Teacher. I am honored."

Watanabe did not respond. He took hold of Okomoto's shoulder and led him a few feet away as the others climbed

onto the platform. He said, "There is a chance we will
not see each other again, my son."

"Only if you die from overexerting yourself with one
of your youthful bedmates."

Watanabe said, "You know what I mean. If they capture
you, you must take the pill I gave you; they must never
have the answers. This act must remain clouded with mystery."

Okomoto said, "Do not worry about me, Teacher. I
will be away from there and out through Mexico, just as
we have planned. It might be a while, but I will return to
our land."

Quietly, Watanabe said, "Banzai!"

Okomoto struggled to avoid yelling out proudly. He
whispered, "Banzai!"

With quick bows, the men parted. Okomoto turned and
joined the others for the ride up to the plane's entrance,
and Watanabe walked across the tarmac to his waiting car
and got in. He wanted to distance himself from the officials because he had nothing to say to them; his statement
would be made soon. The old man told Sano where to go.
He had important things to do and he was not going to
waste time at the Osaka Airport. He did not even look
back to see the final activities at the airplane.

As the loading platform pulled away and the bulbous
nose of the plane was lowered, the four IFP passengers
went up the steep ladder leading to the flight deck and
what would have been the first-class lounge on a passenger
version of the 747. The cargo configuration of the jumbo
jet is spartan, although four rows of seats had been installed to handle the unusual presence of passengers on
this cargo flight. The first officer undertook to brief Okomoto and the others on emergency procedures and what
was to be expected during the long flight to San Francisco.
He also told them that, because of the light weight of the
plane, their flying time for the trip would probably be un-

der twelve hours. Tac Okomoto did not like this: two hours were being added to their California schedule. He began to calculate how he could compensate for the change.

Tori Ito reached out to Okomoto, but he pulled his hand away as if to readjust his seat belt. Since their reunion, Tac had been vocal about the rage he felt because she had been untrue to him; he was convinced she had had a sexual affair with Bart Faber, and he accused her of being with many other men in the two years of his absence.

Tori had been unable to convince him of her fidelity, even though she had had no reason to think he was still alive and that she should remain chaste. In spite of his unreasonable attitude, she still considered him a precious gift she had lost and then found again. She meekly returned her hand to her lap as the plane rolled down the runway and lifted into the black sky. This venture to the World Peace Rally was one last effort to see if he could contribute to their love, to see if they could find what had once been between them. She honestly doubted that it would work, but there was always hope. Perhaps the drama, as it played out, would provide them with a new bond that would help them again find a mutual love.

She was not especially impressed with the extravagant scheme, even though moments of excitement had rekindled the firebrand that had once flamed in her activist heart. When Tac had first told her of the plot to expose the nuclear danger by presenting the artillery shell at the rally, she had suggested that it would be just as impressive to hold the press conference in Tokyo, or better yet, Hiroshima. But he had been adamant, telling her to keep out of the affair. He had insisted on her making the trip so that she could help cover any errors he might make in his impersonation of Raion. She accepted the story that Raion had simply disappeared, and she was amused by Tac's taking the role of an artist. She suspected that Tac wanted her along as a convenient sexual companion. He had been quite demanding in that regard, and she found it confusing that, after two years of abstinence, she was finding no gratification for herself. She had accepted Tac's brutality as a sign that he had, himself, been celibate during their years apart, but she was longing for some demonstration of tenderness. Whenever her thoughts strayed into that area, she found that she would end up thinking of Bart Faber. She never fantasized about Faber, sexually, but she did remember his thoughtful gentleness.

She looked out the window of the plane and caught the lights of Osaka slipping away into the darkness of the night. Would she see Faber in San Francisco? She doubted that; he was gone from her life. She accepted that in the same way she accepted her unhappiness with Tac Okomoto.

Across the aisle, Susumu Kato had caught the rebuff to Tori Ito and he wondered why she put up with Okomoto's nasty manner. Kato felt that Okomoto had been acting like a bastard ever since he had resurfaced, treating people like dirt. Kato could not fault Raion for having pulled out of the IFP. Okomoto kept saying that Kato was running the IFP, but he never allowed Kato to make any decisions. Kato would be glad when the World Peace Rally was over and they were all back in Japan. The only real question was if Tac Okomoto would hold to his word and leave the IFP alone once the great exposé had taken place in San Francisco. Kato had to give credit to Okomoto for engineering the theft of the nuclear weapon; the man had pulled off the coup that had been the goal of every underground anti-nuclear group for the past thirty years.

Once they were back in Japan Kato would force a confrontation with Okomoto; the real battle would be to perform according to the standards of Watanabe.

Next to Kato, Bernie Eby sat rigidly in his seat, hands gripping the armrest tightly enough to show white knuckles. Kato said, "It will not be long. Try to relax."

Eby glared angrily at him. "I do not like being used. You people are a bunch of lunatics."

"Watanabe-san ordered you to come; we all must follow orders."

Eby turned away and looked out into the dark sky. "I'd like to order that old bastard to hell."

Minoru Watanabe was comfortably ensconced in the plush backseat of his limo as it sped towards downtown Osaka. Watanabe had no fear. He had lived a full life, and he was the mastermind of a scheme that would make the world take notice like nothing else he could think of. If he had not been in the boiler room of his factory when The Bomb had exploded over Hiroshima, then he would surely have been incinerated and his life would have terminated in a second. But he had lived, and he had lived lustily as he savored the gift of borrowed time. Now, after years of struggle, he was about to make his own statement. The entire world would respect the old man called Teacher.

Sano handled the long car well as he pushed faster towards the Shin-Osaka railway station. Because it was in the dead hours of the night, there was no traffic and, twenty minutes after leaving the airport, the limousine pulled through a freight gate and came to a stop at a dimly lit platform. Watanabe climbed out, made his way up the freight ramp and entered the private railway car of Isamu Saito.

The car was attached to the rear of an express freight train that would travel over the same tracks used by Japan Railway's Bullet. The freight train could not match the one hundred seventy miles per hour of the Bullet, but it would cover the three hundred and thirty miles to Tokyo in just under three hours. The train pulled out as soon as Watanabe entered.

Isamu Saito's railway car was not a relic of a bygone

era of private train travel; the car was sleek and modern. The rear was set up as a small lounge and observation area defined by a bar and small kitchen. The middle of the car was a large conference room that doubled for dining when the crowd was large enough. In the front were two large bedrooms appointed in the Western fashion but still able to provide a comfortable night's sleep for Japanese guests.

The two men greeted each other formally and then Saito asked, "It went well?"

"It went well." The old man declined the offer of sake but accepted a cup of tea which Saito prepared himself.

Saito said, "I invited a guest for you. She is at the front of the car, waiting."

Watanabe smiled and wondered what young thing was waiting for him in the sleeping compartment. But there were matters of import to be discussed. He said, "I watched the loading and I saw the plane take off. There is nothing more I can do."

Saito sipped delicately at the green tea. "You know, I was furious at you when this all started; most of us in *Kugatsu* were ready to finish you."

Watanabe nodded. "It was a gamble that was necessary. If I had informed the *Kugatsu*, there would have been long periods of soul-searching; I could not afford to waste the time. Tac Okomoto formulated the plan, and the triumvirate of the *Hitori shinzo mittsu* gave the approval and allocated the funds. I feel sure that the *Kugatsu* would have never been able to give total approval."

Saito said, "Well, that is all in back of us and the *Kugatsu* is in accord. It will be a demonstration, once and for all, that we should have won the war."

Watanabe looked at his watch and said, "In thirty hours history will be corrected. Then we can all take a rest. I think we have earned one."

Saito looked out the window. The train was picking up speed as it slipped out of Osaka and began the climb towards Tokyo. "I do not intend to raise questions, Watanabe-san, but you are certain that everything is planned?"

The old man gave a patient smile. "Tac has worked out every detail. All will go as planned."

Saito asked, "And the safety of our own people?"

"The main people from our Institute will be away before the explosion. There is a three-hour time delay once the trigger mechanism is actuated; they will be well clear. Some IFP people, those we could not bring into the plan, will be sacrificed."

Saito said tensely, "There are nearly five thousand people attending the rally from our country."

Watanabe gave a smirk. "Most of them are from the *Gensuikyo* and *Gensuikin*. Little loss. You know, Saito-san, I once spoke to one who served on the Imperial Army's Intelligence Staff. He told me that General Ikeda had three of his top agents working in San Francisco in 1945, and he was willing to leave them there when we dropped the bomb, that is the kind of dedication that wins wars. We must be ready to sacrifice. This will be the final victory. It will end war for ever."

"That is why we do what we must do, Watanabe-san. For the glory of the Empire."

"We have earned our nation's glory."

Saito stood and said, "Then the die is cast." He moved to the bar, picked up a telephone, and tapped out a long series of numbers. Watanabe poured another cup of tea. Saito said, "I'd like a cup too, Watanabe-san. Could you bring it over?"

The old man filled Saito's cup and carried it to the bar. There was no noticeable train movement, even though they were now approaching eighty-five miles per hour. Watanabe looked out at the street lights of a small village in the distance and wished he was back in his own home, but he had to be in Tokyo when the event occurred. He heard Saito saying, "Hello, Clay. How are things in Texas?"

Satellite communications shrank the seven-thousand-mile distance to where a man could whisper, but Clay Morton yelled back, "Hey, good buddy! How's things over there?"

Saito grinned. He was fond of the American and his gruff, unpolished manner. "The plane is gone, Clay. They took off less than an hour ago."

Morton yelled back, "Well, that's just dandy, Isamu. Everything's just fine here. Our people have the 'copter sitting in Frisco waiting to pick up your little old dove of peace, good buddy. I told you I'd take care of everything. I sent that huge Super Stallion, you know the one that can lift an elephant out of shit up to his ass? That's the one."

Saito laughed. "Yes, Clay, but can it lift thirty-one thousand pounds of peace statue?"

"No sweat, good buddy! It's a piece of cake. I sent our best crew from the job in Arizona; they got there yesterday and they're waiting."

"Then that's about all," Saito said, "I can quit worrying."

Morton yelled, "You can bet your boots on that. I'm going up and supervise the whole thing."

"No!" Saito shouted. "No!"

Morton came back, "Hey, take it easy. You asked me to see that your people got that statue in place, and I'm gonna make sure that—"

Saito cut in again. "No, Clay, don't do that, please."

"No trouble. 'Anything for a friend;' ain't that how we always did business?"

Saito's mind was reeling. He pleaded, "Please don't go, Clay. There is no need. Everything will work just fine. You are a very busy man and . . ."

"Hey, good buddy, I've got the plane all set to go; I'll be there in a couple of hours. I'll wait around until that devil arrives, and then I'll make us both look good with them activists. I might even get me some of that anti-nuke nookie while I'm waiting."

Clay Morton could not be easily swayed once he had made a decision. Isamu Saito asked, "Where will you be staying when you get there?"

"Where else? The St. Francis."

"I'll call you there later today."

"Take it easy, good buddy. I'm on the job for both of us."

Saito heard Morton break the connection. He did not like the dead feeling in his stomach.

Watanabe had heard enough to ask, "Is there trouble?"

"I hope not; I pray to God not the trouble I think there could be." Then, almost to himself, he said, "He isn't supposed to be there."

CHAPTER THIRTY-NINE

Charlie Ingersol drove the four-wheel-drive Bronco along the narrow dirt road sliced into the knoll at the north end of the pasture. The road, which was nothing more than a rudimentary emergency path, rose steeply towards the summit of the knoll. A hundred feet from the top, it ended abruptly. Ingersol slammed on the brakes. "This is it," he said. "We walk from here."

Bart Faber was glad to walk. He did not trust Ingersol's driving much more than he liked the man.

At the post office building in Santa Rosa Faber had been escorted to a large basement room where half a dozen people manned telephones, computer terminals and short-wave radio transmitters. Along a wall of banked television monitors, a disorganized team of technicians were making connections and swearing vociferously at wires and switches. It was in that confusion that Faber had met Charlie Ingersol.

The first words from Ingersol had been, "Oh, yeah,

they told me you were coming. We checked you out and you're okay.''

Faber accepted the proffered handshake, wondering how the hell such an arrogant person had risen to any position of authority within the somewhat sensitive CIA. What did Ingersol mean, ''We checked you out?'' *Maybe*, Faber thought, *maybe I'll have Phalanx do some checking on Charlie Ingersol.*

This inauspicious beginning led to nothing better. Ingersol resented this outsider in his operation, even if it was at the behest of the Speaker of the House of Representatives. Ingersol had resented bringing in customs and immigration, too, but the mechanics of examining the baggage and effects of thousands of arrivals for the peace rally was beyond the capabilities of the Agency people in the San Francisco area. Faber did not like the condescending manner of the CIA man, but then he disliked the manner of most professional intelligence workers, who seemed more dedicated to insuring their own retirement than to their jobs.

After establishing what Faber knew of the most dangerous aspect of the operation, Ingersol explained what precautions had been taken to prevent the stolen nuclear weapon being smuggled into the country, at least by any participants arriving for the rally from Japan and Korea. Every piece of luggage, every sleeping bag large enough to hold the weapon was examined and x-rayed. There was a network of Geiger counters installed around the perimeter of the rally site, so if the weapon had been slipped past the arrival inspections—''like in the trunk of one of those Jap cars arriving at Oakland every day''—the device would be detected as soon as it entered the rally grounds.

Ingersol then asked Faber to accompany him for a look at the location.

They had driven south from Santa Rosa to Cotati, then east to the farm being loaned to the organizers. Ingersol said, "You know, Father, this area used to be known as the Egg Capital of the World. I hope those fuckers don't turn it into the scrambled egg of the world."

Faber was quickly tiring of Ingersol's calling the peace activists "fuckers;" after this mess was over he might sit Charlie Ingersol down and try to clarify some facts of life.

Now, at the end of the road, Ingersol and Faber climbed out of the vehicle. Across the hood, Ingersol said, "I've got to hike up to the top; you can come if you want."

"I'll come."

The climb took a full five minutes in the bright, noon-time sun, and both men were damp with perspiration by the time they reached the summit. Below them spread a two-hundred-acre meadow that was showing preparations for the huge population that would be immigrating to the "Field of Peace" in the next few hours. There were groupings of large Army field tents to serve as first aid stations, and round, galvanized stock water tanks were scattered around to supply drinking water. Ingersol said, "The fuckers'll probably go swimming in 'em." At other locations were collections of portable toilets. Ingersol joked, "There are five hundred crappers out there. Now, just figure, three hundred thousand people here for ten hours and each one uses the john twice, that's six hundred thousand trips to the pottie, and that comes out to sixty thousand an hour or one thousand a minute. Those fuckers had better do their business in thirty seconds each, or somebody's gonna be pissing their pants. It ought to be fun."

Bart Faber had nearly reached his level of tolerance with Charlie Ingersol. He said, "Why didn't they simply get more facilities?"

"Look, Father Faber, I'm out here to try and find out who the shit is going to make the grandstand play with an armed nuclear weapon; I don't give a shit if all those dirt-head hippies burst their bladders."

Ingersol turned and looked up at a huge pad of concrete perched at the peak of the knoll. He said, "This is what I'm worried about."

Faber looked at the pedestal on which the statue Yamabato would finally rest after its trip from Japan. "What worries you?"

"If you were wanting to put something on display, wouldn't this be just the right place?"

Faber studied the concrete pad and imagined Yamabato perched there majestically looking down on the gathering of demonstrators. From what Faber knew of the nuclear weapon that had been stolen, it would be too small to be seen from the meadow. He gave that opinion.

"Think, man! There'll be three hundred thousand yahoos down there all just aching to make some great statement. So they can't see all of the gory details; if someone tells them there's a bomb up here and that the big bad United States government is responsible, then they're gonna raise shit. There'll be television and photographers who can get in close with their long lenses, and everything will show up on the big screens down there." Ingersol pointed halfway down the knoll, where workmen were putting the final touches on the scaffolding that would be the platform for the speakers and the rock-and-roll performers who would be entertaining. In addition to the massive speakers and microphones and wires, there were two outdoor television screens that would be used to bring the image of the performers closer to the crowd. Faber could imagine the millions of people who would be watching on national and international television. He looked back at the slab of concrete and tried to remember the configuration of Raion's Yamabato. He thought he could place the claws right at the bottom and they would make a lovely cradle for the bomb. It would be an awesome sight.

Then, unwanted, another image came to Faber's mind— a vision of the bomb exploding with three hundred thousand people all standing within two or three thousand feet. Horror gave an ugly twist inside of his stomach.

Ingersol was speaking, but Faber did not hear the words. He asked the CIA man to repeat what he had said.

"I said: I'm gonna have to get guards up here. We'll have to stop them before they can get it in place."

Faber nodded absently; his own mind was creating an obscene scenario that was almost beyond comprehension.

Ingersol said, "Let's get back to the command post. I've gotta get some bodies up here."

Faber was looking out over the meadow. Now semi-trailer trucks were hauling in equipment to be set up for the rock bands to use, and access aisles were being created with long stretches of rope attached to fence posts. Even some early arrivals were beginning to stake out their turf down close to the speakers' platform.

Faber said, "Look, Charlie, I'd like to hike down. I want to see something."

Ingersol checked his watch with obvious impatience. "Look, *Padre*, I gotta keep to a schedule. Now I don't have to play wet nurse to you just because some fuckin' congressman likes you."

Faber grated, "I don't need a wet nurse, Ingersol. You take off; I'll be back in Santa Rosa when I get there."

Ingersol was irritated that he had been unable to bluff Faber, but there was no way that any government employee would willingly incur the wrath of the Speaker. He said to Faber, "See that big van coming down the road?" Faber nodded. Ingersol said, "I'll pick you up there."

With a nod of acknowledgment, Faber began to work his way down the steep knoll. Halfway down he stopped and looked back towards the summit; he could still see the edge of the concrete pad. He worked his way around the chaotic main-stage area, and when he reached the flat part of the meadow he looked back up again. It was as he had suspected: The base that had been prepared for Yamabato was still in a line of sight.

For the next five minutes, he worked his way around the meadow and confirmed what he had feared: If any explosive device was ignited up at the statue, all of the three hundred thousand people would be exposed. If a nuclear weapon was exploded, mass death would result.

He met Ingersol at the rendezvous but he did not climb into the Bronco. He walked to the driver's side and asked, "Have any of you given any thought to the possibility of that weapon exploding?"

Ingersol leaned forward against the steering wheel. With no effort to hide his exasperation, he replied, "No way, Father. That thing needs a trigger. They didn't get one."

"Suppose they had one from some other source?"

Ingersol looked disgusted. "Look, *Padre*, you can't simply go to a True Value and buy a trigger for a nuclear device."

"Just suppose."

"Well, we're talking about radicals, but they're peace radicals. These are their own people who are coming to this rally. Shit, they'd have to be crazy to set off a nuke here!"

"And people who steal nuclear weapons are sane? Think about it."

Faber walked around the Bronco and climbed into the passenger seat. Ingersol gunned the gas as he said, "Shit! All I needed today was some stupid suggestion like that. I think *you're* crazy, Father. What do you think about that?"

Faber lit a cigarette. He said, "I don't give a shit what you think, Ingersol."

CHAPTER FORTY

Clay Morton fit into the St. Francis with ease. The people at the front desk knew him, the people in the restaurants and bars knew him, and the people in room service knew him. Morton used the St. Francis frequently, especially when he was needed on some nuclear power project along the northern part of the West Coast. Morton liked San Francisco and loved the varied, excellent cuisine unique to the city.

But this trip was different; this time his mission held no promise of pleasure. He was doing a job that was repugnant. He had not told Isamu Saito that he did not want to take part in the preparations for the World Peace Rally; friends did not slight friends that way. When Saito had asked Morton to provide transportation for the stupid peace statue, Morton had not hesitated. He had pulled a company helicopter and crew out of Mexico and sent them to San Francisco, and had sent two excellent—and highly paid—engineers up from Houston just to be on hand if needed. Making the biggest sacrifice of all, he himself was pitching in as the ultimate backstop against anything that might go awry. Morton also harbored a fear that some news types might spot him. The last thing he wanted in life was to get credit for supporting the anti-nuclear movement; years of carefully orchestrated hostility to the nuclear protesters might be erased by one innocent comment on a major network or in one of the big daily newspapers.

Morton had guessed that Saito had become involved for Japanese political reasons; it was not Morton's place to question Saito's motives, because the two men meant so much to each other. But Morton still could not like what he was doing. That was one reason he was not looking forward to the visit from the government man who had called for an appointment and was now coming up to Morton's suite; to Morton's mind, government people were the same kind of whores as journalists.

Coming out of the elevator, Charlie Ingersol said to Bart Faber, "You don't have to come with me, you know. This will just take a couple of minutes; you could wait downstairs in the lobby."

Bart Faber would have liked nothing better than to cut loose from Charlie Ingersol, but there were still things he had to learn about the way things would be handled during the rally.

Faber had not recognized Clay Morton's name until Ingersol remarked that Morton was in nuclear power; Faber remembered that he had read about Morton being an adversary of the anti-nuke movement. Morton helping out with the World Peace Rally? Very strange. Faber repeated what he had told Ingersol twice before; "I'll just tag along."

The door to Morton's suite opened almost immediately after Ingersol pressed the buzzer; Morton's first words were: "You have identification?"

Ingersol produced a CIA I.D. and Morton looked surprised. He said, "Must be some big doings if the Agency has people on this. 'Come in and let's jaw about it."

Bart Faber was uncomfortable because Ingersol neglected to introduce him, and Morton seemed satisfied with the one I.D. card. Morton poured himself a bourbon and water while Ingersol opted for coffee; Faber passed on anything.

The three men sat at the mahogany table in the alcove of the living room. Morton encouraged Faber to go ahead and smoke. "Be my guest."

Ingersol, stirring his coffee, came to the point. "We understand that your company is taking the job of transporting this statue out to the peace rally. Is that right?"

"Well," Morton drawled, "We ain't exactly *takin' the job*. A good friend of mine in Japan asked for some help, and so we're sorta using some of our equipment and talent. That's really all we're doin'."

Ingersol said, "But it *is* your helicopter and it *is* your manpower, and you *are* here in person. So your company is involved."

Morton was not in the habit of being subservient to government employees. "Now listen, boy. I guess you still realize that you work for us, for 'we the people.' You remember that, do you? Now why don't you quit wasting my good tax dollars and get to the fucking point."

Faber rather liked seeing Charlie Ingersol cowed, but he was beginning to wonder what had happened to the slick operatives that had once made the CIA so effective. Ingersol seemed to want to bristle, but he backed off and said, "We'd like some help from you and your people."

Morton snapped, "What help, boy?"

Ingersol said, "I can't go into too many of the details. We'd like a couple of minutes alone with that statue."

Morton sat back. "I ain't got no control over that sort of thing, Mr. Ingersol. All we're doing is picking it up and putting it down. You've come to the wrong man for what you need.''

Faber was pleased that Morton had stopped using ''boy'' when referring to Ingersol; both of the other men were being a bit too aggressive, but Faber decided to let the scene play itself out.

Ingersol said, ''Well, the truth is, Mr. Morton, we need a couple of minutes between the airport to the rally site. If you could just put the statue on the ground for a couple of minutes—''

Morton said, ''Are you fucking crazy, boy? The whole world's going to be watching that transfer!''

Ingersol said nothing.

Morton calmed himself and said, ''Why don't you tell me what your problem is; maybe I can think of something.''

Ingersol struggled with the decision; finally he said to Morton, ''There's a possibility there might be some radioactive material in that statue. We want to check it for radiation, that's all.''

Morton tossed down his drink and walked to the bar to pour another. ''Look, I don't know what you and your friend here are up to . . .'' He interrupted himself to look at Faber. ''Just who the hell are you? I never did catch your name.''

Ingersol jumped in. ''His name is Bart Faber. He's helping me out with this problem. Now, what were you saying, Mr. Morton?''

Morton had poured a healthy belt of liquor and added water as he said, ''Well, I think I can be of some assistance. I've been around the nuclear business for a long time, and I can tell you this: You can bet that there is radioactive material in the fuckin' statue.''

Ingersol's eyes brightened as he glanced at Faber with victory on his face. Morton walked back and sat down as he said, ''From what I understand, that statue was made in Hiroshima, by a sculptor who has done a lot of work in the Peace Park. This sculptor has got to be one of them raging radicals, and I'll put dollars to donuts that he used scrap metal collected near the blast area. Shit, man, just about any piece of steel in Hiroshima is laced with alpha, beta and gamma particles. It'll be a couple of hundred years before you'll be able to take normal readings in that city."

Charlie Ingersol's face showed his disappointment.

Bart Faber had little liking for Charlie Ingersol, but he did respect the CIA man's job. He said, "I had the opportunity to see that statue while it was being built a couple of months ago. The sculptor did have a whole warehouse of old metal that he was using to make the skeletal frame before he poured the concrete."

Morton asked, "You saw it before the pour? Tell me, what did it look like he was using: re-bar?"

Faber replied, "There was some reinforcement bar, and quite a bit of strap steel that he cut with a torch for other supports."

"That's it, then. First, the re-bar could be old stuff and could have picked up radiation from the steelyard, and that other stuff was just what I said, junk from buildings destroyed in the 1945 blast. They'd still be giving off a goodly bit of radiation."

As Faber glanced at Ingersol he saw a change in the CIA man's face; it was as if he had made a major discovery. Just then the telephone rang, and Morton stood, saying, "I'll take that in the other room. Have some more coffee." Morton left.

Faber asked, "What are you thinking about now, Charlie?"

"I just had an idea. Let me work with it for a couple of minutes."

In the master bedroom of the suite, with the door closed for privacy, Morton picked up the phone. It was Isamu

Saito calling from Tokyo. With quick platitudes out of the way, Saito said, "I'm calling about you being up there, Clay. I don't think it's a good idea."

"I don't think any of this whole peace rally is a good thing, good buddy, but I'm here, and I'm going to see that things go right."

"But something bad could happen."

"The whole damned thing is bad, Isamu."

Saito probed, "You could be hurt. I do not want that, my friend."

"I'm not going to get hurt by those shitheads. I'm riding the copter out there, and we'll drop off their piece of shit, and I'll come back here to the St. Francis and find out if I can get laid. That's my plan."

Saito asked, "Then you will not stay at the rally site?"

"I'll be forty miles away from those pagans and their concrete god. Don't worry about that."

Saito pleaded, "You promise?"

"You can bet your ass."

There were a few more platitudes before they finished. After hanging up the phone, Morton stood there for a moment of contemplation. Why on earth was Saito so concerned? It was not Morton's style to delve into Isamu Saito's motivations, but this was the first time in all of their years of business that Morton had not been able to understand Saito's actions.

Ingersol and Faber were standing when Morton returned to the living room. Ingersol said, "We've got to be running, Mr. Morton. Thanks for your help."

The abruptness of the departure pushed Morton slightly off balance, but he recovered. "I didn't do anything, boys. I just think you are on a wild goose chase if you're trying to find radioactive material in that statue. I'll guarantee it's there."

As soon as the door closed behind them, Morton decided to quit worrying about Isamu Saito; his Japanese friend had frequently played the part of a worrier. This was just a particularly bad case of the jitters. He decided to go out for lunch.

Down in the lobby, Ingersol and Faber came out of the elevator. The CIA man said, "I'm onto something, Father. That visit with that old fart was worth the trouble."

Faber asked, "What did he say? The whole thing seemed like an exercise in futility."

"It pulled things together for me," Ingersol said. "It dawned on me that the Japs are using the statue as a smoke screen. There's nothing in that fucking thing; it's being used to throw us off the track!"

Faber looked skeptical. "There's no reason to think that, Charlie. I still feel they're going to sneak that weapon into the rally site and show it to the people." Faber kept private his fear that the weapon might just be exploded in some fanatical gesture of hate for America.

"I'll tell you what they did; I just know it. They disassembled the shell into small pieces and snuck it past our customs inspections. Shit, man, they've brought in rock-and-roll sound gear, they've brought in crates of stuff for displays; it would have been easy. So they figure if we concentrate all of our efforts on that statue, then we'll miss them bringing it in some other way. We've been going kind of gentle on them because, sure as hell, if we don't, they'll begin screaming that we're harassing them because they are anti-nuke people. But, by God, we're going to drop the hammer on them." Then, filled with excitement, he said, "You ready to go?"

"I think I'll break off here, Charlie. There's not much I can do at this point."

Ingersol was obviously relieved to be ridding himself of Bart Faber. "Come out to my vehicle and I'll give you one of the all-area passes. You'll need it to get past security."

At the Bronco, Ingersol gave Faber a plastic laminated card issued by the Department of Justice that identified the bearer as being on official business. After Ingersol sped off on his new quest, Faber went back into the hotel and rented a car. Faber had his own plans for the rest of the day.

CHAPTER FORTY-ONE

Bart Faber stood at the south end of the meadow, looking north towards the knoll and the slab of concrete that was awaiting Raion's Yamabato. He could not purge from his mind the grim vision of an explosion that could kill thousands of peace-loving people. From where he stood, he estimated the distance to the knoll at just under twenty-five hundred feet. The death toll could be disastrous.

He had left the Morton meeting and driven to the Bohemian Club for a briefing with the Speaker and Father Venturi. Both men found it difficult to accept the notion that any peace activists might be willing to sacrifice such large numbers of their own. Faber argued that Tac Okomoto and his cadre of fanatics were far from being peace activists; they were Japanese militarists with an evil sense of mission. Faber reminded them that he had met these people, that he had come to know them and that their mentality was so distant from modern civilization that few could comprehend how mass murder was justified in the name of a political statement.

The Speaker said, "Father Faber, I trust you. If you give me the word, I'll order that the statue be banned from the rally. For God's sake, we're talking about a catastrophe of monumental proportions. Or I could meet privately with Clay Morton and have his helicopter drop the damned thing into San Francisco Bay. It could be passed off as an unfortunate accident."

Faber said, "I think Charlie Ingersol is right, when he says the main body of activists would like nothing more than some obstruction from our government. We could end up with a riot on our hands."

The speaker retorted, "I'd rather try to handle a riot than face the grim prospect of a mass funeral."

Father Venturi said, "There are still about eighteen hours until the statue is to be delivered. The order to abort the delivery can be given at the last minute. Do you think you can be sure by that time, Father Faber?"

"I'll try," was all that Bart Faber could offer; he hoped his voice sounded less doubtful than his mind about the possibility of success.

After leaving the Bohemian Club, he had driven to Cotati, then out to the rally site. The traffic was beginning to build as early participants began arriving. Some were treating the event as a gala happening, to be attended merely for the joy of being a part of history. But most of the patient people in the creeping cars wore the solemn faces of those individuals who were joining hands with other citizens of the world to stop the nuclear madness. Some people were traveling in tour buses, some were packed into tiny economy cars, and some were riding in vans of every description. Peace! The word and symbol were displayed as graffiti on the sides of the vans, and on banners tied to the sides of the buses. The universal sign of greeting was two fingers raised in a V.

It tore at Faber's heart to think that these people of goodwill were completely oblivious of the threat that might be waiting for them.

He stood there at the edge of the meadow as the sun began to make longer shadows in the late afternoon, wishing he was watching the demonstrators leave twenty-four hours hence rather than put themselves unknowingly into danger. He wanted to greet all of them and extend his love to them, to let them know that what they were doing was right, as right as anything anyone had ever done for his fellow man. He was charged with seeing to their safety, and he would not fail them.

Perhaps, he thought, he had manufactured the threat in his own mind. He realized that he felt great hostility towards the Institute For Peace, and the reason was not very attractive in the mind of a priest: A woman. Tori Ito. He wanted to think he did not love her as a husband loves a wife but, rather, as a brother loves a sister; he had tried to convince himself of that, but he had been honest with his confessor and both agreed that Faber might be experiencing the torment of doubt known to many priests, especially in the current atmosphere of the Church. He would have to struggle with that again, soon, because Charlie Ingersol's computers reported that Tori Ito was manifested on the cargo flight bringing Raion and his statue from Japan. Bernie Eby's name was also on the passenger list, and that might be a good omen; Eby might be able to supply some answers.

He had never thought to see Tori Ito again. He had begun a dozen letters to her, saying that he hoped she would find happiness with Tac Okomoto, but it was difficult for him to lie to her. At least Tac Okomoto was not coming on the same plane with Tori Ito; that would make the reunion less harrowing. Had Okomoto been coming,

one of them would get smacked in the face; Faber knew
he would win that encounter.

So, Faber confirmed his plan. He would go to meet the
plane coming from Japan and face Tori Ito. He would also
enlist Bernie Eby's help.

Now, if it would all just work out that way.

CHAPTER FORTY-TWO

The Japan Air Lines 747 cargo plane made landfall just north of Half Moon Bay on the California coast, then darted across San Francisco Bay to begin its final approach into Oakland International Airport. JAL officials had made arrangements to use the Federal Express maintenance base at Oakland to handle the arrival of Yamabato, because San Francisco International was pressed to capacity with commercial and charter flights bringing in people for the rally.

Tori Ito had fallen asleep half an hour before the plane began its descent, and the change in cabin pressure awakened her; she felt depressed and tired. During the flight, Tac Okomoto had sat silently with a grim look on his face and he had rebuffed her frequent efforts at conversation. Early in the flight, she had accepted the pilot's invitation to come and watch a 747 being flown; Tac had rudely refused. He had silently accepted her offer of one of the box lunches that had been provided, but that was all.

She had finally been able to fall asleep because she had

reached a decision about their relationship. She had, with some joy, welcomed Tac back into her life. She had returned to his bed, she had resumed her place in his shadow, she had worked desperately to put back into her life the love she had shared with Tac in the warm, comfortable cocoon of the peace movement. But that cocoon had burst open. Tac did not now seem determined to end the world's military madness; he had turned violent. On one occasion, he had beaten her badly enough for her to remain in seclusion for a week. He had not apologized or even been tender about the injuries he had inflicted on her. He had contended the fault was hers; that she had earned the beating because she had been unfaithful.

Tac had insisted that she sell her home in Tokyo, the one tangible thing that remained of her family, and she had begun the steps needed to do so. He had said they would be needing the money because he was going underground again, but this time he would be taking her along. She had, for a short time, felt that the two of them running together would revitalize their love, that the underground world would be romantic. But that hope had vanished, because she sensed that Tac was planning something obscene at the World Peace Rally, something more than simply proving that he had stolen a nuclear weapon. She feared the man she had once loved.

Well, she had had enough. From a feeling of loyalty, she would see this trip through to the end, but to retain her sanity and dignity she would be done with the man she had loved so dearly.

She did not know what Tac's plans were. She had tried to find out from Bernie Eby, but he was just as ignorant as she. She suspected that Susumu Kato knew the details, but Kato saw Tori as Tac's woman, and she could not even get him to talk to her.

She had no firm plans as to how she would sever her ties to Tac Okomoto; she would let it happen naturally.

She did want to see things through to the end of the rally, because she had been there two years previously when the idea of the mass rally was first discussed; she felt she was a part of this statement to the world.

Tac leaned forward in his seat and peered out the window. He gave a sideways glance at Tori and she shuddered at the look in his eyes; it was hate.

The 747 banked and turned on its final approach; a Fasten Seat Belts/No Smoking sign flickered on at the front of the cabin.

On the ground, in the shadows alongside the huge hangar of Federal Express, Bart Faber was trying his best to be unobtrusive. He wore a set of FedEx mechanic's coveralls and carried a clipboard.

He had gained access to the hangar area with the I.D. card given him by Charlie Ingersol. Once inside the security perimeter, he had found the shift supervisor and used the card again to get permission to observe the arrival of the JAL freighter. The shift supervisor had been doubtful about Faber's authority, and had called the Justice Department number on the card. Verification of Faber's right of entry was given quickly. The FedEx man had no way of knowing that the call had been automatically reswitched to the CIA command station in the basement in Santa Rosa. The supervisor offered his help. As they went to the locker room to get a pair of coveralls for Faber, the man asked, "You FBI?"

Faber replied, "Nope, DEA."

"I should'a figured. Them hippies gonna be bringing one big load of shit with them, right?"

"We'll see."

So Faber had the run of the hangar area. As the 747 taxied toward the unloading equipment, he moved closer but kept in the shadows.

The freighter was chocked into place, three JAL crew

vans pulled up, and workers, along with men in business suits, jumped out. The Federal Express cargo people would handle the mechanical aspects of the unloading; the Japanese Air Lines people were on hand to see that nothing went wrong.

When the nose was elevated, Faber could see four people waiting to be lowered to the ground. He immediately spotted Tori Ito. A change had come to her once lovely, charming face. He saw sadness and pain in her eyes, and a pathetic slackness to the mouth that had once laughed with cheer. Faber realized at that moment that he had nothing to fear from his relationship with Tori Ito; he was feeling a true friend's pain. It came to him that the two-month interval had had a cathartic effect on any romance he might have felt; all he wanted was happiness for a friend.

Bernie Eby was standing beside Tori. Eby looked more dissipated than before, but Faber marked that off to a tiring flight and probably a considerable amount of booze. Susumu Kato was standing back from the edge of the cargo door, but where was Raion? Suddenly, Faber boiled with anger as he recognized Tac Okomoto: *How did he get here? He's not on the manifest.*

As the passengers were brought down to ground level, a long grey Lincoln limousine pulled up and parked less than ten feet from where Faber stood. The back window on the driver's side rolled down and Clay Morton's head popped out. He called to Faber, "Hey, boy! What you up to?"

Faber darted to the car. He didn't want Morton yelling and attracting attention. "What are *you* doing here, Mr. Morton?"

"Aw, I was just heading over to the old Airdrome side of the field to see if my copter crew is ready for the big shindig. How about it? What are you looking for?"

Faber replied, "Just watching."

Morton opened the door. "Good man. Gotta keep our eyes on those inscrutable Japs. Jump in."

Faber did not want people to begin wondering about him standing there, so he climbed in beside Morton. As soon as the door was closed, Morton asked, "Now, what the hell's going on? Where's your partner?"

Faber answered, "Charlie Ingersol is not my partner. I don't know where he is. I'm just here to take a look at what's going on. That's all."

"Right," Morton drawled. "You just happen to be in the area and just happen to be dressed like a mechanic. Right?"

"Think what you like, Mr. Morton." Faber was paying little attention. He was watching the process of getting ready to lower Yamabato.

"Why don't you level with me, son? Just what the shit are you up to?"

Faber pulled his eyes away from the activity at the plane and studied the man sitting back in the plush seat. Faber guessed he had twelve, possibly fourteen hours to stop a possible disaster from happening. He knew he needed help, perhaps some extensive help. Phalanx had imported three operatives, secreted at the Newman Club on the Berkeley campus. They would pitch in when needed. But the other three Phalanx operatives would only be added manpower, not the type of high-powered influence represented by Clay Morton. The Speaker of the House could produce an Army division if that was needed—but what Faber needed was strength allied with a delicate, sensitive hand.

Clay Morton had earlier scoffed at the suggestion that Tac Okomoto and those controlling him had decided to set off a nuclear explosion just to bring attention to their claim that Japan should have won the war. Faber was going to have to handle the difficult task of convincing Morton otherwise.

Faber asked, "Do you have time to listen to a crazy idea?"

Morton gave a quiet laugh. "Son, I've spent my life listening to crazy ideas; they're the only kind that make any money."

Faber smiled. "You'll not make any money with this idea."

"I don't have to make money all of the time. Tell me your story."

Faber began. It took only a few minutes to capsule all of it: the dissension within the peace groups, the startling revelation that the World War II Japanese were intending to bomb San Francisco with their own A-bomb, the mystery of Tac Okomoto's vanishing and, finally, the theft of the nuclear artillery shell in Korea.

Morton cut in. "What you talking about, boy? Have we lost a nuke weapon?"

"It was being kept at a Korean Army post; our people did their job, but the Koreans screwed up. No matter who dropped the ball, someone has a nuclear weapon. They might have a way to arm it."

Faber summarized the other events that had contributed to forming his fears; the mysterious death and fire in the city of Hagi, and, most importantly, the sudden reappearance of Tac Okomoto.

Morton sat for a time, digesting what he had been told. Finally he said, "You know, son, I've got a friend over in Japan who is like a brother to me. I'm gonna get into this fuckin' mess just to make sure that he's not embarrassed. You know, I think he has a suspicion that something might be going wrong with this stupid rally, because he tried to keep me from getting involved. God bless him for that. But I think the two of us together can get this sorted out and that we can make the rally come off okay."

Faber was watching the unloading process.

Morton added, "Now, let's just sit back here and think this thing through."

The pallet holding Yamabato was being lifted by crane onto a flatbed truck. Morton patted Faber's shoulder as he said, "Relax, son. I know where that truck's going: over to the old Oakland Airdrome where my helicopter is parked. You see, son, we've still got a few cards up this old man's sleeve. That's the way I like to play poker."

Faber was studying the activity and the people. Eby and Okomoto moved quickly away from the unloading process and jumped into one of the waiting JAL crew vans. Just as the van was pulling away from the crowd, Tori Ito strolled absently from the parking ramp towards a dark area. She seemed in deep concentration. Faber opened the car door and started out as Morton ordered, "Hold it! I think I've got an idea . . ."

Faber was out the door and did not hear the rest of the sentence. He ran easily and caught up with her in the shadows.

"Tori."

Bart Faber had learned in an early seminary class on human relations that emotions are a strange quirk in man's nature, that there are times in life when one wants desperately to see someone and yet dreads the moment of meeting. That confusing emotion now gripped him.

She stopped walking, paused as she recognized the voice, then turned. The beaten look in her eyes was not what he wanted to see in this woman; he wanted to see happiness.

"Hello, Father," she said with a lifeless voice. "I didn't think I would ever see you again."

He felt barren of words. Before he could speak, she said, "You left me quite alone, you know."

He said, weakly, "It was the only thing I could do."

Some life came into her voice. "Oh, no, Father Faber,

there were several things you could have done besides just running away.''

He tried to counter by saying, "I had to leave; I feared for your life.''

She snapped, "So you condemned me to death. You talk with the logic of your infamous Inquisitors, Father. You also used me.''

"In the beginning, I did," he admitted, then added, "but I also wanted to help you.''

She yelled: "You deserted me!''

From behind him came voices as Susumu Kato heard the scream and began to run to the grassy area where the pair stood.

Quickly, Faber pleaded, "Please, Tori, I must talk to you!''

She spat out, "We have talked . . . too much.''

She made a move to go past him, but he grabbed her by the shoulders and their eyes met. Hers did not speak with the hate spilling out of her mouth. He felt that she wanted to say something tender, something that would bridge the angry gap between them.

Before he could speak, a fist hit into his shoulder. As he swung around, he caught another fist on his chin. Kato was throwing punches at a furious rate. Faber ducked and flicked out a backhand that sent the smaller Kato reeling. Suddenly there was a crowd forming around the two men and Tori Ito as Faber made ready to handle another onslaught.

Faber saw Clay Morton elbowing his way through the crowd that consisted mainly of JAL employees jabbering in their native tongue so rapidly that Faber could not interpret what they were saying.

A vicelike grip closed on his right arm, and he turned to see the Federal Express shift supervisor standing beside him saying, "Take it easy. I'll handle this.''

Faber looked around, but Tori Ito was gone. The supervisor was saying, "Now listen, knock it off!"

Susumu Kato made to launch another charge at Faber, and the supervisor shouted, "Listen up, shithead. You're on my turf now. This man works for me, so git! Go back to what you have to do!"

The angry Japanese did not like to be spoken to in such a manner, but one of the JAL officials hissed out some quick commands and the crowd began a reluctant retreat. Kato followed.

Clay Morton came up to Faber just as the supervisor was releasing his arm. Morton said, "Good job."

The supervisor replied, "Thanks, Mr. Morton. I never have liked those fuckin' Japs."

Morton turned to Faber. "Son, you sure do know how to attract flies. Now, let's skedaddle on away from here and get to our thinking. First, you gotta tell me what all of this fracas was about."

CHAPTER FORTY-THREE

Dawn was breaking over the meadow. Bart Faber stood glaring at Tac Okomoto on the concrete slab that was awaiting Yamabato. Bernie Eby stood close by, trying to lessen the tensions; his efforts had been useless so far and he dreaded the next few minutes.

Faber had arrived well before the sky had grayed; Okomoto and Eby had come just as light was beginning to add color to the day.

Faber had not slept; he had spent the night with Clay Morton in the drafting room of the Simons Engineering Company in downtown San Francisco. Morton had been busy with calculator and sketch pads; Faber had supplied such answers as he knew about the statue. Just after five in the morning, Morton had finally switched off the fluorescent lamp over the drawing table and said, "There's no question about it; there's a fucking bomb in that piece of shit they call a peace memorial. The bastards are either going to leave it there and worry the hell out of our government, or they're going to explode it like some devil's fireworks display.''

Faber asked, ''Is there any way we can tell when it's going to blow?''

''Well, son, we could get them to tell us; that would be the easiest way.''

Faber grinned sourly. ''I doubt they'd be inclined to give us that.''

''No, but we don't need their help.'' Morton added, ''I sure wish we could get a drink in this place.''

Faber was sure he could not handle a drink after the dozens of cups of coffee they had drunk during the night; he waited for Morton to continue. Morton ran his fingers through his short-cut white hair and said, ''No, sir, we don't need their help. Look at this.''

Faber looked again at Morton's sketches. ''This one here.'' Morton pointed to the largest rendering of Yamabato. ''You see, from what you said about the placement of that cradle, the one that was used to hold the shell in place while the concrete was poured, well, it's about twenty inches deep inside. If they are planning to initiate the explosion by remote control, they'll have to be within a hundred feet to push a radio signal into the trigger device. Now, unless we're dealing with a bunch of Khomeini suicide squads, there must be a timing device to allow the guy with the transmitter to get his ass well away from the explosion.''

''I wouldn't discount the suicide aspect. Remember the kamikaze pilots during the war?''

''Well,'' Morton said, ''We can handle that, too, by just putting a sniper near the statue and having him shoot the ass off anyone within a hundred feet. Okay?''

''That's one aspect covered.''

''But they could have some kind of a device that initiates the timer once the statue is set in place. Remember, there's that plug at the bottom that will fit into the hole in the mounting slab.''

Faber said, ''There's that crack that we spotted.''

''Yea,'' Morton agreed. ''But when I called my engineer out at the Oakland Airdrome, he took a look and said it just looked like a flaw in the concrete. No wires, no switches, just a crack.''

Faber asked, ''What's left?''

Morton answered, ''Very simple. We just put a radio scanner in our helicopter and wait to pick up some signal that might be the trigger impulse. Of course, we'll hook it to the 'copter's computer. This won't be any simple home-use scanner that people use to listen in on police calls. I'm talking about a full-spectrum scanner that will catch just about anything that squeaks.''

''Then what?''

''Then, my boy, we either take the damned thing out and dump it into the ocean, or we clear the area and let the thing pop. It'll only yield about one kiloton, and the California countryside can handle that. After the rally we can chop into that concrete lump of death and take the thing out, and no one will be the wiser.''

''Why not do that right now, before the damned thing is taken out to the rally?''

Morton stood and put on his coat. ''I'll tell you, Bart. For a smart guy, you sure are innocent. We go cutting into that statue, and the Japs will begin screaming bloody murder about us desecrating their idol. There's no sweat. I've been around the nuclear business all of my business life, and I guarantee you that we will have time to act. Trust me.''

Faber walked beside Morton as they left the engineering office. He said, ''What choice do I have but to trust you?

''None, son, none at all. Now I want you to go out to that rally site again and I want you to inspect that hole in the slab. They might just put some kind of a device down there that could initiate the timer as we set old Yamabato in place. You need to check it out.''

Faber offered, "I could get Ingersol to put a guard on the slab after I make the inspection.''

Morton said, "If I was you, son, I'd get your friend the Speaker to give that order. Use your friends when you need them. Ingersol isn't going to listen to you; he's convinced the weapon is coming in another way.''

As they parted, Faber said, "Suppose Okomoto has come up with something we haven't thought of?''

Morton had grinned like a wolf. "Then, son, we're all in a lot of trouble.''

Faber had left Morton with the agreement that they would meet at the Oakland Airdrome at nine in the morning. Morton wanted some sleep; Faber knew he could not have handled sleep at that moment.

On the slab, Faber felt rage building as he looked across at Tac Okomoto, because it was very possible that Okomoto had come to deposit the transmitter that would be used to trigger the timer for the bomb.

"You've got a lot of nerve, American," Okomoto yelled across the slab of concrete.

Faber responded calmly, "You're a sick man, Tac Okomoto.''

Bernie Eby pleaded, "Hey, both of you, how about it? There's no reason to get mad at each other.''

Okomoto screamed, "That pig screwed my woman!''

Eby moved closer to Okomoto, saying, "Hey, Tac, that's a rotten thing to say: He's a priest.''

Faber suddenly realized they were all speaking Japanese and that he was understanding and using words and phrases he did not know he knew. He started across the slab, and Eby stepped between the two. "Look! You're acting like a pair of kids. Knock it off!''

Faber stopped within three feet of Eby. "Do you know what's going on with this bunch, Bernie?''

Eby's face showed he was torn between loyalty to a friend and fear of an enemy. He turned and looked at Okomoto, who gave a curt nod granting permission. Eby turned back to Faber and said, "Look, they did steal the nuke weapon in Korea. That might be wrong, but maybe it isn't. All that Tac and his people want to do is to demonstrate the threat to peace . . ." He cut himself off, then added, "That's what Tac wanted me to tell you."

Faber said, "All they're going to do is show it to the people at the rally?"

"Sure, that's all they're going to do—what else?"

"Do you trust them, Bernie?" Faber's question was in English.

Eby hesitated just long enough to contradict his next words: "Sure I trust them."

"You're sure?"

"Look, Bart, I've got a wife and . . ." Eby's face was full of fear. Faber understood. He looked at Okomoto and said, "You're scum, Tac."

Okomoto gave a sardonic grin. "You should learn to relax, Mr. Faber. Believe me, in just a few hours . . ." He looked at his watch and continued. ". . . just nine hours, you and your whore will have all of the answers."

Faber snapped, "Get one thing right in your mind, Okomoto: There was never anything between Tori and me. Believe that!"

Okomoto turned abruptly as he said, "I will believe what is true. In nine hours you will know the truth!" He had taken a few steps before he called to Eby, "Come. We must go."

Eby began to obey, but halted and said to Faber, "I don't know what's going on, Bart. I will tell you to get the hell away from this bunch; they're crazy. He has ruined Tori Ito; don't let him ruin you." Eby ran across the slab and jumped to the ground as he followed Okomoto down the knoll.

Faber watched the pair for a moment, then turned and looked down at the crowd in the meadow below. He guessed there were more than a hundred thousand people encamped on the grass. A cacophony of music was drifting up from hundreds of ghetto blasters that all seemed to be tuned to different pop music stations. It was a poignant sight. In the next couple of hours, another two hundred thousand people would come and join hands to say "End War!" No doubt there would be some joints passed around, too much white wine sipped from bottles hidden in paper bags, and a few incidents of unbridled public sex, but those would not be the essence of the day. Some citizens of the world were going to deliver a message: "Stop!" Faber was proud of these fellow humans. He was equally furious that some madmen were willing to put them at risk.

Faber would not let harm come to them.

The parking ramp in front of the old Oakland Airdrome looked like a helicopter trade show. Near Clay Morton's huge CH53-E cargo transporter a dozen other helicopters were parked, ready to carry television camera crews, peace rally officials and sundry other VIPs to the rally site as Yamabato made the trip to the meadow in Sonoma County.

Clay Morton, wearing a bright orange flight suit, stood with his crew, studying the last-minute details of the flight plan. Bart Faber was with the group.

Morton said to the pilot, "Remember, anything I tell you, do it! If anything happens to me, take your orders from Bart Faber. That's the law for today."

The chief pilot for Clay Morton's company was paid $108 thousand a year to do what Morton told him. So long as there was no threat to life, the man would fly where, when and how Morton ordered. "We'll do the job, sir," the pilot said.

Morton smiled confidently. "I know you will. Let's go."

The flight crew climbed into the cockpit of the Super Stallion and began their preflight checklist. Morton said to Faber, "One more time: Keep in touch. That's why you have that walkie-talkie. We've got to know what's going on."

Faber had had the Speaker use his congressional influence to insure that he would be on the helicopter with Okomoto and the others. He said, "There'll be shit raised when I climb in, but I'll handle that."

Morton looked happy. He was in the middle of busy activity, and that was his lifeblood. He stated, "If you see that Jap do anything that could signal a trigger, you get on that radio to me. If we hear anything, anything at all on our electronic gear, I'll be on to you. We've got to stay in touch, son."

Over their heads, the whine of the helicopter's engines began to build and the rotors started their lazy-looking windmill. Morton said, "I'd better get on board. Take care!"

Impulsively, Faber extended his hand. The old industrialist, shook it sincerely. Faber distrusted everything that Clay Morton stood for, but the two would do the job that had to be done.

Faber turned and ran across the tarmac to a waiting Hughes helicopter. A pert young blonde stood by the entrance ladder with a loading list. The girl seemed to be in her late teens and was wearing a bright yellow T-shirt decorated with a silk-screened image of Yamabato, the logo of the World Peace Rally. Faber gave the girl his name and she looked on the list, then twisted her mouth slightly. "Oh, yes. Mr. Faber . . . you're government, aren't you?"

Faber gave a patient smile and said, "Yes."

"Well, *please* don't do anything unattractive; we're just ordinary people."

Faber grinned. "I'll behave."

Faber climbed into the helicopter and saw Tac Okomoto sitting beside Tori Ito up near the front of the cabin. He took a seat at the rear so that he could keep an eye on Okomoto and still look out and see Yamabato. All of the participating aircraft had their doors locked open to provide camera angles. Across the parking ramp, he could see the cargo copter begin a short roll as it lifted into the sky. Clay Morton was standing in the open door; the old man was watching intently as his plane gained altitude. The hostess entered the cabin and said, "We're going to have to take off now. I'm sorry, but Mr. Eby and Mr. Kato have not arrived."

From the front of the cabin, in stilted English, Okomoto called, "I told you . . . they not coming."

The girl gave a friendly grin. "Oh, that's right. You did say that. Thank you."

As Faber's copter started its engines, all eyes were on Morton's copter. It lifted about a hundred feet into the air, then stabilized for the hoisting operation. From a hatch in the bottom of the Super Stallion, a cable began dropping slowly to where Yamabato lay waiting.

The statue sitting in its wooden frame was draped with a loop of wire rope that spread down under the statue's wings, then spanned the chest of the concrete bird. Hemp ropes secured the harness to the wings. Morton had told Faber that he planned to keep the harness in place after the statue had been set on its pedestal, "Just in case we want to lift him up again. Got it?"

Faber hoped the entire set of precautions initiated by Morton would be unneeded. But, looking across the twelve feet to the front of the cabin, Faber knew there was danger in the person of Tac Okomoto.

To a casual observer, Okomoto looked like any other

glum peace activist; but Faber knew Okomoto was a special case—a man gone mad with a cause, unpredictable, an especially evil enemy. Faber wished desperately to go and talk to Tori Ito. She had seen him when he climbed into the copter, but she had not smiled, and her eyes were vacant. The sight hurt Faber. He pulled his own gaze away and watched as the cables tightened and Yamabato began to rise majestically into the air. Everything was on schedule; Faber hoped that was a good omen.

Yamabato soaring through the bright day was a grand sight. It was carried high enough to be seen for a dozen miles and yet low enough so that it appeared to want to share its message of understanding.

The route sliced across Contra Costa County, then flashed over the waters of San Pablo Bay before it turned northwest at Black Point and headed towards the rally site.

When Morton's helicopter was about to crest a low line of hills east of Cotati, the pilot climbed higher and the statue was dramatically revealed to the meadow. The 342,000 participants at the rally roared a loud, boisterous shout of love.

The heavy metal group that had been filling the time before the noon arrival was drowned out as the screams of happiness paid homage to "Yamabato! Yamabato! Yamabato!"

Looking down at the mass of people in the meadow, Faber grew angrier at Tac Okomoto for having the murderous audacity to scar this celebration of peace. The copter began a rapid descent into a clearing north of the knoll, out of sight of the people attending the rally. Faber was just about to leap to the ground when he was pushed aside by Tac Okomoto, who made it to the ground first. Faber threw a glance back at Tori Ito who was sitting, crying, her head bent down to her knees. He wanted to go to her, but he had an obligation that could not be ignored. He jumped and landed on the ground as he saw Okomoto running up the knoll. Faber ran after him.

Above the knoll, the cargo helicopter eased expertly into position, Morton's engineers on the ground began making hand signals as the hoist lowered Yamabato slowly to the waiting slab.

Jockeying thirty-one thousand pounds of airborne concrete into position seemed, to those watching the spectacle, an impossible task. But in less than a minute, the statue was a mere three feet above the slab. The engineers attached guide ropes and steered Yamabato down the last short distance.

Faber caught up to Okomoto just as the workers were removing the guide ropes. The quick-release hook snapped loudly as the helicopter was freed from its tether.

The workers were so busy they did not notice Faber jump up onto the slab. The voices of the huge crowd were screaming with abandon; the *whop-whop*-ing of the helicopter blades as the craft landed nearby made thinking nearly impossible.

Tac Okomoto had taken out a small calculator and was tapping out numbers with a finger. Faber grabbed him and pulled the man to him; there was arrogant success on Okomoto's face. Faber felt sick.

At that same instant, screaming into the earplug attached to his walkie-talkie, Faber heard Clay Morton imploring: "What's he done? We got a signal!"

Faber yanked at Okomoto's shoulders and demanded, "Tell me! Tell me, you bastard!"

Okomoto gave a smile. "My work is done."

Before Faber could stop him, Okomoto flipped a hand up to his mouth and Faber saw a yellow capsule disappearing between his teeth. In three seconds, Okomoto's body twitched and went limp; he was dead.

Faber let the body drop to the ground and he yelled, as

if Morton could hear the words five hundred feet above, "He did something with a pocket calculator. He's dead!"

"Easy, son, talk lower. You say he's dead? You killed him?"

Faber answered, "He took a pill. What's going on?"

"Look, Bart, we picked up a signal. Now we're picking up a field of clicks; there's a timer running. I don't know how much time we have; but it can't be much."

Faber asked, "What do you want from here?"

Morton ordered, "Tell my men to hook us up again. Tell them to look up for a signal."

Faber ran around the base of Yamabato, found the foreman of the mounting crew, and told him Morton's orders. The man looked up, watched a series of hand signals being given from the copter then yelled, "Okay, lads, it's going back up. Get ready for the hook!"

The people in the crowd were still celebrating the arrival of Yamabato. Faber ran to one of the rally officials and shouted: "Get down there and get on the PA system. Tell them we have to move the statue but that it will be back in a little while."

The official, too young to handle the responsibility and rattled by the excitement of the moment, demanded, "Why are you taking it back?"

Faber summoned up his sternest look as he said, "Do what I tell you. Move!"

Through his earpiece, Clay Morton was saying, "Listen, Bart, I've made a decision. We're going to take this hunk of shit out and dump it in the ocean. That's all we can do. I just hope we clear out of this area before it goes off. If that Jap killed himself, we probably don't have much time."

Faber argued, "He said it would happen at three o'clock!"

"That's what he told you, but I'm not taking any

chances. As soon as we have that thing hooked on, we're leaving.''

Faber pleaded, "I need to come with you."

Morton came back, "Sorry, son. No time."

By then, the ground crew had fastened the hook to the sling. Yamabato began rising back into the sky. There was an ugly murmur beginning in the crowd. Faber could not worry over that; the rally officials would have to make the explanations. He ran down the back of the knoll towards the parked helicopters.

The pilot of the copter that brought Faber to the meadow had shut down his machine. He'd expected an hour or more before he'd start taking VIPs back to the city after the dedication. The pilot called to Faber: "What's up?"

Faber yelled, "There's an emergency."

Tori Ito was sitting on the entrance stairs of the passenger compartment, the small blonde hostess was making a futile effort to comfort her.

Faber stopped in front of the pilot of the copter and yanked out the plastic I.D. card he had been given by Ingersol. He handed it to the pilot, saying, "Read this. I need you to fly me out of here, along with that." He gestured up at Yamabato, which was now free of the slab, being hoisted up into the carrying position. Faber ran back to Tori Ito, who was still crying furiously but was now looking at Faber; he saw hope in her eyes. She stood up.

He took her by the shoulders and said, "Tori, you've got to wait here."

She was sobbing. "What happened?"

"No time, Tori. I'll be back."

She pleaded, "What has Tac done, Bart? Tell me!"

Faber turned to the small blonde. "Take care of her, please. I'll be back."

Tori screamed, "Don't leave me! Not again!"

The blonde began to pull Tori away.

Faber ran back to the pilot and said, "Why aren't you ready? The pilot said, "Yeah, so?"

Faber snapped, "So, I need to be flown out with the other copter. This is an emergency!"

The pilot argued, "Look, mister, I'm paid to fly people back to Frisco. I've got no permission to take this bird anyplace else."

Faber struggled to hold his temper. He calmed his voice and said, "Look, your company will be paid, you won't get in any trouble. I need help!"

Faber's voice had risen just a bit. The pilot said, "You promise no trouble, and you promise payment?"

Faber said, "Agreed."

The pilot answered, "We'll go."

Morton's helicopter carrying Yamabato was out of sight by the time Faber's machine started. But, as his copter lifted above the knoll, they could see Morton and Yamabato heading just a bit south of due west. Faber shouted to his pilot, "Follow them!" The pilot steered west.

Just as Faber's copter was clearing the meadow area, the radio crackled and the CH53-E's pilot radioed: "San Francisco control, this is Stallion Two-four-two. We are declaring an emergency."

The San Francisco controller came back placidly, "Roger Two-four-two. . . . What type of emergency?"

Morton's pilot came back, "Dangerous cargo." The controller demanded clarification. The pilot radioed back, "I'll call you later, Frisco. Out."

The Hughes helicopter was able to fly faster than the Stallion, and, by the time the radio exchange was completed, Faber was within a quarter mile of Morton's plane. Faber pulled the microphone clipped to his lapel and said, "Morton, this is Faber. We're right in back of you."

Looking ahead, Faber saw Morton's bright orange flight suit as Morton leaned out and looked back. The voice came to Faber's earpiece: "Look, son, you can do no good tagging along. We don't know when this little jewel is going to pop. Just get away.''

"I managed to get us into this, Morton, I'm coming."

"Look, Bart, you're risking that copter and the pilot and your own silly ass. Now I can handle this . . . so, scoot!''

Faber's helicopter was nearly alongside Morton's stallion. Faber's pilot asked, "What the hell's going on, mister? We're passing over the coast.''

Faber snapped, "We've got to stay with them. It'll be okay.'' Faber had lied before in his life, but this was the first time the lie had weighed so heavily on him; he wanted to get the pilot safely away, but he felt the need to see the crisis through to the end. They flew on.

They were clearing land over the Point Reyes National Seashore when Morton called over the walkie-talkie, "Damn it, son, back off! I can handle this from here on.''

"What are you going to do?''

"Well, in about ten minutes, we'll be at the Farallon Islands. They've got this nice little nuclear waste dump there. We're gonna put this hunk of concrete to bed down in six hundred feet of water.''

"You can't do that, Morton! Did you get permission?''

Morton's voice seemed to have a laugh to it as he answered, "Ain't time for all that red tape, son. We've been using that dump for years, and there's no sense to stop now.''

Faber knew about the Farallon Island dump site. It was an environmental obscenity where industrial and military waste had been ignorantly deposited for years. Over time many containers had ruptured and cracked, spewing contaminated filth, rife with radiation, out onto the ocean floor.

Faber looked ahead to the low profile of the Farallons; his stomach sickened. He said to his pilot: "Cut them off!''

The pilot looked at Faber. "Mister, I think you're about one egg short of a dozen. Now you just sit back and relax, because we're going to turn around and go home."

Faber snapped, "You can't!"

The pilot moved his control stick and the craft began to turn. "Watch me!"

Faber put the microphone to his lips and said, "Morton, please. Don't put that thing there. If it blows, it could be a disaster for the California coast."

Morton's voice came back, "Faber, I like you; you're a nice young man. But we're getting rid of this Yamabato, and we're doing it my way. See you later."

A minute later, as Faber looked back, he saw the handsome shape of Yamabato plunging to a watery grave in the Pacific.

He felt beaten, drained. He had worked so hard to prevent a calamity, and he might just have been a party to setting the stage for something worse. He wondered when Yamabato might explode.

ACKNOWLEDGEMENTS

As with any work of fiction, *PIKA DON* contains material from the imagination of the author, but it also contains a considerable measure of historical fact. The major fact of significance is that the Japanese government and military were deeply involved in developing an atomic weapon for use against the United States during World War II. Direct references regarding their efforts during the war grow out of that fact and other facts of record concerning their atomic weapon program. As is the prerogative of a fiction author, I chose to use San Francisco as the intended target; other researchers have designated the Panama Canal and General Douglas MacArthur's headquarters in Manila as the intended target.

A few who have helped me with reference material in this work are: LTC Dick Grant (USAF-Ret), former U.S. Army/Air Force Intelligence Operations; Vic Voit, former Chief Pilot, Becthel Corporation, San Francisco, CA; LTC Ray Carlson (USA-Ret), former Chief, Helicopter Standardization Branch, Fort Rucker, AL; CW4 Les Tucker (USN-Ret), former U.S. Navy Nuclear Weapons Specialist; and Charlie Donaldson, Donaldson Brothers Structural Concrete. Those friends are not responsible for any of the author's creation or statements; they did contribute factual items necessary for authenticity.

THE BEST IN SUSPENSE
FROM TOR

☐ ☐	50451-8	THE BEETHOVEN CONSPIRACY *Thomas Hauser*	$3.50 Canada $4.50
☐ ☐	54106-5	BLOOD OF EAGLES *Dean Ing*	$3.95 Canada $4.95
☐ ☐	58794-4	BLUE HERON *Philip Ross*	$3.50 Canada $4.50
☐ ☐	50549-2	THE CHOICE OF EDDIE FRANKS *Brian Freemantle*	$4.95 Canada $5.95
☐ ☐	50105-5	CITADEL RUN *Paul Bishop*	$4.95 Canada $5.95
☐ ☐	50581-6	DAY SEVEN *Jack M. Bickham*	$3.95 Canada $4.95
☐ ☐	50720-7	A FINE LINE *Ken Gross*	$4.50 Canada $5.50
☐ ☐	50911-0	THE HALFLIFE *Sharon Webb*	$4.95 Canada $5.95
☐ ☐	50642-1	RIDE THE LIGHTNING *John Lutz*	$3.95 Canada $4.95
☐ ☐	50906-4	WHITE FLOWER *Philip Ross*	$4.95 Canada $5.95
☐ ☐	50413-5	WITHOUT HONOR *David Hagberg*	$4.95 Canada $5.95

Buy them at your local bookstore or use this handy coupon:
Clip and mail this page with your order.

Publishers Book and Audio Mailing Service
P.O. Box 120159, Staten Island, NY 10312-0004

Please send me the book(s) I have checked above. I am enclosing $ _____
(please add $1.25 for the first book, and $.25 for each additional book to cover postage and handling.
Send check or money order only—no CODs).

Name _____

Address _____

City _____ State/Zip _____

Please allow six weeks for delivery. Prices subject to change without notice.